SAVE THE LAST DANCE FOR ME

THE ASKENES TRILOGY:
BOOK 1

KEITH POLLARD

Published by Keith Pollard

ISBN 9781649697035

First published in 2021

Design and typesetting by Hawk Editorial Ltd, Hull

I have tried to recreate events, locales and conversations from my memories. To maintain their anonymity in some instances, I have changed the names of individuals and places. I may also have changed some identifying characteristics and details such as physical properties, occupations and residences.

To my wife, Jacky – thanks for putting up with being a wannabe writer's widow.

And I would like to thank Sam Hawcroft at Hawk Editorial for all her help and patience with me while proofreading and editing my trilogy, for without her help this would never have happened.

*FOR MOSE – YOU WILL
ALWAYS BE A LEGEND*

CHAPTER 1

THE BEGINNING
1946

As she opened her eyes, she looked up at the single flickering dim light bulb; she could smell the dampness in the air and see the marks on the walls where the wallpaper had peeled off. At first it had all been a dream, but then the realisation set in: she had gone into labour; she was giving birth.

Christine's final push was almost painless. The midwife urging, 'Come on, Chrissie, push! That's it, come on, I can see the head! Come on, just a bit more,' was just background noise to her.

The life in her belly was expelled as the baby emerged from the womb; the relief was immense, as the midwife Freda looked on, but this was not to last.

'Just relax; baby takes some deep breaths, for we have to do it all again – there is the other baby.'

CHAPTER 2

LEIF
Schooldays

It was Saturday, June 29, two days after my birthday, and I was about to take my eleven-plus examination. If I was honest with myself, it was something I was not that bothered about passing.

I was sitting in a classroom at a school down Wheeler Street in Hull, at a desk next to a window, watching the seagulls hovering above the playground, with the sun beating down, wondering what the hell I was doing there on a Saturday morning. Why we had been sent here, a school I had never been to? Must be neutral ground, was the only reason I could think of.

I was about to leave Constable Street junior school and start at Boulevard High School if I did not pass the exam, which would be taken over the next two Saturday mornings. I knew what my first choice would be – Boulevard. Whichever way it went I was about to embark on a long journey, and I had no idea what it would bring.

The test papers were already on the desk, and we were told not to touch them until the allotted time. We were informed that we had to put our name and birth date on top of the form once given the go-ahead.

The teacher looked at his watch, waited a few seconds, then told us to begin. Still in the back of my mind lingered the thought, what the fuck am I doing here on a Saturday morning? It was just not on.

The previous day I had got home from school, was sitting reading my *Eagle* comic when I heard my mate Mike Cooper at the back gate.

'Yow, Leif, are you coming out, yow, Leif?'

'OK, Mike, come in – the back door is open,' I shouted.

'Now then – you coming out or what?'

'Nah, just doing some revision for tomorrow; what do you reckon?'

'Looks like you are… that comic won't be part of the questions, but if it is you will have a good chance of passing.'

'Never mind that – what do you think about tomorrow?'

'Not a lot, to be honest. I am not going to try – fuck 'em. I don't even know why I am doing it; only to keep my old man happy, I suppose.'

I had done a lot of hard work revising for the exam and was quite confident I would do OK.

Mum had spoken of nothing else since she had received a letter telling the parents what it was all about. It read:

'The examination tests a student's ability to solve problems using verbal reasoning and non-verbal reasoning, with most tests now also offering papers in mathematics and English. The intention was that the eleven-plus should be a general test for intelligence similar to an IQ test, but with testing for taught curriculum skills. The test now measures aptitude for schoolwork.'

I passed with flying colours and was offered a place at Hull Grammar School. Mum was over the moon. It was a bit of an uplift for her. Things had been pretty rough over the past twelve months or so.

Mum and Dad had looked like splitting up only a few weeks previously. It seemed things had been OK for the first few years, not that I could remember, for I couldn't recall much until I was about six or seven years of age. They had been married for ten years at the time. It seems I was the reason they got married, for I was the hole in the French letter, or so I was often reminded.

One thing that does stick in the old brain box was the fights they had every time he was home from sea, as he worked as a spare hand on the trawlers.

Mum told me he had come from the North East in the late 1940s looking for work; he was a shipwright by trade, as he had served his time in the shipbuilding industry. But there were few opportunities around the area – only Dunstan's in Hessle, Cook, Welton & Gemmell in Beverley, and a shipbuilder at Paull, to the east of the city. They were all run by strong unions, and if you didn't have the right card, there was no chance of getting a start.

He found it hard to get a job, and with Mum pregnant, he had even more pressure on him. He had been drinking in Rayners and someone who knew someone put a word in for him, and he was given a chance to go to sea fishing as a deckie learner. Although a bit older than usual, he took the job; it was like being an apprentice or semi-skilled labour, and meant starting at the bottom. He soon got into a fisherman's life, away nineteen days, home for three, then out again for another trip.

During the three days home the majority of his time was spent in the pubs and clubs on Hessle Road. Being new to the game, his friends came from the younger lads that generally made up the ranks like him. Live for today – you can imagine how that went down with Mum.

Over the years, which I don't know much about, they went through more good times than bad. The money coming into the house was never regular; at times he was loaded, sometimes more than others, dependent on the settling pay, as they were only paid on what the catch was worth after the skippers and owners had taken their cut. The rest was split among the crew; the higher up the chain you were, the more money you received.

It was generally more than most jobs paid 'on shore', but with only three days to spend it in and the majority of them single, trawlermen earned the name 'Three-day Millionaires'.

There was a time when Dad was out of a ship; sometimes, he sailed out of Grimsby. It seems he must have worked for most of the six trawler companies in Hull. But he had settled down with his latest company, having been employed by them before. He had been lucky to be given a chance again by 'looking after' one of the runners. Because if you fell out with them, you had no chance of getting a ship – they would make sure of that.

It got to me, having to listen to Mum and Dad arguing every time he was home; he treated me like shit. He blamed me for him being tied down because he thought he was god's gift to women. I hated the bastard; he used to beat her, and I often had to listen to them at loggerheads when he was home from the sea; only back three days, but it was hell.

Things had got so bad over the years that my Mum had found a boyfriend when Dad was away; I used to hear them in the next bedroom to me, making love. Mind, that wasn't hard to do, in a small terraced house.

Then Dad would come home. The boyfriend knew him, but he was another one who hated him. It made me wonder whether he was seeing my mother out of spite.

CHAPTER 3

LEIF

Missing

The night it all kicked off big-time was just after Christmas in 1956. Everything had been great. Dad had been OK, not being abusive to Mum or me; he seemed like a real father for the first time. But it had to happen.

I had gone to bed at about half-past nine; Mum was listening to the radio, as he had gone out with his mates for a night on the beer before he went away the next day.

I must have gone to sleep; as I woke up, I looked at the clock; it was only half-past ten. I could hear this commotion going on downstairs. It sounded like Dad was trying to rape Mum. I could hear her shouting and screaming; she was making a terrible sound like she was choking, gasping for air. It was unreal; I had never heard anything like it.

When I came down, he had his back to me, and Mum was on the floor. I could see her legs, and he was bent over her. I jumped on him, grabbed him by the hair, and tried to pull him off her. I hung on to him like a baby gorilla on a silverback's back, and he was turning and trying to get hold of me, but I kept avoiding his grasp; he was staggering around, pissed. Mum had got up from the floor, blood coming from her nose. Her eyes were full of hatred; this bastard was trying to kill her firstborn child. As we were staggering around the kitchen, there was not that much room as it was; he picked up a carving knife from the draining board.

'You little bastard, get off me,' he shouted, but I held on, and as he spun around I saw Mum's rolling pin on the tabletop. She had been baking that day and luckily not put it away. He pushed me back to the table, so I kind of sat on it for a split-second, long enough for me to grab the pin. He twisted away from me and turned to look at me.

'Now, you fucking little bastard, I am going to fucking kill you!'

With that, I swung at him with the rolling pin. I only hit him on the shoulder, but with him being pissed he staggered away from me, tripped up and fell spinning backwards, turning towards the cooker and hitting his head on the side of the temple. He dropped to the floor, not moving.

I jumped on him, hitting him with the rolling pin, but missed his head again; fucking useless. I threw it away and started punching him. Ten years of hatred was coming out of me, punch after punch. My mother was trying to pull me off him, but I had gone now. The red mist had taken over. She eventually managed to get me off him. I sat on the floor next to him, sobbing like a baby who had had a favourite toy taken from him.

Mum bent over him; she put her finger on his neck to feel for a pulse.

'He's dead! You have killed him!' my mother screamed.

I screamed too, and there was only one person not crying – my old man; he was not making a sound.

I was thinking, I am only ten. OK, I was well built at five foot six, but how could I have killed him?

'I only hit his shoulder,' I shouted. I didn't think my punches had been that hard. Then I looked at him, and I realised I had been punching a dead man.

My mother panicked, and started to shake with shock. I didn't give a fuck – he was dead, which was great in my mind, but deep down she loved him, I suppose. I took hold of her, shaking her, trying to get her to stop screaming, but she was inconsolable. Her eyes were like marbles, tears streaming down her face, just staring at his body on the floor.

Then it hit me. I grabbed Mum's arm. 'Oh, fucking hell, Mum, we have to get rid of his body!'

She was not listening, still trembling with the shock.

'Mum! Can you hear me?' I shouted. 'Listen – we must get rid! I have killed him.' How I was so calm and collected in the nightmare that had unfolded, I will never know, but someone had to be. 'Mum, he is supposed to be going back to sea in the morning; we will just act as though he has gone, and we don't know any more, OK, Mum? Are you listening?'

I told her I'd go and see Billy, her boyfriend. 'He will know what to do,' I said. I didn't know if he would, but he was the only one I could think of. We had not seen any of our close family for years; you would not believe we lived in the same town. I did not even know where they lived.

I got to Billy's house and banged on the door; he opened it, bleary-eyed. I had lost track of time and had forgotten that it was almost eleven o'clock and he was in bed. He had to be up at twelve to go down the dock for a two o'clock start; he was what was known as a bobber, who unloaded the trawlers.

'What the fuck you doing? Do you realise what time it is? You know damn well I have to be down dock early – why the panic?'

Fucking panic, I thought, you'll panic in a second when I tell you what's happened. 'It's Peter; he's dead – he has had an accident.'

He couldn't quite grasp what I had said, so I repeated myself; three times, I told him the same thing.

'OK, OK! What you mean, dead?'

Now, how many ways can you mean dead? 'He is dead – stopped breathing, no response, not moving, that sort of dead,' I told him.

Billy passed out. That was all I needed, another lifeless body. It is incredible how quickly you grow up. I went under his kitchen sink; they always had a bucket under there behind a curtain. I filled it with water and threw it over his head, slapping his face a few times; he came round, coughing and spluttering.

'What the fuck happened?'

'You passed out; you fainted when I told you about Peter.'

'Oh, fuck, yes, what happened?'

'I killed him; hit him with a rolling pin – he was raping Mum. The bastard deserved it.'

'You said he had had an accident, not that you had murdered him.'

'I don't have time to explain now – are you coming to help us or not?'

'Yes, OK, let me get dressed.'

We got back to our house; it was a good job next door was away on holiday, and the other side both in their eighties and deaf as a post, or we would have been in real bother. Billy went into the house first; Mum was still standing in the same place just staring at the body.

He grabbed her, pulled her towards him, and said, 'Don't worry, everything will be OK. I know what to do.'

I thought, you know what to do? How many bodies, other than those of dead fish, have you disposed of in your career on the dock?

Billy stood over Dad. 'Hmm… right,' he said, rubbing his chin. 'We need to get rid of the body.'

Wow, the brain of Britain. 'Billy, we know that, but how?'

Mum had calmed down now and was thinking straight, 'OK, OK, hang on, I'll get something to wrap him in,' she said.

'What do you mean wrap him in?' I said to them both. We duly wrapped him up in an old blanket and tied him up in a sort of parcel with some old net braiding twine; every house on Hessle Road had some in the shed.

We dragged him out into the back. 'That will do for now; we need to get rid of him tonight,' said Billy, at the same time consoling my Mum as if it happened every day. 'I will go round and see my mate – he has a van. He will lend it to me; as he is a bit dodgy, he won't ask questions about the rush. He often helps people do a flit in the middle of the night when they do a runner from the rent man.'

One good thing was it did not take a lot of cleaning up – no blood to get rid of; not that it would have mattered as we only had lino on the floor.

Opening the back door, Bill took him by his legs and dragged him along the back alley to the corner. It was a struggle, lifting a dead weight, but we managed to get him in the back of the van. 'Now get back inside – I will take care of him; go on, get in.'

Off he went, and we went back inside out of the cold to await his return; we made sure he had taken Dad's kit bag and everything that was in it, ready for his nineteen days away at sea.

After cleaning out the van and taking it back to his mates, Billy returned later that night, no questions asked or given. Mum never asked where he had put him or anything; she just said, 'I am going to bed.'

He must have thought that was an invitation as he stood up, but she said, 'Billy, no, not tonight; besides, you have to go to work, don't forget.' He nodded his head and raised his hands, realising what he had just done.

'Yes, you are right. I must get going, it's getting late. Night, babe.'

He turned to me and said, 'I'm off; see you, mate.'

'No, Billy, don't,' I told him. 'Please stay a bit, please stop; I don't want to be alone right now.'

I was feeling a bit frightened; being quite honest I just needed someone to talk to. My father had never spoken to me; I might as well not have had one as I only saw him about eighteen times a year, and most of that time, he was pissed.

'Billy, please tell me about you. I know you love my mother, or you would not be doing what you are doing to help us. You could easily have just walked away, not even come when we asked you to.'

He kind of shrugged his shoulders and gave that daft grin he always had on his big red face. I don't know if that was through too much beer or being out in all weathers working on the fish dock.

'What do you want to know, son? And yes, you are right – I would do anything for your mum. I love her more than anything.'

'Tell me about you, who your dad is, what did he do? I know nothing about your mum – where do they live? I know you live alone – are they both dead? Please, Billy, I would love to know.'

He told me both his parents were gone; his father had been a bobber same as him; in fact, it was the reason he went on the dock rather than being a fisherman.

'I started on the dock as a barrow lad, then picked up filleting, wasn't much good at that until I was of age. Twenty-one, you had to be, to become a bobber, hmm, six years ago now. I love it, you know, the job, a great set of blokes, all mates, some are relations, like me – that is how we got a start, having family in the know.' He tapped the side of his nose and winked.

'Following in my old man's footsteps, or clog steps,' he laughed. 'I take after Dad – he was my double, big ginger-haired clumsy oaf, but would have given you his last penny. Mum was a devoted wife and mother; they only ever had me. She had problems after I was born and never really was the same after that.'

'When did they die? How long ago?'

'Mum died five years ago when I was twenty-two and Dad never really got over her passing. He only lasted a couple of years, and then he died, some say of a broken heart. He missed her so much, he hit the bottle. I still live in the same house; I took over the rent when they'd both gone. Nowhere else to go, I suppose; I was an orphan.'

I got out of my chair, went over to him and hugged him. 'Oh, I am so sorry.' He looked so sad telling me his story; I wished I had never asked.

'Anyway, apart from all that I think we have a lot in common,' said Billy. 'I also lost a brother; well, not lost one – he was also stillborn. You see, my father was married before. Sadly his wife Elizabeth died along with the baby in childbirth.'

'What do you mean I had another brother? Mum's never mentioned this. I know she was young when she had me and Peter was my father, but when did she have another baby? How do you know this? Why has she told you and not me?'

'I am sorry, Leif, you had better ask Christine; it's not my place, and I just thought you knew.'

'Please, Billy, tell me.'

'Leif, please don't ask me – if Christine hasn't told you there must be a reason. I think it's better if it comes from her. She would never forgive me if she thought I had been poking my nose in; please don't ask me again.'

'But, Billy...'

'No, please, I will say this last thing. There must be some reason why she hasn't told you and please do not push her for an answer while all this is going on. Let her get over the loss of your father; it might just push her over the edge. Will you do this for her?'

'OK, I suppose you are right.'

'Good man. Leave it a while. I am sure she will tell you one day when she is ready. I better get going now; it's been great talking with you. We will be OK; it will get sorted, don't worry. I must be going now, son, thank you for listening to me. I have never discussed it before. We will get over this, so don't you go worrying – you hear me now, OK?'

He got up and left.

Not being able to sleep I took my eiderdown and went downstairs. The fire was still going so I banked it up and settled down on the couch; I must have gone off.

When I woke up it was freezing; there were icicles on the inside of the windows and the fire had gone out. I had to clean out the ashes and mend the fire. This was my job anyway; I did it every morning before I went to school. With that done, it was starting to warm up a bit and I was sitting having my breakfast when there was a knock at the door. My heart started beating faster. Don't panic, I was thinking. Who could it be? Possibly the police? I was shitting myself as I opened the door.

'Hello, mister, can I help you?'

'Good morning, is your Dad in, son? I need to speak to him.'

'No, he went away this morning. What do you want him for?'

'Is your mum in, then – could I have a word with her, please?'

I was worried, but did not want to show it. 'Can I ask who you are, please?'

'Tell her I am Mr Tavistock, the ship's husband from your father's company.'

I felt my face going red. I was nervous now. What did he know? Oh, Jesus. 'Why, what has happened? Is Dad... is he OK? What's wrong?' I asked.

'Please can I speak with your mother, son? I won't keep her long.'

With that, Mum came to the door.

'Hello, can I help you? What's happened?'

'Sorry to bother you, Mrs Daniels – may I come in, please? I would like to speak to you about your husband, Peter. I am Mr Tavistock, the ship's husband for the company that Peter works for.'

'Yes, please come in – what is it you want to know? I don't understand. He went away last night. What's wrong?'

'We seem to have a bit of a situation. I must point out I don't usually handle the crew's problems apart from the skipper, mate, and the like, who are the crew's senior members. The remaining personnel are looked after by the ship's runner, but he was rather busy and seeing I would be in the area I said I would call by. I was hoping to have a word with Peter, but your son here…'

He looked at down at me and Mum said, 'Leif.'

'Ah yes, Leif – he tells me he is not here. Have you any idea where Peter might be and why he did not turn up to sail on his ship this morning?'

'It seems the taxi that was ordered to pick your husband up came for him, the driver knocked on the door a couple of times, but no one answered. He had another job – one of the other lads from the ship was getting picked up and sharing the taxi. When he came to the dock to drop the other lad off, he let us know that Peter would not be coming. Our runner for that ship, Tommy, took the cab and went to pick one of our people on standby to take his place.'

'What do you mean he missed the tide? He left here early. You know what fishermen are like; they don't like saying goodbye. I never even heard him leave.'

Mum was right; it was frowned on. If you said goodbye, it could bring bad luck, the same as bringing a woman on board before sailing was a bad omen. It was also said that fishermen never wished each other good luck as it was considered to bring the opposite; it just showed how superstitious seamen were.

'He never orders a taxi – he always walks down to the dock, as we live so near. I can't understand it – his kit bag had gone; as far as I am aware he had gone down the dock. I have not spoken to him since yesterday dinner time when he went in Rayners for the last few pints, not that he hadn't had enough; I'd not seen him much the past couple of days. He never came home for his tea either. I was expecting him home at three when they chucked out, but he didn't turn up. It is not the first time he has not come home; I'm getting fed up with it. He must have gone back to someone's house after chucking out time for a few more beers; he got home after we had gone to bed, must have been after eleven, I think. I did not get up as there would only have been another row; that is all we seem to do nowadays.'

'So you did not speak to him then?'

'No, I just told you that. Peter slept on the couch – look, there is the spare eiderdown we keep,' she said, pointing at the back of the couch. 'He must have got up and gone straight out; he never came up for any other clothes, or I would have heard him. Mind, he would still have been pissed; it was an early morning tide, I think.'

'What was he wearing, do you know?'

'What difference is that to you? Why are you asking me that sort of question, what are you getting at? He had his new suit on, sky-blue with box pleats and belt on the back of the jacket, with twenty-six-inch bell-bottom trousers, if you must know. What difference does that make?'

'Did he wear an overcoat? It is winter, after all?'

'No, never – it was always a big thing for him; he said it was a sissy who wore topcoats, hard man and all that.'

'I will ask around if anyone spotted him on the dock; it seems odd that he never turned up, that's all.'

'Well, if you see him, tell him to get his arse home, OK?'

'OK, I understand, but you must know the company frowns on this sort of behaviour by its employees. It could cost him his job; if we had not got a replacement it would mean they were a spare hand down, which would have put the other members of the crew under greater pressure. It is not good enough, you understand?'

'I am sorry, Mr Tavistock, but I haven't a clue where he is. All I know is he was in a good mood when I last spoke to him. Peter was looking forward to going back; he was happy in his job and grateful that the company had given him a chance and taken him on.'

'It may be possible he could be blacked for a while; he would be added to the "walkabout list" – you do realise that?'

'Sorry, Mr Tavistock, I don't know how things work; I did not know there was a standby list, but how could I know?'

'Yes, we keep a list of what you might call "characters" on standby who are, shall we say, are not reliable; it is one way of keeping them in line. Peter has been very good for us. I know he has floated about a bit from company to company, even sailing out of Grimsby on a few occasions, but since he has been with us his behaviour has been exemplary, hence me taking the trouble to call on you today.'

'I am sorry for your trouble and appreciate you coming round.'

'OK, when you see him next will you ask him to come to the office, please? We need to have a word with him. I will bid you a good day – thank you for your time, and I would not worry too much, he will turn up, I am sure.'

Mum closed the door. 'Fucking arsehole, who does he think he is coming round here with his high and mighty attitude? Well, that is the last we will see of him. Did you hear anyone knocking last night? You slept down here, surely you heard the taxi driver?'

'No, Mum, I never heard anything. Well, not while I was awake. I must have fallen asleep at some time.' I started crying; tears were rolling down my cheeks.

'It's OK, baby; hey, come on, don't cry, you did the right thing. We must stay strong and stick to our story, OK?'

It was common knowledge that my old man was a bully and a thug, and that things were not going well between them. Mr Tavistock knew this, but what he didn't realise was that it did not matter about him losing his job; he would not be going back anyway.

I went to school that day acting as nothing had happened, but the jungle telegraph was already working. One of my classmates, Kenny, came up to me with a worried look on his face.

'What's this about your old man? Is he ill or what?'

'No… why do you ask? He missed his ship, that's all.'

Another one joined in the conversation. 'Well, I heard he had disappeared, gone back to Newcastle, left you and your old lady, the bastard.'

'You know fuck all, Tony, so don't start spreading rumours about; it is bad enough without a load of shit being spread.'

'OK, Leif, it is just what I heard.'

'Well, don't believe everything you hear, OK?'

I don't know how I got through that day – it was the hardest day of my life. When I got home from school that night Mum was sitting in the kitchen, sort of staring at nothing.

I could see she was worried sick; she had had a few drinks to calm her nerves. We sat there in silence. I tried to make conversation, but she just couldn't talk; she was still in shock, I suppose. I don't know how I was standing up to the strain, but I was.

We heard nothing from anyone; not the police, no one. Mum thought we should go to the law and tell them we were worried that Dad had gone missing but were unsure what to do.

The next day Mum had gone shopping on road to get some normality back into her life when she bumped into one of her old friends in Boyes on the corner of Constable Street.

'Hiya, Christine, how are you, love? You OK? I heard about Peter not being well. Must have been bad if he missed his ship – is that right, love?'

'Hiya, Mary. He is not ill, so if you can let anyone know that wants to gossip about him, tell them that.'

'No need to get the shits, Christine, I am your friend; I know what an arsehole he can be. You don't have to get on to me, it's not my fault.'

'Sorry, Mary, it's just that I don't know where he is and I'm worried sick about him.'

Mum told her the story about him walking out without talking to her, and as far as she was aware he had gone back to sea, but he had missed the tide.

'OK, love, well you know where I am if you need anything. You know us Hessle Roaders must stick together – we are one big family. Don't you forget now, will you?'

'No, Mary, salt of the earth us lot, I know. Now I must get on – bye for now and thanks, Mary.'

A week went past with no news; no one came back from the company, nothing. We were trying to act like Dad had gone back up to Newcastle, or he was just lying low.

Then Mum had been on road again and met another old workmate, Elise; she had advised Mum to go to the police station and report Dad missing.

'What are you going to do, Mum? Are you going to Gordon Street – can you handle that?'

'I suppose I will have to do something, or it will look suspicious if I don't. I will have a cup of tea before I go – put the kettle on, love. I will try and think of what I am going to say in the statement. It will have to be the same as I told Mr Tavistock, just in case the police go and see him.'

CHAPTER 4

LEIF
The Police

'**G**ood morning, madam, how can I help you? Is there a problem?'

'I don't know how to put it… I think my husband has disappeared. I am worried sick. I thought I had better come and tell you – I believe he has gone missing.'

'OK, just a minute – I will get a lady constable to come and see you. Please take a seat, won't be a second. Can I take your name, dear?'

'Christine Askenes. My husband is Peter – please help me.' She broke down in tears.

Christine was sobbing with her head in her hands, a handkerchief collecting the tears.

She felt a hand on her shoulder, and a woman's voice, soft and gentle, said, 'Hello, Christine, how can we help?'

Christine opened her eyes and looked up. 'Sorry, I am at my wit's end… I don't know what to say. He was supposed to have gone back to sea, but he hasn't.'

'OK, now don't fret; we are here to help you. My name is Constable Holmes; we will do all we can to find… Peter, isn't it? Mrs Daniels, you say your husband has disappeared; what makes you think that?'

'As I said, he was home from sea and was due to go back, but we had a row. He had been on the drink, again, and came home after closing time, pissed. I had gone to bed with Leif. He is my son.' She then told them the story she had told Mr Tavistock and her friends on road.

'Right, come with me, let me take some detail; we need this to make it formal. OK, that's all the basics complete. Did your husband have anything particular about him that was different from other men from Hull? Or have you any idea where your husband might have gone without telling you?'

'He had a Geordie accent but wasn't from there; he came from Fleetwood. I don't think he would have gone up there. I can't remember him ever mentioning any relations. Even when we got married, no one from his side came down for the wedding. Peter is a bit of a loner, a bit of a dark horse; he doesn't have many what you would call close friends. I did not know him that well myself, which may sound strange. I met him in a pub, started going out with him and then it had to happen – Leif came along.'

'OK, we must tell you that the procedures for treating a disappearance are varied as the circumstances change from case to case. But you have done the right thing in contacting us so quickly. Christine, was it out of character that he should go away without informing you where he was going?'

'No, he has never done this before. He is only home three days every month with him going to sea. I don't see that much of him.'

'Is he on any medication, or has he been ill lately? Have you seen any change in him?'

'No, I rarely see him sober, to be honest. You know what fishermen are like – three-day millionaires… I am not being very helpful, am I?'

'It's OK, Christine, don't cry. I know it's a worry. We will find him; don't fret. I think that will do for now. Is it OK if we come to your house and take a look around? It is just to look for any clues, all sorts of stuff, to try and get a picture of what happened that night.'

'Yes, please – you are welcome to do whatever is necessary.'

The next day they came round and searched the house; you would have thought we were criminals trying to hide something. I was off school – I could not go and leave Mum on her own. I was pleased when they went upstairs. Mum was feeling the strain; she just sat there holding my hand.

About half an hour later, they came back down with looks on their faces that said, 'Well, that was a waste of time.'

'Well, Mrs…'

'Call me Christine.'

'Well, Christine, I would suggest that you keep a diary of events, try and think back over the past few weeks if anything has changed. Has there been anything different in how he acted, did he meet anyone you know of who was different from his usual friends? Also, if he tries to contact you, let us know as soon as possible. There's not much more I can add – we will be in touch if anything comes up. We will be leaving now, so thank you for your time, Christine – goodbye.'

Not much chance of that, I thought, for as far as we knew, he was dead, and Billy still hadn't told us what he had done with his body.

The police came back a few days later. I had just got back from school and there was a police car outside the house. My arse fell out when I saw it. I went inside, and there were two of them, a man in plain clothes and a woman in uniform.

'Hi, babe, this is Detective Nestrick.' He looked like the coppers you saw on the films at the cinema – a big bloke, well over six foot, grey trilby hat, gabardine macintosh, grey suit, tie, hands like shovels. When he shook hands with me, I thought he was going to crush my bones.

'Hello, Leif, how are you? How you coping? OK?'

'Yes, thanks – any news on my dad yet?' I had tears in my eyes as I spoke to them, thinking I should be an actor when I grow up, I like this pretending game. The woman just smiled, never said a word, and just sat there making notes; she was the same policewoman, Constable Holmes, Mum had met at the station.

'We have been handed the case as a missing person; we will be your contact from now, OK?' They then explained what the next steps would be.

'Did you get anything back from up north?'

'No, Christine, nothing came back from the North East. We enquired in South Shields, where we thought he was from, but none of the other forces had come forth with anything under his name. We are at a loss as to his whereabouts.'

SAVE THE LAST DANCE FOR ME

They bid us a good day and off they went, saying they would be back if anything else came up.

A couple of days later, there was an article in the *Hull Daily Mail* about the local constabulary looking for information about a missing person. 'Mr Peter Daniels, aged 34, last seen on the 30th of December 1956. Anyone with any information should contact Gordon Street police station.'

Two weeks passed, and then another police visit. Detective Nestrick and Constable Holmes came back to see us.

'Hello – have you any news about Peter? Have you found him? Where is he?'

'Christine, we have reason to believe we have found Peter's kit bag on the banks of the Humber, washed up on the foreshore, up near the lock gates to Albert Dock.'

'Would you be willing to come to Gordon Street to try to identify the bag and its contents?'

'Yes, of course – when do you want me to come?'

'Now, if it is possible – do you mind?'

'No – I will get my coat. Will you be OK, Leif, if you stay here on your own?'

I nodded my head, trying to look sad and heartbroken. Off she went, to come back in a police car an hour or so later.

'Yes, it was his bag; most of the stuff was in it, nothing had gone missing. They had said there was no sign of any violence and left the case still open, as a missing person. I had better tell you something, son – the truth, before it goes any further.'

I sat, silent.

'He wasn't from the North East, which is why they couldn't find any trace of him up there. He wasn't born up there at all; he was from Lancashire.'

I couldn't believe what I was hearing. 'What you talking about? Lancashire? When did this all happen? Mum, please tell me what you are talking about – you mean you have lied to me all these years? Everyone knows he came from South Shields.'

She looked so sad, sitting there. I'd never, ever seen that look on her face. She just looked tired; her face was drawn, with dark rings under her eyes. The pressure must have been getting to her.

'I had run away from home when I was fifteen; my father Hans was a right bastard to me, Mum, and the kids. He had tried to rape me one night; once again, he was pissed. It was one night when Grandma was at work.'

'He tore the clothes off me; it had been happening for a while; the first time was when I was only fourteen. I never told Mum because he was always full of remorse every time; he always swore it would never happen again. He begged me not to say anything. I kept it to myself, but I couldn't stand being in the same house as him. I told Mum I was leaving home, and I went to Blackpool; in those days that was the end of the Earth to a fifteen-year-old girl.' She was in tears now.

'I got a job in a café. I had a few quid I had saved up over the years, and Mum gave me a hundred pounds to help get me started in my working life; that was a fortune back then.' I got a room in a bed and breakfast boarding house; I had told them I was eighteen and had left home to find a better life.'

If I say it myself, Mum was a beauty, tall, gorgeous-looking, with a look of Anita Ekberg. Her genes had been passed on to me, for I was five foot eight at the age of eleven, with blond hair.

'Why didn't you tell me the truth about Dad?'

'I met your dad in a pub in Blackpool; he came from Fleetwood and sailed out of there on trawlers, not the North East. He had a Geordie accent because when he was adopted as a baby, the people who brought him up were from the North East.'

'That makes sense, Mum. Is that why they can't find any records about him up there?'

'Yes. Then I got pregnant with him.'

'Brilliant – that means I am a Lancashire bastard, not a Yorkshire one.'

'I came home to Hull after having you; I couldn't cope on my own. I had a tough time with my father and after a while moved out again, and my parents disowned me. Then, your dad came over and took some responsibility.'

'When did you get married to him, then, in Blackpool?'

'No, we never got married; we just never got round to it. Everyone believed we were married, so why bother?'

'Mum, why have you never told me all this?'

Mum stood up and walked away, looking out of the window as if she was hoping no one could hear. 'Listen, I am telling you now as I said your father followed me here, and I introduced him to your grandparents. You can imagine how that went down. Peter managed to get a job on trawlers here; as I said he had sailed out of Fleetwood, but had to start from the bottom here as a spare hand until he got worked in.'

'But we told the police he was into shipbuilding – you mean that was another lie?'

'Only a little one, to put them off the trail. Don't ask me why I said it; I don't know… just panic, I suppose.'

'When were you going to let me into the secret? Why not tell me before? I have a right to know. I know I'm only a kid, but I should have been told.'

'I know, I am sorry, Leif, I did not want to hurt you; I thought it best if you did not know. I am so sorry. But now you do know, am I forgiven?'

She put her arms around me and hugged me; this must be serious, I thought – she had not done that for a long while.

'OK, Mum, I forgive you, but please don't do it again. There is only you and me now.'

CHAPTER 5

LEIF

Family History Lesson

T hen as we talked, she came out with this story that had been passed down through generations. 'When I was little,' said Mum, 'the old people used to sit around telling stories; there weren't the radios and televisions like today. One of the stories that had been told for many years was how they came to Hull, as your great-great-grandfather was from Norway.

'There was a relation who was alive during the great famine in Scandinavia in the late 1800s. They had a small farm just outside a village in the south of Norway. Having a rough time of it, they had just had their first baby, but things had turned sour after around six years or so – the crops failed. Having eaten everything they had, the husband went to the neighbours in the hope of begging some more, but without any luck, because they had only a few days' food left. One of the neighbours suggested that he go to the next village, twenty or twenty-five miles away.

'He set off, but about halfway there he took a short cut that not many knew; he was sure it would cut his walk by nearly half, but he got caught up in a storm. Due to the cold, weakness and hunger, he collapsed and died.

'There was a couple, Jarle and Inger Askenes, who, a few days later when travelling with their horse and trailer, found and recognised the frozen body. They had met the man before in the village, but didn't know his name or where he lived.

'When they arrived at the village they made enquiries with some of the local people. Most of them knew him and told them it was Peter Olson and that he had lived up in the hills north of the village with his wife, Anna.

'One of them offered to take Jarle and Inger up to show them the way to his hut. It is said that when they finally arrived, there was a stillness in the air, peaceful, no sign of anyone.

'Inger called out to Anna, but no sound came back, and on entering the hut, they found Anna dead – but, unbelievably, her baby boy was still alive. In his struggle against hunger, he had consumed nearly half of his dead mother's breast, which had kept him alive.

'That baby, who was born in 1843, it is said was your great-great granddad, and his name was Jarle Askenes.

'That's where our name comes from; the local people didn't know a lot about the family, only that they had come to the village a few years earlier, before the famine, and started a small farm growing crops. No one knew where they came from or of any relatives, so the baby was an orphan.

'There was a local church in the village, and the priest offered to take the child in until they could find someone to adopt him, but things were hard, and often people didn't have enough to feed themselves, never mind another mouth. The two people who had found the body did not have any children, and they offered to take the child as their own, giving him their name.

'They had been planning to emigrate to America and were just waiting for the nod, and they would be gone. It was their dream to make a new life for themselves and now their child.'

'Wow, so I am of Viking blood, then? Is that where the blond comes from?'

'Yes, the couple who were your great-great-great-grandparents, Jarle Askenes, and his wife Inger Seljord, by adoption had named him as part of their family. In 1852, having saved enough money, they set off for a new life. It took four days to get to Hull; the conditions were not that good. The immigrants were often seen as second-class passengers, and not treated much better than cattle.'

She had a tear in her eyes as she continued with the story.

'It seems that the Norwegian names in those days weren't hereditary; you could almost name them anything. Askenes comes from "the ash tree on a headland" – it was an old western Norwegian name. They had funny ways of naming children, and I won't go into great detail. But in 1923, it became law that each family should have a hereditary last name – and only one last name. Some families took a patronymic surname, which means that it was based on the given name of a father, or an avonymic, which means a name based on that of a grandfather or earlier male ancestor.

'Others took a farm name and, of course, the old hereditary titles lived on. But it resulted in significant numbers of families called Olsen, Hansen, Nielsen and names like that – old patronymics. It was the same as it is here – women lost their last name.

'During the period that the emigrants where in transit, the people of Hull had a fear of catching diseases, the reason being the shipping agents used to march the emigrants through the streets of Hull from the dock en masse, often unwashed and in a terrible state after the journey across the North Sea.'

She was starting to get upset, as the memories of her forefathers came flowing back.

She told me that the North Eastern Railway had agreed to transport the emigrants from Victoria Dock by rail to a new purpose-built waiting room at Paragon Station in the city centre. There were facilities for them to meet ticket agents, wash, use toilets and shelter from the weather after being cooped up on the ships.

Mum finished off the story by telling me the family's ancestry 'Luckily, your great-great-great grandparents did not go any further than Hull. The journey was so horrific they decided they had done enough travel and that England was the place to be, so they settled here.'

She listed all of their names, like she was reading from a school register; how she could recall all this I did not know. She named them all, from Jarle Askenes Snr and Inger Seljord, who adopted the orphan

Jarle. Their family grew, and had a son, Hartor; he met and married Audrid Estem, who had been born in Norway. They had a son, Olaf, who married Solvild Neilsen. They had two kids, Audrid and Gustav; sadly, he only lived three years.

Jarle married Helga Axberg. They had one son, Olaf, who married Christine Christensen; they had Hans, my grandfather, and he married Elizabeth Webb, a local girl from Hull.

'They had me in 1930, and before me, three other boys – Olaf, born 1926; Arkvid, born 1924, who married Mary Stephens (they had one child, Jason); and Hans Jnr, born in 1925, who married Angela Peterson.'

'But why did you fall out with Grandad? Was he that bad a father?'

'He was an oddball. We had some terrible arguments about little things; he used to put a padlock on the larder so that we could only eat a certain amount of food.'

'But why was he greedy? Did he want it all for himself?'

'No… I think it went back to the days of the famine when they had a fear of not having enough food in the house. After he left school at the age of fourteen, his father took him away to sea with him to work on a steamship as a coal trimmer, working in the ships' boilers shovelling coal; he was away three years. That trip was in 1909, and he sailed all over the west coast of the USA on a tramp steamer from Newfoundland down to New York. He came back in 1912 only because he had had enough and had managed to get a ship that sailed from the USA to Norway, working his passage.'

'What did he do then? Did he stay in Norway?'

'No, he then got a job with a company that sailed from Norway to Sweden regularly. He only got that because his father knew someone at that company. He worked with them until he came back to England.

'When did he come back home then? Was he away a long time?'

'I am not sure how and when, but when he got back he was in the Merchant Navy during the first war. He was then in it during the second, but this time he was torpedoed; the crew managed to get to the lifeboats, and were picked up by a hospital ship. He had lost his left eye.'

'God, he was lucky being picked up.'

'Not so lucky – the hospital ship was also torpedoed and sunk, which was supposed to happen, but some U-boat captains had no scruples; it was an unwritten law.'

'Was that it then he managed to get home safe? Did he go back to sea after that?'

'No, that ended his career in the Merchant Navy. He managed to get a job as a fish bobber after the war ended. It was all casual labour; he never knew until the day before if they were required to work. It all depended on how many ships had arrived on the previous tide.

'He had a terrible accident one day. He was in the fish room and the hook of the winch caught in his glove, just as the control lever on the winch jammed, and it lifted him high up and hit the winch block. The sudden stop made his glove rip, and he fell about twenty feet to the deck below. He fractured his skull, his pelvis, and his left arm was never the same again. He called it his one wing – the right arm, that is; he was off work for a very, very long time and people said he was lucky to have lived through it.

'With him being so strong, that was what pulled him through, and because of this he managed to get back to work, on light duties, as they called it in those days, and was given a permanent job for life as part of his compensation.'

I was so intrigued about my ancestry I went to the local library down Boulevard, only a street away, to see if I could find anything to back up this story Mum was telling.

It seems that during the 'emigrant season' between 1836 and 1914, Hull had more than twenty-two million migrants pass through from Norway, Denmark, Sweden, Finland, Germany and Russia. It was no cruise line luxury; on quite a few occasions the Hull Board of Health wrote to the Wilson Line with concerns regarding the unacceptable standard of accommodation offered to the emigrants.

In 1915, the passing of immigration acts in South Africa and the USA brought an end almost overnight to mass immigration from Europe. In 1918, transmigration commenced again but on a much lesser scale and would never reach the numbers previously seen.

The newspapers in Norway were full of stories about passengers suffering and dying on the transatlantic crossing. There were stories about people who had been tempted to emigrate, even though they did not have enough money for their passage. Quite a few had signed contracts to work for companies in America, and paid their fee by providing labour after arrival. Often many of them had been duped to sign contracts that they could not free themselves from.

The Norwegian government decided to monitor the transportation companies' activities and their agents. As a result of this, the first emigration records commenced as a temporary arrangement in May 1867.

Mum knew the story off by heart; she told me that the emigrants' waiting room was still standing, now a social club for railway workers.

CHAPTER 6

LEIF
More Questions

Back to my father's death, the police had paid us several visits but could not tie anything down as no body had been found. Even me and Mum had no idea what Billy had done with him; he would not tell us. Every time we asked, we got the same answer – 'The less you know, the better.'

It was a week or so since Billy had been round to see Mum, and then out of the blue, he walked in. 'Hiya – where's your mum?'

'She has gone round to see Hans; he is home from sea. Why, what's up? You look worried.'

'That is what I had heard too, that he was home, and that is what worries me – whether your mum can keep shtum about what's gone on.'

'I don't think you need to worry, Billy, she seems OK with it now; even when the police come round she just acts relaxed, yet still the concerned wife act comes out.'

With that, who walks in? Mum and Hans.

'Hello, Billy, what are you doing sniffing around my sister?' Hans laughed.

'Not so lucky.'

'Lying bastard – you would love to get into her knickers. You have been trying long enough.'

'Hans, shut the fuck up,' Mum chipped in. 'If you think you can talk like that in front of the boy, you think wrong; you can get out of my house.'

Hans realised he had said something wrong and his face went bright red, but still came back with, 'Bit touchy there, sis – did it hit a nerve or what? Everyone knows he is around here as soon as Peter has gone through the lock gates. By the way, Billy, be careful, mate – he is due home next week.'

'Listen, Hans, shut up and listen good; you have got your dates wrong. Peter has been home and was due to go back but disappeared; his kit bag has been found but no sign of him, and that was a week or so ago.'

Hans sat down and went grey. I thought he was going to pass out.

'What happened, then? Where is he? Have they found his body?'

'Why would there be a body?' Billy asked. 'Who said he is dead? He has just gone missing.'

That was the first time I had heard Billy sound nervous. I looked at Hans, and his face had changed; I think he smelt a rat.

Mum also could see the change in Hans and butted in. 'Billy, forget what Hans has said about you coming round, and you, Hans, no one is saying Peter is dead, apart from that I like Billy coming round when he's away. I need a grown-up for company.'

'Whoa, grown-up company – is that what they call it, then?' Hans laughed. 'I am only kidding. Don't take it to heart, mate; you have always been easy to wind up. Peter must have gone to see his mates in Newcastle, but it seems odd that his kit bag was found in the river all the same. Come on, Billy, let's go to Rayners, I am gagging for a pint. Come on, I'll treat you to make up for winding you up.' He then grabbed Billy's arm, saying to Mum, 'OK, sis, we're off. I hope Peter turns up. I am away again on Thursday, so let me know if you hear owt, OK?'

With that off went Hans, none the wiser about Peter's disappearance. Nothing more was heard from the police for quite a few weeks. No one seemed to give two fucks about my old man; it seemed odd to me that someone could just disappear like that, and nothing happened.

Mum had gone back to Gordon Street and asked to speak to Detective Nestrick.

'Hello, Christine – I can call you Christine, can't I?'

'Yes, of course, I don't mind,' she said; she probably thought that was a good sign she was not under suspicion.

'There is no change as of yet; we are still treating this as a missing person as there is no evidence anywhere of any crime being committed.'

'What will happen now if he doesn't come back? He has gone missing before during his three days at home, but usually due to him being on the drink most of the time. He always turned up to go away, and always came home on his return.'

'Christine, I must ask you something. You say Peter went missing now and again when he was home – now, please don't take this the wrong way, but was your husband ever unfaithful?'

'What, you mean did he go bagging off other women? I don't know, and that is the truth. Why ask that? What have you found out?'

'The taxi he ordered on the night he went missing – we went to the taxi company and enquired about the booking. It seems they went to a different address, not yours. It might have just been a mistake, but they showed us their ledger, and it was not your address. I am sorry, but I had to ask.'

'What address was it – can you tell me?'

'No – I am sorry, it is part of our investigation. There may be nothing in it, as I say; it could be just a mistake – the girl in the office could have written the wrong address. I am sorry, Christine, but I had to ask.'

'He has always been a ladies' man, a proper flirt, but I didn't think he was seeing another woman. I have had my suspicions, but just shrugged them off. Thinking about it now, though, when he was out of a ship, he used to disappear for a few days at a time, and when I asked him where he had been he had always been looking for work. He could turn his hand to anything, sometimes on building sites; he often worked away down the smoke, but always came back. He loved the sea, but you just never know, do you? At home, the woman is always the last to find out. Thank you for telling me; it makes sense. Like I told you, we did have a row before he went out the night before, and it's the first time he has just left in the middle of the night.'

'OK, you did the right thing, but having said that, you could have informed us earlier. Seeing he had done it before, it doesn't matter. The one thing that does worry us is that we found his kit bag in the river. We had considered a search of the area, but with it being so vast and the rise and fall of the currents, it is just out of the question. If it had been in the river Hull, we would have brought in a search team, but even then we would be lucky to find anyone. We have put bulletins out to the pilot cutters who use the river; they work twenty-four hours, seven days a week, and also the coastguard and lifeboat crews.'

'What about hospitals – have they been informed?'

'Yes, we have contacted all forces as far as the North East, who in turn contacted all the hospitals in their area. We have put out media and press releases appealing for help, but up to now no response.'

'I can't thank you enough; from the bottom of my heart, we thank you.'

'OK – if we hear anything, we will be back, and you will be the first to know.'

There was nothing more for weeks, possibly a couple of months, until one Sunday morning a police car turned up. We were in bed – luckily Billy was not there; he had gone home after the pub and not even come back with Mum.

I went down when I heard a knock on the door. Still a bit sleepy, I opened it and said, 'Hello… er, can I help you? What's happened.'

'Is your mum home, Leif? We need to talk to her – it's a rather urgent matter.'

'She is still in bed asleep… can you come back?'

'No, sorry, son – we need to speak to her now. Can you ask her to come down? We will wait.'

I went upstairs and tapped on the door. I wouldn't say I liked going in without knocking as she slept in the nude, always had done, and to be honest, she was gorgeous. I know lads should not think like that about their mothers, but she was a beauty.

I tapped on the door again, but there was no sound. I knocked again; no sound. I peered around the door – she was lying there face-down with no bedclothes on. I cleared my head, and went over to shake her.

She rolled over and looked at me. Then, realising who it was, she yelped and pulled the bedclothes up. 'What are you doing, Leif? Coming in here without knocking – you know the rules.'

'I'm sorry, Mum. I knocked a few times, but you did not reply.'

She had always kept the door locked, even when Dad was home. It went back to the times when she was younger to save her abusive father coming into her room. She told me once about it and said I was never to mention it again.

'Mum, you've got to get up – the police are downstairs.' The look of terror in her eyes told me she was going to panic.

'What you mean the police are here? Why? What for? What did they say?'

'They haven't told me anything; just that they needed to talk to you right now.'

I went back downstairs and told them she was getting dressed and would come down as quickly as possible. I asked them again, 'What has happened? What have you found? Why are you here? I have the right to know; after all, Peter is my father.'

Constable Holmes stood up, took hold of my hand, and said, 'Look, Leif, we know it's hard, but please just wait until your mum comes in, then we can tell you both, OK?'

With that, Mum came in, still looking frightened to death of what they were going to say. Were they going to say that they had found Dad, and that they believed he had been murdered and would be furthering their enquiries?

Detective Nestrick started to talk. 'OK, it's like this – we have found a body in the river but up towards Spurn Point near Sunk Island.'

Mum started sobbing, and Constable Holmes offered her a handkerchief. Mum took it and wiped away the tears. I was thinking she was putting on a good act as she already knew he was dead. Or was it the reality of the situation that had got to her? I thought I had better start to cry or they might smell a rat, so I burst into tears as well.

The detective continued. 'With regards to whether it is your husband, it is not quite certain. The body is at the Hull mortuary, and at this moment in time we are carrying out a post-mortem. You must understand the body is not in a good state because of the submergence in water, we think for a long period. We can't identify him from just looking at him, but from what you told us he was dressed in the last time you saw him, it fits the description of clothes he is wearing.'

He told us that an autopsy was being carried out on the body to try to determine the cause of death, but that there could be problems, which he did not elaborate on.

He then asked the critical question. 'Did your husband have any distinguishing marks on his body, like birthmarks or tattoos, for instance?'

Mum kind of went quiet; I wondered what she was doing by not answering the question. She had a funny look on her face, then she said: 'Yes, he did, he had two tattoos.' I had never seen any tattoo on him in the eleven years I had known him; we had been swimming together when I was younger, and had even been to the local swimming baths in Madeley Street.

'Under his balls.' The room went silent. Not a word was said; you could have heard the proverbial pin drop. I was the first to speak.

'Under his balls? You've got to be joking, Mum. Why… when did he get that? What's it say? I don't believe it.' I started laughing.

The policewoman went red. Detective Nestrick eventually broke the silence.

'Are you sure, Mrs Daniels, that he had a tattoo on his balls – I mean, testicles?'

'Yes, definitely – two words put on his balls; he had it done when we were in Fleetwood, one on each side of his dick.'

We were all dying to know what it said, and waited with bated breath for the punchline. Then Mum started laughing, and said, 'Semper fidelis.' We looked at each other, not a clue. 'Always faithful,' Mum said, then burst out crying again.

That was the end of the conversation; they closed their notebooks, looked at each other, and told us they would be back after visiting the mortuary.

The following day they came back and confirmed that the body they had found was indeed Dad. There was no doubt whatsoever that the information Mum had given confirmed it, and there would be no need to identify the body physically. I don't suppose many guys were walking around with a tattoo on their scrotum.

Detective Nestrick told us that a report would be sent to the coroner and they would be in touch within a couple of weeks. He also explained what the procedures were. 'Only a coroner can order an inquest; relatives of the loved-one cannot insist that one is carried out. Those who can attend an inquest are, of course, you, the close relatives or, where there is a will, the executors of the deceased. Did Peter make a will, do you know?'

'No, I don't think so – not that I know of. If he had, he never told me, and we don't have any copies here if he did.'

'OK – details will be given to you of the time and place the inquest is to be held. You do not have to attend unless you have been called as a witness.'

He did advise that, although it was distressing, most families chose to participate, because above all, 'You need to know how, where and when your loved-one died. To find out who, if anyone, is responsible.'

I hope they never find out, I thought, or we are in deep shit, that's for sure.

He continued to lay out the rules. 'If the coroner did call an inquest, they would consider the information we have gathered over the weeks, statements from us, and the results of the post-mortem that showed Peter had drowned, as his lungs had water in them. They found quite a lot of alcohol in his stomach, but not a lot of food other than that. It seems this is the reason he died as he had no real injuries apart from a bump on his forehead, which did not suggest he had been in a fight or there would have been more bruises on his face.'

I don't know how our faces looked when he told us that he had drowned; as far as we were aware, he had been dead when we put him in the van.

'Also, during an inquest hearing, the coroner will decide which witnesses to call and the order in which they give their evidence. You may write to the coroner in advance of the inquest, suggesting that a particular witness may be required. Sometimes written statements are accepted if witnesses cannot add any further information by being questioned at the hearing; for example, an identification statement can be read aloud. There are a lot more rules and regulations, but I don't think there is any need to go into detail.'

'Wow,' said Mum, 'I did not realise there was so much involved, but I just need to know what happened to Peter. You have been very kind; we appreciate all you have done for us – thank you.'

'No problem, Christine, we will be in touch to let you know what the coroner says, but we think there will be an inquest and further statements could be required. We will get going now.'

CHAPTER 7

LEIF
The Truth

'What do you think about that, son? That lying toe rag Billy. We need to get hold of him, the lying bastard – he did not tell us he was still alive when getting rid of his body. Well, it wasn't his body – he was still alive.'

After a few weeks, the inquest was called, and as predicted they took further statements from us two, plus Billy; his statement said he had seen Dad going down the dock with his kit bag at two o'clock that morning when he was on his way to work. He had been riding his bike towards the tunnel that led to St Andrew's Dock, and had seen him walking and thought he looked a bit rough. He'd said hello to him but got no reply, so he had thought, fuck you, then, and kept on riding. He had thought it was odd because tide time hadn't been for another four hours and his trawler the Kingston Onyx was at the back of the list to sail. They could get out into the river four hours before high tide and four hours after, but there had been a bit of a backlog due to Christmas.

The inquest sat on the 15th of April 1957 with coroner Mr Michael Toogood taking the proceedings. He was a small fat man with bright ginger hair; if you'd put him in a green pixie outfit and buckled shoes he would have made a good leprechaun.

He opened the trial by stating that we were there because of, well, I won't go into all that again.

We were all asked to say what had happened that night he went missing; well, we didn't know he had gone – as far as we knew he had left to go away on the Kingston Onyx for nineteen days. We didn't know he was missing until the ship's husband came round to ask why he hadn't met up to sail. It went on and on until Mr Toogood said, 'I will adjourn to consider my findings and we will reconvene at ten tomorrow morning.'

We got home; the house was silent. Grandma Lizzy came round; it was the first time she had got in touch after all her daughter had been through. There was still no sign of Grandad, and she never even knocked – she just walked straight in.

'How are you, Christine?'

My mother looked at her; she couldn't believe what she'd heard. 'How am I? How the fuck do you think I am, Mother? We have not seen hide nor hair of you for months – no, fucking years – and now you dare to ask how the fuck I am! I will tell you how I am, Mum; I am sick to death of you and my so-called father, that's what I am. Now just go and leave us alone.'

Grandma was about to say something, but Mum cut her short. Mum stood up and walked to the door, opening it. 'Now, please, Mum, do not say another word – get out. I never want to see you again. You have been nowhere near us through all this tragedy. I have lost my husband and him his father. OK, I can accept you didn't like him. Well, stiff shit, mother, he didn't like you either; he thought you were a pair of arseholes, treating their only daughter the way you did. I married Peter not because I was pregnant but because I loved him.' I looked at Mum, thinking, you tell me not to tell lies.

'So just go, will you? Please go. Oh, and while I am on a roll, you can tell my so-called brothers not to bother either, if they are still alive.'

With that, Grandma turned and left without saying another word. Mum slammed the door behind them. 'Fucking good riddance.'

They never stepped foot in the house again, nor did we visit them.

The next day we went back to the inquest. Mr Toogood came out of his room and asked us to take a seat. He started off telling us about what had gone on the previous day, etc.

He then stated, 'After some consideration, I have concluded that Peter Daniels died through accident or misadventure.'

He gave us his condolences and said we could all leave.

Detective Nestrick and Constable Holmes came up to us. 'Well, Christine, that is it – case closed. No further meetings will be needed. We will organise a death certificate for you, and you can go ahead and arrange a funeral. We are so sorry for your loss.'

'Thank you for your help,' said Mum. 'We as a family could not have asked for anything more; thank you.'

She kissed the detective on the cheek and hugged Constable Holmes. It may not have been the right thing to do, but it seemed fitting. They never flinched or backed away, just smiled and left.

We went home. Mum was numb, and so was I. Billy was very quiet. He knew he had got away with murder.

Mum was sitting on the sofa and looked over at Billy. She stood up and said, 'OK, Billy, now are you going to tell us what did happen that night? You were supposed to dispose of my husband's body.'

Billy looked down at the floor, not saying a word, just mumbling to himself.

'Billy!' Mum shouted at him. 'Billy, please – what happened? Why didn't you tell us that he was still alive? Why keep it to yourself? You should have told us.'

He looked so sad; he had aged ten years in a few months. He must have been wondering how he got himself into this mess.

'OK, yes, I should have said something. I know I was wrong, but I thought he was dead same as you did. I believed he had died due to an accident. I had taken the van up near the jetty near Propeller Graveyard, as no one would be around that time of night and the copper at the gate was asleep. Although the docks work twenty-four seven, they always get their heads down that time of night. As I dragged him out of the van, I took the blanket and twine off him; I didn't want to leave him wrapped up – that would have been suspicious. Then, as I lowered him on to the ground, he moaned. I thought it was air in his body coming out, but his arm moved. I was just lifting his legs to push him over the side, and his eyes opened, but it was too late – I had let him go. I will never forget the look on his face as he disappeared into the water. I am so sorry, believe me, so sorry.'

We just sat there, looking at each other. No one said anything. I was about to speak, when Billy said, 'But you wanted rid of him – you wanted him out of your life, Christine, didn't you? He was a right bastard to you – or why did we get together when he was at sea, it wasn't because of spite, was it? We love each other, don't we? I would have killed him for you if you had asked me to.' Tears were rolling down his cheeks now. 'I would do anything for you, you know that, don't you? Well, I did, I killed him. I was willing to go to jail if we got caught, but we didn't. He is gone – we are free of him, be thankful.'

That had broken the silence; but then no one uttered another word for what seemed like an eternity.

Mum was just looking at Billy; he was sobbing. I did not know what to say. I felt sorry for him; he had done his best for us. Still, in the end, he had killed my father. My mind was in turmoil now. Why did we get rid of his body? Why didn't we call an ambulance? We knew it was an accident – he'd banged his head on the stove, but I was hitting him with the rolling pin. I thought I had killed him, as Billy did. I would have – I wanted to at the time; I wanted him dead.

Mum seemed pleased that he was dead after we'd put him in the van and Billy had gone off to get rid of the body, to places we did not know where. But if we had known he was still alive, what would we have done? Finished him off?

Then Mum broke the silence. Almost whispering, she said, 'We can't change things now. What's done is done. We can't bring Peter back and, to be frank, I am glad he is dead, so we must stick together, and tell no one the truth. We must live this lie until we are dead ourselves – understand?' We all stood up, and we were holding hands, just the three of us in the middle of the room. 'Now you must swear that this is the end of the matter – it's never to be repeated to anyone, OK?'

Billy dried his eyes, hugged me and Mum, and turned to leave. As he was going, Mum said, 'Billy, don't stop coming round, will you?' and blew him a kiss.

He left and never looked back as he closed the front door.

That just left Mum and me. We held hands, and she put her arms around me and said, 'Just you and me, kiddo – fuck the rest of them.'

We cremated Dad on Monday, April 29, 1957 at Hull Crematorium; his ashes were taken and scattered off the Bullnose near the lock gates of St Andrew's Dock.

CHAPTER 8

LEIF

Passing the Eleven-plus

As I said earlier, I passed my scholarship and left behind the few mates I'd had at Constable Street, along with those who had moved to the new estates in East Hull to enable the slum houses in West Hull to be demolished.

I started at Hull Grammar School in September 1957, with a new uniform, the whole works; the first day went OK, I suppose. We met our new teacher, Mr Jackson.

Now, I wouldn't say I liked the guy from the first time I saw him. He had the most prominent nose I had ever seen, and used to perch his half-rimmed spectacles on the end of it. He looked like a pelican looking down on you. There was one story they told at school – and I do not know how true it was – that when he got married, he stood up to give his speech, nodded to the guests, and cut the cake.

Along with all my new school friends, he took us to our classroom. Something just didn't seem right.

I was sitting next to a guy I had never met; he was from the other side of Hull, and a Hull Kingston Rovers supporter. God, I thought, can this get any worse? During the first break, he followed me around like a lost puppy. 'What do you think then?' I said. 'I'm not sure that I have made the right decision in accepting a place here – are you?'

'What? I worked my socks off to get here, and you think you might have made the wrong decision? Are you crazy?' He whispered so that no one else could hear what he was saying. 'Do you realise the history of this school? It was founded in 1330 as a secondary school and endowed by Dr John Alcock, who was later to become Lord Chancellor of England and founder of Jesus College Cambridge.'

'Give over, I'm not interested – just shut the fuck up.'

'It was first built in 1479 in a brand-new building on the Market Square in South Church Side near Holy Trinity Church. Nearly 100 years later it was falling to bits and it took another five years to renovate and rebuild the school; it was completed in 1583.'

I was almost falling asleep listening to this kid; oh fuck, what had I let myself in for? My head was buzzing. He went on and on about how the school was bought by the vicar of Holy Trinity Church in 1785, which meant that it had to move to temporary accommodation until 1891. It then moved to another new building in Leicester Street in 1892, when the Lord Mayor of the day, a Mr E Robson JP, opened it on the 27th of January. He went on, believe it or not, to give me the sizes of the fucking rooms and how many there were.

I gave up. 'Shut up, for fuck's sake, you are doing my head in.' He looked aghast; I don't think he had ever had anyone swear in front of him. 'Come on, it's time to go back in the classroom.' I thought, I have got to get rid of this kid. I will kill him if they keep me with him.

The teacher then took over where mastermind beside me had finished; he started talking about who the notable former pupils were, including Andrew Marvell, the English metaphysical poet and patriot. As the teacher spoke, the parrot on my shoulder whispered, 'His father, the Rev Andrew Marvell MA, was a former master at the school.'

Mr Jackson, or 'Old Jacko', as I had christened him, then mentioned some more notorious ones such as the guy who founded the National Boxing Association of America, William Gavin, and Sir Linton Andrews, who finished up as editor of the Yorkshire Post.

I had heard enough of this bullshit; I was glad when the first day was over.

I arrived home to be welcomed with, 'Hi, dear, how was it? How did it go? Who were your new friends? What are the teachers like?'

That was all I needed. Oh my god, talk about an inquisition. 'Mum, I hate it; I wish I hadn't taken up the offer.' I then broke down and cried and went upstairs to my room.

Mum came up, and she held me in her arms like she hadn't done for years. I smelt her perfume and felt her body hugging me, and it was not like any feeling I had ever had for her. She was rocking me back and forward, telling me, 'It will be OK, baby, don't worry. Don't go back if you don't want to.'

'What? I only went for you, Mum. I didn't want to go, but with all that had gone on I thought you wanted it more than me.'

We talked about it most of the night, and we decided we would – or I would – give it a go, for at least as long as it took. I went back the next day, but it did not get any better by the end of the week. I knew I had been wrong when I'd promised I would give it a go, but this was going to be some tester.

I was at the end of my rope and, after a few weeks, I went home and said, 'Mum, that's it. I have to get away.'

What I did not know was that in the meantime, Mum had been to the Boulevard School and met with the headmaster, Mr Gillies; she'd asked him if I could leave Hull Grammar and go there. She pointed out it would have been the school I would have gone to if I had not passed the exams. He advised her that he had never heard of anyone leaving Hull Grammar School to return to a secondary modern, but he would look into it for her. He did say that the education department would not be too pleased to hear that I had not given it a go.

Mr Gillies knew of the situation we had been in, with my father leaving us, so he was sympathetic to her request and said he would make some enquiries. He told my mum that he thought I should give it a bit more time to make sure I was making the right choice, for it was my future that I should be thinking about, not just this time in my life, and I could be making a big mistake.

Mum told me he was a lovely man. 'I am sure you will like him – he is not like any headmaster I have met,' she said. I am not sure what that meant, for she did not do that well at school.

I was adamant I that I wanted to leave as soon as possible. We argued about it for days after she had been to see Mr Gillies, but she could not convince me to stay.

A couple of weeks later, I came home from hell, and there was a letter from the education department in Hull, addressed to Mum; she had left it until I got home before opening it.

'Here you are, Leif, you open it – I am sure it is regarding my request for you to leave grammar school and go to Boulevard.'

'But I did not know you had written to them? When did you do that? You didn't tell me; you thought I should give it longer.'

I opened the letter, which was full of official jargon. I was trying to read fast to get to the crux of what it was saying, but it was just a load of bullshit typical council stuff. Mum kept asking, 'What's it say? Come on, tell me!'

'Hang on, Mum, I'm trying to understand it.' I read the rest of it – two full pages about it not being the usual thing to leave after passing the eleven-plus, and it being a waste of time taking a position that could have gone to another child.

Then it came to the nitty-gritty. 'If your son is 100% certain he wants to give up his position at Hull Grammar School and go to the Boulevard Secondary Modern, due to personal circumstances, you have two weeks to consider the option shown below in paragraph 5.1.1.'

I turned over the page, and there it was – an offer to leave Hull Grammar School at half-term in October and transfer to Boulevard.

'Yes! That's it, Mum – I am leaving. Write back to them and accept the offer.'

Mum had that 'are you sure?' look on her face.

'Mum, before you say anything, I am positive. I hate it at Grammar – they're not my type of lads, or teachers. It's too posh for me. I will never see the time out there – please let me go to Boulevard where I belong.'

So it was done; she succumbed to my will and filled in the attached form, sending it back the next day.

We got an answer with a week, and at half-term I left. I went back for one more week and said my goodbyes; the staff were a bit pissed off that someone didn't want to be at their school. I was interviewed by the headmaster and explained the situation. Lo and behold, he fully understood my request, shook my hand and bid me farewell on the 25th of October 1957.

I started the autumn term at the Boulevard on the 4th of November. It was great to get back and meet some of my old mates. They put me in the B stream for the first year; I was a bit pissed off, as I had been smart enough to pass the eleven-plus, but I think it was a bit of, 'We will show you who's boss, son,' sort of thing.

I did OK. I found it too easy, to be honest, and not too big-headed, but I got 100% in every exam and finished top of the class in all subjects.

During the first winter, I was not that sports-orientated; I played a few football games, but did not enjoy it. I won't bore you with the full details.

The new term came, and they put me in 2A, which was the form of Mr Boulton, who was a bit of a disciplinarian. His primary subject was maths, but he was also coach of the under-twelves football team. When you talked to him you felt like nodding off; he had the most annoying voice, and just seemed to go on and on a never-ending drawl.

He tried to talk me into playing football, but I was not interested. I went one Saturday to watch them play as a few of my mates were in the team, but I had never been so bored in my life.

There was a rugby league game going on at the same time, but not from our school; St Andrew's and Maybury from East Hull were the teams. I started watching the game with interest. I had never paid much attention before – I classed myself as a Hull FC supporter, but this was only because their ground was near where I lived and all my mates supported them. I'd often thought about going to watch them, but never had enough time; there'd always been other things to do.

All I knew about rugby league was the clubs; I had once found an old Hull FC programme, and after reading it I was amazed at how far and wide the clubs were. They were spread from Hull in the east as far as Workington and Whitehaven in the west. There were no regional divisions like in football.

I was instructed by my mates that I was never to go and watch Rovers. There was a deep hatred from those in West Hull, but I couldn't understand it, to be honest. I thought that, if both teams were from the same city, you should hope they both did well – but I once said this and was looked at like I was from another planet. Hence my comment earlier about the boy at grammar school who was a Rovers supporter. Mind, he would have sent a glass eye to sleep. If they were all like him, I could understand why no one wanted to know them.

The new form teacher was a bit of an arse, and I did not like him one bit. All of his blue-eyed boys were the ones who starred in his beloved football team; the rest of the rubbing rags did not matter. He was having a go at me one day, about something or nothing, and for some unknown reason I blurted out, 'One day I will play a professional sport.'

'You have no chance; you need to start very young to make it in any sport. You have never kicked a football, never mind good or hard enough to play rugby league.'

Hmm, we will see, smart arse, we will see, I thought.

Anyway, I watched this game, and another older boy from Boulevard, whose brother played in the football team, came up to me. He asked me who I was.

'Why are you asking? Who are you?'

'I am Mike, Peter's brother – I believe he is in your class. He mentioned that a new lad had come to the school last year from Hull Grammar, and it sounded like you, that's all.'

I was OK with him; it was just after what had gone on with Dad and everything, I didn't want to start answering questions.

'Don't you play football, then? Is rugby your game?'

'No, I don't like football, and I'd never actually seen a rugby game until now; it looks much better.'

'I play in the A team for us – why don't you try out for the C team? I know they are looking for players. When is your birthday? Because it depends on when you were born.'

'The 27th of June 1946,' I said.

He thought for a moment. 'Bloody hell; you're a big lad. How tall are you?'

'About six foot, I think.'

'I am not 100% sure, but I think you would be in the C team age group – do you want me to ask for you on Monday?'

'Will you? That would be great.'

Wow! I had met a new mate and an older boy as well. I went home and told Mum what had happened. 'You are not playing rugby,' she said. 'It is too dangerous – no chance.'

'Oh, Mum, come on, let me at least try a game. I won't get hurt. I'm miles bigger than most kids in my class. I will be OK, I promise! Oh, come on, Mum, let me, please.'

Anyway, after a bit of convincing, I went to school the following Monday full of hope that I was to start rugby training.

We were seeing more and more of Billy; he was staying over now and again, usually at weekends because of work, but still, things were beginning to change in my life – new school, new friends and possibly a new man in my life.

One day, I arrived home and, to my surprise, Grandma Lizzy and Grandad Hans were sitting in the living room. 'Come and say hello to your Grandma, give us a hug,' she said as I walked through the door. Wow – this was a change of heart; it was not long ago Mum was telling them she never wanted to see them again.

'Hi, how are you? Is everything OK?'

'Yes, we thought we would come round – it's been a while now since Peter died.' It was not often they mentioned his name; Grandad hadn't spoken yet.

'Hi, Grandad, how are you?' I said to him, trying to get him to talk, but he just grunted; that was his way of saying hello.

Mum asked them if they wanted a drink, and they accepted. Jesus, that was something – they had never had a drink in our house, not that I knew of, anyway. 'Go put the kettle on, Leif, will you, please; make us a nice cuppa.'

After a few minutes, I returned with a tray and teapot, cups and saucers. The tray had never been out of the cupboard for years; I even brought milk in a jug and sugar in a separate little pot. They looked impressed, which they should have been as I had put in a lot of effort.

Also, to find the cups was a trial of endurance.

Mum played mother, so to speak, and we all sat there not saying a lot; we even had some garibaldi biscuits on the side.

Then Grandma broke the silence. 'Christine, we had to come round. It has gone on too long, this gap between us, hasn't it, Hans?' Grandad grunted again. 'For god's sake, man, speak up – you always have plenty to say at home. Come on, tell her what you have been telling me – how much you miss her and Leif, how we should stop this stupid argument.'

I was amazed at what she'd said, and so was Mum. As usual, Mum started to cry, and then Grandma began to as well. I just sat there watching Grandad for his reaction.

Then the voice from thunder spoke. 'OK, you two, that's enough of that sniffling. I just want to say, Christine, I am truly sorry for being a bastard to you and the boy. I hope you will forgive me. I know it will be difficult for you and I will understand if you tell me to eff off, but I want to make it up to you and Leif. You have suffered enough over the past years; please let us back into your lives, before it is too late.'

Grandma and Mum stopped crying almost immediately. I sat there open-mouthed; I couldn't say a word. I don't think I had heard him say so many words in one go in my life. I know he hadn't when I had been in his company, although I had never really met him.

He walked over to the two of them and put his arm around them; he looked over at me and smiled. It was the first time he had ever shown any feelings at all towards our family. I stood up and went over to join the gathering. He put his arm around me, and pulled me towards him. It was like being gathered in by a machine – he was still so powerful, like he was chiselled out of Norwegian rock. He kissed me on my forehead and said, 'I love you, son. Please, please forgive me.'

We talked for hours that teatime. Everything came out. We all promised to see more of each other, as families do at weddings, not just at funerals when they haven't met up for years. They stood up to leave, we said our goodbyes, and then they were gone.

'Well, what about that, Leif? What do you think happened there? That was a surprise, wasn't it?'

Now, that was the biggest understatement since Noah said it looked like rain.

We talked for ages after discussing what Mum should do. She explained in greater detail more than she ever had about what had happened with her and Grandad, how he had abused her from being aged about thirteen.

'Mum, you should go to the police and report him even now. You can't let him get away with it. You can't just wash the memory of it away and forget what he did over a few cups of tea. Did Grandma know what was going on?'

'No, baby – no one knew, only me. I have not uttered a word to anyone. I kept it all a secret, and even now you are the only other person in the world who knows what he has done. It is gone; let's just forget it ever happened. We have our lives to live now.'

He'd kissed me earlier; why did he say sorry to me? I just could not comprehend it; it was beyond me. I was eleven, and he was saying sorry to me – why?

Back at school, one of the boys introduced me to the teacher who coached the C rugby team, as my birthday fell into that age group. Mr Allan Adams was a teacher in the third year, so I hadn't met up with him before; I had seen him but not had a chance to talk to him.

After we discussed the possibility of me playing, I pointed out that I did not have much experience, but he said quite a few of the boys had not played the game in the past, which he liked, as he then had a blank canvas to work with, so to speak.

He asked me if I could stay back a couple of evenings a week and go through the game's basics in the playground, starting tomorrow with the rest of the squad. I told him I would have to let Mum know, but couldn't see any problem as long as she knew where I was.

Oh, how wrong I was.

I got home from school. Mum wasn't in; she was working now, having got a job at Hammonds shop in the town centre. There hadn't been much money coming into the house since my dad had disappeared. Billy had been kind to Mum, but she needed an income to pay the bills.

As I was always home, I used to get my own tea ready; Mum had shown me how to cook the basics – how to boil spuds and open a tin of corned beef, which was still my favourite, with a can of garden peas and salad cream on the potatoes.

I had got everything ready for when she got home, about six o'clock. She walked through the door, with the usual, 'Hello, how was your day?' greeting, followed by a kiss on the cheek and a hug.

'Oh, hi, Mum. OK, I've got something to ask you – the rugby team coach asked if I was interested in playing in the school C team.'

'No, definitely not – I told you, you aren't playing rugby. No way.'

'But, Mum.'

'No buts. No way.'

I stormed out of the kitchen and went upstairs to my room, not saying another word to her. I heard her shout, 'Leif, get your backside down here! Don't you ever ignore me! Get down here, now.'

I went back down. 'Sorry, Mum, but I want to try this rugby game. Please, let me give it a go. They will think I am a sissy if I tell them my mum won't let me play'

That seemed to do the trick. 'OK, but the first time you get hurt or injured, you're finished – understand? Finished.'

That was a result. I couldn't wait to get to school the next day to tell Mr Adams it was OK for me to join the team.

After everyone had left for the day, we got changed in the gym at the southern end of the school and met in the playground.

Mr Adams got us all together and said, 'OK, lads, how many of you have ever actually played rugby at all?' No one put a hand up. 'Well, let's see how we get on then, eh?' He muttered something about it being a challenge.

There was no such thing as an academy or youth teams; you learnt to play at school. There were no under-six or eight teams; we were the virgin players in those days, and starting at eleven was the youngest age group.

We began to throw a ball about, which was new to most of us. Some lads used to play in the street throwing rolled-up newspapers secured with insulation tape or cut-off stuff they had pinched from the tip in Hessle.

We had a few sessions and, yes, I enjoyed it; it was the first real sport that I had ever put my hand to. I did like swimming and was quite good at that; it must have been down to my Nordic blood.

I was the least experienced; although they had never played, most of the other lads knew the rules and had a basic idea of the sport, and they all had dreams of what positions they should play.

The scrum-half was always small, so Willie Hargreaves was the choice there. He was a real cheeky chappie – another thing that scrum-halves tended to be.

Props were the big fat lads in the team – the plodders who were not quick enough to play anywhere else, but their weight and size was an advantage in the scrums.

That left the others; one of them, John Norman, was really good with a ball – he was a great passer, and could throw it at least twenty feet, which, for a kid, was unreal. He became the loose forward.

Carl Marks – now, he could tackle anything. His timing was spot on. He wasn't the fastest, but he became the full-back.

It is often said that hookers are born for the position, or so they say. Peter Jackson was a hooker; he was hard as nails, frightened of nothing, and would run all day. He was a natural, and in the scrum, his feet were like a chameleon's tongue – they could hook the ball out before the opposition realised it was in the scrimmage.

That left Billy Wright and Mike Smith, who were nearly as tall as me, and they were put in the second row.

Two other lads who were pretty quick, Sam Peters and Dennis Oakes, were chosen to play in the centres, leaving me and another lad who had no game experience to play on the wings.

Our remit from Mr Adams was to get the ball and just run, using the touchline as our guide, and when in doubt step out, which meant that if you looked like getting clobbered by the opposition, stepping into touch would save you a hammering. It was sound advice, as you were open season for the defences covering across.

We trained for about four weeks before the actual season started, which turned out not to be too bad. We were in Section A of the Hull Schools C league, and played ten games, winning eight of them, scoring 98 points with only 17 against, finishing top of the league.

I loved it. I was smitten, and had even started going to the Boulevard to watch Hull FC; I had found an entirely new existence.

One of the first games I ever saw was Hull FC against Wigan; their team was full of international players. The highlight of that game was watching Billy Boston. To see him taking the ball on the burst, scattering players aside like rag dolls, his sidestep as he beat the full-back and scoring under the post, was out of this world. Another player, his centre and captain, was six foot three Eric Ashton. Strong as an ox, he could sidestep off either foot, and watching him run, every step was a sidestep, and the opposition had no idea which way he was going. Then a deft pass to put Boston over… oh how I wished I could play like them one day.

I was doing well in my school classes too. It seems odd but maths was my favourite subject along with history; it's something I have always loved, having a 'foreign' background. I finished top of the class in all subjects except religious instruction; I just could not grasp all that Jesus and God thing. As my grandfather Hans used to say, if there was a god he would not let all these bad things in the world happen.

I was now thirteen and had moved up to Mr Parker's year three class. He was a history teacher, and I liked him; I could listen to his stories for hours. He made everything sound as if you were there. Whether it was the battle of Hastings in 1066 when old Harold Godwinson, or King Harold II, lost his eye, or King Richard and his adventures on the crusades, I relived every moment.

Also, in a significant change to the school curriculum, a foreign language was to be included. A German teacher came to the school and – a first for us – she was a woman, a Mrs Ashcroft, or should I say, Frau Ashcroft. I was starting to notice girls now; they were no longer the victims of ridicule, but something about them was beginning to catch my eye, and this German woman was having a hell of an influence on me.

She was tall, blonde and well-proportioned. Mum used to say, laughing at me, 'Leif, why are you always talking about Mrs Ashcroft all of a sudden? I think you have a crush on her!' I thought, you might be right, Mum, maybe I have. 'I heard you dreaming the other night, and it seems you were making love to Mrs Ashcroft, or so it sounded.'

I went bright red. 'Mum, do you have to?'

'Only kidding, stupid, it's natural. Don't you think I haven't noticed the marks on your bedsheets? All boys go through this stage in their lives.'

Now, we had never discussed sex education at school, never mind at home; it was something you learnt in the school playground or reading dirty magazines, that's if you could find any in those days. *Lady Chatterley's Lover* was the nearest thing to porn back then.

I could not believe it – my mother now knew I masturbated. In her eyes, I was a wanker! But, as she said, all boys went through it, though I must admit I did enjoy it.

I came home from school one day and was surprised when Mum had asked me if it was OK. Billy came to visit a bit more. 'Leif I want to ask you something,' she said. 'You know Billy and I have been seeing each other for a while now, don't you? Well, I was hoping you would consider letting him come to stay with us?'

It seemed a bit early to me, to be fair, although thinking about it, it was two years since Dad had died. 'Of course, yes, why not?' I said. 'He spends enough time here. It's OK by me.'

A few weeks later Billy moved in with us. It was great to have a man about the house all the time; I never really felt like I'd had a real dad, as he was always either away at sea or home pissed. Everything had turned out well up to now; I was loving school and Mum was the happiest I had seen her for years. I was even getting to see my grandparents more often, and old Hans was starting to be more like a grandad. He used to come out with some things related to dates in his life; he reminded me that when I was born in 1946, Alistair Cook had broadcast his first programme of A Letter from America, and it was still going.

The B team was my other love now. Some new players came in as others had left the school and migrated east to the new council estates, as their houses on Hessle Road had been knocked down to build industrial units and factories.

John Norman had gone up to Longhill Estate along with a few of my classmates. However, life went on. I was still a winger and even scoring tries. I'd had a couple of games as a centre and enjoyed being involved a bit more, getting to learn how to pass a ball as well as catching it; after all, it is a ball-handling game.

I often think about what Mr Adams used to say: that there were only six things you needed to remember in the game of rugby league – run, pass, backup, catch, tackle and kick now and again, but only those who have the skills to kick, not everyone – and he was right.

Although we failed to win any silverware, we had another reasonably successful season, and three of the squad had been chosen for the Hull and District Intermediates representative team.

Another change had taken place: the SMC, or Kingston upon Hull Secondary Modern Schools Certificate, came into being. It seemed that this would be the ultimate examination for boys and girls in Hull, much like GCSEs today.

The school offered a choice of three courses to those in their final year – technical, nautical or commercial, each designed to give preliminary training and background for their careers. It was a gigantic step forward, for there were few schools that offered such opportunities.

I went through that year with flying colours. I liked my friends and had got to love a new sport – life could not be better. I gained useful reports for my end-of-year exams, and was looking forward to going into the fourth year and the new format.

CHAPTER 9

LEIF

Holiday Time – Three Years Later

For the summer holidays in 1960, we went away, and like most families from Hull we took the train to Withernsea on the east coast. 'Withn'sea,' as it is pronounced, was to Hull people what Southend or Brighton were to Londoners.

We had rented an old railway carriage converted into a caravan on Nettleton's field, right on the clifftop looking out to the North Sea.

It was decided we would go by train this time; it was easier with the luggage for three of us, as Billy had become part of the fixtures. He and Mum were now like two peas in a pod, and always together – it was great to see her so happy. She had been promoted to a supervisor at work, so we had more money coming in, and Billy paid his fair share. He had moved in permanently, and had got rid of his house and sold all his furniture – well, Mum got rid of most of hers and brought his to our house; we even had carpets.

This was only the second time we had ever had a holiday away; the first was in 1956 when we – I say 'we' as Peter was on the scene then – went to Skipsea, near Hornsea, on the east coast, and it had taken us ages to get there. We'd gone by bus, taking one from Hull to Hornsea, and then another from Hornsea to Skipsea up the coast road via Atwick and Skirlington. There were only three buses a day, so there was a long wait for the next if you missed it. For me, it had been an adventure; it was the only holiday we'd had with Peter. He had had a trip off during the school holidays to try to sort himself out.

We'd arrived at the site – if you could call it a site; it was right on the cliff top, with no running water, and the only tap was fifty yards away, where you went to fill up an old army fuel container. The toilets were the old chemical type which, believe it or not, you emptied over the cliff edge as far away from your van, but not too near any other. The wind was so strong; coming straight off the North Sea, it hit you like a sledgehammer, and you could only just keep your footing.

The accommodation was a converted single-decker bus with the one double bed at the back end and one single bed near the front, next to the door. As I said, it was right on the cliff, twenty yards from the edge, and steps had been cut into the cliff face running down to the beach. There was a rope alongside in irons to help you climb up and down.

The week turned out to be terrible; Mum and Dad argued the all the time, about just about everything – some things never changed.

The nearest shop had been about a mile's walk back to the village. It was unbelievable, for this was where we had picked the keys up for the van, having paid the postmaster. Then we had to borrow a wheelbarrow from him to take our bags up to the field.

The road ran due east and ended at the cliff edge. There were no bar-riers, nothing – just the end of the road. This area suffered from coastal erosion on a big scale, and still does, with yards being lost to the sea every year.

There were only two good things that stick in my memory about that holiday; the first was the fact that I had an air rifle that Dad had bought me for Christmas. Mum went crazy when she found out. I was over the moon, and used to spend hours shooting targets in the back yard. I say yard; I had to leave the back door open and stand as far back as I could against the wall in the kitchen with the target pinned to the back door. Anyway, I had it with me on this trip. The second thing was that there was a song being played on the radio all the time – *Que Sera Sera*, by Doris Day or, in English, 'Whatever Will Be, Will Be'.

The highlight of the holiday was when Peter tried emptying the toilet. He misjudged the wind direction and got covered in human excrement.

I nearly pissed myself; he was not amused and, to make things worse, he had to strip off outside the bus as he was not allowed in. Mum washed him down with cold water, having sent me to get a refill halfway through. It was pissing down as well. I was laughing like hell; you couldn't have written a film script better.

Anyway, back to our holiday in Withernsea. After we arrived at the station, a group of lads about my age came over with trolleys that had been homemade out of old prams to help carry our luggage to the site. They did this on school holidays and weekends to make some pocket money. Billy went over to discuss terms, driving a bit of a hard bargain. Still, we finished up with Ben, a lad a bit younger than me but not as big.

We got to the caravan, paid young Ben his half-crown and he disappeared with a smile. The old railway carriage had been converted to have two bedrooms and a living area. The lighting was gas-fired, with no central heating, and it got quite chilly even in summer. Luckily, as it was a glorious summer that year, we did not need it.

We spent hours on the beach, climbing the steps dug out of the cliff face, with a rope-type banister stuck in with iron rods, which gave you some feeling of safety as you struggled to keep your feet on the uneven surface. You could walk along the beach into the centre of Withernsea, with its arrangement of pubs, cafés and fish and chip shops; I always remember Redferns on the front corner of Seaside Road and the promenade.

The biggest of the amusement arcades was on Memorial Avenue. The Pier Hotel was just up from the fish shop, and then there was Butterfly Inn on the T-junction. Turn right from there and our favourite, the Spread Eagle, was on the corner of Hull Road and Queen Street with its kids' room and beer garden.

We had some fantastic nights in there. Mum would give me a few bob to go to the amusements, with the order, 'Be back as soon as it gets dark.'

We would then walk back together along the cliff top to the van, always taking a torch with us to light the way, or there was a chance you could fall over the cliff edge in the dark – more than ever if you were pissed like Mum and Billy often were.

We were on our own the first week, but unknown to Billy and me,

Mum had asked Grandad and Grandma to come for the second week. I lost my bed as I had been sleeping on my own in one of the bedrooms; that was given to them, and I was put outside in an old tent, complete with a paraffin lamp that stunk when you lit it.

I had met up with a lad who was staying in another caravan just along the way from us. He was from Pontefract, in West Yorkshire; funny how you meet up with other kids when you are on holidays, isn't it?

It was the first Monday, and I was kicking an old football I had found in a sort of shed attached to the van. I had kicked it over his way, so he kicked it back. 'Wanna play, t'owld cock?' was his call. Now to me, he spoke another language; it like he was from another planet. 'Old cock' seemed like an odd way to make a friend, but OK.

'Hi, yes, OK – fancy going down the beach away from the vans?' I said.

So off we went to the beach. We got talking, chattering away about this and that; he was a bit older than me – only a few months, but still older.

He was already in the fourth form; he had started just after Christmas.

'I'm Dougie – Dougie Dickinson, by the way.'

'Leif,' I said.

'Fucking Leif? What sort of name's that? Never heard that one afore!'

I told him it was Norwegian, and he seemed impressed.

We kicked the ball around a bit, and then he said he played rugby at school and Featherstone Rovers was his favourite team; his Dad used to take him all the time to Post Office Road.

We were getting on OK; at least I would have someone to play with for the rest of the week, I thought.

'Where is thy van, t'owld cock?'

'Over there – the old railway carriage.' I pointed over to it. 'But I am sleeping in that tent as there is no room for me inside.'

'Hey, bets that's fucking great – can I come and sleep in tit wit thee if I ask t'owld Mam 'n' Dad?'

'Yes, it's big enough for two of us – it will be fun.'

He got the nod, and I was now sleeping in a tent with a new mate.

We were in the tent alone, and you know what boys are like, talking away about this and that, about no subject in particular, when all of a sudden Dougie said, 'Have tha had a jump yet?'

'What you on about, a jump? What's a jump when it's all there?'

'Tha knows – with a girl, a jump, your leg over. Bloody hell, Leif – sex?'

Talk about being dumbstruck. Once again I thought he was talking in a foreign language; some of these expressions these West Riding people came out with just killed me.

'No, I haven't.'

'Tha means tha's a virgin, then? Bloody hell, bit slow you Hull lads, aren't thee! I had one when I was twelve – my first jump. Tha don't know what tha's missing, t'owld cock. Oh, by the way, my cousin Dot is coming tomorrow for a few days – she will put thee reet, tha knows; she's a reet cracker.'

'What do you mean, put me right? There is nothing wrong with me.'

''Cos thee is, t'owld cock – tha's a fucking virgin, that can't be reet.'

I did not know what to expect with this Dot due to arrive tomorrow, but I could not wait to find out.

'How old is this Dot?' I asked.

'Fifteen, nearly sixteen,' he replied. 'And as horny as hell.'

We talked for ages until the battery ran out on the torch. I woke up during the night; it was raining – you could hear it beating on the canvas.

Dougie was lying on top of his sleeping bag, snoring, dead to the world – and naked, with the biggest erection I had ever seen; not that I had ever seen another boy hard.

I rolled over, trying to get back to sleep, thinking about what the next few days were going to bring.

We were up early the next morning. Dougie had his head out of the tent door, watching what was going on outside, with his bare arse stuck up in the air in front of me.

'Dougie! Hey, get dressed – what are you doing?' I shouted at him.

'Shh,' he whispered back. 'Some girls are walking across t'field – come and look. They are gorgeous – come and watch.'

How can I get my head through the same gap he's looking through, I thought.

'Come on, hurry – or you will miss them!'

I got out of my sleeping bag. I still had on my Y-fronts. 'Mind out the way, then,' I said, as I pushed him aside.

'Na, get underneath me – go between my legs,' he said.

'Oh, OK,' I said, as I dropped to my knees. He opened his legs wide so that I could crawl under him. It felt weird crawling beneath a naked boy; when I felt his skin against mine, I felt uneasy – it did not seem right.

I got my head out of the tent and, sure enough, three girls carrying duffle bags and towels were walking along the clifftop towards where the steps went down to the beach.

'Come on, get thisen ready – we are going t'beach.'

Like hell I am, I thought; I'm having breakfast first, I'm starving.

He pulled his head in and closed the gap, and as he came back he fell on me once again. He was sitting more or less on my chest as we got tangled up, our bodies wrapped together, all arms and legs.

We untangled ourselves and looked at each other. It felt odd, the look he was giving me, and he was now sitting on the floor holding his penis. He started to stroke it. It was like it was during the night – but now he was masturbating, in front of me, blatantly wanking, his eyes closed; he was in a world of his own.

Now, this was the first time I had never seen another boy doing it. I always thought it was a private thing, something you did alone in the privacy of your bedroom, not sitting in front of your mates. At least there were no sheets to stain on this occasion. I just sat and watched Dougie reach a happy ending; there was a grunt, he said, 'Yessssss', and it was all over.

'OK, come on then, let's go – we must find them girls.'

'No, I need something to eat.'

Mum had got up with Grandma and was cooking bacon – it smelt great. The smell of the bacon in the sea air is so much different.

Billy had been down to Watt's bakery near the Alma pub. Now, these breadcakes were the best in the world, believe me, and bacon and egg sarnies, washed down with hot tea, made a perfect start to the day.

'We are off, Mum – just going to Dougie's van to get his cozzie and towel. We are going down to the beach, OK?' Before she could answer back we were gone.

When we got to the beach there was no sign of the three girls. I must admit this Dougie was leading me astray, for I had not had a lot to do with girls up to now in my life. Now I was thirteen, nearly fourteen, and without a doubt starting to notice the opposite sex.

We never found the girls, for they'd just disappeared, so we went for a swim. Now the North Sea is not the best place in the world to swim, even in summer, and it was bloody freezing. We ran straight in, and my balls disappeared inside my body as the water reached them. 'Oh, fuck!' I heard Dougie shout, as the smart twat dived in head first as a breaker hit the beach, and he tried to stand up. Still, the current took his feet from under him; the pebbles were loose, and he could not get a grip. I was pissing myself watching him flounder like a beached whale.

He eventually stood up, sand in his mouth, coughing and spluttering and spitting out salt water.

'Jesus, thot I weer fucking drowning there, t'owld cock! Thot I weer a goner.'

'I thought so too, but I couldn't have helped you.' I was still laughing. 'Never mind, you're here now. Come on, let's walk into town.'

'No, not yet – let's just stay here for a bit,' he said.

We got dried off, and put towels around us so that no one could see our beautiful bodies – well, mine was anyway. It's stupid how you do that even when there is no one around to see you.

Dougie had gone quiet for the first time, kind of shy on me, as we slipped off our trunks under our towels. Or perhaps was I imagining it; he did not say much, which made a change from the bouncy lad I had met.

We hung about, lying on our damp towels; the sun was just getting a bit hotter, so we were OK in our shorts.

After an hour or so, we were getting bored, and we talked about everything again. We were getting on great. I liked my new mate – he was more worldly than me, and had been and done things I had never heard of, never mind dreamed about. Or so he said, anyway; he was back to the guy who was full of himself again.

It wasn't long until we were back in the town; we hung around at the amusements for a while, then went up to the Spread Eagle to sit in the beer garden. I had enough to get us a couple of cokes.

The next day we had been into the amusements again, got fed up, and decided to head back to the caravan site. We were walking down Hull Road towards Arthur Street, nearly up to the lighthouse, and I decided I would like to go inside it. 'Come on, let's go in and see if we can have a look.'

'Why, I'm not that interested – it's only a leet.'

'OK, you go back – I'm gonna see if I can get in. See you back at the van.'

CHAPTER 10

LEIF
The Lighthouse

I walked up to the lighthouse keeper's cottage and was about to knock on the door when it opened.

'Now then, son, what you up to – mischief, no doubt?'

'No, sorry, mister – I just wanted to have a look at the lighthouse. Is it open? Can you go in? I was hoping I could go to the top.'

'Not on your own – you need to be with a grown-up.'

'I'm fourteen – that old enough? I am not a kid.'

'Wow, fourteen… are you now? That is old.' He started to laugh; his belly wobbled under his blue Trinity House jumper. 'OK, I'm going up myself. Come on, and don't touch anything, OK?'

'I won't, I promise – thanks, mister.'

'Less of the mister. I am Harry – what's your name, son?'

'Leif. Leif Askenes.' I did not tell him my father's name; I always used Mum's name.

'Right then, what do you want to know?'

'How high is it and how many steps are there to climb? Can you see far?'

'The views from the lamp room are breathtaking, Leif, especially after you have climbed the 144 steps. It is 127 feet high and took eighteen months to build between 1892 and 1894. It is owned and run by Trinity House.'

'Why is it so far from the sands? Why isn't it built on the front?'

'Good question – it is nearly a quarter of a mile from the seafront.

There was nothing between it and the sea but dunes, and fear of coastal erosion led to it being built back here.'

'What's coastal erosion?'

'You have seen the cliffs along from the prom going north and south, and how they are collapsing into the sea?'

'Yes.'

'Well, collapsing is called erosion; it means the sea beating against the cliffs at high tide is eating away the land.'

I nodded my head as if I knew what he was talking about, but I did understand him, a bit.

'What is the light? How big is the bulb?'

'Come on, let's get up there; it is going to rain.'

I did not understand – it was a beautiful day, with a few clouds out to sea, but it was OK.

'Why do you say that? It doesn't look like rain.'

'It will, believe me – look out to sea. You can see it is coming in, and within the hour we will get a shower or two; the barometer has dropped.'

'How do you know that?'

'Don't you learn anything at school? The stable high pressure indicates good, fair weather, while the low-pressure system alerts you to rain, snowfall, or storm. The barometer readings rise when the weather is fair because the air is dry and cool. The barometric pressure falls if the weather is gloomy as the air is warm, yet wet.'

'I never heard that before; we don't get taught that at my school, Boulevard, in Hull.'

'Oh, so you are a black and white, are you?'

'Yes, why? Are you a Rovers supporter?'

'No, I am not into the sport; this job keeps me busy without going to watch a load of blokes chasing a pigskin about.' He wobbled again. 'But I do know Boulevard is where the rugby ground is, and the black and whites play there. We get a lot of them in Spread Eagle always singing their song, "Old Faithful", when they are pissed.'

We got to the top – and what a view. He was right; it was fantastic.

I'd never seen anything like it.

'Right, now then – here we have the light, or lantern, giving it its correct name. Originally, it contained an eight-wick paraffin lamp within a fixed Fresnel lens optic. It was an occulting light.'

'What does that mean, occult?'

'It means the lamp being eclipsed, or covered, three times in quick succession every minute. The occulting mechanism was clockwork. A petroleum vapour one was introduced in the early 20th century; the triple-occulting arrangement remained in place until 1936.'

'In 1936 the light was electrified: it was given a hundred-volt, 1,500-watt bulb set within an eight-sided revolving Fresnel lens array, which displayed a white flash every three seconds with a range of seventeen nautical miles or twenty miles.'

'How do you know all this? You sound as if you are reading it from some book.'

'It is my job to know the answers to any question. I take a lot of people around the lighthouse, and I have said it all so many times it's easy. Now, next question.'

'What's the difference between nautical and normal miles?'

'Well, the main difference between a land mile and a nautical mile, as their names suggest, is what they are used to measure. The land mile is mostly used for expressing the distance between points on the land surface, while nautical miles are mostly used for distances at sea, or through historical reasons.'

'Yes, but what is the difference in length?'

'Let me think; ah, yes, a mile is 5,280 feet, whereas a nautical mile is 6,076 feet. Are you happy now? God, you are nosy.'

'Yes, thank you – but what else can you tell me? I love history.'

'OK – Withernsea Lighthouse was the first in the north of England to be converted from oil to electricity. It runs off mains electricity, but if the main lamp fails, an automatic lamp changer brings a battery-powered lamp into action.'

'Who made the light? Was it a local company?'

'No, the arrangement was provided by the Chloride Electrical Storage Company, an American firm. It was the first electrical emergency lighting system adopted by Trinity House for a lighthouse. A similar system was installed at Lowestoft two years later, and subsequently, it was widely adopted across the service.'

'It's massive – how heavy is it?'

'The lens weighs two tons and floats in a mercury bath; as I said before, it is turned by clockwork. I don't think there is any more I can tell you, Leif; you are a very bright young man, nearly as brilliant as the lantern.' He wobbled again.

'Thank you for letting me come up here – it has been exciting. Just wait while I tell my mate what he has missed – he will be right pissed off.'

'Mind your language, young man, you are not old enough to swear. Now, have you had enough? Fancy a cup of tea before you go? I will put the kettle on, OK?'

'Yes, thank you, Harry – you have been great. Have you any children? I bet they love living in the lighthouse.'

'No, son, I am a widower. I lost my wife five years ago; we never had any children, sorry to say, that's why I love showing kids around the lighthouse. I enjoy the company – mind, some of them can be little bastards. Whoops, sorry, son. I will put the kettle on. We need to go down a couple of flights of stairs to the workshop.'

We walked down the stairs, Harry still telling me about the history of the building.

'Right then, pull up a chair; I will mash the tea.'

I was looking at some old photographs of Withernsea taken when there were no cars, just horses and carts. 'How old are these photos, Harry? There are no cars.'

'Oh, must be early 1900s, I suppose, just after the lighthouse was finished. They were in a cupboard in the cottage and have never been on show, as far as I know. I have been meaning to frame them and put them up on the walls, but never got round to it. You sure have a hell of a brain on you, son – what do you want to do when you leave school? Most of the children who visit ask, "Why is that rusty? How do you paint the outside of the lighthouse?" That sort of thing.'

'I want to get an apprenticeship in engineering. I read a lot about it; I don't want to finish up on fish dock like a lot of the lads.'

'Here, get that down you.' He handed me the mug of tea.

I took a mouthful; it tasted different from the tea I drank at home. I pulled a face.

'What's wrong with it? Don't you like Earl Grey?'

'Earl Grey? Who is he? What has he got to do with tea?'

'Well, Earl Grey tea is a blend that has been flavoured with bergamot, a type of orange mainly grown in Italy. The rind's fragrant oil is added to black tea to give Earl Grey its unique taste. Traditionally, Earl Grey was made from black teas such as Chinese Keemun, and it was intended to be drunk without milk.'

'Is there nothing you don't know?'

'You asked, and I know the answer. You can't have enough knowledge, young man. Now, do you want a biscuit – like a garibaldi?'

'No thanks, Harry, they always remind me of dead flies; my old man loved them. Harry, tell me, after you retired from the sea, did you miss it?'

'Yes, I do. I was a ship's master, sailed the seven seas as they call them, from the Atlantic run, then across the Pacific to the coast of Australia.'

'What about your wife? Bet she didn't like you being away all the time?'

'Oh, Margaret – she came with me. As I said, we had no children, so there was nothing to keep her in this country. She was an only child, and her parents had died quite young, I suppose, at around fifty.' He looked up at the ceiling as he spoke. 'It must have been in the genes; she died aged fifty-two.'

He looked so sad; I did not know what to say.

'Anyway, as I was saying, we had had a great life travelling the world, and we decided to retire early and come back home to enjoy life onshore.'

'Wow, I bet that was a great life. No wonder you miss her. What was the best place you went to? Where would you have liked to live, and why did you come back here to this?'

'What do you mean, "to this"? Withernsea, you mean?'

'Yes, why here?'

'Because it's my home – I was born and brought up here. Margaret was born here too; we went to school together, and were childhood sweethearts. That's why I love the place – lots of great memories. This job is perfect for me'.

'You must have been to some place better than this?'

'OK if you want me to choose a second place, somewhere that I think we would have loved – it's the most beautiful harbour in the world.'

'Where is that?'

'Sydney in Australia. As you sail into the harbour and see the arch of the bridge, it's unreal; the city is there, laid out in front of you – unbelievable. Want some more tea, Leif?' Tea Leif!' He laughed again, and then his eyes filled with tears. 'Margaret would have loved a boy like you, son. Your mother must be so proud of you; what does your father do?'

'He died not long ago; he had an accident.'

'Oh, I'm so sorry to hear that, son; can I ask how it happened?'

'I am sorry, Harry, I would rather not talk about it.'

'That's OK, son, sorry to ask. Anyway, as I say, we came back here as Trinity House needed a lighthouse keeper. I put in for the job, and got it. Margaret loved it – it was the first house we had ever owned; well, not really owned, we had always rented it, but it felt like it was ours as we didn't have to pay for it.' That laugh again. 'Then Margaret was taken ill, and after a short time, she passed away.'

'I am so sorry, Harry, I don't want to upset you asking all of these questions.'

'No, you are OK, Leif, I have never talked to anyone about my past – it's nice having someone to listen.'

I looked at the clock on the wall; it was nearly half-past five. I thought I would be in bother if I didn't go soon.

'I'm sorry, Harry, I have to go – it's getting late. Thank you for a great afternoon.'

'My pleasure, Leif. I hope I didn't bore you with all the details about the lighthouse. I have been telling people about it for so long; as you said, it sounds like I am reading it out of a book, but it's all in here.' He tapped the side of his head.

I left him sitting with his mug and his memories, and as I got to the bottom of the stairs, Harry was right – it was chucking it down.

CHAPTER 11

LEIF
Dorothy

The following day we once again had been into the town, having walked down Arthur Street; I was hoping to see my new mate Harry at the lighthouse, but there was no one around. Going on to the prom, having a bag of chips and a bottle of Coke for our dinner, we just killed time.

'What do you reckon? Shall we go back now? You said your cousin was coming today, didn't you?'

'Yes, OK. I have had enough of losing my money in the arcade; them machines are fucking fixed, I am sure of it,' said Dougie.

We had started walking back along the prom to the caravan park when this girl walked up to us. I had spotted her coming; she was stunning, with short shorts and a tight T-shirt with 'LOVE' written across the most beautiful bust I had ever seen on a girl so young.

As she got closer, she shouted, 'Dougie, there you are! I bin waiting for ages for thee to come back! Thought I would come looking for thee, where's tha bin?'

No, not another one, I thought; didn't anyone speak English in Pontefract?

'Stop moaning, here's ma new pal, Leif. Well, say hello.'

I was dumbstruck just looking at her; she was a real beauty.

'Oh, hello – you must be Dot. Doug has told me so much about you. Pleased to meet you', I held out my hand to greet her, but she ignored it, and came up to me and hugged me, giving me a peck on the cheek.

79

'Hiya, Leif – I never heard that name afore – how is thee?'

'I, er… I am fine, thanks.' I was still drooling over her body, and hoped she didn't notice me staring. I still hadn't made eye contact yet.

'How old are you, Leif?' she asked.

'Fourteen.'

She looked at Doug. 'Bloody hell, they breed 'em big round here, Doug, don't thee? Is he as big all round?' she said, laughing.

'That is for thee to find out, Dot,' said Dougie, and walked away.

Well, I thought things couldn't get any better than this – two new friends and now Dorothy had arrived. Was I pleased? Oh yes, too right I was. I think I was in love.

We all got on well together, but on the Wednesday Dougie told me they had to go home, as his granny had been taken seriously ill. I was so disappointed he was leaving when we were just getting to know each other. The good news, though, was that Dot was staying with her mum and dad as they were keeping the van; well, I say van – they were in a converted double-decker bus. Upstairs were the so-called bedrooms, two of them, and she was sleeping on a pull-out bed downstairs with Dougie, who was on a bunk bed that was part of the diner.

We said our goodbyes, promised to write to each other, and that was it – Dougie was gone. I felt very sad; I hadn't taken to a lad like that before; was I getting old? God, I was going to be fifteen next year and leaving school. Dot still had not sorted me out, as Dougie had said – until the Thursday morning; now, that was the D-day.

Dot's mum and dad had booked a bus trip to Bridlington, and Dot decided she did not want to go. She came over to tell me and, smiling, she said, 'We can be alone, Leif; there's no one to bother us with Dougie gone as well.'

We were sitting outside their 'van' when her parents came out and her dad said, 'Reet, we are off. You be OK now, you Dot, you hear, and behave yourself. Here –' he gave her a half a crown – 'that's for tha snap today, OK?'

'OK, Dad, stop mithering and get thiself going, or thee will miss tha bus.'

We watched them walk away to the path that led down to the road and waved as they turned to the left.

'Give them ten minutes,' she said, without even looking at me. The time seemed like an hour before she said, 'Reet – in t'bus, t'owld cock.'

I must have gone red as I blushed, wondering what I was supposed to do; the procedure of being 'sorted out' was a bit of a mystery to me. I still had thoughts about pictures I had seen, but other than that I knew nothing about sex. I was a virgin.

We went into the bus, and as I turned left, Dot said, 'No, not down here – upstairs, where no one can see us.' I was panicking a bit; nervous was not the word. I was about to be deflowered by a sixteen-year-old temptress, or so I thought.

I had never kissed a girl properly, never mind made love to one. OK, I was now nearly six feet tall and starting to mature. I looked older than I was, or so they told me, but in my head I was still a boy. Was I ready for sex? Or anything that was even remotely like sex? I was shitting myself, if the truth be known.

I stood there in front of Dot; I didn't know how to make the first move. She stood there waiting, and I waited – it was like a couple of boxers weighing the opponent up. Who was going to throw the first punch?

She came towards me, and took hold of my hand. I could not believe this was happening, and neither could my penis, which started to grow inside my shorts. She was bang in front of me, looking up at me, and her face and eyes were so beautiful. She gently went on her tiptoes and kissed my lips – oh my god; I had never felt anything like it.

Then it happened. She put her arms around my neck and kissed me again. For the first time, I was kissing a woman. For this was no innocent girl; her lips tasted so sweet. I still wasn't sure how to do it – kissing, I mean. I opened my mouth a little, and her tongue entered my mouth; our tongues touched. She started to suck my tongue. What the fuck was she doing? I'd never had this happen before. I did not even know this was what people did. I felt her breast against my body; she was breathing deeper as our lips were welded together. I was rock hard now; she was rubbing her groin against me. I pulled away.

'Sorry, Dot, I am not sure about this – we should not be doing it; I am not old enough.' I had never done it before. I was waffling like a stupid kid, which is what I was, I suppose.

She started to undress. She kicked off her sandals – and, oh my god, I suddenly had a foot fetish. I had never noticed a girl's feet before; she had perfect, straight toes. What was I thinking? That had never entered my head – where did that come from? My mind was going crazy.

Then she lifted her top, and what made it worse – or better, which-ever way you want to look at it – she did it slowly, and threw it on a chair. I was gone now; I had my very own stripper. Then she removed her shorts, but she had turned her back to me, and was lowering them down to the floor and bending over to pick them up, exposing her arse and small white panties; she had the most perfect bum that you could ever have seen. Then she undid her bra fasteners behind her back; I thought that was clever to do that without looking. She then turned around to face me and I almost had a happy ending right then.

'Leif, now it's your turn – you strip for me, please.' I did not know where to start; there wasn't much to take off – just my T-shirt and shorts, that was it. I took off my shirt and threw it on the chair with Dot's clothes; I undid my belt on my shorts, then the top button and let them drop.

My underpants were all I had left. 'Mmm,' Dot said. 'Now them – off now.' As she said that, she slipped hers off, and stood there naked as the proverbial day she was born, a small tuft of hair above her vagina.

I could not take my eyes off the hair; it was like it was hypnotising me, drawing me towards it. I dropped my underpants, and my penis shot up as the elastic went past it.

'Mmmmm,' she said, as she came to me. 'Now, that's much better.' Better than what? I thought. She touched me, stroked me… oh my god, this wasn't happening. She went down on her knees in front of me.

I had my eyes closed and to this day I don't how I did not come. I felt her soft lips touch; I was now having a lesson in oral sex.

'Now, Leif, I am going to tell thee something that thee must always do when tha ist shagging.'

82

'When tha is int girl, or even when tha feels tha is going ta come, try thinking about summat or nowt. Dunt matter what it is – anything, as long as tis not fuckin'. Tha knows, I tell thee what, a lad who I bin with a few times tries to think of all rugby teams and tha grounds, alphabetical like, tha knows. He ses it works for him – tha try it when we get back in ta it, OK?'

After I'd had my first sex lesson ever, even in a foreign West Riding accent, I started to think of all the teams in the rugby league competition. In those days there were thirty clubs; bloody hell, this was going to be some task, for sure. I did not know a lot of them; my next job would have to be to find an old sports mail and read up on all the teams.

With that, Dot stood up and took my hand. She led me to the bed, and pushed me back on it. She then got on top of me, and straddled her legs either side of me; I felt the heat of her as she positioned herself. I had gone limp, but not for long.

Within seconds I was standing to attention like a guardsman at Buckingham Palace, and, using her hand, she guided me into her and lowered her body down.

She started to ride me like a horse, taking the weight on her legs and holding my shoulders. Dot was fucking me – this girl was taking my virginity, and I did not care one little bit.

'Leif, please, please, don't come inside me, Leif – please don't come inside me.' She was repeating this as she rode me faster; she kept saying those words. Now, I thought I would have come a lot quicker than I did, but I was so determined; I did not want it to end. I loved it.

Bradford came to mind, then Barrow – I knew those two. Bramley, yes – that was in Leeds. Now, what were their grounds called? Bloody hell – it was working.

I got hold of her and pushed her off me I stood at the side of the bed, and, pulling her towards me, I lifted her legs and entered her again. This time I was going to fuck her; it was my turn to be boss.

I didn't take me long to reach the happy end; I had only got to Dewsbury. Now, this sex thing I could take a liking to.

I dropped down on the bed, sweat running off our bodies. I was lying face down and Dot ran her hand over the cheeks of my arse, then up my back. She rolled over on top of my back, and I felt her breasts, her nipples still erect, pushing into me. She lay there on my back, kissing my neck and running her hands up and down my arms.

Well, I was no longer a virgin. I was proud of myself. We had a drink, sitting around the bus naked. It was great – I felt so free, just my new girlfriend and me. She was mine now; well, for a few more days anyway.

We made love again that afternoon, but did not have to get stripped again. We were all ready for when the moment happened; it was great not to go through all that ritual. All we did was do it when it felt right for us both. I knew when I started to get erect just looking at Dot.

That night I went back to my tent again and thought about what had happened that day. I was alone; no Doug to watch me wanking. I found myself saying hello to man's best friend when he is alone – the five-fingered widow; yes, it was a very happy ending to a beautiful day.

The next day, we were up early. I went over to her bus; I couldn't wait to see her again. I was in love – or was it just lust? She had seduced me, her younger lover.

It was a gorgeous morning, and we decided to go for a walk along the clifftop and see how far we could get. Walking along hand in hand felt incredible. I loved it – my first girlfriend.

We had taken our swimming costumes and towels with us in case we decided to go for a swim, and Mum had made us some sandwiches; we were all set for the day. We walked for ages, climbing over fences, not sure if it was OK; still, we did anyway. We had been walking about an hour when we came to some steps carved in the cliff.

'Come on, let's go down to the beach,' I said. 'Be careful, though – they look a bit dodgy. Don't think anyone has been down them for a while.'

'You sure it is safe? I don't like heights that much; they always send me dizzy.'

Anyway, we managed to climb down; there had been quite a bit of coastal erosion around the area and the clifftop wasn't that high. It took a bit of doing, and where the cliff had fallen into the sea, it had created a bit of a headland. Dot decided she fancied a swim.

'Come on, let's go in here.' I was a bit unsure; I didn't know the beach and had read somewhere that you had to careful of currents.

'OK,' I said, 'but don't go in too deep – just over paddling depth.'

'Don't be such a baby, Leif – we can both swim.'

'Yes, in the pool, but I've but not had a lot of sea experience.' None, in fact.

'Ast tha ever did skinny dipping?'

'What is that, then?'

'Tha knows – swimmin' int nude. Naked, no cossie?'

It sounded a bit iffy to me. 'What if someone comes along the beach?'

'Don't worry, we'll si them coming'.

What a fucking girl this was; unreal. She was already stripping off as I was putting our towels on the sand. 'Come on, get thisen naked – it feels great, sun on t'body, look at me.'

That was all I needed. I stripped off, and she was right – it felt great. Off she ran – well, kind of ran, as the beach was more pebbles than sand nearer the water. At least the tide was out, and once you got over the stones, it was OK – flat, hard sand. There was not much of a swell in the water anyway.

I was getting a little of a swell on myself, watching Dot jumping up and down, tits bouncing. Once again, although the sun was hot, the water was freezing. Once I got my balls in, my hard-on soon disappeared.

We played about in the water, and got used to it, but no way could you call it warm. She jumped on my back, and pulled me down into the water, diving on top of me. God, it was good feeling her body next to mine naked, so natural. After a while, I said, 'Come on, I have had enough. Let's go sunbathe for a bit.' We got out and dried each other off; it was so beautiful just to be naked as nature intended.

We lay down on towels next to each other, holding hands, the sun beating down on our bodies.

I had nodded off and was soon asleep; I thought I was dreaming that I was on a beach with Dot.

We were making love – she was now down on me, but then realised I wasn't dreaming. She was doing it while I was asleep. What a horny bitch this girl was. Who had taught her all of this at such a tender age? You never saw anything like that on TV if you had one.

She got on top again; there was something about her riding me, but who was I to complain? It ended a bit quicker than the previous day, but still fabulous.

We decided to walk along the beach back to the caravan site, which was not the right decision as walking on the sand took far longer, and the tide was coming in.

I started to get a bit worried as we tramped on. I could see the gap between the water and the cliffs narrowing. I knew we had not seen any other steps carved in the cliff face along the way; well, there were no posts stuck in the grass at the top of them anyway. The sun was going down as well; there was a bit of a chill in the air. We came to a bit of headland, and we had to get around this point. The problem was, the water was lapping at the cliff for about a hundred yards or more until it opened up again. I could see the panic in Dot's face when we rounded the head.

'What are we going to do? Oh, Leif, I am frightened.' She started to cry.

'Put your swimmers on,' I said. 'We will wade through the surf – it won't take long.'

There was no one around to ask for help, so we quickly undressed, put our costumes on and set off, holding hands as we walked. God, it was hard work; the water was breaking against the cliff and was getting a bit deeper, and the tide was coming in fast. We had no idea what we were getting ourselves into.

It really was a struggle now, and we had only got halfway, for the gap in front of us was getting narrower too; the water was well past our waists and it was hard to walk.

I did not want to swim just in case it took us away from the cliffs. Then about five yards away spotted a rope lying on the rise halfway up. It was what remained of some steps; there had been a cliff fall at some time, and the bottom half had been washed away. All that was left was the top set of steps. They had put a turn in them, and they looked OK, but we had to climb the bottom half on the rough face.

I told Dot to follow me; I would go first to test the ground. I set off, and it was not good, but I tried not to show fear as I clambered up the cliff, now and then stopping to grab Dot's hand as she followed me up. 'It is OK, Dot, come on – don't look down whatever you do.' Which, of course, she then did, and panic set in when she realised how high it was – but we were nearly at the steps.

She froze. 'I can't, Leif – I can't do it.'

'Now listen, Dot, you can – you have to, or you'll die.' After I had said that, I thought it might have been a bit over the top, but still. 'Now, come on, just a bit more – come on, please. Try, please – I love you; I can't leave you here.'

Now, the word love had never been mentioned, not that I could remember, even in the height of passion, but anyway it came out. 'Close your eyes,' I said. 'I will guide you; just hold my hand.' We managed to get to the steps and still with her eyes closed we climbed to the top.

We sat on the grass on top of the cliff edge, watching the waves crashing against the cliffs that we had just come past. 'We were lucky, Dot, that we left when we did, or we would have drowned, without a doubt.' She hugged my arm and kissed my cheek.

We got back to the bus and van a bit later than we thought we would; our parents were panicking as we strolled across the grass. They had been talking about calling the police, as it was nine o'clock. We hadn't known the time, for neither of us had taken a watch.

I got back into my tent that night and lay back naked; I could feel a gentle breeze coming in. It was hot, and I was dreaming of my experience that day. I was that tired I must have nodded off.

I was dreaming of Dot and what she had shown me since we'd first met only three days before, and how she had taken my virginity. When she took me between her lips, I know there is a first time for everything but, believe me, I will never forget that. I was dreaming, but it felt so real.

I opened my eyes, and I wasn't dreaming, after all – there was Dot again, naked and on her knees inside my tent. She had sneaked in when I was asleep, taking me in her mouth once more, without waking me. I never spoke; I just laid back and thought, you are one fortunate boy,

Leif Askenes, one lucky boy. Dot stayed with me all night, cuddled up in my sleeping bag. We fell asleep together, and it felt so natural wrapped in each other's arms, knowing that we would not have many more days together as she was only here for a week.

We spent the rest of the week together, and Mum said to me, 'You like Dot, don't you? I have never seen you so friendly with any of the girls down our street. I have never even seen you with a girl – what's so special about her?'

'I don't know, Mum, I suppose it's because she is not like the Hessle Road lasses. I don't know – I just like her.' If you only knew how close we were, I thought to myself.

It was Saturday, and Dot and her parents were going back to the West Riding. They had got friendly with Mum and Billy, and had been to the pub a few times with them. We even went in the fish restaurant down near the front for Friday night's tea together – the last supper, so to speak.

I was besotted with this girl; I did not want her to go. Yes, I was in love, which is stupid, I know – fourteen and in love with a sixteen-year-old. She had made me a man, and even though we'd done things that may not have been right by the law, it had seemed just so right to both of us. I had found my sex therapist, and she was departing; she had taught me something I would never have dreamed of – rugby and sex going together. She was leaving me, to go back to the land of the funny accent, liquorice cakes and black pudding.

They had booked a taxi to take them back to Hull – they must be worth a few bob, I thought. That was another thing – I knew nothing about her family; just Mr and Mrs Ward, that is all I ever called them.

The due time came, and we said our goodbyes. Dot's mum hugged me, and her dad shook hands with me. Then Dot hugged me; we were standing alone as Mum and Billy were walking back to our railway carriage, and Mr and Mrs Ward were walking down to the road with their cases. I could see the black cab near the gate. We gave our final hug, holding each other so tight, and we kissed; we did not care who saw us.

Dot whispered in my ear. 'Leif Askenes, I love you so much – please,

please keep in touch. Write to me.' She put a piece of paper in my hand, and as she pulled away from me, I could see the tears rolling down her cheeks.

Then my girl was gone. I got my composure as she reached the gate and I ran down to the car just as it was pulling away. I was crying now. I waved, but Dorothy Ward had gone.

I went back to the seclusion of my tent, and opened the piece of paper she had given me. It was a love letter. It said:

24 Castleford Rd
Pontefract
West Yorkshire

Dear Leif,

I just wanted to say how pleased I was to find you these last few days, pleased that you had made friends with Doug, my cousin – for if you had not, we might never have had such a fantastic holiday. I know we may never meet again, but here is my address. I hope you write to me and we can keep in touch. Pontefract is not a million miles away; maybe we can visit each other. We have a big house and lots of room. I will ask Mum and Dad if you can visit.

I start work in an office at a factory in Pontefract in two weeks' time, having finished my schooling – we did not talk much about what we did at school or anything like that – we were having too good a time, I suppose, but please, Leif, please write to me.

Love You,
Dot Ward xxxxxxxxxxx

CHAPTER 12

LEIF

Mrs Wilson

I used to go round to my grandparents' house more now and sit and talk to Grandad. He used to tell some great stories about his father and Norway; I was enthralled just listening to him.

We were sitting chatting one day, and he was saying how his father, Olaf Victor, used to tell him about the old days when Jarle, my great-great-grandfather, came to Hull during the famine. I used to say, 'Mum told us, Grandad.'

'I suppose she did, son, but she didn't know the suffering those families went through; how they gave up everything to get a new life – leaving all their farms and possessions in the old land and walking days, sometimes weeks, to get to the ports to organise a crossing.'

He used to talk about his life at sea, and the mates he had, especially in the fishing industry. For that was the principal employer in the Hessle Road area of Hull; everyone knew everyone else. It was a village in a city, as it was often called. It was a hard life, trying to earn a living. Often trawlers went missing, and even men went missing, having either been washed overboard during storms or injured when hauling in the nets. But work still went on, as catching fish was the foremost priority. Safety did not come into it – and then the real tragedies happened.

We had never talked so much before. I enjoyed his company; he seemed like a father to me – the one I had never had. Even though he was ancient, Grandad was excellent company and, after all, he was my flesh and blood.

I was talking to Mum one day, and I asked her, 'Can I tell you something that has been bothering me – upsetting me, to be honest.'

'Hey, what's the problem? You look as if you are about to cry. Come on, baby, what's wrong? You know you can ask me anything.'

'It's Grandad Hans. You know I have been going round more and more lately, especially weekends.'

'Yes, why? Has he done something to upset you? I will kill him if he has.'

'No, nothing… it is just – well, I feel close to him now we have got to know each other, but I feel there is something wrong. I often sense him looking at me when I am not looking. He turns away when he sees; he is watching me, and I don't get it, Mum.'

Mum went kind of red, with a worried expression. 'No, don't worry – he is just like that... he is – well, no, it doesn't matter.'

I knew that she was hiding something but could not figure out what.

I had been swimming a lot during the summer, going to Madeley Street baths and Albert Avenue lido. This was a vast open-air pool, and the water was always cold, but I loved it whenever I could get there; fitting it in was the big problem.

I was getting leaner and healthier with this form of exercise, and I felt a lot fitter. I was looking forward to the rugby season starting again, that was for sure. I'd also grown a couple of more inches, and was now just over six feet and thirteen stones.

I was at the lido one day, and was swimming alone; only a few people would venture outside because of the water being too cold. There were three lanes separated from the rest of the pool for people who did not want to keep bumping into others as they swam.

I was doing my lengths, just continual swimming – the crawl stroke, up and down. I used to keep going until I was so tired I could not go on. I was pushing myself to the limit – I do not know why; I just did it for my satisfaction, I suppose.

There was this girl – well, not so much a girl, but a woman, doing more or less the same. I passed her a few times in the next lane as she was swimming breaststroke, much slower than me. At one point at the low end when I did not do a tumble turn, she had stopped to take a breather and was putting her swimming cap back on as it had come off. As I turned, I looked at her. She smiled and said, 'Hello – how many is that today?'

'Forty up to now',

'That's over a mile.'

'Yes,' I said. 'Thirty-two lengths is a mile, near enough.' I had stopped now, so had sort of lost my rhythm.

'Oh, sorry – I don't want to stop you.'

'That's OK – I was just about to stop anyway. I like to go as far as I can but was getting a bit tired anyway.' I was lying; I could have kept going, but she was a good-looking sort and I did not want to pass up the chance of talking to her.

'Do you come here a lot?' she asked.

'Yes, a couple of times a week at least during the summer months, and it's the school holidays, anyway.'

'Oh, are you still at school? You look older – whoops, sorry.' She kind of blushed.

'It's OK – people always say that. It's because I am tall for my age. I'm, er, sixteen and six foot tall.' I lied; I did not want to tell her the truth, that I was not quite fifteen. 'I work for my uncle – he is a builder, but when we are not very busy he lets me have days off during the week.'

'My, you are a big boy.' She touched my shoulder as she said it, and my nether regions twitched.

'I come here quite often as well. Do you live locally?'

'Yes, on Hessle Rd, near Boulevard – Rosamond Street.'

'Oh, I live down South Boulevard – been there six months. We moved here from London with my husband's job.'

'You like it?'

'Yes, it's OK. Bit lonely, though, I don't know many people; don't get out much what with his job and all.'

'Why did you pick South Boulevard?'

'Oh, we rent a place – we are having a house built up in Kirkella, and it was near to the docks. My husband is a ship's master and he is away quite a bit. He is also from up this way and wanted to come back to Yorkshire to live.'

Bloody hell – Kirkella! They must have a few quid; that is the poshest place around these parts, I thought. 'Oh,' I said. I didn't know what else to say. 'I have never been to Kirkella; I heard it is nice up there.'

'Yes, it's a quiet area, but nice.'

'Anyway, I have had enough now; I will go and get changed. It was nice meeting you. Oh, I am Leif, by the way.'

'Karen.' She put her hand out. 'Karen Wilson – very pleased to meet you.' She held my hand and looked into my eyes a little bit longer than you would normally. She was lovely.

'Right, see you again, I hope,' I said as she got out of the pool. Now, what a body she had; what a great arse – it was right in front of my face as she climbed out. I jumped up in one movement and stood beside her.

She took off her swimming cap, and her long red hair tumbled out, falling almost to her shoulders; she ran her fingers through it. She was stunning. I just stood looking at her. 'OK, bye,' I said, and off she went.

I went to get changed and set off for home, walking along Albert Avenue towards Anlaby Road, and this car stopped beside me.

'Hi, Leif – can I give you a lift? I am going your way. I am going home – hop in.'

'No, it's OK, I will walk.' What was I saying? Idiot – of course I wanted a lift!

'No, come on, I insist. Don't be silly – why walk?'

'OK, cheers,' I said, and got in the car. It was a little MG sports car. It was a struggle to get in at first – more than ever when my eyes were on the most beautiful legs I had ever seen. She only had shorts on; her legs had looked good in swimmers, but now – fuck me, she was beautiful. Her red hair, now it was dry, was down past her shoulders.

'Thanks for the lift, Mrs Wilson.'

'No, call me Karen – please, Leif, it's Karen,' she said, as she touched my leg. It did not take long to get to Hessle Road; only a few minutes.

'Please just drop me off at your place,' I said. 'I am going on road anyway; no need to stop twice.'

'Would you like to come to mine for a coffee or something? I am not doing anything else today; I would love to chat more. It gets lonely on my own.'

'Can we make it another time? I am sorry, I can't today.' I have no idea why I said that. Why was I playing hard to get? Bloody fool that I was.

'OK – look forward to seeing you again – when are you at swimming?'

'I will be there on Thursday.'

'Fancy doing it together?' she giggled. 'Swimming, I mean.'

'OK, yes, I will be there. What time?'

'Let's make it early, before the crowds get in – say eight, OK?'

'OK. Bye for now.' I got out of the car.

'Byeee!' she said.

Oh, fuck, what have I done, I thought – I'd made a date with an older woman. I was fourteen, for god's sake. I was running it all through my head. It must be a wind-up, or I was dreaming?

I was walking down Hessle Road, asking myself why I hadn't gone in. Was I afraid of her and what might happen? A married woman did not ask a boy to come in for coffee... or did she? What did she want? She kept touching me – why? All these things were running around in my head. Go back, I thought – say you think you dropped your house key in her car – that's a great excuse.

But, no – I did not go back. I decided not to rush and make a fool of myself, so I waited until the Thursday.

Thursday morning came, and I got up nice and early. Mum was getting ready to go to work; Billy had already gone.

'Bloody hell – have you shit the bed, son? You're up early.'

'Yes, I'm going to the lido – I want to get there early before all the kids get there.'

'Hmm... now listen to your old mam, kid. You are only fourteen going on bloody forty yourself, Leif.'

I said nothing in reply.

'Get your breakfast before you go – I am off.'

She kissed my cheek and was gone. I woofed some toast down with some milk and rushed off – if I got to Rayners there was a bus that took you down Albert Avenue. I just managed to catch it as it was leaving, jumping on the platform to a look of disdain from the conductor.

I got off at the baths and was in the water by eight o'clock – but no Karen. There were a couple of older guys in their fifties swimming up and down in both lanes. Bloody hell, she hasn't turned up; you're a fool to think she would, I thought.

I started doing my laps; I do not know how long I had been swimming, but the two old guys had gone, and I had the pool to myself. I was into it now, concentrating, and had got into a rhythm – a nice, steady pace, only breathing in and out on the fourth stroke as I turned my head, then breathing in on the rolling turn as I came up out of the water.

As I got back to the shallow end, there was a hand on my shoulder; it was Karen.

'Sorry I am late, but I got held up – I see you have started, Leif.' She remembered my name – wow.

'Oh, hi, Karen, yes – I have not long been here.'

She lowered herself into the water; she was already wet from the shower and foot bath at the entrance. She smelt wonderful. I hadn't noticed that the other day.

'That smells nice,' I said, but why, I don't know; I suppose I was nervous, on my first date with an older woman.

We swam up and down together for a while, both doing the breaststroke, chatting as we swam. She said: 'I can tell I am holding you up; you go and do your mile and then we can chat again, OK?'

Off I went, and was soon back in my rhythm. I just loved swimming.

Karen was sitting on the edge of the pool as I came up to the shallow end again. I had done more than a mile. 'Hi, you finished then?' I asked.

'Yes, just waiting for you – we're having that coffee at mine today. No arguing, OK?'

I nodded in agreement, and we went to get changed. I waited outside

Karen's entrance; then she appeared in those shorts again. Fuck, she looked beautiful.

I opened the door for her like the gentleman I was, and as she bent down to get in the car her T-shirt rode up her back, showing the bottom of her spine. It was so smooth and tanned – oh my, she was gorgeous. I shut the door when she was inside; those long, slender legs – wow.

We drove back to her house, and got out of the car; there was no one around in the street – not that it mattered. I could have been her son. As we went in the house, she locked the door behind her, smiled and said, 'I always do that. London habit, I suppose, but you never know. Come into the kitchen – what would you like? Tea, coffee, soft drink?'

'Can I have an orange drink, please, if you have any?'

'Sure.' She handed me the glass, and as she did so her fingers touched mine. 'I won't be a second,' she said, and disappeared up the stairs. It was a big old house with large entrance hall and a sweeping staircase.

A couple of minutes later, she returned. 'There, that's better – needed a pee, sorry!' She also smelt good again; she had put some perfume on while she was gone. 'Come into the lounge,' she said. We walked into the front room, which was a large room with two three-seater settees, one by the side of a big old fireplace. Karen put her coffee on the table and sat down next to me, curling her long legs up underneath her. 'That's better. Now, Leif, tell me about yourself. You know all about me – you know I am married, he is away and I get lonely being here on my own most of the time. One thing you did not know is that I love younger men.'

Then she touched my leg; I was wearing old football shorts, and I looked at her as I put my hand on hers. 'You are beautiful, Karen.' I was trembling; it wasn't going to be Wigan today.

She moved closer, stroked my face and kissed my lips softly, just touching hers on mine. She put her hand underneath the front of my T-shirt, stroking my belly. I shuddered at her touch. 'Come on,' she said, and grabbed my hand and led me upstairs.

Now, I had never had sex in a real bedroom, only on a bus with Dot, so this was going to be unique. We walked in, kissing; she opened the door. The bed was about nine feet wide; I'd never seen one so big. She took her top off, leaving her black bra, and black panties with frills that looked like silk, but there again I was no knickers specialist. I stripped down to my underpants; being one of the old Y-fronts brigade, mine were blue with a white Y.

We moved together now, kissing. Oh, that fragrance – fucking hell, it was driving me mad; I'd never smelt anything like it. Her lips were everywhere, kissing, licking me all over my face down to my nipples. Oh god, that felt good. We kissed again, and I undid her bra. I was getting the knack of that – and without much practice, too, I thought. Her breasts were unreal – no drop, firm to the touch and nipples like the proverbial chapel hat pegs.

We walked to the bed, and lay down together, still kissing. Then she stopped and put both hands each side of my waist, sliding my pants down; my cock stood to attention.

'Mmmm,' she said as she began to stroke it, 'You are a beautiful young boy, Leif – I have never made love to a sixteen-year-old before. I am going to make a man out of you.'

And with that, her lips touched me. Barrow, Craven Park... oh, Jesus, down she went. Oh my god, Karen knew what she was doing. Oh, where now? Bradford, Odsal... Bramley, Barley Mowe... control yourself, Leif – oh yes, Castleford... no, Batley... you missed Batley, Mount Pleasant. Too late – Wigan arrived, and without stopping at the station.

Karen just kept me on track, then with a flash I found out what mine tasted like as she kissed me, tongue in my mouth, the lot. I didn't know what to do – gag, throw up or what, but she just smiled at me, licking her lips. 'Mmm, that tasted divine, Leif.'

I cringed, not sure what to say.

'Don't you like the taste, Leif? My hubby loves me doing that to him when he is home. Every time we make love, we do that.' It made me wonder what he did when he was alone in his cabin in the middle of the Pacific Ocean.

It was afternoon, and I had to go – no rest for these men of mystery! I made my apologies, and we arranged to meet at the lido the next week.

The day came around and I met Karen again, going through the same ritual, but there was something different about her this time. It was as if she wanted to say something, then changed her mind.

We had set off from Albert Avenue to go to her place; we came to the junction with Anlaby Road, and she turned right instead of left. I said, 'Where are we going now, Karen?'

'Got a little surprise for you, babe – just wait.'

We drove along Anlaby Road on to Anlaby High Road, then up to Kirkella. I had never been up here. As we passed the sign for the village I asked if we were going to see where their new house was being built. 'No,' was the answer. 'Just wait, I was going to ask you in the pool if you wanted to.' Then she stopped talking.

'Wanted to what, Karen? What are you talking about?'

'Meet a friend of mine, Leif – a very close friend. I was telling her about you on Saturday, and she is dying to meet you. I thought we would have a run out here to see her. You're not busy this afternoon, are you?'

'No, I'm not busy; it's a nice day for a ride out, anyway. When you say "she" – who is she?'

'One of my oldest girlfriends; I've known her for quite a few years. We were at boarding school together – it was a finishing school, Brown-hills in Bristol.'

'Nice, sounds posh.' She laughed when I said posh. We pulled in a driveway, just outside the village, of a large house that looked more like a hotel.

'Here we are. Come on, let's meet Helen.' As we got out of the car, the front door opened and a woman came out. She was tall, with dark hair in a bun, and looked more like an old-fashioned school teacher, like the ones you saw at the cinema.

'Helen, this is Leif I was telling you all about. Leif, this is Helen.'

'Hello, Leif, I've heard so much about you – delighted to meet you,' said Helen, in the sexiest voice I had ever heard. It almost melted me when she spoke; she uttered every word very slowly. I reached Castle-ford without even trying.

'You were right, Karen – such a beautiful boy and only sixteen.'

'Hi,' is all that came out.

'Come in, come in – let's have a drink, shall we?' We went into the hallway, where there was a massive sweeping staircase which must have been six feet wide, with a handrail either side. It was the one in Hammonds, and, I assumed, led up to the bedrooms. Helen turned and smiled at me as I was looking up the stairs.

'Come out to the garden – why sit inside on such a nice day?' she said.

Wow – the garden; it was like West Park. Unbelievable. 'What is that down there?' I asked, pointing to a building about a hundred yards away.

'Oh, that's the indoor pool; we had it built last year. The tennis courts are just beyond it.'

It was awe-inspiring. An indoor pool – we did not even have a bath or hot water, never mind a swimming pool; how the other half lived.

'Want to go down and have a look, Leif? We can if you want.'

'I'd love to.'

We walked down to the poolhouse and went inside. 'I don't suppose you want to try it, Leif? I hear you are a good swimmer – you certainly have swimmers' shoulders,' said Helen, as she touched my arm, squeezing my biceps. 'Wow – hard, too.'

'My cossie is in the car; shall I go back and get it?'

'No need for a costume – we never use them. No one can see us, and we love swimming naked; you feel so free.' My mind went back to Dot on Withernsea beach; a bit of an upgrade here, I thought.

'Told you you would like Helen, didn't I, Leif?' said Karen, and with that they both started to strip off.

'Come on, get stripped, Leif,' said Helen. 'Don't be shy – I heard that was the last thing you were.'

We were all stood there naked, the three of us, and Karen came over and kissed me.

'Come on, let us have some fun. Helen wants you, babe.'

Helen then came to me, and I was about to try to kiss her, but she turned to Karen, and they kissed. Oh my god, what's going on, I thought – I had never seen two girls or women kiss like they were; they were really kissing, and I liked it. Believe me, I loved it.

Helen had a thing in her hand that I'd never seen before; I now know it was a remote control, and it had a lead on it like a microphone. She pressed a switch on it, and behind her, a sliding door moved to the right. It was a double door and it opened to reveal a double bed. It didn't have sheets or bedclothes; it was covered in what looked like a giant towel.

They grabbed a hand each and walked me to the bed. When we got there, they let go of me and jumped on the bed, lying side by side, but with a space in between them. They both patted the gap and said, 'Here, come here, Leif.'

I got between them, my head on the pillow as they moved closer to me. I had an arm around each one, and they were kissing and touching me. I was at Doncaster already. We did everything you could dream of.

It seems they had done it a few times, working a man; they made quite a team. Talk about knowing what the other one was thinking – it was the best thing I had ever experienced in my short life. I even got to Wigan. They shared the spoils. I will say no more.

That was the ultimate experience, but unfortunately, it was the last time I ever saw Helen. In fact, it was the last time I met Karen, too – but I had enjoyed another lesson in the art of making love.

CHAPTER 13

LEIF
The Club

I went back to school in the A form with a Mr Loveless; he was a big man, must have been about six foot two, with a shock of red hair – he looked like Jerry Lee Lewis. He was a great teacher; I looked forward to going to school every day. If there was such a thing as a man-crush, this was it – I loved this man; he was more like a father figure to me. Maybe it was, because I never really had a man to look up to apart from Billy; he was OK as a guy, but you would not call him inspirational. Old Lovelace, as we called him, was the bee's knees. I learnt more from him than any other tutor I had at school.

We had started the new curriculum, and I had picked the technical course. This covered maths, English, science, technical drawing, metalwork and art. I loved every lesson. It was part of my dream; I had to do well if I was to reach the targets I had set myself. Technical drawing I found to be my best subject, and maths was another of my favourites, which fell in line with what I wanted to be when I left school.

I was asked to become a prefect, which was a great honour. Mum was over the moon when she found out. I was not head boy – Tommy James had got that job; he was on the commercial course. Still, I was his assistant, which meant I was in charge of issuing the milk out to all the classes, and also meant I missed assembly every morning as I had to make the crates of milk up. Two boys from each classroom would come out from the assembly and collect the relevant crate from me.

Another task I took on was to take charge of the sports equipment, meaning we had to make sure that all the footballs and rugby balls were inflated to the right pressure and ready for Thursday's sports days.

The school used to transport the boys by bus to the playing fields at Anlaby Park Road North. There were no changing rooms or showers, but when we got back we were allowed to go home early to get a wash, or a bath – if you had one, that is.

The equipment was stored in a small staff-only room between the ground floor and the top floor in the central stairway. Our task was to maintain the equipment during our dinner breaks. For those who stayed school dinners, this was easy – and I was one of those boys.

There were six prefects – me, Tommy James, Jimmy Rogers, Mike Walters, Clive Jones, and Billy Watson, all from the same year. Tommy and Billy were commercial, Jimmy nautical, and the others on the technical with me.

I did not know two of the others that well, for they had been in a B form the year before; I knew them to say hello to. Only Mike played rugby; the others played football. Anyway, the first time we went up to look at the sports gear, we all said, 'Hey, this is a good spot – beats hanging around the playground, tossing it off.' With that, Clive said, 'Great place for a wank.'

We all kind of looked at him at the same time. 'What you on about, Jonesy – a wank?' I said.

'Yes, come on lads – we are all men of the world, and don't give me that. You don't mind pulling one off now and again.'

No one commented on the subject until Billy said, 'Well, I suppose you are right, Jonesy, it is out of the way, and we can lock the door from the inside so we won't be disturbed.'

I could not believe what I was hearing. I knew I had led a sheltered life, I suppose, but to hear five boys discussing mass wanking sessions was beyond belief.

Then the head boy spoke. I was expecting some sense to come from this pillar of society, the top boy in the school, but he said, 'We used to have wanking competitions with my mates at one of their old man's allotments.'

'Fucking wanking competitions? I have never heard fuck-all like it,' was my next comment.

'Oh, come on, Leif, I bet you wank yourself daft having a mother like yours; she is a film star, man,' said Mike. 'I would if she was my old lady. Mind, I must admit my sister gives me one now and again.'

Oh my god, this was a den of vice – they were supposed to be the top six boys in the school, but they were nothing short of wankers.

I had heard stories about public schools where the prefects used to abuse some of the other boys, but they were all much older, in their late teens, some of them at Eton and the like – but a secondary modern in the north of England? No way.

Tommy then chipped in, 'What do you think of the competitions, then? Who fancies that? If you do, put your hand up.'

This is democracy at work, I thought – the Prime Minister asking the cabinet who were the wankers among us. I could not believe it as everyone, but me, put their hand up.

'What's wrong, Leif? You not up for it?' said Tommy, who seemed a bit too keen on this so-called wanking competition, OK, on reflection, it seemed not too bad an idea.

'But as long as it is kept as a secret – how or when does it happen? How can you have a competition when it is you doing the wanking?' Or did this entail some other form of masturbation? 'Tell us more, Tommy, how do we compete in this mass masturbation game?'

'Oh, it is easy, Leif – we just wank together and whoever lasts longest without shooting his load wins. Or we all lie on the floor and whoever comes the highest up against the wall wins. There are different variations.'

How the hell this guy had got the head boy position was just way beyond me. He went on to tell us he was involved with three of his mates, one of whose fathers was a trawler skipper. They were at one of their houses, up Hessle way, and they had a shed in the garden. One of the boys was of West Indian birth, having come here a couple of years earlier; his father was a GP. One might call him an international wanker. They were duly having a 'session', shall we call it, and then, Tommy said, laughing like fuck, 'The door to the shed opened and Kev's father, who was home from sea, looked in. "What the fuck is going on here? No, don't answer that – and is that a black pudding you got there, Leroy? OK, that's enough – out, the lot of you. Don't let me catch you again. Kevin, get a bolt put on that door so you can lock it; at least it will keep your mother or sisters out – now fuck off, the lot of you."'

So the Boulevard Honourable Wankers club was born; it met every lunchtime, Mondays, Tuesdays, Wednesdays and Fridays, 12.15pm to 1.15pm.

The only rules were that you brought your own small towel or cloth, and there no discussions about what went on; it was our very own secret society. As it happened, I won most of the game; must have been the extra tuition I'd had from Dorothy.

CHAPTER 14

LEIF

The Mind of a Fourteen-year-old Boy

The school year was going well. I was now regularly playing centre in the A team, and we had an excellent side. Melvin Neilson was top try scorer with eighteen; Tommy Francis scored sixteen. He kicked fifty goals and was also selected, along with captain Bill Lavery (thirteen tries), for both the Hull Boys and Yorkshire Boys teams, Bill being selected as Hull City Boys player of the year.

A third member of the team, Gordon Hopper, was chosen for Hull Boys. I scored twelve tries. OK, even if I must say it myself, I was really enjoying the game now and was also a regular supporter of Hull FC.

I was doing some homework given to me by our history teacher; we had to put into words or write down our thoughts on the country's past social history. I was telling Mum about the exercise.

'That sounds exciting, dear; have you ever thought about it – they have some funny ways to teach nowadays. Well, have you?'

'Yes, I have; it's not only what I have read, but one thing that has always got to me is I have noticed that anyone wealthy is also influential; anyone who is a so-called leader also has lots of money.'

'Well, that's just a fact of life, son; once you are wealthy, you tend to stay wealthy, unless you are a fool, that is – remember the old saying: a fool and his money are soon parted. That says it all.'

'Yes, but what I can't understand is why are people so toffee-nosed when they get rich? They look down on us poor people.'

'It is called "them and us"; the reason being is because "them" have more money than "us".'

'I can't understand how it works. I have read in the history books that there is a class system in the UK; it was the same worldwide. OK, they have different names, like socialism, or communism, or religion.'

'Wow, you are into this, son – I never realised you were so deep.'

'Why is it that some people became leaders by convincing other people that they were all equal? Only, some of them are just that little bit better than others because they can talk better, as in socialism. Another thing I noticed is the ones who can speak "proper English". They seem not to do anything but somehow have convinced the lower class that they do.'

'Yes, dear; quite a number of these people became politicians. Either in local government or sometimes they go to London to represent the local community, as an MP.'

'Must be a good job sitting around in a big house just discussing "things" and getting lots of money for doing it; that would do me, Mum.'

'They seem to do OK out of it, son, and when they finish being an MP, they never seem to work again; it has always been the same.'

'One other thing I need to write about in my project is communism; it seems to me most of the people are told, "We are all equal, and we all should live together sharing our wealth" – but with some people being greedy, it just can't work, and I think the leaders in communism make sure that they had more of the common denominator money.'

'Jesus, Leif – how does your brain work, son? I did not realise I had a genius as a child.' She started laughing.

'Don't laugh, Mum, I'm serious. It seems to me that money is a big difference in every form of any class system. It appears to me as a boy that those that have more of this stuff become leaders – keeping those that do not have a lot of money in their place. Am I right or not?'

'You certainly have a point; I can't argue with you there.'

'Good. They do this either by making laws to ensure that the lower classes can't get any higher up the ladder, or in some cases use force to keep them down, making sure that the lower-level working class, as it is known, do all the work.'

'Is there nothing you have not looked at? This is amazing, the things they teach you at school nowadays.'

'No, Mum – one other form of a class system, I feel, is religion; this subject always confuses me. It seems to me that the lower classes in the world are always kept in fear by men who walk about in dresses, or who wear their collars back to front. I used to think they can't be that clever, they can't even dress proper. The preacher or priest or vicar, whatever the relevant name being used is, is always talking about some invisible person called God, who lives in the sky. Who no one ever saw walking down the street, whose son was born to a woman who had never had sex. However, she was married to a guy called Joe; now, God, who has never been here, somehow made her pregnant. I have seen some good magicians but never as smart as this.'

'Oh, give over, you are making me laugh now.'

'It's true, Mum; now, this Jesus came for a visit nearly two thousand years ago, right? Stopped for thirty-odd years, finishing up talking twelve other guys into joining his gang. He fell out with some other people from Italy; they got fed up with him having meetings to show his magic tricks. They had him killed because of one of his band who got greedy and was offered some money to dob him in.'

'Sending you to Sunday School didn't do much good, did it?'

'Mum, things have changed. Along with all that I have said, part of this was the fear they put into people. They told them that if you did not do as they were told you would not go up in the clouds to some place called Heaven. You would go to hell. Where is this place? I have no idea, for no one has ever come back from either to tell us what it is we should expect when we go there. We only have the guys in the dresses, or who wear their collars back to front, telling us it's the bee's knees, and when we get there we will love it. Come on, Mum.'

'You are evil – how come you think like this? I never brought you up to be talking like this?'

'Don't get upset; I understand there are different versions of religion. We are Christian in the Church of England; some of my mates at school are Roman Catholics, some practising, some not. How they practise I don't know, but that is what they say they are. Then there is the Methodists, whose leaders do not wear dresses or walk about with their handbags on fire, throwing smoke at people sitting in the crowd waiting to hear them talk about their version of the same guy up in the clouds.'

'Oh, my, you do talk some shite at times, Leif; you should be an MP – you would do well.'

'It is not shite – what about the other lot? There are lads who I go to school with who are Jewish. Now, they all seem to be wealthy, always seem to have lots of money. Seems to me that somehow they are not liked by all the other religions. I don't know why; I never had any problem with them, and what gets me is Jesus was always called king of the Jews. If he was the king, why did he not get the same treatment as our Royal Family? Mind, having said that, I would not like to be Jewish for they have to go to Sunday school on a Saturday – now, fuck that.'

'Stop swearing – you might be old enough to come out with all this stuff you just told me, but not old enough to swear in this house, OK? Anyway, we have a relation of ours who is Jewish – he was once a trawler skipper who kind of saw the light, I suppose. He made a few quid, then chucked the sea and became a money lender; he worked out he could make more money by lending it to lads who were at sea.'

'Why lend them money? I always thought they were on good money?'

'Most of them are, but they only get paid when they come home and even then they might not get a lot if the catch isn't big enough when they settle, or there isn't a big enough share after the owners and the skippers have taken their bit. He used to sub them a few quid so that their wives had enough money to feed the families, and he then used to charge them money for borrowing the cash.'

'Is that what they call interest? Because they showed interest in borrowing it, or something like that?'

'Yes, that's the idea – when they come home, they pay him back what they owed plus a bit on top for having the luxury of borrowing the money.'

'It seems to me these Jewish guys had their heads screwed on the right way. It has gone on for years, this money thing. I read somewhere in one of the history books at school that it started when people used to barter or swap things, mostly animals like horses or cattle or sheep, or goods like wheat, anything that someone else wanted, they used to exchange items. Say you had a cow that someone with sheep wanted, then because your cow was bigger you could get three sheep for one cow, and vice versa; then someone had an idea that they could make something that was worth, say, a cow, but you did not have to swap the cow – you gave them some of these little round things that they decided to call coins. Now, a cow might be worth sixty of these coins, so if it was worth sixty, a sheep was worth twenty, so to get a cow you had to sell three sheep for sixty coins. Who decided how many coins each thing was worth I do not know, but they worked it out among themselves. Some bright spark – I think they were Jewish – decided to collect these coins that everyone needed, and then lend them to those that did not have enough, but they charged them for the luxury of borrowing them. Say they borrowed ten, they had to pay back twelve, seems fair to me – but sometimes they could not pay back in the allotted time. They then had to pay back thirteen, and if longer, say, fourteen. This all got a bit too much for me; all I knew was that if you did not have enough of these coins, you would always be in the working class.'

'Have you quite finished? I have got work to do, and you need to finish that homework. Just write down what you have told me for the past bloody half-hour, that will do!'

'There is one other thing that still confuses me – the Royal Family.'

'Oh, no, don't get on about them – my father used to moan about them, and he is Norwegian.'

'No, he's right – how come this lot seem to get all the special treatment, which gives them the right to live in big houses, have servants at their beck and call just because their parents did the same? They have done it for hundreds of years, just because it has been handed down. I was born and live with you, Mum; the house was not given to us by Grandad. You have to pay rent for it; we only borrow it. Why do these

Royals, not just the top ones like the Queen and her brothers and sisters, but their cousins and other hangers-on get all the exclusive stuff? Like going to the cup final, for instance, and not having to pay? Or to the theatre where all the best singers perform for them and a load more upper-class people – it just does not seem right to me. While I am on the subject, one other thing that pisses me off – sorry, Mum… gets to me, as a kid, is that the upper class seem to be there because their fathers were there. Not because they did anything special to be in that club, but because some years ago it was decided that the upper class were better than the middle class. Now, these middle class were only working class that had been given jobs to manage the working class to make sure they did the right thing and work hard, to make sure the upper class kept the working class down.'

'Wow, one thing, babe – I only hope your teacher does not forget these are the thoughts of a boy looking from the outside, considering you were being brought up in a working-class family? The majority of those around us have worked in the fishing industry; they work for people who have more money for one reason or another, which enables them to live in big and better houses. They do not have to worry about having enough money to clothe and feed their children.'

'Yes, Mum, you are right – one day I will do something about this so-called system; how, I don't know. Still, there must be something that a working-class lad can do to make things better or more equal, without using socialism, communism or religion, for as far as I can see it hasn't worked up to now.'

CHAPTER 15

LEIF

Jenny Johnson

The end of the year came so quickly it was not true; spring had passed, and summer was on its way. I had found myself my first girlfriend, Jenny Johnson. She was a sweet girl who lived in Hessle. We'd met at a youth club some of my mates from school attended; it was called Constable Street Youth Club, but was actually down Bean Street, not far from where I lived.

I had gone along just for a change as Mum said I was not getting out enough; too much work and no play.

It was a Friday night; they used to have a dance on the last one of the month. We had been in Engineers Arms, which was also down Bean Street; the landlady had a good idea we were under age, but she did not bother as long as you looked eighteen, or near enough. I honestly believed that as long as we were spending money, she was OK with it.

We did not have that much to drink; only a couple of pints of bitter, when we got into the club. I had to join as I was not a member, and had to complete a registration form before getting through the door.

It was bouncing; they only played records, but there were no live bands in those days, anyway; we were standing around, and the girls were dancing together, bopping, as they called it. Mike, who was in the rugby team with me, was a club member and talked about playing rugby for them in the Hull and District RL under-seventeens competition when he left school, and he had been telling me about the club, going on about coming with him.

He was a great dancer; his sisters had shown him how to bop, and he was trying to get me to take this other girl who was dancing with the one he fancied, or split them, as the saying went.

'But I can't dance,' I kept telling him.

'Doesn't matter, just pretend you can.'

I looked older than my age, but if you could not dance at the age I was supposed to be, there must be something wrong with you, get my drift?

'Come on,' Mike said, 'it's a slow one – just hold her close, you don't have to bop.' He started to walk towards them and split them up, taking Barbara, the one he fancied, leaving this other poor girl standing like a spare dick at a wedding; she did not turn to walk away but stood looking, expecting me to move in. I went up to her; she put her arm on my shoulder, and I grabbed her waist. She then put both arms around my neck. Her head was resting on my chest as I was much taller than her. We started to move around the floor, not dancing but nevertheless I was managing. We were chatting away and getting on quite well. I liked this girl; she was the first girl I had met since Dot. I had written to Dot a couple of times, but had no reply.

To hold a girl in my arms again felt so good; so natural. Her hair smelt terrific – fresh and clean, and she had a solid body, if somewhat slim, but she still felt good against me; her breasts felt firm.

The music stopped, and I expected her to let go, but she didn't; she stood there for at least two minutes just holding on. I thought she had fallen asleep. Another record started to play – a bit faster this time. I thought, that's me done – if she expects Fred Astaire, she has had it.

I will never forget "Save the Last Dance for Me" by the Drifters. She started singing it softly under her breath. I could just hear her; I was hooked, line and sinker. 'What a beautiful voice,' I said. 'What's your name?'

'Jenny – Jenny Johnson,' she replied. 'And thank you, Leif.'

I was puzzled as to how she knew my name. I had never seen her before. 'You have one on me, Jenny Johnson – how come you know my name?'

'Mike told me you were coming. I know his sister; I was at his house yesterday and he said he was coming here tonight, and that a mate would be coming. He described you to a tee, Leif.' She giggled, because she had said, 'Tee leaf.'

'Oh, did he now? And was I what you expected?'

'Even better,' she said, blushing.

I was flattered and chuffed all at the same time; once again, at only the second attempt, I had hooked a gorgeous girl. She wasn't all tits and arse like Dot, but the opposite – smaller and slender, but equally as good looking.

I did not dance with any other girl in the hall that night; we sat chatting, drinking coffee or lemonade in the classroom set up as a café. She told me she lived in Hessle, and her father worked on the fish dock dry side, which meant he worked on the dock's engineering side.

She was the only child of Frank and Ruth Johnson of First Lane, Hessle, and she was fifteen – a little older than me, but only by a few months. We talked and talked; I was smitten. Her friend, Barbara Quinn, who had been instrumental in our getting together, was now out in the playground welded to Mike's lips.

Barbara was also from Hessle and also lived down First Lane. This Hessle was the place to be. When the dance had finished, it was not a case of, 'Can I take you home?' We just left together, the four of us, hand in hand down Bean Street, as we walked the girls to the bus stop on the opposite side of Hessle Road. Mike and Barbara were in one shop doorway, and we were in another.

I had not attempted to kiss Jenny at all that evening, even when we were smooching during a slow dance. There were plenty of them towards the end of the night.

We stood there looking into each other's eyes; I did not want to spoil it by touching her breasts or anything; I didn't want to put her off me. She made the first move – her lips touched mine, oh my god… it was unreal. I licked my lips and then kissed her, and it seemed like an eternity before our lips parted. It was the longest snog I had ever had, including with Dot, who was my first anyway. Jenny just smiled the most beautiful smile you have ever seen, believe me.

I wanted this girl not only sexually, but to be mine and mine alone. The bus came, and she said, 'Whoops, got to go – this is the last one.' She kissed me, and then she was gone. I did not know her address; was she on the telephone? I didn't know how I could see her again; my mind was in turmoil. I had just met the love of my short life and had no clue how I could get in touch with her.

I never slept that night, tossing and turning, thinking about the new love in my life; I never even thought of masturbating. However, yes, I had an erection – who would not? No red-blooded male could have had the experience I had had that night and not have got a hard-on with just the thought of it.

Saturday morning arrived, and I was still in bed about 10.30am. Mum came to the bottom of the stairs, shouting, 'Are you up, babe? Someone here to see you.'

'Oh, who is it, Mum? I am having a lie-in.'

I opened my eyes, squinting at the sun which was blazing in through my bedroom window.

I slowly got up, naked; I always slept naked. I stretched, scratched – the usual male thing when one gets up – and would have gone to the bathroom if we had one, so went and pissed in the bucket on the landing. Oh, how primitive these houses were.

'Are you coming down, or shall I ask her to come back?'

Her? What was Mum talking about? Who had come? I heard Mum coming up the stairs so I quickly pulled on a pair of shorts.

'Who is it, Mum? Who is here? I do not know anyone who knows my address.'

'I don't know, I've never seen her before, but she is a pretty girl, that is for sure.'

'Did you ask her name, Mum?'

She bent to down pick up my clothes from the floor, where I had left them last night.

'Oh, yes, sorry, babe, it's... er... Jenny – she said she was with you at the dance last night and was on road, so she thought she would call around and see you as she hadn't given you her telephone number.' She pulled that, 'mmm, must be posh' look.

'What? Why didn't you say who it was?' I was panicking now, trying to get dressed and comb my hair, rubbing my teeth with my finger as I hadn't cleaned them; the toothbrush and stuff were on the window ledge near the kitchen sink.

'Quick, pass me a T-shirt, Mum – I look all right, don't I?'

'Jesus Christ, is she royalty or something? Never seen you like this. Go on; you will do. Get down before she changes her mind and goes.'

I shot down the stairs, and Jenny was sitting in the living room; well, it was the only other room we lived in, so it had to be the living room.

'Hi, Jenny.'

She stood up, and I gave her a peck on the cheek, ever the gentleman.

'Hi, Leif, hope you don't mind me just calling like this.'

'No, no, it is fantastic to see you. I was worried we might not be able to get in touch.'

'Oh, that's sweet; what are you doing today?'

'Nothing planned… was thinking of going in town. What about you, fancy coming?'

'Yes, OK.'

I was over the moon that Jenny had gone out of her way to look for me.

'How did you find me?'

'On the way home on the bus I asked Barbara if she knew where you lived, and she said her mum would have an idea because she knows your mother; they have been old friends for years, or so she believes. She rang me this morning; she didn't know the full address as such but knew it was Rosamond Street, the first terrace on the right, number six. I went to the fruit shop, Danby's, on the corner to ask if they knew where you lived, and they knew you, so here I am – happy?' she said, smiling.

She would make a good copper, this girl.

We had some breakfast, as Mum would not let me go out on an empty belly; then Billy came in the back door.

'Hey up, son, and who might this gorgeous young thing be? Kept this one quiet, didn't you?'

'Billy, meet Jenny; Jenny, meet Billy – he is my stepfather.'

I had never referred to Billy as my father before to anyone, never needed to, but the look on Billy's face was a picture; he looked chuffed. Mum said he had tears in his eyes when he told her later what I had said.

We caught the trolleybus into town, getting off down Carr Lane, which was the dropping-off place; the bus then would go round past the front of City Hall into Paragon Street, which was the picking-up point for the return journey.

We walked into Queen's Gardens, had a while there, then went off to the open market and got some chips from Bob Carvers, before heading down Queen Street to the Corporation Pier. We watched the Winfield Castle coming in, all the time holding hands; it was a beautiful day. We walked everywhere, completely losing track of time.

On the way back, stopping off at Queen's Gardens to sit on the grass, it was then I said, 'Jenny, can I ask you something?'

She looked puzzled. 'Mmm… depends on what it is, but go on, ask anyway.'

I took a deep breath. 'Will you go out with me, please?'

She looked away. I thought I had dropped a clanger; I'd got bad vibes. 'I hope I haven't upset you. I know we haven't known each other long, only days?' It was hours, never mind days.

She turned and looked at me. 'Oh, Leif, of course I will, of course.'

My heart started beating faster – oh my god, she had said yes. Now, this might not seem much, but when a lad asked a girl to go out with him it was the first step on the ladder of courting – a huge step, and for a fourteen and fifteen-year-old boy and girl to be going out together was something. You were still children in the eyes of your parents, and I had not even met hers yet.

Our next step would be the big one – telling our parents we were 'going out together'.

I did not see Jenny at all on the Sunday. She was going to her aunt's in Bridlington; they had a pub there. But I told Mum and Billy as soon as I got up; I could not keep a secret.

Mum looked shocked. 'Don't you think it is a bit soon to be getting serious, Leif? You are only fourteen, you know; maybe you should have waited for a bit before you asked her to go out with you?'

'No way,' Billy butted in. 'Grab her while you can, son, she is a little cracker – get in before someone else does.'

Mum thumped him on the arm; he played at being hurt and pretend-ed to wince, winking at me at the same time.

'Shut up you, Billy, trust you men, you are all the same – but if you love her, then it's OK by me, baby.'

Who had mentioned love? I hadn't thought about love – it was such a big word. Still, when Mum said it, I thought, yes, do I love her. I had not slept last night thinking about her. I could see that gorgeous – no, stunning – face in my mind, and her beautiful smile. I loved the smell of her hair, her soft kiss when our lips met, the electricity that ran be-tween us when we held hands.

'Yes, I am sure I love her, Mum,' I said.

As I was walking through the city centre with Jenny the previous day, I'd noticed the looks other boys had given her; the envy on their faces. When we sat in Queen's Gardens, when she wasn't looking directly at me, I'd looked at her profile, the cute way her nose turned up, her gorgeous blue eyes, and naturally tanned smooth skin. If this was love, then, yes, I loved her all right, without a doubt. The next day, when I went to school, I never told anyone I was courting the most beautiful girl in the world.

Mick came up to me 'Good night Friday, wasn't it? Glad you got on with Jenny. She is a cracking lass. When are you seeing her again?'

'Er... not sure, mate, she gave me her telephone number; will ring her tonight, maybe.'

Will ring her – too right, I will ring her. There was a telephone box at the top of Rosamond Street. It was a white one; they all were in Hull, as the telephone system was owned and run by the council, not British Telecom.

It was two pence to make a call; there was a big black box you put your money in, and then you dialled your number. When the other end answered, you pressed button A; if they did not answer, you pressed button B and got your money back. There was no time limit on the call.

As kids, we did not pass a phone booth without pushing button B on the off-chance the last caller had forgotten to collect their leftover coins. It worked more often than you might have thought, and 2d bought you a lot of sweets.

There was often a queue, and it was slightly off-putting to try to chat while people were waiting outside, possibly even banging on the window if they thought that a conversation was taking too long. Sometimes there would be people waiting outside the boxes because they were expecting a call. Public phone boxes had their own numbers, which meant you could give them to people as if they were your own phone.

Later on, I would arrange to phone Jenny at an agreed time. I'd go in to the box, call her number, wait for it to ring, and then hang up and press button B; then she'd call me back. I mean, two pence was a lot of money to a boy of fourteen.

Sometimes there would be someone using it and you had to wait your turn. It was so frustrating if this happened when you had arranged a call.

Anyway, I called Jenny that night; it was a thrill just to hear her voice. I can't explain how I felt. That question again – yes, I loved this girl. We arranged to meet the following Wednesday, and I said I would come to Hessle after tea and meet her at the top of First Lane. 'No,' she said. 'Come to the house.'

'Are you sure you want me to meet your mum and dad yet?'

'Why not? I am not ashamed of you, silly, you are my boyfriend. Why shouldn't you come to my house?'

My boyfriend... you don't know how good that sounded. My first girlfriend. I was 'as chuffed as a dog with three dicks', as Billy used to say.

Wednesday came, and I rushed home from school. I even missed rugby practice that night to ensure I got there in time. I had a quick strip wash in the kitchen sink – there were no baths or showers in those days: shirt off, hands, face and armpits was the routine; no deodorants, just the smell of soap.

I pushed a sandwich down for tea, and was gone.

I waited at the bus stop outside Rayners pub, top of West Dock Avenue, to catch the East Yorkshire bus up to Hessle. My heart was racing, not just from running, but the thought of 'my girlfriend'.

I got off the bus and started to walk down First Lane, past Belvedere Road. Then it was Cottesmore Road, and the next street was the one – Seaton Road, on the left, and there was Jenny's house, the sixth on the right.

I stood, just looking at the house; nervous was not the word. I was shitting myself. It made my home look like a slum, which was what it was, as they eventually pulled them all down.

I rang the doorbell, and no one answered. Fuck – had I got the right house, the right street? My mind was whirling. I rang it again; nothing. I thought I hadn't heard a sound when I'd rung the bell, so I knocked, and bingo, it started to open.

'Hello, Leif, how are you? Nice to meet you, son, come on in.' It was her father. Now, I was tall, but this bloke was a giant of least six feet six.

I walked in; they had a hallway. I'd never been in a house with an entrance, as most terraced houses were two up, two down.

This house stood on its own, and it had a garage – unreal. Her dad showed me into the middle room. Middle? We just had the living room and kitchen, plus an old pantry, an extension with shelves, where we stored the boiler.

I could hear music coming from somewhere. It wasn't a radio; I thought it might be a record being played, but just as it stopped, her dad said: 'Jenny won't be a minute – she is just practising.'

'Practising what?'

'Oh, didn't you know? She plays the piano and guitar, has done since she was four or five; she wants to be an entertainer. She has a beautiful voice – have you heard her sing?'

'No,' I lied; a white lie, but nevertheless a lie. Then she came into the room, and kissed me on the cheek as she took hold of my hand – in front of her father. He just smiled and said, 'I will leave you two kids to it, then. See you later, Leif; great to meet you.'

'And you too, sir.'

'No need for the sir thing, son, I'm just Frank, OK?'

'OK, Frank.' He tapped me on the shoulder and winked, then left the room.

'Well, what do you think, Leif, are you listening to me?'

My mind was wandering. 'Oh, yes, sorry – was miles away. He seems a nice guy. Bloody hell he is big – I thought I was tall, but he makes me look small. Is that why you like me? I remind you of your dad?'

She just smiled that smile again, and it had the same effect as always.

With that, her mother knocked on the door. 'Hi, can I come in?'

Mmm, these people have manners, I thought; it wasn't something I had been used to, and that was no offence to my family.

'Mum, this is Leif.' Jenny stood up, kind of dragging me with her.

'Hello, Mrs Johnson.'

'No, it's Ruth – please call me Ruth, and my hubby is Frank.'

'OK, hello, Ruth – nice of you to invite me to your home.'

'That's OK. Any friend of our daughter's is always welcome; please feel free to call any time. You live down Rosamond Street, don't you? I grew up down Walcott Street – my dad was on trawlers, so we have a lot in common, Leif. That's Norwegian, isn't it? My maiden name is Skogstad – my family came from Norway after the great famine; do you know anything about your family? I have always been interested in it; what about you?'

'Mother, please don't start on that again; Mum's obsessed with it.'

'That's OK, Jenny; as a matter of fact, yes, I do know a bit.'

'That's enough now; maybe some other time,' Ruth said, taking the hint from her daughter, just by the look on her face. She left the room.

'Thank god for that,' said Jenny. 'Now we are left in peace for a bit. What do you fancy doing today?'

'I'm easy – up to you.'

'Can you ride a bike?'

She must have thought I was thick. 'Of course I can, but haven't had one for years – why?'

'We have two bikes in the garage – mine and an old one of Dad's. We could go for a ride to Little Switzerland – you ever been there?'

'No, where's that? Never heard of it.'

'Come on, let's go.'

We set off. I was a bit shaky, to say the least, but after a few yards I was soon back into it. I'd had to lower the bike's seat down as a bit it was too high, even for me. We headed for the foreshore, which I'd often heard mentioned by lads at school but I had never ventured up there.

We rode up to the old mill, and under the railway line, and we were then in Little Switzerland.

'You sure you never been here before?'

'No, honestly – but I can see where the name comes from.'

'Yes, it is a former chalk quarry. There is a famous pond called Hessle Newt Ponds – it is the nearest thing to the countryside in the Hull area. I have been coming here to play for a long time; it's great getting lost on the tracks that lead off the main paths. You sure you never been here before? Everyone has been here.'

'No, I've never been to Hessle. Never needed to, until I met you.' She touched my hand; there went the electricity again.

'Follow me.' She shot off down this trail; we went into the woodland and came to a little clearing, and she stopped and got off her bike.

'Bring all your ex-boyfriends here, then?' I said, teasing her. She gave me a black look; the pet lip dropped. Whoops, I thought. That was the first time I had seen that look.

'I'm only kidding, Jenny – no need to get upset.'

'Leif… to be honest, I have never had a boyfriend; well, not one like you. I have always been too busy with the music lessons and study to bother with boys.'

I did not know what to say. No one like me – what did she mean by that? We sat on the grass; it was a gorgeous day, the sun was beating down. I took off my T-shirt; I had a good body, even if I say it myself, what with all the training and swimming I did.

She just looked at me, never said a word.

'What's wrong? Never seen a guy with no shirt on?'

'Not in real life or this close,' she said.

I thought I was embarrassing her; I started to put it back on.

'No, leave it off. I like you like that; you look nice.'

'Your dad told me you had been playing piano and guitar since you were five; is that right?'

'Four. I started playing by ear when I was little at my grandma's house. She had an upright, the one we now have at our house; she gave it to me when I was nine, that's when I picked up the stringed instruments.'

'Instruments? Like, there is more than one?'

'Oh, yes – violin, cello, bass. Plus I have been learning twelve-string banjos in the past two years, only because of Dad; he likes country music, especially bluegrass.'

I saw a musical genius in front of me. The only thing I could play with was myself. I felt useless. What had I ever done? OK, I was good at school, brainy I suppose, but nothing like this girl. Along with being beautiful, she was the perfect package.

'Jenny, if you have never had a so-called proper boyfriend, why did you meet me at the club, and how did you know my name?'

'I told you – I heard about you from Mike. He suggested I go to Cunny on Friday as it was the monthly dance. I never went anywhere, socially, that is, so I tagged along with Barb, and that was it – when I met you, I knew you were the one.' She blushed and looked down.

'So when I asked you to go out with me it meant, er… was I the first lad ever to ask you that question?'

'Yes, you were – all the other boys I have met, not that there were many – two – were boys from music class and nothing like you. You were just something different, my dream boy.' She blushed again when she realised what she had just said.

I honestly could not believe what I was hearing.

'Mum and Dad were concerned that I did not go anywhere; I was just stuck in my room or at the piano. They used to annoy me about going out with my friends – what friends? I did not have any, really; I was not like all the other girls at school, and I felt like the ugly duckling in the Hans Christian Andersen story and song by Danny Kaye. Then you came along and I just wanted to get to know you better, that's all, so if you're going to stop seeing me, please just say so.'

'Stop seeing you? Don't be stupid – why should I want to do that? Come here.'

She leaned forward; I hugged her, kissing her forehead. God, she felt so good in my arms. I didn't want it to end. She looked up at me with tears in her eyes; she looked so innocent, so fragile – how could I hurt her?

We kissed a proper kiss – a lover's kiss – and lay back on the grass in each other's arms. If there was anything better, God kept it for himself. We stayed there alone, with not a sound but the birds singing; no other humans to be heard, no one telling us what to do. It was idyllic; had I found my perfect partner? I didn't know; I was only fourteen, but I was growing up fast. Things had changed so much over the past year, what with a crash course on sex from Doug and Dot, only the summer before.

CHAPTER 16

LEIF
Deep in Love

I was now seeing the proverbial virgin, untouched both mentally and physically, as far as I knew, that is. It wasn't the right time to broach the subject anyway. 'Get that out of your mind; treat her right, mate,' I was telling myself.

We got home to her house, put the bikes back in the garage, and I was just about to go when her mother opened the back door. 'Will you stay for tea, Leif? There is plenty.' Then she giggled just like Jenny had when she too realised what she had said.

I declined the offer. 'No, sorry, Ruth, I would love to, but Mum's expecting me home, and I can't get in touch with her as we don't have a phone.'

'Oh, Frank can run you home if you want – it's only ten minutes down the road. You can stop the night if you want; we have a spare room.'

They are trying to palm her off on to me, that is for sure, I thought. Frank appeared from out of the garden shed. 'Yes, come on; it'd be good to have a man to talk to for a change.' Man? I was fourteen, for fuck's sake. It was getting serious, this, but what could I do? Mr Johnson came out of the house with his car keys. 'Come on; let's go.'

Things were happening so fast; maybe too soon. I didn't know, as I had nothing to measure it against; I was the virgin last year, and no one had given me any directions. My mother wasn't trying to match me up with the first girl I had met. My head was in a spin.

As we travelled along Hessle High Road, Jenny's dad pulled the car up to the side of the road near Pickering Park's gates, just outside the Maritime Museum. I thought he was going to suggest we go in for a look.

He turned in his seat, looking at me. 'Right, Leif, my son – I just wanted to have a quiet word with you, man to man sort of thing; it is about Jenny. I just want you to know if you so much as hurt her in any way, shape or form, I will rip you apart limb from limb – is that clear?'

'Er, well… Er, yes, Mr Johnson.' I was struggling here. I was in uncharted waters; nothing like this had ever happened to me. I didn't have a clue what to say or do.

'Look, Leif, you don't have to say anything. I know it is early days, and you are the first boy to set foot in my house, but I just want you to know she is the most precious thing in my life. She's my only daughter and I want everything she wants, and at this moment in time, it seems you are the one she wants. You are good for her, Leif; we have seen such a change in her over the past few days. That is the most important thing. Jenny's happiness in both her and our lives, that's it – you understand? OK, great, now to your house.'

A few minutes later we turned in to Rosamond Street and pulled up at the end of our terrace.

'Mind if I come in to meet your mum and dad, Leif? I would love to say hello.'

How could I argue? He was out of the car, which was only a small Hillman Imp saloon, and he stooped to get his giant frame out of it. He kind of stumbled as he got out, saying, 'Bloody knee is playing me up.' He was rubbing his knee as he walked.

He followed me up to the front door, and we walked in; there was no one in the living room, so I shouted, 'It's me, Mum, are you in? I have a visitor to see you.'

With that, Mum came through the back door. 'Just been for a crap.' She clearly hadn't heard me. 'Oh, hello! Just need to wash my hands; be back in a second. Take a seat, please.'

Mr Johnson sat down in one of the two chairs, and I told him I would go and get my stuff from upstairs. What things to take I hadn't a clue, as I slept in the nude, so I didn't need any pyjamas. Better take clean underpants to put on tonight, I supposed.

I went in the back kitchen, and Mum whispered, 'Who is that? He's a fucking giant – who is he?' I told her what had happened that day and the story about being asked to stay the night.

'You must take some of Billy's pyjamas; the ones he got when he was going to go into the hospital that time. Take clean underpants, and your toothbrush – I think we have a spare tube of toothpaste...' She was panicking like a madwoman.

I went upstairs, got my duffle bag and stuffed my gear in it, and when I came down Mum was sitting chatting with Mr Johnson. He stood up, towering over her, offered his hand, and said, 'Right, best get going – tea will be ready. Pleased to meet you, Christine. I can call you Christine, can't I? See you again some time – you must come for tea one Sunday, you and Mr...'

Before he could get the words out, Mum said, 'Billy.'

'Right, yes, Billy. OK, come on, son, let's go.' We headed for the door.

'Goodbye, Frank, nice to meet you,' said Mum, and we were back in the car.

'My, good-looking woman, your mother – I see where you get your looks from,' said Mr Johnson, laughing, which sounded like thunder coming from him.

We got back to his house without actually having said much to each other. Ruth was buzzing around like a mother hen with her brood. 'Be back in a sec; just checking on the meat.'

Things were going just a bit too fast for me; I could not keep up with the pace of it. I felt like they were trying to get us married off, and we were only kids. We'd only known each other a matter of days.

I was questioning myself. Had I jumped in too quickly when I'd asked Jenny to go out with me, or was this a cunning plan of her parents to put me off her? Only time would tell.

We went into the dining kitchen, as they called it – it was bigger than the downstairs of my house. I sat down opposite Mr Johnson. Jenny was on my right. Seeing as it was warm, I had changed into a pair of old rugby shorts and a clean T-shirt; it was all I had with me. No comments were made about my attire, so I assumed it was OK and that I hadn't been expected to dress for dinner.

The food was terrific – roast beef, Yorkshire puddings, the full bifter; we only had this on special occasions at home. I could get used to this. What was I doing? I was starting to think like them.

We didn't say grace before we started eating, so that was a relief. One of the hardest things when dining with someone you have just met is knowing what do at the table.

Then out came apple crumble and custard; could things get any better?

We retired to the front room this time, where there was no TV but one of the biggest radiograms I had ever seen. There were records and LPs all around the room – this family clearly loved their music.

'What's your taste in music, Leif?' Ruth asked.

Now, I had to be careful here. 'No real preference, Ruth… I like Elvis, the Drifters' – I had to mention that one – 'Roy Orbison, that sort of music.'

'Do you like country music? Jim Reeves, for instance?'

'Oh, Mum, give over – he's fifteen, not fifty.'

Why had Jenny said fifteen, not fourteen? Was it just a slip of the tongue? I was questioning everything that was going on, starting to become paranoid.

We spent a pleasant evening listening to records and chatting; there were lots of questions – what did my parents do; what were their backgrounds?

About ten o'clock, Ruth got up and said, nudging Frank, 'Well, I am ready for bed; come on, sleepy head. Let's leave these kids alone for a while.'

'Goodnight – don't be too long, you two,' said Frank.

'OK, Dad.'

They left the room. I had been sitting on one of the chairs, and Jenny was on the settee. 'Come over here, Leif, sit with me,' she said. I moved over; she took my hand and kissed my fingers. 'You like my parents,

Leif? Mum loves you, and I think Dad likes you or he wouldn't have offered to run you home.'

If she had only known what had been said in the car; I wondered if she would have the same opinion. Still, there was no need for her to know that.

She cuddled up to me, I put my arm around her, and we sat quietly, listening to Ray Charles's album, *What'd I Say*. It has stuck in my mind ever since.

We eventually nodded off in each other's arms. I woke up first. Jenny was lying with her head on my shoulder, and I just watched her sleep; the rise and fall of her breasts, the smell of her hair – she was so beautiful. Yes, I was in love. No matter what her father thought, I could never do anything to hurt this girl.

We went upstairs, kissed tenderly on the landing and held hands until the final second that we parted. I disappeared into my room, and Jenny into hers. Oh, how I wanted to follow her to lie with her all night, and feel her naked body next to mine, but no – that magic moment must wait until she is ready; she deserves that, I thought.

I woke up as the sun rose. I did not know what time it was, but I could hear some church bells in the distance. There was a knock on the door; a voice said, 'Leif, are you awake, dear? Would you like a cup of tea?' I giggled to myself as she hadn't said 'tea, Leif' this time.

'Yes please,' I said, and with that, the door opened. I was still half-asleep and hadn't realised that I had thrown my underpants on the chair and was naked in bed with just the sheet covering one leg and half my groin, a touch of morning glory showing. Ruth nearly dropped the tray when she saw me. I quickly pulled the sheet to cover my modesty, but it was too late.

She left the room, blushing, and went a lot quicker than she'd come. Nothing more was said of the incident that morning. It wasn't until later that afternoon after lunch, when Jenny and I had gone for a walk into Hessle Square, that Jenny said: 'Mum told me what happened this morning.'

'Oh, Jesus, what did she say? Was she annoyed? I am so sorry – I didn't mean it to happen.'

'Don't be silly, it's OK. She has seen one before; not yours, mind. I haven't seen yours yet! It's OK, don't worry.'

Her comment about not having seen mine yet surprised me, and I did not elaborate on it, but certainly made a mental note of it.

I left after tea; her father had offered to run me home, but I said I would rather walk. I thanked them for letting me stay the night and for feeding me; it had been great. Ruth seemed to look at me differently – or was that just my imagination running wild?

Of course, when I got home I got the numerous third-degree questions – what are they like? What's the house like? Everything you would expect and more, but I had had enough was ready for my bed; no matter where you go your bed is the best, and the only thing missing was Jenny.

I sat reading the next day and hummed the tune that Jenny had sung as we danced; I could not get it out of my head.

'Hey, that is my favourite song!' Mum said. '*Save the Last Dance for Me* – why are you humming that? I just love it.'

'Jenny was singing along to the record as we danced on the night we met, Mum; she has a beautiful voice. I can't get it out of my head.'

I went to school the next day. Mick came straight over when he spotted me. 'How did you get on with Jenny's dad, then? He is fucking massive, isn't he?'

'Oh, OK, thanks – had a great day; even stopped the night Saturday.'

'Bloody hell, getting your feet under the table – is it serious, you and Jen then?'

'I don't know about serious; she is only the second girl I have ever met, but I must admit I do like her. I like her a lot.'

'Oh, God, you are in love, I can tell by the look on your face. Wow, wait till I tell all the lads.'

'Hang on, Mick, just you wait a minute. Keep your mouth shut, or I will make sure you don't have anything to eat your tea with. She is special, and I don't want any rumours started about Jenny, OK? You understand?' It was the first time he had seen the serious side of me and soon shut up.

'OK, Leif, wow – you are serious about her, aren't you? I promise I won't say owt, don't worry.'

Everything was going along fine at school. I loved it. Mum asked me how Mrs Ashcroft was doing, as she hadn't heard me talking about her in my sleep lately. I told her she was OK; mind, the German language was a bit hard to get a grip of. I had just started getting used to make the 'ch' sound like you were clearing your throat and when pronouncing the U-umlaut, you had to pout like a child. Also when a German writes 'sie' he means 'she', and when he writes 'Sie', he means 'you' – but when you begin a sentence with it, there is no difference. It was doing my head in. It got even worse as the sexes were even more confusing. Take, say, a letter B or a bat is masculine; a young lady is neuter and police feminine. Then this made Mum freak. In German, the word 'the' has six different forms, according to the case and gender of the word that follows it, and all the adjectives are just as complicated. Apart from this, it was going well. Mum just shrugged her shoulders and left.

I could not wait to meet Jenny again; she was always on my mind. I couldn't get her vision and her comment, 'I haven't seen yours yet', kept coming back to me, mostly when I was alone at night in bed, if you know what I mean.

One day, when I was in my final year at school, Mum asked me if I thought I had made the right choice in leaving Hull Grammar. I told her that yes, I believed I had, for I did not think I could have got the opportunity to take a course that would give me preliminary training and a background for my career when I left. I must say I take pride in the fact that the Boulevard was only one of a few schools that offered such opportunities.

The systems allowed us boys not to be tethered to as many subjects as in regular secondary school, and I felt that leaving earlier at fifteen would allow me to get out there and obtain an apprenticeship and experience that the grammar boy would always lack.

I believed that the theory side could still be learnt at further education on an evening, or day release if possible. All I needed was the right results of my SMC, and I would make sure I did the work to gain those results. The school, even in its short time, was noted for its turnout of practically minded boys.

I was also enjoying my rugby and was now one of the first to be picked as an inside centre. I had worked on my game with Mr Adams, who had looked after me through my previous season as a novice and turned me into an accomplished player, even if I say it myself. He did a great job, old Allan. We used to call him by his first name – there was none of this 'Sir' waffle. We respected the man, along with Lovelace – they both had a significant influence on my life.

I was also the vice-captain of the school's Yellow House. We were very successful in our last year, winning the senior rugby competition, and finishing runner-up in the football school championship.

Many boys from our house represented the school in various sports; there were too many to remember, to be honest, but it was still an outstanding achievement.

The school year was flying by, and my relationship with Jenny had just got better and better.

Billy came in one day, but Mum was out, and we got to talking. 'You given Jenny one yet, Leif?' he said. 'Come on, you can tell me, you know – man to man.'

'Mind your own business, Billy; it's got nowt to do with you.'

'You haven't, have you? What's wrong with you?'

'Listen, it has got nothing to do with you. I do not want to discuss Jenny with you. I have more respect for her than to tell tales to you, for everyone in Rayners would know about it before the week was out. Her old man drinks in there – imagine what he would think if he heard some sordid tales about his only daughter. Now fuck off and don't ask again.' I got up and went to my room.

When Mum got home, Billy told her what had gone on, and she gave him a right reaming as well. She came upstairs, knocked on my door and asked if she could enter. I said, 'Yes, OK.' She sat on my bed beside me.

She could see I was upset with dickhead downstairs. 'Come on, babe, cheer up,' she said, holding my hand. 'Billy didn't mean anything. You know what he is like. You did right not discussing Jenny with him – it is nothing to do with us what you have done.' Before she could say anymore, I interrupted.

'Mum, we haven't "done" anything. I love her, Mum. I think the world of her, I would not dream of trying anything on with her in case I lose her.' With that, I started crying.

Now, I had always been a bit of a sensitive boy; I suppose that being brought up more or less by my mother, not having a father to speak of, wasn't always easy.

However, I looked older than I was, and I still needed that shoulder to cry on; someone to bounce things off and share my secrets – but Jenny wasn't one of the secrets I wanted to talk about with anyone else but Jenny. I told Mum that. She hugged me and kissed me, more in thanks for praising her and respecting Jenny.

I had been to see my grandad a few more times, and I would always finish up talking about his forefathers and his life at sea. Oh, how I loved listening to his never-ending tales.

'I hear you have a young lady, my boy,' he said. 'When am I going to meet her?'

'I will bring her one day, Grandad, don't worry – she will love you as I do.' Now what made me say that I do not know, but the look in Pops' eyes changed instantly. Had I hit a nerve or hit something? He gave me a look just like a father gives his son. Was I the son he never had? I don't know, but I liked it, and we were now the best of friends.

I had put aside the hatred I had for him, but was I right to do that? He had been so hard on my mother, and she had left home to get away from him. How could this older man have been such a monster to make her do that? There was something missing; something I did not know, and something Mum was not telling me. But right now, Jenny was my life; she was all I could think of night and day.

The school had been invited to send a group of boys to Hull Training College to watch a performance by students of Shakespeare's Richard III. This was the college's appreciation that their students had carried out teaching practice at the Boulevard High School.

I was lucky enough to be chosen as one of the two from the technical course. It was based on work and exam results that had been taken up to the present time.

Mr Prentice, who was now the head of our English department and a real old-fashioned arty type, warned us to be early as the play was due to commence at 2.30pm on Wednesday.

We were told to make sure we came to school wearing decent clothes, no jeans, and a shirt and tie; this was supposed to be compulsory, but the rule had wavered lately.

We were there in good time, enough to obtain seats on the front row. From this vantage point, we had a perfect view of the whole of the action. Indeed, at one point, we were almost too close, for when the Duke of Clarence was drowned in a barrel of Malmsey wine, he was inundated with so much enthusiasm by the members of the cast that we were liberally sprinkled with the contents of the barrel, which was not wine, I must add.

I must confess that some of the dialogue was difficult to understand as it was not quite 'Ull', but this did not detract from my enjoyment. I found no problem following the plot of this exciting story of Richard, Duke of Gloucester, the murder of his two children in the Tower of London, and his greed for power to eventually become King of England and the hatred he created against himself until his death on the battlefield.

I thought the performance was brilliant, and one thing that helped was that the costumes had been loaned to the college from the Shakespeare Theatre in Stratford-upon-Avon. It was pointed out that some famous actors had worn those very same costumes, including Sir Laurence Olivier, Sam Wanamaker and Yvonne Mitchell, all stars of the day. I left with a much greater appreciation of Shakespeare's great plays and writings – but still preferred new stuff.

The school organised various other visits to companies around the area in what would now be called a form of work experience. The commercial group visited Hammonds department store and the Hull Daily Mail, the technical group visited Browns Printing Works and Scunthorpe Steelworks, the boys who were taking woodwork visited Armstrong's cabinet makers, while the Nautical Group made visits to a couple of shipping and fish processing companies and visited various docks.

I recall one of the lads in our class went pleasuring on Lord Alexander, a trawler sailing out of Hull. 'Pleasuring' meant you were allowed to go away for a full trip fishing, always during the summer holidays, and you were classed as part of the crew, helping the cook with his duties. It was quite challenging for boys to learn what it was like to go into the fishing industry, for they always started as galley lads.

Mike Read was the boy in question, and I talked to him when he got back.

'How did you get on, Mike? Any good?'

'Yes, it was unreal – it took five hours to reach the Spurn Point Lightship.'

'How soon did the seasickness get to you?'

'Fucking terrible – until you have had it, you do not realise how bad it can be. I thought I was dying.'

'How long did it take from Spurn to get to the fishing grounds?'

'It was then a full day steaming, or travel, as you landlubbers would call it, to the White Sea fishing grounds. But we had trouble with the engine – it had a fault and had to be repaired by the ship's engineer; he fixed it OK, but he was a bit worried in case we had to be towed into the nearest port, which was Thurso in Scotland. When we got there we trawled for about eighteen hours without sleep looking for good fishing, but we didn't really get a good haul. The Old Man, as the crew called him – the skipper – had decided to move to Bear Island twenty-four hours away, and when we got there, we caught fuck all. The lads were pissed off.'

'Is it right that if they do not catch anything, they get no pay?'

'Yes. Nowt – it all depends on what the catch is worth when they get back.'

'Balls to that – you would not get me to do that for a job. All that work and nowt at the end of it.'

'Anyway, reports were coming in on the radio that the fishing was good at Spitsbergen, but to get there we had to sail through rough seas. I was quite frightened at times. Things got better. The fishing was excellent in this area when the lads were hard at it. I had to keep them supplied with mugs of tea, and in between I did some sightseeing. You could see the mountains looming up around you, rising to 4,000 feet and covered in thick snow even in summer; it was beautiful.'

'Did you get a chance to work on deck or any other jobs – not just a glorified tea boy?'

'Oh, yes, I was taught how to gut and clean fish before it went down into the fish room. The lads reckoned I was a natural at it. After three days of good catches, it was time to head for home, for it was five days' steaming to get back to Hull, hoping to be back in time to meet the afternoon tide.'

'What did you get out of it? Did the company pay you for going?'

'No, you do not get paid for any of this work experience, but it is usual for the crew to all put money in the 'hat' at the end of the trip when they settle or get paid; the amount depended on how well I performed.'

'How much did you get, then? Come on, tell me – how much?'

'I did OK, but I am not saying how much I got. The lads reckon it is an unwritten law so that no one feels let down if they know what other blokes get – OK?'

'Will you be doing it when you leave school, then? Will you be a fisherman?'

'No way am I going to do that for the rest of my life, not a fucking chance.'

'So it opened your eyes – glad you did it, then?'

'Oh, yes, without doubt. I was dead set on going to sea, but that trip made my mind up for me. You have no idea what those blokes go through, and to get back and not get a decent wage out of it must be so sickening. No way was I putting myself through that for the rest of my life.'

CHAPTER 17

LEIF

Happy Fifteenth Birthday

I saw Jenny as much as I could, and my fifteenth birthday was looming. I would soon be leaving school and ending the ritual of going down the Boulevard every morning. My life in the big wide world was about to begin.

I was getting frustrated, I suppose the word is; my sexual needs were growing along with my body. I was nearly six foot two now and filling out, as they say, with all the training. My hormones were running riot. Every time I sat and thought of Jenny, I got a feeling in my groin that would just not go away.

We were lucky that, in the Swinging Sixties, the younger generation had more awareness of sexual activities. There was no actual sex education other than tales in the playground, but no longer would children be seen and not heard – times were changing, as Bob Dylan once sang.

I was with Jenny one night; her mum and dad had gone to the pictures and we kissed on the settee. As we were close, I had, of course, got an erection. I tried to move away from Jenny and she said, 'No, Leif, I like it – hug me again.' As I put my arm around her, she touched me – actually touched me. It was through my clothes, but nevertheless, she touched me. A shudder ran through my body. She smiled and said, 'Wow, it's like a stick of rock.' She then closed her fingers around it and smiled at me. 'You like that, don't you? How does it feel? I have never touched a boy before. What does it do to you, Leif, what does it feel like?'

Now, I had never been asked these questions before, and I could not give a real answer. I just said, 'It is so wonderful that you have now touched me. You told me that your mum had seen me, but you had not, so do you want to see him?'

She bit her bottom lip and closed her eyes. I thought she was going to cry. She wasn't looking at me. You stupid bastard, I thought, now look what you have done. A few moments passed, which seemed like hours, and then she turned and looked at me with those beautiful eyes.

'Can I see you, please, Leif? Will you undress for me? I want to see him. Not just get him out – I want to see your beautiful naked body in all its glory, for I have wanted to for months now, but did not know how to ask. I did not want you to think I was easy like some girls are. I am a virgin, Leif – I've never been touched. I have always said I would only give my body to the man I intend to marry. I know that must sound stupid, as we are both still children, but I love you so very much; you are my world. I can't see me ever wanting any other man. Is it OK that we don't do it just yet – but I want to see you naked. Will you, please, Leif, just for me?'

I stood up. I kicked off my baseball boots and pulled my T-shirt off, exposing my pecs and six-pack, and looked at her as her eyes seemed to get bigger. I took my jeans off, and, standing in my Y-fronts and socks, I stopped. It felt foolish, thinking about it now, but then I bent over and took off my socks.

Jenny spoke for the first time since I had started to undress. 'Oh, baby, now, please, now – do it.'

I slipped my briefs down to my thighs, and then let them drop to the floor. Standing there naked felt so good; my penis was throbbing, solid as a lump of steel. I moved towards Jenny; she was mesmerised by my cock. I was watching her face. 'You like him, Jenny? He is yours if you want him?'

She then touched me, and it twitched to her warm hand, which was so small her fingers did not go right round it. She had not a clue what to do next, but I was that close to ejaculating I was hoping she didn't try.

I was standing there with my eyes closed, and she was stroking it like you would a cat or a dog, lightly running her fingers up and down me, exploring my body. She then cupped my scrotum with the other hand, lifting my ball bag, kind of weighing them in her hand.

I could not believe this was happening. Oh my God, I did not want to shoot. I tried to remember what Dot had said to me. 'Think of anything when tha' ist fucking me – anything, so it makes you last longer.'

I was trying to think of every rugby team in the league and the name of their ground in alphabetical order. Bradford Northern – Odsal; Barrow – Craven Park; Castleford – Wheldon Road… it worked every time; I knew them off by heart. Dot was right.

Jenny was absorbed in my body. 'Leif, what happens when you come? I have heard that that is how babies are made when you come inside a girl's vagina.'

She did not know anything; she had no idea of how to make love. She could have been taking the piss out of me, but I did not think she was. I didn't think she knew how.

Then a question I never expected. 'Can I wank you off, Leif? Some of the girls at school say they do it, wank their boyfriends off – one girl says she sucks him… gives him blow jobs. But, Leif – how can you blow and suck at the same time? If you blow, does it mean your belly will blow up like a balloon? What if I blow too hard? Will you explode? What's the difference between blowing and sucking?'

I was silent.

'Leif, tell me, please – I want to do it right.'

I took her hand from me. 'This is how you wank – the proper name is masturbating; some people call it a hand job.' I started to wank, showing her how to do it… Bradford Northern.

She put her hand on mine as I was stroking it. 'Do you always go the same speed, Leif? Or do you go faster sometimes?'

My balls were aching; I was so close it was not funny. Jenny stopped holding my hand and took my hand from me, taking over; it felt so beautiful. 'I can't get my fingers right round as you did,' she said. I told her it did not matter, and to use both hands. I did not get as far as Doncaster and it shot out of me – all over her arms, and hands; she jumped back like she had been scalded.

'Wow, what's that? Is that semen, Leif? Have you done it?'

'Oh, yes, baby – I have done it all right. You were perfect; fantastic, in fact.'

'Mmm, I like that, Leif. I like wanking you, seeing you smile the way you did; the look of pleasure on your face. I did please you, Leif, didn't I?'

'Yes, Jenny, you sure did.' I kissed her as we had never kissed before.

She went and got a towel from the bathroom to clean herself and me a bit; I told her to find an old one from somewhere, as we did not want to leave smelly towels about; we could always throw it away. People did not keep tissues in those days; even toilet paper was not that common a thing.

I got dressed and was sitting listening to Jenny play the piano when her mum and dad walked in with fish and chips. I had taken the towel upstairs and put it in my duffle bag with the intention of throwing it away on my way home in the morning, to get rid of the evidence, again. Unreal, I thought; it had been the end to a perfect night. It couldn't get any better than this – or could it?

The next week at school was mock exams for the SMC examinations to be taken in a month's time, so I had some revision to do. I hated it, like most kids. I thought I knew everything. Mum was nagging me to do it. 'You see too much of Jenny. I suggest you don't see her for two weeks while you do some revision.'

What? I thought – just when were now having sex. OK, kind of; a lot more than I had been getting, anyway. Then I thought Mum would only stress out if I didn't stop seeing her.

'OK, I will tell her, but it will have to be in person, not on the phone.'

I rang Jenny the next night and told her the situation; she was OK with it. She was used to studying different subjects with various musical instruments; she understood the problem.

I was worried; she had taken the first step forward, and now she might think I was trying to pack her in. I told her I loved her repeatedly, and said I would see her at the weekend, for sure; it was only a short while away.

It was two and a half weeks before I managed to see Jenny, and a week before my birthday. I had done all the swotting until I was exhausted by it all; my head was full of information. I told Mum, that's it, no more – if I don't pass it is not without trying.

I took the exams, and now all we had to do was wait for the results. I had finished my school education; it had had its ups and downs, but I had come through it without much drama.

A few days later, I came home, and Mum asked me, 'Do you want a party for your birthday?'

'No, thanks – I don't know who I would invite. I do not have a big circle of friends. I go to the youth club, but still I am not really "friends", so to speak, with that many of those who go there. Anyway, our house is not big enough to accommodate a lot of people. Just think when Jenny's mum and dad, Ruth and Frank, visited – it was full then, with six of us sitting in the living room.'

I knew Mum was not ashamed, but a bit conscious of her home; it was clean and tidy but still no palace.

'I just want to spend the day with Jenny. Is that OK, Mum?'

I could see she was upset, but she said, 'Yes, OK, I understand – but let me make you a birthday cake at least.'

My birthday was on a Tuesday in 1961; we decided to celebrate it on the following Saturday. Well, celebrate is not quite the right word.

On the day Mum and Billy gave me their presents – a new shirt from Mum and five pounds from Billy. I also received a fiver from Grandma and Grandad, so I was really pleased with that lot.

I rang Jenny on my way to school.

'Hi, Jenny, how are you? OK?'

'Oh, hi, babe, happy birthday – when are we meeting? Tonight, I hope?'

'Yes, of course. I told Mum I wanted to spend the night with you. Well, I don't mean all night.'

'That's wonderful, Leif – Mum and Dad are going out to some function or other in Leeds, it has been booked for months, and they told me to tell you they were sorry that they would not see you as they will not be back until very late.'

'That is no bother; it is you I want to spend my birthday with, anyway.'

Jenny just giggled in the way that only she could. 'I am sorry, it is getting late. I have to go.' She blew me a kiss; how you could blow a kiss on the phone was beyond me, but she always did it.

I had a good day at school, with lots of cards from all my classmates. I did not realise how many friends I had, or should I say how much the lads in the class thought of me; it was very humbling.

I could not wait to get home. I had a quick sandwich, as I always stayed school dinners and that was enough for me, then a quick wash and out I ran to the top of the street, knowing there was a Hessle bus in five minutes. I got to Jenny's house in record time after running from the bus stop.

As I got to the back doorstep, Jenny greeted me with a beautiful birthday kiss. Oh, how good it felt to have her in my arms once again. I cannot explain what went through my mind and body whenever I was with my Jenny; she meant the world to me. OK, I had not had many girlfriends, in fact not any if you do not include Dot, but I did not want anyone else.

It was a lovely day, the sun was shining and there was not a breeze to be had – perfect in every way – and to top it off, I was fifteen.

We went inside and into the middle room. Jenny was looking gorgeous that day, wearing short shorts and a tank top, but no bra; I could see her nipples pressing against the material, and was getting excited just looking at her.

She went to a cupboard and brought out a gift and a card from her parents. 'Go on, open it,' she said. It was a new pair of expensive shoes, more than I could afford to buy. They were wonderful. 'They bought them for your first interview,' Jenny said.

'Gee, I am a lucky guy having friends around me like this.'

'You will have to come upstairs with me for your present – it is special.'

My first thought was, what has she got me? She'd already given me my card and the words inside it were so beautiful; she had written a poem straight from her heart.

I headed towards the room I usually slept in. 'No, in my room – it is in here,' said Jenny. We went in, and laid out on the bed was a silk black bra along with suspender belt, stockings, the full works – even some high heels she had borrowed from her mother's collection.

I looked at her, and she smiled. She told me to go into my room; she would be there in a few minutes. What the hell was going on here? Was I dreaming? She turned me and pushed me out of her room and closed the door. As she closed the door, she whispered, 'Get ready.'

I quickly stripped off and lay on top of the bed, waiting for her.

She walked in – oh my fucking god, what a vision. 'It is all for you, Leif. I could not think of a better present to give you than me. I am ready to be a real woman for you. Do you like me like this? I thought you would like the new version of your Jenny.'

The bra was see-through; her breasts were so perfect – I could see her nipples with that dark brown areola just visible around them. I so wanted to put them between my lips. Her smooth, naturally tanned body was beautifully proportioned.

She stood there, pure sex – I'd never seen anything so beautiful. Not even photographs of film stars could have looked any better.

I got off the bed and went to her.

'Leif, open your present – undress me, please. I want you.'

There was a full-length mirror on the wall. I was standing behind her just looking at us both, like watching a movie, but we were the actors. I was cupping her breast with one hand, while stroking her belly with the other. She threw her head back. I kissed her neck; it seemed so natural. No one had taught us this; it just happened. I undid her bra. It fell to the floor. She turned her head, looking up at me, and we kissed a real lovers' kiss. She slipped her panties off, stepping out of them. I could not believe this was happening – two kids. If Frank could have seen me I would have been a dead man.

I turned her towards me, and she put her arms around my neck. I picked her up – she weighed nothing – and carried her to the bed, as she kicked off her shoes. I laid her down, taking off her stockings one by one, kissing her toes as I pulled them off. Then the present was ready. The wait had been worth it, for now, Jenny and I were going to make love.

We lay there in each other's arms, just gazing into each other's eyes. She smiled and then started giggling.

'What you laughing at? Why are you giggling? Come on, tell me.'

'Why did I wait so long for that, baby? It was out of this world. Well, I know why – because I wanted to give it to the man who would live the rest of my life with me, that's why.' She started to cry. I looked at her beautiful face and kissed her nose.

'Come on, baby, don't cry; it was perfect. You were wonderful to share your body with me, it was the ultimate any girl can give. I love you so very much, my sweet, sweet Jenny.'

Then I kissed her lips and I could taste the salt from her tears.

This had to be the best birthday any boy could wish for. We did it twice more before getting in the bath together, which was the icing on the cake. Then we went downstairs for a drink before I had to get the last bus home.

After our first love-in, we made love whenever we got the chance – always getting off before we got to Wigan. Her mum and dad often had days away and left us alone in the house.

I was forever staying over, and when I did, Jenny used to sneak into my room and then go back to hers before her parents got up.

Mum said I should move in with them as I was spending more time at Jenny's house than my own, but such is young love, as she kept saying. One thing was for certain – Jenny had found something she liked playing more than a piano.

CHAPTER 18

LEIF
Devon

The day I had been waiting for. My SMC results. I received a pass in every subject with credits in maths, English, and the one I wanted most – technical drawing. For I knew if I got that I would have a high chance of an apprenticeship with one of the companies I had written to for a job – Paratec Ltd in Hull.

I wrote to them as soon as I got my results. A week later, I got a reply asking me to go for an interview the following Wednesday; this was mid-July. Two weeks later I had a letter offering me a position as apprentice draughtsman in their Hull office.

I was, as they say, over the moon; I had got what I had worked so hard to achieve. Mum was in tears when I had asked her to open the letter, but I knew as soon as I saw the beaming smile on her face.

I was now the same age as Jenny. However, she was going on sixteen and still at high school hoping to go to university to study for a degree in music.

Knowing this was breaking my heart now, for I knew I would lose my best friend and soulmate not too far off in the future, perhaps when she was eighteen, or nineteen if she took a gap year. It was getting to me. I knew it was a long time away, but the thought of it still hurt. I had never mentioned this to Jenny, for I knew she would worry.

As the school year was coming to an end, and the summer holidays were approaching, Jenny's dad asked me if I wanted to go on holiday with them to North Devon. They were renting a three-bed cottage in

Woolacombe and thought I might like to go. I had asked Mum, and she'd said no problem. Frank had emphasised the separate bedrooms bit when describing the cottage, as if he suspected something was going on between us kids. Good job he did not know the truth, or I would have been dead.

Anyway, I went with them. It took ages to get there, nearly a full day with only one break, as the traffic was unreal. Woolacombe was a beautiful place; we were not far out of the town and the beach we were nearest to was Croyde Bay only four miles away; some great spots with loads to do.

Jenny's mum and dad loved touring the area, whereas we were more interested in the beaches and exploring small coves and the like. We used to all go out in the car, and they would drop us off at one of the little beach areas, then we would walk back or get the local bus. Frank had a bad knee and couldn't walk long distances, so we were all happy with the situation.

Saunton Sands was one beach we visited. It was only seven miles away. Another was Putsborough Sands, four miles away; we went in the car and they dropped us off. Jenny's mum and dad were going a bit further south and we did not want to be stuck in the car all the time – plus, it gave us time to be alone, something we weren't getting a lot of.

If I had not agreed to come along, Jenny would have had to go with them on her own; there was no way would they have allowed her to stay at home, I am sorry to say. We had talked about offering to let her stay at our house, but there was not enough room.

One of the most beautiful days out and to one of the prettiest beaches was when we visited Wild Pearl Beach only four miles away. As per usual we got dropped off and walked to the beach, which it was in a cove and had a deep descent to get to it. When we got down from the rocky path one thing was immediately noticeable – everyone was naked, not a stitch on. All ages, all sorts of bodies, some families – but all starkers.

Now Jenny wanted to go straight away, but I thought, no – this could be fun. 'Come on, Jen, get your kit off,' I said.

'No,' she said emphatically. 'No way. I am not going to do it.'

'Well, I am,' I said, and started to strip off. Jenny just stood looking at me as I got naked. 'There – what's the harm in that? Look, no one's staring, no one's pointing or giggling saying, "look at them".' Jenny looked around and saw that I was right; no one was taking any notice of us.

'Jenny, come on, please, babe – have a sense of adventure. Get naked – it feels great.' The breeze around my arse was an unreal feeling.

'Oh, OK, I will, but hold the towel up – I am not just stripping off as you did; you love people looking at your cock.'

I held the towel up, and she slowly undressed. Why she should have been ashamed of her body was anyone's guess, but I suppose she was shy. After all, it was only a few months ago that no one had seen her until I did.

She was now naked, and I was still holding the towel. 'What's that over there?' I said, nodding in another direction. She turned her head to look, and when she looked back the sheet was on the sand, and she was open to view. I was pissing myself laughing. Her look of surprise was priceless; she didn't know what to try to cover first, her breasts or her groin. 'Calm down, Jenny, look around – who is looking at you? No one. Now, come on, let us walk over there where there aren't many people; come on.'

We set off walking, and there was a couple was walking towards us. 'Hello! Lovely day, isn't it?'

'Hi – yes, it is a fantastic beach; we love it,' Jenny replied. I looked at her, and she added, 'We always come here too,' and then just walked on.

We had some sun cream with us; we both had a bit of a tan, but more white bits that needed some. When I offered to do Jenny's white bits, she declined.

I would not have hesitated to go to a naturist beach again. It was great; it wasn't a suggestive environment. Most people who went there just loved being nude, as I did when I was at home in my bedroom alone. I just loved lying on my bed naked; it felt so free. I wouldn't have said Jenny would have chosen to go there, but she thoroughly enjoyed our day as Adam and Eve.

When we got home from Devon, her dad dropped me at home.

There was no one there, mind; it was late, nearly nine o'clock, and Mum and Billy must have gone to the pub or maybe Gipsyville Tavern – Mum liked it in there. It felt so strange being alone. It was the first time for a long time that I had been in a room with no one to talk to; usually, it did not bother me, having been an only one, but I had got used to having another to share my life with, share my laughter… yes, I was in love.

I had a couple of hours to myself, so I put the TV on. In those days it was Rediffusion cable TV, which also was cable radio but only four stations. It had just two TV channels. I must have nodded off as I felt Mum shaking me. 'Leif, come on, son – wake up, sleepy head, and get yourself to bed.'

I woke up late the next morning; the journey must have taken more out of me than I'd thought. Having been cramped up in that small car for that length of time, I needed to stretch my legs. I had started going for runs as I was beginning to put weight on around my waist – too much food on holiday, despite the walking we'd done. Ruth had been to blame all the time. 'Here you are, Leif, have some more…' Seconds, thirds – she just wouldn't take no for an answer.

I went for a run up to the top of our street on to Woodcock Street, then up Boulevard, across the road and into West Park; a couple of laps of the park then back home. That was better; I thought I would start doing more of this; it couldn't do me any harm and would help me get fit for when rugby season started with Cunny again in September.

I went for this run three times a week during the school holidays until I started working. The rest of my time was spent with my beloved Jennifer; we had a great summer together, going on bike rides to Little Switzerland or on walks along the river Humber, nearly up to North Ferriby or until the footpath ran out. I was gradually getting my weight back to normal and my abs back.

Jenny often came back to my house, but we had limited time alone; when Mum was at work regularly, Billy would be in as he worked early mornings as a bobber. He was often in bed early as he had to be up at two in the morning to get to work for around three o'clock.

We had been doing some work at school on local modern history and, being on Hessle Road it was the Cod Wars, which was of great interest to me, I knew it was a hard life working on the fish dock but not as hard as that of the fishermen, for the Icelandic Cod Wars had been going on since 1958, and there had been various disagreements since the 1400s. The first so-called Cod War started in 1958 when Iceland extended its four-mile limit to twelve miles, therefore cutting down the fishing field area.

There were lots more arguments for years, with Iceland threatening to pull out of Nato at one point, and the UK and Iceland came to a settlement in late February 1961. The deal was very similar to one that Iceland had offered in the weeks and days leading up to its single extension in 1958. As part of the agreement, it was stipulated that any future disagreement between Iceland and Britain over fishery zones would be sent to the International Court of Justice in The Hague.

But this was not the end, for I intended to try to improve things, one day – but how, I did not know.

CHAPTER 19

LEIF
The Big Wide World

My summer holidays over, I started my new job with Paratec as an apprentice draughtsman. The firm was a contractor in the oil industry, working worldwide on petrochemical plants and oil refineries, which interested me, as I could see a future in this.

I had done my homework looking at possible prospects, something my form master had emphasised we should do in my last year. I can recall our conversation.

'I have been thinking about what you said about doing my homework in the future; what I wanted to do for work.'

'Don't just look at the fish dock and the fishing industry as your only employer, for one day that could dry up. Look at what is in the future for you, possibly fifty years from now and what you will be doing in the coming years. As an example, my father had been a joiner. As he got older, his body had worn out as well as his tools. His body was his main tool as it was a physical job, involving lots of lifting, carrying and manual work, and once he could not do the work, he was put on the scrap heap.'

Now, these words of wisdom had stuck in my mind. I had seen my mother struggle all her life to make ends meet, living from day to day, and this was not going to happen to me, that was for sure.

I had met Jenny; she had made a big difference in my life. I was hoping we would still be together in the future, but deep down I doubted it – her father wanted her to go to university and so did her mum. I wasn't sure about Jenny herself; it was early days yet.

I just did not want to be stuck on Hessle Road. It was no fun living there. It had often been said how friendly the people were, but still, the conditions were far from good; most people lived in back-to-back houses, nearly all two up and two down, with no central heating, no hot water, an outside toilet, no bathroom and an outside tap, although most had had a sink and inside tap fitted as a luxury. When there were large families, most of the children all slept in one bed; sometimes tip to toe came into the equation.

I had thought, right – what is the most used commodity that everyone needs today and will always be wanted? Water was one, food was another, but I didn't want to be a farmer. Air it was free, so there was no real money in that, but air conditioning was a big thing – not so much in the UK, but in hotter countries it was a must. I knew nothing about it, only that in places like Australia it was a growing industry. Having looked at quite a few options that I thought may give me a future, most of my mates were talking about getting jobs on the fish dock as barrow lads, as the money was good, or going to sea fishing, but that was not for me.

The number of cars on the roads was increasing; now, I was no genius, but even I could see another commodity was petrol. Yes, this was the business to get in to. I read as many books as I could on where it came from, and how it was produced, and decided that I would try to get into that industry. How, I didn't have a clue, but I had to do something with my life. I had the opportunity here to do it, and intended to take it with both hands.

On my first day at work, I was introduced to the head designer, Mr Peterson, who seemed like a decent sort of bloke, and the fabrication shop manager, Mr Collins. Now, I was not so sure about this guy; on first sight he had a bit of a limp handshake, something Grandad always said was a sign of weakness in a man. Still, I gave him the benefit of the doubt.

Paratec had taken on another apprentice to their workforce, Dave McAlister, who started as an apprentice mechanical fitter. He had come from Ainthorpe High School as he lived in Anlaby. I was introduced to him at the induction meeting on the first morning.

We were sitting in Mr Peterson's office as he began the induction.

'OK, boys – welcome to Paratec. I will start by telling you what is expected of you, along with what the company can give you in return and what they want from you, not only here in the works – but also as good citizens, for any misdemeanours will not be tolerated, either as an employee of ours here, or away from the workplace. I will also cover the company's safety policy and other rules. Also, more importantly, how much you are going to be paid will be laid out in a structure, year by year from the age you are now at fifteen, and every year until you are twenty-one – that is a six-year tied apprenticeship or indenture. I will explain how the taxation and National Insurance system works – does either of you know this? To possibly save me going over something they taught you at school.'

We both replied that we knew a little and that the youth employment officer had given us some brochures on the UK's taxation system. We were asked to take the document home that night and bring it back signed by our parent or guardian.

'Finally, boys, last of all – it is the usual practice to have a period of three months' trial, either way, when each side can pull out of the agreement. After this period you are then tied in for the duration; do you understand?'

We both nodded and said, 'Yes, we understand.'

He then laid out the training plan. 'You will do so many months in each discipline of the works. You, Leif, you will be starting in the fabrication shop with Mr Collins, where you will learn the estimating and commercial side of the business for six months. Then for the remaining six months you'll work on the shop floor with either a dedicated trades-man, or a mixture of trades. You, David, will be the opposite – you will start on the shop floor and the same as Leif here, but in reverse – OK?

'After the first twelve months, both of you will then be allocated to an outside gang working in and around Hull for six months, then across the UK for another six months, coming home every weekend.

'Continuing after the first two years, Leif, you will then go to the drawing office and, David, you'll start your four years of training as a mechanical fitter dedicated to your apprenticeship.

'I must point out that we work on the same principles as most companies, in that we expected you to go to night school and day release in your second year when working around Hull. You are expected to have passed everything in eighteen months at night school for day release in your third year; understand that it is compulsory to pass the night school exams. Are there any questions up to now? Don't be afraid to ask – I won't bite. I work for the company the same as you do, and we are all here to help you in your working life. OK, then I will continue.

'Then during your four years in the office or works shop you would also be expected to gain your ONC, then your HNC – they are national certificates in engineering in your particular trade.'

I put my hand up. 'Can I ask when we have finished our apprenticeship, what happens then? Are we just let go, sacked or what? Are we just sent on our way, so to speak?'

'Good point, Leif. After your training period is complete, the company then decides to either keep you on or let you go – or sometimes they could give you a promotion to site management working up from foreman to supervisor if you were on the tools, or as a site manager or QC (quality control) or QS (quantity surveyor). Cost control is another important side of the company; there are lots of opportunities, as long as you work hard for them, which would also mean further education, or possibly university or the Open University.'

'Have I missed anything?' he asked Mr Collins, who had not said a word; he just looked fucking miserable.

'No, I don't think so – you have covered everything.'

'Right then, all this information will be handed to you in a package to take home to your parents as a reference to what you will be doing. You will also be given an apprenticeship plan, week by week, year by year, which you are expected to keep up to date similar to a diary. This is to be signed each week by your immediate supervisor at the time.'

I took the plan home that night and gave it to Mum. After reading it, she said, 'Well, I am confused by it all.'

Billy agreed. 'I am glad I am only a bobber – I could not handle all that shit.'

I went round to Jenny's house after ringing her on our home telephone – which Mum had had put in that day. It was so great to be a member of the twentieth century at last. Still, we didn't have hot water or a bathroom, but there again you can't have everything.

My apprenticeship went well in the first year; I loved working in the fabrication shop, getting my hands dirty and finding out what the company was all about. They manufactured various materials from copper, brass, aluminium, stainless steel and carbon steel in different forms, such as pipework, structural steel, vessels and expansion bellows. Working on the shop floor under the foreman – a guy called Jack Brownhill, whom I did not like or get on with, but that is another story – were tradesmen who covered quite a few disciplines from coppersmiths and sheet metal workers to platers and welders.

We apprentices were expected to work with these guys and learn our trade from them. Some of them were quite good and wanted to teach the tricks of the trade; others were more interested in what production bonus they were making or losing by explaining the different processes – especially the coppersmiths, who were a dying breed; all of them were in the later years of their lives and ready for retirement.

You took it in turns to work with each of them; the idea was that if you worked with different men, they all had different techniques of doing things so the more ways you were taught, the better you would be at the job. We had to be ready when required to give a hand, say, working on pipework. A tradesman could not lift and carry pipe pieces – or spools, as they are called in the trade – on their own, so inevitably they needed a mate to assist them.

Now, you have all heard of the piss being taken out of young lads in their early years of their apprenticeships – such as being told to go and ask the storeman for a long wait, and he would leave you standing there for ages, totally ignoring you when others came to the serving hatch, until you got pissed off with waiting and asked what was going on, how long was he going to be, that sort of thing. The coppersmith's favourite was a coppersmith's clout. This was a tool used when creating a branch or outlet in a length of the copper pipe. It was shaped like a carrot – a round steel rod that gradually tapered to a point, not just a chamfer on one end, if you get what I mean. It was around an inch and a half in diameter with a flat side that you hit with a hammer. I won't go into a great deal of detail as it will only bore you, but they would send you to one of the other coppersmiths and tell you to ask him for his clout. And then he would clip you round the ear.

There were five coppersmiths in the shop. Ray Waddle had a bad knee, which was, for want of a better word, fucked; he had to keep lifting it and resting it on the bench to ease the pain, and he used to nod off standing up. I'd never seen anything like him. Stan Clarkson had had an accident working for another company; he said he'd got caught up in a belt-drive which was fifteen feet long and that carried him around four rotations. He was lucky he was not killed. It left him with a twisted spine and one leg longer than the other; he had to wear a club boot with a sole about four inches thick, and you had to be wary when you worked with him, for he was a right nasty bastard. If you did something wrong, he just belted you. Bob Forth was another coppersmith, and he was a great bloke to work with – really keen, and always wanted to show you in great detail how to do some aspects of the job.

We were working away one day fabricating some pipe spools. Bob was welding a branch on to a piece of pipe. I was standing with my welding screen on, waiting for the green light to appear. I waited and waited, but nothing happened, so I lifted my screen – and then saw that Bob was lying on the floor unconscious, with the pipe on top of him. It had toppled over and hit him on the head. Unbeknown to me, he was not amused. I did not know I was supposed to hold the branch piece to stop it falling.

Geordie was another guy I worked with quite a bit; we used to do a forty-two-hour week in those days, and half of the Saturday morning was on single pay and then time and a half for the other two hours. I never knew his real name – just Geordie, for he came from Newcastle upon Tyne, was a big drinker and Friday was his big night out. It was not unusual for him to come in on Saturday still half-pissed. He was a good welder, even when he was pissed – especially on aluminium.

Without going into great detail, when you were welding with TIG, or tungsten inert gas, you used what was called the filler rod. This had to be extremely clean, and it was my job to rub the rods with emery cloth and methylated spirits. It was usual that, halfway through the morning, Geordie needed the hair of the dog or livener, and he would take a swig of the meths just to keep him going until he got to the pub at lunchtime.

It was funny how some of the guys had nicknames; there was Deaf and Dumb Billy, Willy Mac, Young Billy and Billy the Giant – this was so we knew which Billy was being referred to, as they were all welders. There was Wally the stutter; for no apparent reason, he had a terrible stutter. I remember one Monday morning going into the shop, and the guys who used to get there early, often because the bus times, were assembled around one of the coke fires that were used in fabricating copper pipe bellows.

We were standing there drinking mugs of tea when Wally came in looking very exasperated.

'Now then, Wally – you look pissed off. What's wrong?'

'Y-y-y-ou, w-w-w-w-w-would, n-n-n-not, b-b-b-b-believe it!'

He had missed out on winning the treble chance football pools, and just one team had let him down.

'B-b-b-b-b-b-b-b-bastard...' He was trying to get the name out. 'B-b-b-b-b-b-b...'

Still he kept trying to say the name of the team. Well, we went right through all the football league clubs beginning with B. Someone said, 'Birmingham?'

'N-n-n-n-no.'

The more we went on naming teams, the more he stuttered. 'Bradford City?'

'N-n-n-n-no.'

'Burnley... Barnsley?'

'N-n-n-n-no.'

Well, we went through the lot, and the more we called out, the more frustrated poor old Wally got – and then he finally managed to get the name out.

'B-b-b-b-b-b-bastard Arsenal!'

Well, we fell about laughing.

Billy the Giant was a huge man who was a plater; he used to fabricate all the big carbon steel pressure vessels. Willy Mac built all the smaller vessels. A lot of them had nicknames related to what they did in the shop, and everyone was a character in his own right; it was a great place to work.

I loved the second year too, which involved going to different jobs and sites with four other men – a supervisor, a tradesman, a mate and a rigger. Most of the work was pipework, which I became very interested in, but that will explain itself later.

A year later

My sixteenth birthday was coming up, and once again Mum suggested a party, but as before I declined the offer as all I wanted to do was spend the day with Jenny. She had said she had a special present for me – mmm… not again…?

My birthday was a Wednesday that year and I was still working in the fabrication shop. I left work at 4.30pm and got home about five, said my hellos to Mum, opened my present from her, rushed my tea down, and was soon out of the door to catch the bus around six o'clock to get up to Jenny's house.

I knocked on the front door and Jenny opened it. She looked stunning – wearing a black top, red mini-skirt and stockings, and bright red high heels. Oh my god… was this my special present?

'Fuck me, Jenny, you look beautiful.'

She did not answer me; she just took my hand and pulled me into the hallway, putting her arms around my neck as she kissed me. 'Happy birthday, Leif, come on – Mum and Dad are out; the house is ours for a few hours. Come and get your present.'

She led me upstairs into her bedroom, then let go of my hand. I was standing with my back to the bed; she pushed me. I sat down on the edge. She had a record player in her room and turned it on; the record dropped on to the turntable, and our song came on. Save the Last Dance for Me. She started singing the words, and as she sang she began to strip; first of all she undid the buttons down the front of her black blouse, one by one, and that came off. Then the red skirt fell to the floor. Her movements were so erotic, in time with the music, I reckoned Jenny must have been rehearsing this for weeks. The music played on, she retook my hand, and I stood up.

'OK, Leif, I am yours – happy birthday. Take your present, it's all yours.'

'Oh, baby,' I said as I unhooked her bra and slipped it off, then slipped down her small black silk panties, stroking the cheeks of her bottom as I did so; her skin felt as smooth as the panties.

She moved away from me, sat on the bed and undid the fasteners on her suspender belt; she lifted one leg for me to take her shoe off and slide the stocking down. I kissed her toes as they appeared, then did the same with the other leg. After my fifteenth birthday present, I was beginning to like this feet business.

She was naked; my present stood up and came to me. The feeling of her skin against mine was unreal.

'Now, Leif, take me, please. I am all yours. Happy birthday, darling – now make love to me. Don't just fuck me; make love to me.'

Going back to my fifteenth birthday again, I never thought this one could better it, but how wrong I was. I picked her up in my arms, carried her the few steps to the bed, lay her on it, and then knelt beside her. I started to explore her body softly, kissing her lips. First I worked my way down her body to those dark nipples, licking them in turn, then taking them between my lips, sucking and just nibbling them. She gave out a little moan as I worked down that flat, smooth belly, running my tongue around her navel. I was savouring every inch of her; I had got to Doncaster without stopping, so I was doing well. She moaned again as I gently touched her. I felt her body stiffen as her first orgasm arrived. Oh, fuck, this was so good. She moaned again, 'Oh, Leif, yes, Leif! Yes, oh, baby, yes! Now, Leif now!'

Always wanting to do as I am told, I came up and lifted her bottom, putting a pillow under the small of her back then holding her legs I entered her. Her warmth... wow – she was so hot. I pushed forward with my arse, and she was writhing and lifting her little body to take me. Oh, it felt so good. The train arrived at Wakefield Trinity's Belle View. I was looking into her eyes, but she was not there – she was somewhere in her mind. Wherever it was, Jenny was happy. I then began moving, and she climaxed again. 'Oh yes, oh yes, fuck yes, Leif, oh baby!' she shouted.

It was the first time I'd ever heard her swear. I was in heaven, but I was not there yet; I was at Warrington now. I was on my elbows and toes to keep the weight off her body, and I was getting close; Jenny had her legs wrapped around my waist, holding me. 'Oh, Leif, please, just stop now, please – please, just keep him there. Oh, I want to have this moment forever. Mmm, oh god! It is so fucking good... oh, yes, oh, fuck, yes, mmm, oh, Leif.'

Widnes Naughton Park passed by; Wigan was coming into view – oh, yes – Central Park. I was not pushing as hard as I could to get as far to Wigan as possible; maybe the end of the line in Workington. I can't remember ever reaching Derwent Park.

'Oh, yes, baby!' Jenny was gripping me.

I arrived at Wigan and withdrew from Jenny. I looked down; I had gone limp. My present had been gratefully accepted; we were both covered in sweat as we lay next to each other, I gently touching her beautiful flat belly. That was my first legal fuck – and the best one ever.

CHAPTER 20

LEIF

Decision Time

I was now enjoying playing rugby for Cunny YC under-seventeens in the Hull and District League.

We played against Craven Park Juniors one Saturday afternoon, and this guy came up to me and asked my name; he told me he was a scout for Hull Kingston Rovers. I had come to their attention, and now I was sixteen they could approach me. Would I be willing to talk to them, as they were interested in signing me on. My first reaction was 'fuck off' – but I kept my cool and said I would think about it. The man gave me a card with his name and telephone number and told me to call him when I had talked to my parents about it.

I went home after the game and told Mum about what had happened, and like all mothers she was chuffed about the prospect of her son going to play professional sport and possibly being another Johnny Whiteley.

'I am not interested,' I said.

'What you mean you are not interested?'

'I am not going to play for them red-and-whites, I'm an FC fan, Mum! I would be a traitor.'

'Traitor, my arse.'

'FC – have they come to see you? No. Are they interested in you? No. Now, don't be stupid – ring the man up.' She looked at the name on the card – Billy Erskine. 'Go ring this Billy up and tell him yes, you are keen to talk with them – what harm can it do?'

I thought, boy, this is a change; it was not long back that she did not want me to play rugby in case I got hurt. Now she wants me killed in action playing against giants. Women!

I was thinking, what if I did get injured and I had to be off work through playing rugby – how would Paratec react? Would they be happy about me having time off? I doubted it. No, I would speak to them before I did anything. I told Mum this, and she agreed.

I went into work the following Monday and asked the foreman, Len, if he saw our supervisor, Jack, to ask him if he was coming to the site – and if he was, I would like to have a word. I knew full well that Jack would be coming to the site that day to pick up the weekly timesheets.

Lunchtime came and, sure enough, Jack showed up.

'Now then, young Leif – what are you after, son? Put somebody up the stick, have you?'

What was he on about? Where did he get that from? Oh, right, Len must have told him I had a personal problem, and two and two made five. 'No, Jack, I haven't – what's Len been telling you?'

'Only kidding, son – what's the problem? How can I help? Come on, tell me.'

I told him the situation with Rovers, and that I wanted to know the company's stance on it.

'Well, now,' he said, 'I think to be honest they might not be too happy, but that is only my opinion; the company is a sponsor of Hull FC – only in a minor way, admittedly – but still follows them. They may not like the thought of you being red and white. Another factor is whether you'd have to have time off work through injury or having to travel away for matches. But I will ask for you when I get back to the office; I can't do more than that. By the way, well done, son. I did not know you were that good. I had heard you were not a bad player, though; I'm surprised that FC haven't tapped you up.'

I left, happy in the knowledge that he was interested enough to put my case to the management; I'd wait and see what happened.

I was not seeing Jenny as often as I would have liked, what with work and training at Cunny. It was getting to be a bind, rushing home and grabbing something to eat, and Mum was still working. Hence, meals were always a bit later at around half six at night, and by the time I had eaten, rushed to catch a bus up to Hessle, then got back home to get some sleep, I was shagged. This work was not supposed to be like this; no one warned me about this at school. Then playing rugby on Saturday only left Sunday to see Jenny; something had to give, and I did not want it to be her.

About two weeks later Len told me the result of his enquiry into me playing rugby and possibly going to Rovers; mind, that was a bit of a long shot. He had a letter for me from the managing director, Mr P S Smith. 'Here you are, Leif, it is addressed to you; I don't know what they said. Open it, son, be interesting to know.'

I opened the envelope, and the letter inside it read:

'We did not realise you had been playing amateur rugby league, and we would rather you not play any sport that could be a risk to injury by collision or impact, for the loss of time could influence the running of the company's workforce. Should the occasion arise we would have to look at your employment status, and you should look at your employment pack and the apprenticeship plan issued to you at the commencement of my employment, stating the page and paragraph number.'

Len took the letter from me and said, 'Hmm, they won't let you – or they would rather you did not play. I can understand it as well. Sorry, son – it is up to you.'

I was gutted, to be honest – who were they to say what I could and could not do in my own time? Why did I bother asking?

I went home that night and gave Mum the letter, telling her I was not taking any notice of them; I was still going to play – they were not telling me what to do.

Billy agreed with me. 'Fuck 'em, Leif.'

Mum, the ever-composed; Mum, who always thought things through realistically, said, 'No, Leif – it is not worth it if you lose your job through it. Don't forget, it is a good job you have with Paratec; you have a big future with them. Why throw it away for a game of rugby? You might not be good enough to play professionally after all, and you can get injured playing for Cunny as quickly, if not more easily, as you would not be as fit and well-trained as you would with Rovers. For they have physio and trainers who know what they are doing; they would get you back from injury a lot quicker than the lad at Cunny who carries the bucket of water and sponge. My advice is no. Sorry, but no – let the rugby go.'

Why do mothers always look at things differently to children? 'Your mum's right,' Billy said. I agreed they were both right, but then I said, 'I can get insured for loss of earnings.'

'No, Leif, it is not about the loss of earnings with Paratec; you still get paid, but not all companies pay their people if they are off. They are more worried about the disruption to their workforce. No, end of story – you are not playing any more.'

I went to training on Thursday and told Ronnie I was not playing again; he was gutted, the same as me. All the lads gathered around; some said 'fuck 'em', and others agreed it was the right decision, for they were also thinking about giving up playing. I said my goodbyes and left. I was going to miss all my new mates, but it was for the best.

Jenny was upset that I was not going to play, but deep down she was pleased because she would see more of me. I suppose that was the only good thing to come out of the whole situation. Life was still good. I was now seventeen, a little bit taller at six foot three, and around fourteen stone, keeping fit with swimming and running, and my job was excellent. I was still doing manual work with the site crews on a maintenance contract at one of the edible oil refineries in Hull – mostly pipework, the odd bit of structural work and mechanical installations.

I was learning more and more every week, and I had gotten into the industry's welding side. Welding pipes was an art as much as a skill, as I found out. The most skilful of these welders were called coded welders, needed, for example, when tubes had to be welded together. Then a percentage of the total welds each welder had completed had to be non-destructive tested, mostly by X-ray, but I won't go too much into that. Still, only the most highly skilled welders could do the work.

I had got that proficient at welding that I was working with the pipefitter welding the spools, fabricating spool or pieces of pipe made from measurements taken on site, and manufacturing them in the shop, before installing them on the plant. Our work was not high pressure and did not require NDT inspection, but was still not expected to leak when online or used in the process plant. I was asked if I would take a weld test but declined the offer as I did not want to be a welder all my life, and next year would be office-bound learning my job as a design draughtsman.

I was still going out with Jenny and deeply in love with her; we went everywhere together. Although I was under-age, we still went to pubs around the town. Halfway on Spring Bank West was a great place, and the Ferry Boat in Hessle was a fantastic Saturday night, just to name two of them.

But one of the really fun nights out was going out to Withernsea Pavilion dances, as they had live bands on, and Jenny loved that. Being a budding entertainer she loved listening to guitarists playing, often saying, 'I am better than him!' or 'He is not in tune!' (They always seemed OK to my ear, but she was a perfectionist.) She sometimes got a bit too much with the smart, know-all attitude, and I did not like that one bit.

It was a great adventure, the train ride to Withernsea, before Dr Beeching thought it an excellent idea to dismember the railway system in 1964, mostly in rural areas with over half of stations closing. People thought this would be the death of such seaside resorts as Withernsea and Hornsea, the two closest to Hull.

We were at 'With Pavil', as it was known, one Saturday night with the last train leaving after the dance finished around 11pm. It was a mad dash to stay in the Pavilion drinking as long as you could, then get on the train for the journey home. There was always someone who left it too late, and one night this was my mate Kenny, who was with a girl and giving her what could be called a goodnight kiss.

As the train was pulling out, he started running along the platform, trying to catch the train. We were holding one of the carriage doors open for him to jump on, but as the train speeded up, he was gradually getting further behind. Still, he had a chance, as the station platform was a decent length, and we were in one of the carriages at the back of the train; they were the old-type carriages with single compartments and individual doors. As he ran along, his chance had gone. He disappeared down the ramp, and spent the night in a shelter in the sunken gardens on the front.

I saw him in Rayners the following lunchtime; he had just got back, and he was pissed off. He reckoned that as he stumbled he'd nearly gone under the train, and he was only just realising how lucky he was.

Things were getting a bit edgy between Jenny and me; she wanted to see more of me, but there was nothing I could do – I was busy working and studying one night at night school.

She was also very busy; maybe it was getting to her a bit, the pressure of 'must do good' for mummy and daddy. As I said, I still loved her to bits, but yes – the 'buts' were beginning to appear. She was starting to try to dictate when we met on her terms, and I wasn't having any of it. I was quite an easy-going type of guy but to be quite honest she was beginning to bore me; I was seventeen now, and wanted a bit more freedom; she kept talking about which university she would like to go to, and which was the best music academy.

There was no doubt she was outstanding – but she was starting to tell me she was, a lot. That had always been one of the things I hated – big heads – and Jenny was going that way. Trinity College London was her number one choice if she did well in her exams. I was sick of hearing about how good it was. It was founded in 1872 by the Reverend Henry George Bonavia Hunt, fellow of the Royal Society of Edinburgh and author of *A Concise History of Music*.

Jenny went on and on about Sir Frederick A Gore Ousley, Professor of Music at Oxford University, who established the Church Choral Society and College of Church Music London, created for teaching, practising and testing. This was later to become Trinity College of Music. If I heard this once, I heard it a hundred times.

I kept forgetting she was that little bit older than me. Jenny was eighteen – nine months older than me. We were just not the same any more; she was becoming a bit of a snob. We had not seen each other for about two weeks, and then it happened.

It was tea-time; I was home early having got a flyer, which we often did on a Friday afternoon, and I was hoping we could go out to the pictures for a change, just the two of us alone. I thought it might be useful to ease the tension.

I rang her up, and her mum was a bit strange on the phone with me. 'Ruth, what's wrong?' I said. 'You seem a bit edgy in your voice… is there something you want to say? Be honest now. We have always been straight; what's wrong?'

With that, Frank came on the phone. 'Hi, son, how are you, OK? Not seen you for a while.'

'It has only been two weeks, Frank, what are you talking about, "a while"? What the fuck is going on, Frank? Tell me!'

'Don't swear at me, Leif; it is not my fault if Jenny does not want to see you again.'

Talk about a hammer blow.

'Hang on – what are you talking about? When did she say this? She has not mentioned this to me. We were OK six weeks ago. OK, it has been a bit rocky of late but, hey, not that bad – nothing we could not talk out. Come on, Frank, what has been going on?'

'Leif, she got the pass for her exams; she got great results, and, well, she got a place at the TCM London.'

I went silent. I knew this was going to happen but had hoped it would not.

'Leif? You still there, son? Leif, talk to me,' was coming down the phone.

'Yes… I am OK, Frank.' I had a croak in my voice and my eyes were filling up. How could she not tell me herself? Talk about gutted… it is not the word. 'Frank, can I come and see her, please? I do not want it to end like this – we are good together. I love her, Frank, more than anything in the world. I will do anything to keep her, Frank. Please, can I?'

The phone went dead. 'Fucking bastard.' I started to cry. I was heartbroken.

Mum walked in from work. 'What's happened, Leif? What's wrong?'

'It is Jenny, Mum; she has blown me out, wiped me like a shitty arse,

Mum. She has packed me in – can you believe it?'

'Come here, babe.' She put her arms around me, looking up at me. 'Leif, I am sorry, son. Jenny rang up three weeks ago; you were out. On the phone, Jenny was hysterical, crying her eyes out; it took me ages to console her. She told me she had got her results from her exams and got her placement, but did not want it; she did not want to go to London and not see you any more.'

I looked at her. 'You mean you knew three weeks ago and never told me? What sort of fucking mother are you, Mum? Why? Why? I don't understand.'

'Listen, Leif; it was for the best.'

'The fucking best? Fucking best? How do you work that out? Mum, are you mad? Have you lost your senses? It is Jenny you are talking about – my fucking girlfriend, not some bird I have been shagging for a few weeks.'

'Stop swearing. There is no need for it, and have some respect, for I'm your mother. Calm down and just think about it – all her life she has worked, from being four years old, playing the piano and the rest, learning how to read and play music, and then she meets you, her dream lover, and falls madly in love. You were good for each other, but I knew one day you would be second-best, son. One day her other dream would come true; she would get that place over the rainbow. It would not have worked. If she had knocked it back and told them, no, she would never have forgiven you for stopping her go to uni. Every time you had a fallout, it would come up, believe me, Leif. Let her go, son. Please don't hate her; she is an angel, the most wonderful girl I have ever met – but it's just not to be. It was in the stars, baby.'

I went to my room and lay on the bed; my mind was in turmoil. Why? Why? I kept asking myself. All I could see was my Jenny, but she was not mine any more. I then just broke down in tears. I cried myself to sleep that night – well, I say sleep – I didn't get that much. When I woke up the pillow was soaking and my eyes red, and there was a lump in my throat like someone close had died – for she might have well had; she had gone out of my life.

I got up for a drink, and Billy was having his breakfast. He didn't say much; what could he say? He just came up to me and hugged me. 'So sorry, Leif,' he said, and kissed my cheek.

'Thanks, Billy.' That is all that was said between us. I made myself a tea and sat next to him on the settee. We did not have a table in the living room; there wasn't any room for one – we always ate off trays or just plates balanced on our knees.

There was still no conversation. Billy did not say much when he spoke, to be honest, but I could feel that Billy was feeling my pain, too; he had got used to Jenny. I think he thought of her as the daughter he was never going to get.

I went to Wharrams the florist the next day and bought a massive bunch of flowers, as well as a card from the paper shop, and caught the bus up to Hessle. I had rung work and told them I was ill – more like dying; it was the first day I had had off since I started there, but I could not face work. I knew Jenny would be in, and she would not be expecting me to turn up.

I was walking down toward her house when I saw the front door opening; I ducked behind the telephone box. Jenny came out, but… hang on – who was this? She was seeing someone. Who was this bastard? I watched as she gave him a peck on the cheek before he got into a car. I waited until he drove off past me, and she was waving at him as he disappeared.

I watched her go back in the house, and waited a few minutes. Oh, boy, was I going to enjoy this. I did not feel so bad now. I wanted to be rid of the slut – how long had this been going on? How long had I been sharing her with him?

I went to the house and knocked on the front door, but there was no answer. I knocked again, and heard this voice call, 'Who is it? I'm busy.'

I tried to put on a voice that did not sound like me. 'Delivery for a Miss J Johnson.'

It must have worked for I heard her unlock the door and take the bolt off. The look of surprise on her face was priceless.

'Leif, what are you doing here? Why aren't you at work? What do you want? I don't want to see you, sorry.' She started to close the door in my face. Did she hate me that much? Why was she doing this to me?

I put my foot in the door to stop her closing it; she was pushing against me, but there was no chance of stopping me, and I pushed it open and walked inside.

'Jenny, why the look of terror in your eyes? What the hell happened between us to make you react to seeing me in such a way?'

I put the flowers on the table in the hallway and moved towards her. She slunk away from me as if she was going to drop to the floor. I grabbed her hands before she did and lifted her to her feet. 'Baby, please talk to me. Why are you acting like this? I have never hurt you, have I? What the hell is going on? I am not leaving until you tell me. And who the hell is the bloke you just kissed goodbye to out there? How long you been seeing him behind my back?'

'Michael, you mean?'

'Michael, Schmichael, whatever his name is – who the fuck is he? How long you have been going with him? Has he shagged you as well?'

In retrospect that was not the right thing to say, but at the time it fitted.

'No, he has not! How you dare think that of me? Do you think I am some sort of slut? You know me better than that, Leif.'

'Jenny, please, I am sorry. I did not mean that – but who is he? Why were you kissing him? OK, it was on the cheek, fair enough – but who is he? You leave messages with your mum and dad saying you don't want me any more; please, Jenny – we need to talk. We need to sort this mess out once and for all. You told my mum three weeks ago you were going to finish it. Why not tell me to my face? At least I deserve that, don't I?'

She was crying now; tears were rolling down her cheeks, and she looked so sad. I pulled her towards me; oh, how good that felt to hold her in my arms again. She was sobbing like a baby, and mumbled something that I did not catch, like when a child tries to say something and sob at the same time. I stroked her hair and held her tight to my chest, feeling the sobbing subsiding; she sniffed, resting her head on my chest, like times before when we were lovers.

She looked up at me. 'Oh, Leif – I did not want it to end like this. I love you so much, but I need to go to London. I did not want to have to say goodbye, and I thought it best to end it without the turmoil of seeing your face for the last time. I knew you would be upset, as much as I am, but just thought it best. I am so, so sorry, Leif.'

'OK, OK, I get it now. I do understand why you want to go to London, but let's not stop being friends. We had too much together. We loved – no, still love – each other, and that will never end. We can always love each other, maybe not physically, but please, Jenny, do not leave me this way.'

A little smile came on her face – that beautiful, sweet face, the look that I loved, the face that had given me such joy and happiness.

'Are you sure, Leif? Do you think you can still be my friend if we part, even if you meet some other girl and become as we were, or if I meet someone – when I'm back home, if you see me in town or a pub with another boy? Look how you just reacted to Michael – who, by the way, happens to be my cousin back from Australia. He is here working; he emigrated with his parents when he was five, and it's the first time I have seen him since. He's twenty-three now. Also, he's with an orchestra – he's a musician, that's why he is here. Look at how you reacted to seeing me with him.'

I had to be honest with myself; I had overreacted, but I was annoyed, because of what had happened between us.

'Jenny, I have no intentions of pushing you into something you do not want. All I want is for you to be happy and to be a success in whatever you do in the future. If I am not part of that future, so be it, but I beg of you, please, please do not just push me to one side like a dirty rag. I also think I deserve better than that.'

We hugged again, this time with feeling; she looked up at me, and our lips met. The taste of her lips was so beautiful, but she pulled away before our kissing became the beginning of a happy ending for both of us. I still held both of her hands in mine – those beautiful fingers, fingers that could make so much happiness from a piano or a violin; when they touched anything it brought great to joy to everyone.

I picked up the flowers and handed them to her. 'Please take these, Jenny, as a farewell gift. I hope you have a great time in London with all your new uni friends that you will no doubt make, but do not forget I will always love you from the bottom of my heart until the day I die. There will always be a place in my heart for you, for I do love you, Jenny Johnson.'

With that, I opened the door to leave. 'Give my love to Frank and Ruth,' I said. 'Tell them I will call round some time to say hello. If you find the time, please ring me or write me a letter. Bye, baby.'

As I closed the door behind me I heard her crying, and I was close to tears, for closing that door without looking back was the hardest thing I had done in my seventeen years. But now I was OK with it; I had to move on. My life was directly in front of me.

CHAPTER 21

LEIF
New Opening or Not

It was now July 1963 and I had started the next year of my apprenticeship, entering the world of the draughtsman; I loved it.

The company had a modern drawing office and was hoping to bring into the systems a new form of working – CAD, or computer-aided design. I was taken into the manager's office on my first day, and he said, 'Leif we are going – well, hoping – to use a new way of working, son, and we want you as our first apprentice to come through the ranks, to be taught CAD working systems. We believe, looking at your school results, that you are well capable of taking this on, going forward. We believe that, should everything turn out as we expect, you will become our head of the drawing office and design department, possibly taking over from me.' He smiled. 'But not too quickly, I hope! What do you think to that?'

I was gobsmacked. 'Well, what can I say? You certainly know how to put pressure on a guy, and I do appreciate that you think I will be good enough. I am not going to stand here and say that you are right; all I can say is I will do my best and look forward to the challenge.' How I thought of all that bull, I do not know, but I guess it sounded all right.

'That's the spirit! Very well spoken. I will start by giving you a brief overview of what CAD is all about, as it is all brand new to me.'

He went on about how it all started around the mid-1960s, how it would be a cost-benefit for us to switch to CAD-integrated circuits, interference checking, and many others. During this transition, calculations would be still performed either by hand or by those who could run computer programs; they needed to train me and some of the existing team.

'OK, so far, Leif, I know it may sound a lot of waffle to you right now, but I am sure you will get a grasp of it once we get under way. Now, where was I? Oh, yes. It won't eliminate departments as much as it will unite them, and will it empower draughtsmen, designers and engineers. CAD is an example of the effect computers are beginning to have on our industry. It is expected that future computer-aided design software packages will range from 2D drafting systems to 3D solid and surface modellers. Some CAD software they hope will be capable of dynamic mathematical modelling; it will revolutionise the design industry, without doubt, what do you think to that?'

'Jesus... that sounds a bit much for me to pick up,' was my response.

'Don't worry, Leif – we will ensure you get the finest training possible. All I need to add is that we need to bring this into line with the way the company wants to go and this will enable us to compete cost-effectively. For the world is becoming smaller; air travel is now the norm. They have been flying scheduled flights from the UK since 1958 when BOAC flew from London to New York. This has opened up a whole new world for commerce. And the company needs to be in that marketplace. Well, young man – we understand it is a lot to take on board, and you might be a bit worried by what I have just explained to you, but we honestly believe you are capable of becoming an important part of this company. If we did not, you would not be sitting there now in that chair. So – any questions?'

'Mmm... Er... wow. I do not know what to say, to be honest. I am... what can I say? Humbled, I suppose, that you think so highly of me. I just hope I can live up to your expectations, for I am only seventeen after all, and still wet behind the ears, so to speak.'

'Don't worry about that, Leif. That is why we want you to start now because you are so young. We believe that not too far in the future every home will have computers, and children will be able to use them in schools; the world is changing, Leif, and we need young boys like you to help take Paratec into the twenty-first century. Will you come with us?'

I believed this bloke could sell ice cream to Eskimos. I could not say no; Paratec clearly thought I was the next best thing to sliced bread. 'OK, count me in,' I said, which sounded a bit like John Wayne, but that was all I could think of.

Mr Peterson came around his desk and shook my hand. 'Thank you, Leif – welcome to Paratec's new world.'

I was now getting day release to go to college for adult education, but it was a way behind what the company was teaching me. I went to Mr Peterson midterm and explained the situation. I thought that I was better off working five days a week rather than the four I was doing. He said he would have a think about it and let me know; he needed to contact the tutors at college to see what their views were on the subject, but appreciated my concern.

A few weeks passed, then one day out of the blue, my tutor Mr Jackson collared me and asked me to stay behind after class, and go to his office.

I knocked on the door; a voice called out, 'Come in, Leif – thanks for staying back a bit; it's hard to talk with others around. Please sit down.'

'Thank you – what's wrong? Why did you want me to stay? Is there something I have done?'

'No, Leif, no – just needed a word, son. I have been talking to your manager, Mike Peterson.'

'Mike?' I did not know his first name, so it did not ring a bell at first. 'Oh, yes, Mr Peterson; you mean at Paratec.'

'Yes, him – Mike. Well, we have agreed that it is in your best interest that you will get a lot more from your apprenticeship by learning their requirements for the future and what they have in mind for you. I believe you have already discussed this with him? We think this will help both you and your company, which is paying your wages, after all, so it's not necessary for you to come here any more. There is one proviso – we both agree that you should study at home in your own time to gain your ONC and HNC certificates. We are quite willing to set you the work for you to complete and submit to us every week, should you be willing.'

My first thought was I was not too keen on that, but I told him I would consider the offer and get back to him next week. He agreed that it was OK.

I went back to work the following Monday and asked Mr Peterson if I could have a word. I told him what Mr Jackson had said and Mr Peterson was not over keen on my doing 'homework'. I had thought I my suggestion would help both myself and the company and expecting me to do the said homework was a bit too much to ask.

'Leif, I thank you for your honesty and appreciate what you are saying. How about if we say you did your coursework here in the office, perhaps one half-day a week? I was thinking of putting you in an office of your own anyway, to let you concentrate on this CAD system work. I know you need to be out with the guys, who are a bit further advanced than you are, to learn from them. I want you to be picking up on future systems; we will be sending you on courses anyway, at the providers of the new systems we will be introducing. How does that sound to you, OK?'

'Yes, fine by me, Mr Peterson.'

'It is Mike, Leif – let us cut out the "Mr" bit, shall we?' He offered me his hand to shake; we were becoming friends, not just boss and worker, but mates.

Mike turned out to be one of the best managers I ever worked for; he really taught me a lot about man-management. 'Treat people as you would like to be treated yourself' was one of his favourite sayings, and how right he was.

That was settled – no more days off, and the college did know about the agreement I had set up with Mike; they set me the course up to enable me to gain my engineering diplomas.

There was only one problem. One of the senior guys, Jack Mackman, hated me; he believed he should have been given the job that I had been brought in to do, and he made no bones about telling everyone of his discontent.

He fronted me one day in the toilets, saying he would do whatever he had to do to get me sacked. Now, OK, I was only a kid, a big kid, but still a kid, and I had never been threatened in my life. I was not frightened of him, but I wasn't sure how to handle it. Should I go to Mike and tell him what was going on, or should I try to see what happened and take care of him myself?

I decided to give it a few weeks, possibly months, and see what happened; I think one or two of the other staff members was thinking along the same lines. Had I made the right choice in taking this on? If I was going to get all this grief, yes, I was sure – I had goals in life to make sure I never had to live in near-poverty again. I'd said I would never go through what my forefathers had suffered. I would be rich, live in a big house, drive an expensive car, travel the world – and this twat was not going to stop me.

Things came to a halt when a new accounts manager joined the company, and it was discovered that the cost of installing even a 2D CAD system was way beyond the company's budget, and they decided to put it on hold it for a while.

Mike called me into his office to give me the bad news. We had been doing groundwork on it, but along with the managing director they had done a feasibility study, and they had decided it was not worthwhile just yet.

I was disappointed. Mike told me not to worry, and that all the work I had put in would be worth it in the end. The company had not aborted the idea; it was just not the right time.

It seemed to me that all that Mike had said about the company needing the system to go forward and be a leader in the industry had been a load of shit. I had been thinking about it and just had to know, so I went back to Mike's office and knocked on his door. His secretary must have gone to powder her nose, as they say.

'Come in. Now then, young Leif, what can I do for you?'

'Sorry to bother you, Mike, but it has been getting to me about the computer thing. Can I ask you a question, please?'

'Yes, sure. Don't look so serious, son, it is not the end of the world; we are not going to get rid of you just because we have decided on shelving it for a while.'

'It is getting to me; I am sorry, it is just the way I am. I can't stand uncertainty. There is no grey area with me; it is either black or white. What happens if you don't go with it? And how long do you think it will take for us to get it on board? I just need to know in my mind, that's all.'

'Hey, look, son, you need to learn the economics of running a company, and at this moment in time you are, sorry to say it, not ready for that worry. Just leave that part to us – that is what we get paid for. Just you concentrate on doing what you are doing, and you will be fine. I have told you – the work you have done will hold you in good stead; it won't be wasted. Is that good enough for you?'

'Well, yes, I suppose so. OK, thanks, Mike. Sorry to bother you again. Thanks.'

He came over to me, put his arm around my shoulders, and hugged me.

'Leif. I wish everyone in this company were as conscientious as you, son; now, off you go. I am busy, OK?'

I came out of his office with a different approach; I was happy with the outcome.

I reverted to what you might call the standard way of producing drawings. It used to take days to complete them by manual drafting, and reproducing it meant recreating the item from the beginning. But with CAD, you could reproduce the drawing in no time and make as many copies as you wanted; this was why Mike was so keen to get it on board. He was gutted the same as I was when he got the news, but as he said, we would just have to wait.

As it seemed there was no alternative yet, we had to carry on producing engineering drawings on sheets of paper using drawing boards. Our engineers and toolmakers used to draft all things on paper with the help of drafting tools and pens.

So, Jack got his wish, and I was reduced to ranks. The only good thing was that Mike kept to his word and let me do my studies for my ONC and HNC in the office, as the tech college had already set up the course.

One other good point was the company had now a piping division to drive its refinery and petrochemical plant design business forward; it was taken away from the general mechanical division. Luckily for me,

Mike headed the new division and picked his crew from the ones already employed, including myself and two other guys he had recruited from BP – a piping designer called Terry Foster, and a piping draughtsman called Neil Goodway.

Mike also brought into the crew an old guy named Johnny Capelin; he was an older man to me, anyway, as he was in his sixties, which was ancient to a seventeen-year-old lad. He was a master tradesman plumber/pipefitter/welder. Johnny was also a welding instructor at the Hull Technical College, and what he did not know about pipes was not worth knowing; he was going to be the fabrication shop foreman. I wanted to learn as much as I could from him but he always seemed to be a bit wary about the office staff, and didn't say much, just kind of answered in monosyllables, yes or no. I'd heard he had been a staunch union man and could only get jobs as supervision because he was a bit of a redneck. But with the guys on the tools, he was brilliant.

As 1964 came, I was now going on eighteen, and we had started the year with the loss just after the new year of Mum's mother, Elizabeth. She was sixty-eight, and she had been ill for a few years. She'd been found to have emphysema, mainly caused by smoking, which she had done all her life. All the family smoked except Mum and me, and she always made sure that I never tried it. 'I ever catch you smoking, you will eat them, OK?' she would say. That was good enough for me.

Grandma was the second one of my family to have passed away, along with my father. The service was at St Barnabas Church, and the funeral was at the Western Cemetery down Chanterlands Avenue in the eastern part of the burial ground. I had never been to a burial, and at the time, it was the last one I ever wanted to go to; it was terrible standing around the graveside.

I was holding Mum's arm; she was trembling as the vicar said the prayers. He went on and on until the time came for the coffin to be lowered into the ground. Then all the close family members threw a rose or some soil on to the coffin as the vicar said: 'In the sweat of thy face shalt thou eat bread, till thou return unto the ground; for out of it wast thou has taken: for dust thou art, and unto dust shalt thou return.'

I was in tears, as was everyone else, for you do not know what people think about you until you are dead.

Grandad was very quiet; he was on one side of me, my mother on the other. He took my hand in his; it was the first time I can say that he ever showed any manner of affection. We had had a lot of conversations lately but he never did hold me or touch me. It was as if he was afraid to show anything.

There were people there that I did not really know or had ever met; there were two cousins – thirteen-year-old Jason, son of Arkvid, my mother's brother, and her other brother Hans's son Hans Jnr, who was eleven. I had not known they existed.

Two new aunties that I had never met, Mary and Angela, were introduced to me by Mum; why we had never been closer to them I do not know. It was troubling me, and I needed to understand why they were never included in my family. I had been the only one who did not know of these other people – people who were part of my flesh and blood. What made it even worse was I never saw them go to Grandad and talk to him one-to-one; they just nodded as they came into eye contact.

As at all funerals, we promised to get together more, 'You must come for tea one day, or we must have a family day sometime soon,' we said, knowing full well it would never happen. We never had a wake; Grandad did not want one. He'd said Grandma wouldn't have wanted any fuss, so we all said our goodbyes at the gates to the cemetery and went on our way.

I went back with Mum and Billy for a drink in Rayners with some of Billy's friends who had been to pay their respects, but the other two parts of the family just disappeared as quickly as they arrived.

I had met Hans before when Dad died, but Arkvid had never been near. OK, Hans went to sea fishing. I knew he would not be around much, but what did Arkvid do? Where did they live? I vowed I would find out somehow.

I was not seeing anyone regular in the girlfriend stakes. I had gone off women altogether; they were a pain in the arse – too much trouble, and Jenny had hurt me. I had seen a couple of girls who were OK, but one wanted to smother me, and the other wanted to marry me – you could hear church bells ringing in her head whenever we talked, so I had to get rid of her.

The romances never lasted more than three weeks. I do not want to sound awful, but they were easy. They wanted sex more than me, I think. I was not a prude by any imagination, but these two could not get my pants off quick enough.

I was not used to this but was getting to like it, for it thrilled me, in a funny way, the fact that girls wanted sex as some sort of standard thing you did after being out for a drink; some way of paying you back what you had spent on them. Being involved with girls who were that forward led me astray when I went with my first prostitute when I was nineteen; she was a working girl called Rachel – but more of that later.

CHAPTER 22

LEIF

First Time for Everything: June 1964

I could now go into pubs legally, although I was not that keen on beer; I preferred spirits. I loved whisky – I'd got the taste for it once and loved it, even though it was expensive. A single malt was often twice the price of beer, and I had found a favourite tipple in Lagavulin. There are thousands of whiskies, but in my mind, you can't beat Lagavulin.

I met a guy in The Olde White Hart in Hull one night, and we got chatting. I had ordered my drink, and he smiled at me. 'Good choice, mate – ya cannae beat a single malt.'

'No, I agree – never been a beer lover but this one I do like.'

'Aye – why Lagavulin, how come that particular drop?'

'I found it one day and have drunk it ever since.'

'I come from the wee village it is distilled in. Just about everyone in the area works there and always has done. Do you want to know all about it? You ever looked into its history? Got an hour to kill?' he laughed.

I could not believe my ears; this guy could not have been any more Scottish – red hair, bushy beard, hands like shovels, the works. All he needed was a kilt and sporran.

'How come you are sitting in a bar in East Yorkshire instead of working in the distillery?'

'Nah, fuck that – I got out. I decided I didn't mind drinking the stuff, but no way was I tying myself down in a wee village. I wanted to see the world. I ran away to sea, finished up as a ship's master, made a few quid and retired. Now I am here working for a shipping firm and looking at buying out a company in Hull – but enough of that, let me tell you about the stuff you are drinking, son. Hey, set us another couple up, mate,' he said to the barman.

'Now, Lagavulin is a real old whisky first produced in 1816 when John Johnston and Archibald Campbell built two distilleries on the site. One of them became Lagavulin, taking over the other – which one is not exactly known, because records show there were at least ten illegal distilleries on the site going as far back as 1742. You want to know more? If not, just tell me to shut up.'

'No, carry on – it's interesting.'

'However, in the nineteenth century, several legal battles ensued with its neighbour Laphroaig, brought about after the distiller at Lagavulin, Sir Peter Mackie, leased the Laphroaig distillery. It is said that Mackie attempted to copy the Laphroaig style. Since the water and peat at Lagavulin premises were different from that at Laphroaig, the result was different. Now, as I said, the Lagavulin distillery is located in the village of the same name. After all these years it is still one of the finest malts in the world. I may sound a bit biased, but there you go. I think I have bored you enough!'

'Not at all – as I said, it's fascinating. I would love to hear more, but I have to go. It's been great chatting to you. Hope everything goes well with the purchase; might catch you in here again in the future.' With that, I left him.

I could now go into pubs without the fear of being asked for identity, and I was also taking driving lessons with BSM, or the British School of Motoring, which was based down Carr Lane near the King Edward pub, which was now my local. I had had four driving lessons and was quite good, even though I say it myself. I was learning in a Vauxhall VX 490, which was a big car – but I was a big boy now, standing six foot four and nearly fifteen stone. My instructor Ken – I never knew his last name – said I was a natural and suggested putting in for my test there and then as it would take three or four weeks to get a slot. He told me to try to get it at Hessle; it was a bit 'easier' to pass there. He was spot on; four weeks came and after eight lessons, I was to take my first driving test.

Test day came – Wednesday, September 16, 1964 at 10am. It was a doddle. I pissed it, with only one error. I had done everything – reversing around corners, three-point turn, all the usual – and then the examiner said, 'When I slam my pad, you do an emergency stop; but I won't tell you when I am going to do it – OK?'

'No problem,' I said. I did all the preparation – looking in all three mirrors, and so on – and as I pulled away from the kerb a little kid ran out from behind a parked car. I slammed all on, and the examiner nearly went through the windscreen. There were no seat belts in those days. His glasses had fallen; he looked shaken, 'That will do for an emergency stop – well done.'

We drove back to the square. He finished writing on his pad and turned to me, smiling for the first time, and said, 'Congratulations, Mr Askenes-Daniels, you have passed.' He handed me a paper with my details to take and get my driving licence.

A year later

I was now in the fourth year of my apprenticeship and loving every minute of it. As well as being an apprentice draughtsman, I was also learning design work from Terry. How to follow company specifications, what all the terminology was as shown in inquiries – it seemed endless, but I had a young mind. I was absorbing everything they could give me.

I kept a diary of what I had done, along with my plan that had been issued to me when I started. I was still doing my college work, and the reports I got back at the end of every term were perfect, so I was not missing out in any way by not going to day release. My tutor thought I was further in front than most of the guys who would have been in my class.

I had sent for my driving licence; all I needed now was a car. But there was no way I could afford one. Mum said she could get the money for a decent deposit, not an old banger but a second-hand one if I could afford the HP.

I asked around at work, but not a lot of people had cars; most used the bus or a bike. I asked Mike, the manager, who had a company car. 'Are you asking for a raise?' he said.

Like a fool, I said, 'No.'

'Why?'

'Then I am.'

'There's not a lot I can do about giving you more money, mate – the wage structure for apprentices is set in stone. Still, maybe I can look into it as I know you are doing more than you should be doing; I will ask.'

That is how we left it. I did not expect much joy, but dumb boys do not get anything.

In the meantime I went to a couple of insurance brokers and they gave me some quotes for third party, fire and theft, and fully comprehensive; the latter was not too bad for an eighteen-year-old at about £25, but it was no good – I still could not afford one.

Mum said Grandad would give me the deposit as she had been talking to him, and he was not broke. 'He owes you something, Leif, so he will cough up the money.'

'What do you mean, Mum, by he owes me something?'

'Oh, just that you have had nothing off him all your life; it is about time he got his finger out, that's all.'

But Mum had an odd look on her face as if she had said something wrong.

About three weeks had passed, and Mike came back to me. 'Can you come to my office at two-thirty, please? I have some news about your request.'

'Great!'

'Don't get too excited. I am waiting for a phone call from the accountant who has all the details.'

I was on tenterhooks now could not wait until two-thirty, but it eventually came.

'Hi, Tracy – Mike asked me to come to see him, OK?'

'Oh, hi, Leif, yes – he told me you were coming. Take a seat; he is on the phone.'

She was a beauty, was Tracy. She was about thirty-two, and married, but fit as a butcher's dog. She used to wear short skirts, even at work, as was the fashion in those days. She knew she was good-looking and flaunted it, to the enjoyment of all the lads on the shop floor.

The phone rang. 'Yes, he is here.' She nodded towards the door. 'I will send him in.'

Mike was standing over a drawing board looking at some documents, and he walked over to his desk. 'Right, sit down and listen,' he said. 'They have decided, that seeing you are not far off your fifth year' – I had eight months to go – 'your salary would be going up by 10%, and they will increase it to 18%, putting you on the equivalent to a year six rate, which will give you £10.75 a week for forty hours. Is that OK?'

I was on £8.50 before stoppages, and the tradesmen in the shop were only earning £12 per week.

'There is one proviso, Leif; you do not tell a soul. If anyone comes back to me complaining that you are getting X amount, that is the last time I will do anything for you – understand?'

'Er, yes – thank you very much. I appreciate it.'

'Stop grovelling and get back to work,' he said with a smile on his face.

Not long later, I bought my first car, a Ford Classic Cortina 1962 model with 2,000 miles on the clock. It had been owned by a friend of Mike's who had sadly passed away and his wife wanted to be rid of it as she could not drive, and it held too many memories for her; she wanted it to go to the right home.

It had cost about £780 new, but she only wanted £500 for it. Grandad forked out the money; he said I could have the deposit of £200, and he wanted the other £300 back plus interest of £45 at £10 a month.

When I was earning £10.75 a week, that was OK; I still had money left; petrol was pretty cheap so that I could run it easily.

Nineteen, single, own car – I was king of the road. It was a real fanny puller, as most lads only had pushbikes, or had to use the bus – old Leif here was mobile.

I was out one night driving down Waterhouse Lane in Hull; it was pissing down with rain. A girl was standing at the side of the road, and she looked a bit wet, to say the least. She was under an umbrella that wasn't looking very happy.

I pulled over, and she just got in the car. 'Thank fuck for that! I didn't think I was going to do any good tonight in this weather. So what are you looking for? Three pounds for a short time or blow job, or back to mine for a full session for eight quid.'

'I am sorry – what are you on about? I don't follow you, sorry.'

She looked at me kind of funny, then put her hand on my penis. 'Mmm, you are a big boy. I don't usually get young guys like you; mostly dirty old men. Why do you want to pay for it? You must be knocking them off like dead flies, a good-looking boy like you – not that I will be complaining, you understand.'

'Pay for it…? You mean you are a prostitute?'

She started to laugh; she held her hand over her mouth like women do when they laugh; why, I do not know. 'OK, sorry, babe, for the fucking misunderstanding. I thought you were a punter looking for a good time – my mistake,' She started to get out of the car; it was chucking it down now, the proverbial cats and dogs-type rain. 'Oh, Jesus, look at that lot.'

'You don't have to get out yet if you don't want to.'

'I am going home anyway; I won't get my leg over in this weather.'

'Can I give you a lift home? I am not doing much, anyway; it is up to you.'

'That's nice of you. My name is Rachel. What's yours, babe?'

'Leif; my name is Leif.'

'OK, Leif – take me home.'

We arrived at her house; it was on Airlie Street, off the Boulevard, it was not far from the main entrance to the Boulevard ground.

'Here we are, babe – are you sure you won't come in for some fun? I will do you a special deal seeing as you have been kind to me. I can't pay your taxi fare, but can pay you in kind, if you want it. I'd love to fuck a younger boy for a change. Come on, three quid – there you are; that is a good deal.'

I went to the house; it was a small two up, two down, similar to my house, except this one had a little garden at the front. I was thinking that three quid was half a week's wages after tax, but she did look lovely in the light. She was about thirty-five, with a beautiful body, and was wearing a mini-skirt. Oh, fuck it, why not?

'Sit your arse over in that chair, Leif, I need to get these wet clothes off before I catch my death.'

Around the living room I could see photos of her and a guy, who, by the look of it, was a fisherman by the style of his suit. I'd just picked one picture up as she came in with a robe around her.

'Oh, that's my hubby, Ken – you know him?'

'Er, no, I don't think so. You are married? How does he feel about you being a working girl?'

'Oh, he doesn't know I do it; only when he is away at sea. I love cock; I can't get enough. It's not my fault he is in the wrong fucking job. I have always been the same – I started when I was eighteen, with a man who went to sea with my dad. So, Leif, baby – how can I pay you for the lift home?'

She pushed me towards the settee. She undid the belt on her robe, and it opened – she was naked, with a shaved vagina, not a hair to be seen. I had never seen a shaven one before. She started rubbing herself and smiling at me. 'Well, do you want me or not?'

I was sitting on the settee now; she undid my jacket and stood back, still stroking herself.

'Get your kit off. Let's see what you've got for Rachel.'

I was already at Doncaster; I stripped off in front of her, solid as a rock.

'Oh my god, that is nice, Leif – I want that.' She went over to the sideboard, opened the top drawer and took out a condom. I had never used one, so I wasn't sure of the procedure.

'You must wear this, Leif, OK? Don't want to get preggy or a dose, do we, babe?'

A dose? A dose of what, I wondered.

She came to me. 'I don't usually kiss punters, babe, but for you – well, it's different.'

She kissed me hard – no soft pre-kiss but bang, straight on like a limpet. Fuck, this was nice.

She turned her back on me and bent over, showing all she had. I didn't see her put the condom into her mouth; turning, she dropped to her knees. When she came up, the condom was on. Now, that was a smart trick. She then went astride me, guiding me inside her. Hunslet Parkside came to mind as she started to move up and down. Fuck, these prostitutes knew their jobs; I was hooked. I could feel her gripping me as she slid up and down.

Wigan Central Park arrived, and I did not have to get off. I lifted her as I arched my back – no hands, just the strength of my legs and upper body. The look on her face was worth the three pounds as I reached the happy ending. She was still grinding me as it went limp and flopped out with a full-to-the-brim French letter still attached. That was the first sex I had ever had where I did not withdraw. I was not that keen on the sheath but nevertheless, for the first time I must say it was delightful.

CHAPTER 23

LEIF
Coming of Age: A Year Later

I t was now 1966. I was well established at work in a draughtsman's role, working alongside the company's more senior members. I was also doing a bit of estimating in conjunction with one of the new project managers the company had brought on board, a guy called Paul Doward; he was from what we in Hull called 'over the river' – a 'yellow-belly' from Lincolnshire. The nickname is thought to have come from the colours of the tunic of the old Lincolnshire Regiment, and it has stuck through the years.

Paul was running a couple of more significant projects, and our estimator was on sick and been away from work for a few weeks, so they needed a hand in that department. He taught me a hell of a lot in a short time and was a great guy to work with; what he didn't know wasn't worth knowing.

Once again, I loved this work, doing material take-offs from some isometric drawings, which I had produced along with general arrangement drawings. It was a whole new world to me; yet another string to my bow. I had always thought I would try to get as much experience in various disciplines as possible, which would give me higher bargaining power when looking for a job.

My social life was OK; I was doing things I had never done before, including ten pin bowling. I had been talked into going with a guy from work who was really into it. He played in the local league in Hull, and it sounded good, so I went along.

One of his team was a girl the same age as me who lived in Anlaby and was in one of the offices. I had never met her; her name was Carina, and she was training to be a process engineer. She was a bonny little thing, very petite, loads of freckles but sexy with it, with ashen skin and gorgeous red hair. It was another first as I had never met a ginger girl before.

I could not get over her long slim fingers on such a petite body. Anyway, we met and got on really well.

Over the next few weeks, I took her out a few times, and went for drives to Hornsea, Withernsea and as far as Whitby one Sunday. We also went to York for a day out, which was bastard of a place to park, so we parked up outside the city and caught a bus into the centre. Carina was really into her history so we went around all the museums. I really enjoyed the day out with her; she was great company.

We stopped for a meal on the way back to Hull. It was almost nine when we got back to her parents' house in Anlaby. We pulled up and she asked me in for coffee. Her parents were away for the weekend and not back home until Tuesday, this was Saturday night, and it was a bank holiday weekend. Was I on a promise here? I had never touched her up to now and it had been almost six weeks since we first met. She unlocked the door and said, 'Come in – there's no one home but me and you.' We went inside, and it was a lovely house – well furnished, somewhat old-fashioned, but expensive.

I know I keep going on about sizes, but once again it made me think a bit. I was not getting paranoid but certainly envious about where I lived on Hessle Road. Carina's house made mine look like a garden shed; well, maybe not that small, but you know what I mean.

We were in the kitchen sitting at a table, me and Cary – I had cut it short and she liked being called that. I had the idea from the way she talked that her parents were a bit old-fashioned in their ways; her father worked in a bank, and her mum was a social worker.

'Come on, Leif,' she said, 'let's go in the lounge; it's cosier in there.'

I did hear the word cosy much; whatever could she have meant by that? We went into a large room with a big three-seater sofa and two enormous chairs; once again, it was very expensive-looking. We sat on the couch; in front of us was a coffee table with drawers in it.

We put our cups down, and she took hold of my hand, hers looking so small in mine. 'Leif, I like you… can I ask you a personal question, please?'

I wondered what was coming next.

'It's like this – I have never been with a man before.'

Oh no, not again, I thought – how do I pick them? First Jenny, now Cary. I had seen a few girls since Jennifer, but Cary was the only one I had got to like.

'And I want to make love before I am too old. I have never had a boy-friend. I do not think I am attractive being ginger and white as a ghost; I think it turns men off me.'

'You are only twenty, for god's sake – you are not ancient, and besides that, I think you are beautiful.' Now, that was not supposed to come out, but it did, and I meant it.

'Do you honestly mean it, Leif? You think I am good-looking, freck-les and all?'

'Yes, why not? You are cute.' A puppy is also cute, but in a different way.

That was the key. After that she just leapt on me, kissing me – and what a kisser. We stripped each other there on the mat, and had some of the best sex ever. Her skinny pale body was placed in every position possible, and I reached Wigan in record time. I got off the train before the end, just in case, but all the same it was the start of what I hoped would be a perfect relationship.

We carried on seeing each other for quite a while until she started getting wedding bells in her ears, and her mum hated me. 'Not good enough for my little Carina…' I could hear her saying it. Her father was just a meek fool; he would stand for bricks breaking on his head. It was a shame, but I must be honest – I was never really in love with Cary. Yes, at first she was different. I got on well with her, but there were not the same feelings that I had for Jenny. Maybe I was hoping to find another Jennifer Johnson, I don't know, but I thought it best to end it before Cary would get too starry-eyed.

It was not a pleasant situation to be in, but it had to be done. We had gone for a drive and had a drink in a country pub out near Beverley. I did not want to be too far from her home as I would have to take her back after I had broken the news to her.

We set off for home after being in the pub; I pulled up in a secluded lay-by on the way back. She moved around in her car seat and started to undo the zip on my jeans. I went to stop her; she got hold of my hand. 'Cary, I need to talk to you, it is important,' I said, with my serious face on. 'I want you to know I think a lot about you, babe, and I am so glad we got together, but – yes, there has to be a but. I feel you may want more from me, but I have to be honest, Cary, I do not want to settle down and get married. I have the vibes from you that that is what you want, if not now, but eventually. I think we should take a break from each other, see how we feel in say a month; no phone calls, no letters, no contact for a month, and see how we feel then.'

She had tears in her eyes; I was feeling pretty shit about having to do this to her, for, yes, I had feelings for her, no doubt about that, but they were not the same feelings I'd had for Jenny – and she was my yardstick, the only girl that I had loved. Until I got that 'wham' in my heart, if I ever did, then I would just have to keep trying, maybe having some fun on the way. But I didn't want to break too many hearts of sweet girls like Cary; she, for one, needed letting down slowly.

We drove to her house in silence. She was crying a little, but she was OK by the time we arrived outside her home. We did not take time saying goodnight as it could have been goodbye, but she gave me a peck on the cheek and said, 'Bye, Leif – I love you,' and then was gone. I think she knew deep down it was the end of our relationship. Well, I did, for I never made contact again apart from a bunch of flowers a month to the day with a card saying, 'Thank you, love Leif xxx.'

It was my twenty-first birthday; Mum had organised a party for me at Dee Street Club, which was a typical working men's club, with cheap beer, a bar downstairs where the men drank, a lounge-type room where women were allowed in, and a concert room upstairs. It was one of those holy places where all the regulars who went in week in, week out always sat in same areas, and got very pissed off if anyone dared sit in their seats.

It was not a big do, but all my friends from work were there, and some of my old school friends came. It was great to see everyone and everyone had a good night.

We got home; Billy was smashed and had gone to bed, and then Mum said, 'Leif, I need to talk to you. I feel that now you are old enough to know the real truth – the truth about your past your life up to now.'

Hello, Mum's pissed again, I thought. 'Oh, Mum, come on, don't start getting sentimental now I am of age,' I said.

'No, I mean it, and I am not pissed,' she said, slurring her words.

'You sure it can't wait until the morning? I am tired, Mum.'

'No – it has to be said now.'

'Oh, OK, but make it short, please. I am just not in the mood for a lecture.'

'Can you recall when you were younger? When we thought you had killed your father? Well, it was not the whole truth.' She was crying now; I'll never forget the look on her face. 'I have been keeping a secret from you for twenty-one years; it was not what I told you. Now, Grandma was a bit of a girl in her day, and she had had two affairs with other men during her life with Grandad, one with a guy called Harry Neil from Hull, who was the actual father of my brother Arkvid. Harry was already married and loved being the centre of attention, and he was always in the local pubs buying drinks for everyone; he was a fish merchant and it was well known he was worth a few quid, but a fool and his money are soon parted, and that is what happened to him. His wife found out one day and walked out on him, taking everything. She left him a letter, or so the story goes, saying, "You don't deserve me – do not feel sorry for me; I am gone." She was right – she emptied the bank accounts and disappeared, never to be heard of again.'

'Mum, what's this got to do with me being twenty-one? Come on, I want to go to bed.'

'Listen, the other guy was also from Hull: Robert Fisher, he was the father of Hans Jnr. He was another "good friend" of Grandma Elizabeth, and he worked the night shift at Hull fish meal factory but was never there. Robert also owned a couple of houses where the ladies of the night used to "entertain" their guests. He spent more time with them and Grandma than at work.'

Now, that was bad enough, but then the real bombshell hit.

'Leif, now listen. Peter was not your father. He had been duped into thinking he was. Your grandfather, Hans Snr, is your real father. He abused me for quite a few years, then I fell pregnant to him. I did not run away from home; I had been sent to Grandma Lizzie's sister Freda's B&B in Blackpool to have the child. Freda was the local go-to for abortions and midwifery. I did not know much about Freda; I have never been back. In fact, someone did tell me she had died in a house fire. Both she and her live-in "gentleman friend" were victims of an arson attack; oh, years ago that was. I found out that the child turned out to be twins, one of which was Lars, who was sold to a couple unknown to me; well, not unknown – I had thought the child was stillborn, but I later found he had lived. When I was in early pregnancy, I met Peter, who I conned into believing the children were his. He accepted this, and he also had accepted the other child, Lars, was dead. I gave birth in the B&B, and Grandma's sister was there to deliver the babies; she was also the one who told me that Lars had died. We'd had an idea I was having twins by the size of my belly, so we had already picked the names, in case it was two boys, and Christine if a girl had been the other. Peter was at sea when the birth took place and did not find out about the death of Lars until he got home.

'I had a rough time during the birth. You came out normally, but Lars was different; he was a breech baby, which mean he came out feet first. I was in agony. Freda kept saying it's OK, Chris, just keep pushing, I was in so much pain, I don't know what happened – I must have passed out, for the next thing I can remember I was lying with you on my belly, and then they told me that Lars was dead. He hadn't even told his parents about me until he came back from sea and told them the truth about what had happened.'

'We lied to you. Lars, as he was known, was sold to a couple from

Manchester who were very well-to-do, from a good family, but there were no records kept of who they were. All the time Peter was with me, until the accident, he never knew that Lars was still alive somewhere, no one knows where.'

I was mortified that Mum could live this lie for twenty-one years. I realised now why Grandad used to look at me in a funny way. I was his son – his only son, for he knew the other two, Arkvid and Hans, were not his.

I was devastated. Could it get any worse? I had killed my stepfather; OK, it was by accident, but my mother's boyfriend had thrown him in the river. I had two uncles who were not really my uncles, my grandma had been the local bike, and, to top it all, my grandfather had molested my mother, made her pregnant, then drove her away at the age of sixteen. Fucking marvellous. It was beyond belief. What a fucking family.

CHAPTER 24

LEIF

After the Revelation

I now had another goal in life – to find my brother Lars; but how the hell would I do that? Where would I start? There were no records: no birth certificates, no death certificates, for if he did not have one for being born, he did not exist. Was he dead? Well, at least we thought he was still alive for he would be twenty-one, same as me.

Apart from all this going on, my life changed dramatically. At the beginning of the following year, seven months later, something happened that would live with me forever as a black day for my home town and the village that was Hessle Road.

I remember a few lads I went to school with were lost at sea in the city's most famous maritime disaster – if that's the right word – the Triple Trawler Disaster of 1968.

It began in the January. The conditions were terrible as the vessels battled through towering waves. Their radio operators continued to put out mayday signals, but sadly the three trawlers sank with the loss of fifty-eight lives. The headlines in the local and national papers read, "The Triple Trawler Tragedy." The first vessel to be lost was the St Romanus, which went down in the North Sea 110 miles off Spurn Point on January 11. All twenty crew members died. Then on January 26, the Kingston Peridot sank off Skagagrunn on the Icelandic coast, claiming the lives of another twenty men. The final loss was the Ross Cleveland on February 4. The boat had sought refuge from a storm in the natural inlet of Isafjord in northern Iceland. Dozens of other trawlers were also in the fjord, so the Ross Cleveland had to stay further out. Three crewmen made it to a life raft, but only one, Harry Eddom, survived the bitter cold.

After twelve hours in the raft, he was washed ashore and found help at a remote farmhouse. The trawler was swamped by mountainous waves and sank. The last message from the skipper, Phil Gay, was, 'I am going over. We are laying over, help me. I'm going over… give my love and the crew's love to the wives and families.'

Eighteen lives were lost. Spray had turned to ice as it hit the trawler's rigging; steel cables just half an inch thick swelled to six, seven and eight inches as the ice built up, and they couldn't chip it off quick enough. As they broke the ice off, it just gathered up again.

After the initial shock of the losses, the mood in Hull turned to anger. Many of the wives of fishermen began to campaign for better safety conditions on trawlers. One of the campaign leaders was Lillian Bilocca who lived in the Hessle Road fishing community's heart. 'Big Lil', as she was known, organised a 10,000-signature petition calling for reform. She and her supporters carried out direct action, trying to stop boats leaving St Andrew's Dock. They led a delegation to Parliament and demanded a meeting with Harold Wilson, the prime minister, even threatening to picket the PM's house if there weren't reforms. Speaking to a BBC reporter, she said: 'If I don't get satisfaction I'll be at that Wilson's private house until I do get satisfaction in some shape or form.' She did not get to meet Wilson, as he was away at the time, but she did meet up with the Secretary of State. The campaign was successful with many new safety measures introduced, including making it compulsory for every trawler to have a full-time radio operator.

At the time, I was working away from home, down in the south of England. I had been sent on a small job to see how I performed as a project manager. The news was sparse; it hardly got a mention. The only time I managed to get the full story was when I rang home; I thought something needed to be done about this – that the government should be forcing companies to act on safety standards. It was around this time I started to take an interest in politics.

The families all rallied round, as they usually did when this sort of thing happened. A few younger men involved in the fishing industry at the time got in touch with Hull Round Table, part of the national organisation of Round Tables. There were three groups in Hull – Humberside, Hull and Hull White – which used to meet every fortnight for a meal with a guest speaker. One of the organisation's main aims was to help people in the region as much as they possibly could.

The feeling was that the Triple Trawler Tragedy was a national disaster, so they contacted the National Council, the main body, to launch a national appeal. They agreed to do this and, as there were approximately 960 Round Tables, the money started to roll in, and within three weeks they had collected £10,500. Also, a number of businesses owed money by dependants of the fifty-eight men lost agreed not to chase them and instead pledged to cancel any overdue accounts. It was not just money; the Round Tables organised free coal deliveries, and opened accounts at banks; one unborn child was given a deed of covenant to be paid at a certain age. The families of the lost trawlermen were well looked after. The help they received from the Round Tables would never bring their men back, but eased the burden of finance a great deal.

Men should never be asked to go to work, whether in a factory, office or construction site, and have the danger of never going home. These men who went to the North Sea's farthest points to put fish on our tables deserved better. It lived with me for a very long time; I resolved one day that I would try to make a difference if I was in a position to do so.

I worked for most of that year with not a lot happening. My life had been work, work, work and more work for nearly eighteen months on sites in the UK from Scotland to Southampton. We also were providing labour to Germany and Holland, for the offshore boom had begun.

There was one contractor in the Netherlands where we just could not get enough labour for them, for this was a new type of working environment – the offshore platform. It was the latest gold rush; the North Sea was the new Klondike. Money was no object; men were paid cash in hand on most jobs at the beginning.

I remember one incident when lads used to come in from offshore and go to an Amsterdam hotel to collect their pay. I stayed at the same hotel. The company men or paymasters were under enormous pressure to check the lads' ID, if they had any, and pay them in cash; they had thousands of pounds on a table. The contractor would say his name; the paymaster looked it up on a list and how much he was due. They would then pay him by counting out the money in front of him; he did not have to sign anything, and he was gone.

There were that many men and sometimes, under pressure, the paymaster forgot to tick the name off. The lads would take note and watch if he failed to do it, and would be straight in there to hassle him. I am sure it was a setup – the lads would harass the paymasters, and after they had left the queue they would go outside and tell the guy who had already been paid to go back in and ask for his pay again. He would wait a few minutes, then go back in, often coming out with a wad to share the spoils. There was no secrecy to it all, and it was not breaking any Dutch laws to pay men cash in hand for they were not working in Dutch waters.

Often the men would come in on supply boats. Now, getting on and off these rigs was a deadly practice. In the beginning, they would be lifted on and off the platform using the crane and what was called a Billy Pugh, a cone-shaped basket with three netted sides. The men used to throw their kit bags into the net and stand on the outside ring, holding on to the netting, and then would be winched up possibly a hundred feet, maybe more, into the air and dropped on to the platform. Not all companies used this system. Eventually, it was banned in the North Sea when helicopters became the norm.

I wanted more out of life than the hassle of chasing companies up for payments owed, and the aggravation of my bosses always wanting more. I made the big decision to get out of the UK.

I went home and told Mum I was going to emigrate. She looked shocked. She got up off the sofa and came over to me, holding me. 'Why? What's wrong with what you've got here?'

'Now, you have got to be joking, Mum. I am still living at home in a two up, two down terraced house working 100 hours a week. I deserve more than this. OK, I get to travel up and down the country or in

Europe, and I get to live in decent hotels, but it is not what I want. I want to get something out of life, not make a man wealthy living in a big house that I helped him buy, and run a brand-new car that I helped him buy. No, Mum, I want those things too and I am not going to get them working for Paratec.'

I handed in my notice to the personnel department the following Monday. By that time I had just become a number, for the firm had grown out of all proportion from the company I had joined from school. They said they needed six months' notice due to the time I had been with them. I told them to fuck right off. 'One month – that is all you are getting. Take off the holidays you owe me, from not only this year but last year when I was working in Scotland, and you would not let me take them. That is six weeks' holiday pay you owe me as I am taking all my holidays as from Friday, OK? I have never had a contract; you lot did not exist when I started here. Now I want what's owed to me.'

Mike tried to talk me round, but I was adamant I was going. I was a bit stupid as I'd already jacked my job in before even applying for residency in Australia, but I sent for my application to Australia House, and they wrote back and asked me to contact the Leeds offices in the Headrow. The number was included in the letter, so I rang them; they were brilliant, and said could I go for an interview the following week. It seemed that a spot had become vacant as someone had pulled out, so they could fit me in short notice, no problem.

I went, and it went well. After my medicals and injections I was to be on my way in just eight weeks. They said I could either fly or go by boat for £10, which was a no-brainer. A month's holiday cruise for a tenner? A cruise it would be.

They sent me the option of leaving on March 18 from Southampton on the Ellinis, or waiting a few extra weeks and going on the Marco Polo, but I wanted to be off as soon as possible.

I told Mum and got what I expected – tears. I was her only son, and I knew it would be hard on her. Still, I told her I was twenty-two, and if I did not go now I would never go. I was only going for two years, which was the minimum time you could stay or you paid the Australian government your fare back; after the two years you were free to come home.

They stamped my passport 'COM NOM', which stood for Commonwealth Nominee. It gave them the opportunity, if you tried to get out of Australia before your two years were up, to stop you leaving if you had not paid them your fare back.

Once I had decided to get away from England, my mind was settled now. I needed to travel to see the world. I needed some sun on my back, and I knew the weather would be fantastic as I intended to follow the sun around while on this vast continent.

I arrived in Perth on April 18, 1968, on the RHMS Ellinis after being at sea for the past month sailing from Southampton to Amsterdam, Las Palmas, and Cape Town, and ten days' sailing across the Indian Ocean to Fremantle, then on to Melbourne and finally Sydney.

She carried 1,668 one-class passengers, but there were lots of cabins of different standards, from those used by the more wealthy on the upper decks, where fare-paying passengers were staying, down to the lower decks where the six-bunk cabins were segregated into male and female. Well, at the start anyway.

I was allocated one of these cabins, and met my 'cabin boys' – the name we gave ourselves – when we checked in at Southampton. After going through the embarking procedures and receiving our boarding cards, once on board we had to go to the purser's office where we were issued our cabin keys. Our cabins for single emigrants were down on D deck, more or less the bottom of the hull. We put our bags in the cabin, and our suitcases were placed in the hold; you never saw them again until reached your final disembarking port, which in our case was Perth.

We lived for the month, sailing from the UK, in just what we could carry on board. I only wore T-shirts and shorts. There were a couple of formal dinners, but we did not go as we never had the correct attire.

The trip was brilliant. The crew were all Greek; they were fantastic, and the food was spot on. And, to top it all, the beer was ten pence a can.

The guys in my cabin were a mixture of ages; twenty-one was the youngest that you could emigrate as a single person. Mike was from

Leeds, Gerry was from Glasgow, and there was Tom from Birmingham and Ted from Manchester, plus Londoner Cliff, so there was a real mixture and they were all different in every way. I seemed to hit it off more with Mike, maybe because he was a Yorkie. The other guys were all OK, though; I had no problems with any of them.

We had some great times on our way down under. Our first port of call was Rotterdam to pick up some more European emigrants, mainly French and Dutch, with a mingling of Germans.

We then sailed on to Las Palmas in the Canaries before heading down to Cape Town in South Africa. By this time we had fantastic weather, and enjoyed lying around the pool swimming and sunbathing; my tan was unreal, and some of the women were awesome, to say the least. As I said earlier the cabins were segregated but had somehow got mixed as people decided to move in with friends. Not all the time, I will admit, but odd nights were very crowded in some of the cabins, and you did not need to have any inhibitions,

There was one girl, an American, who was on holiday with her gran; I think she had every guy in our cabin and most of the ones in another two cabins over the twenty-eight days; if she had got pregnant, the kid would have come out like a zebra with striped hair.

On arrival in Perth, we went through immigration procedures within an hour of entering the port buildings; we were then taken by bus to our temporary accommodation at Graylands in the suburban City of Nedlands.

Graylands had once had numerous uses, from prison camp to mental hospital, before it was turned in to a migrant hostel. Basic was the word, but I did not intend to stay there long; I'd had enough after being there three days. I had been given several contacts by the migrant officers for employment opportunities in Perth, so I moved into the city and booked into a hotel for a week at first, to get my bearings.

I had a skill, and they seemed to think I had a good background at most of the agencies I contacted; they all asked me to give them a few days to see if they could find something that may interest me.

During my time off, I did the tourist thing – looking around the area;

finding things to do wasn't hard, so I had a few more days on holiday.

I made a phone call to a guy at one of the agencies about positions with companies involved with projects on extensive Western Australia mining facilities at Port Hedland, Dampier and Port Walcott. The following day I went round to see him. He gave me a list of contacts at several companies looking for staff. I got back to the hotel and made half a dozen calls, all bearing fruit; I could not believe it – everyone wanted me to do a phone interview. If that worked out OK then I had to take my details around for them, along with my CV. I'd never heard the word before; it was a new one on me. I needed to investigate this CV thing and asked at reception where the nearest library was; they gave me directions and off I went.

In the reference section, I looked up 'CV' and found a description:

A curriculum vitae, often shortened as CV, is a written overview of someone's life's work (academic formation, publications, qualifications, etc.). It usually aims to be a complete record of someone's career and can be extensive, as opposed to a resumé, which is typically a brief one or two-page summary of qualifications and recent work experience. In many countries, a resumé is typically the first item that a potential employer encounters and is generally used to screen applicants, often followed by an interview. CVs may also be requested for applicants to scholarships, grants and bursaries.

I could soon knock up a CV – but all I needed was a typewriter. I asked if the library had that facility, which it did, and I was pointed towards a small room with a couple of typewriters in it, and A4 paper was ten cents a sheet.

CHAPTER 25

LEIF

Donna

I went back to my hotel and gathered up my paperwork – references, indentures, everything I had supplied to Australia House to get my emigration application granted – and returned to the library.

A young lady called Donna was on duty, and she was quite lovely too, I might add.

'G'day, how are ya mate?' she said as I walked up to the reception.

'Very well thank you,' I replied.

'Oh, right, a Pommie! How long you been in Oz, then?'

Did I look brand-new? What made her think I was straight off the boat?

'A couple of weeks; I was looking for employment and was in here yesterday.'

I told her what had happened, and she was accommodating; she told me they often got 'Poms' in here to do the same thing as I'd wanted to do, and if I needed any help to give her a shout, as she put it.

An amiable lot, were the Australian people; I was impressed. I went into the typing room and started writing my CV, following the reference book which showed the most popular layout: name on top, followed by address – which I did not have, so I put my home address – followed by my qualifications and then schooling. I left out Hull Grammar School, and just put Boulevard Secondary Modern High School, including the fact I was prefect and assistant head boy. Interests: reading, rugby league, swimming; work history in order of years from last to first; well, that was easy, as I'd only had one job since leaving school.

With that, Donna came into the room. 'How ya doing mate, OK? Got it done yet?'

'Yes, thanks – here, what do you reckon?'

'Nah, needs a bit of doctoring, mate. Now then, let us see, you're what – six feet four, I reckon? What you weigh, mate?'

'About fifteen stones, I think.'

'Single, I hope; no kids, right? Mmm… what else? Oh, yes – willing to travel, can drive; you can, can't you?'

'Yes, I can drive, but no car yet; that's next thing on my list.'

'There ya go, that's better; got to give them a bit of bullshit, mate, this is your first step through the door. Have you not made one out before? You got to impress.'

She had noticed I was a draughtsman, so she added in assistant drawing office manager, leading hand, whatever that was.

'Yes, that's great – thank you so much for your help; you are very kind.'

'Don't need to thank me; it was a pleasure meeting you. Now retype it like that and job's a good un.'

I did as I was told and took it to show my new friend; she looked through it and agreed it was OK.

'You will need some copies, the machine's in the print room. Here, pass it to me; how many? A dollar's worth, or more? Better make it two bucks.'

Off she went, and as I watched her walking away from me, I did not see a woman standing next to me as I was following Donna's beautiful rump. 'Nice arse ain't she, mate,' the lady said, and chuckled.

I had to agree; she did have a nice arse.

'Hey, Donna, this guy fancies you, girl? Seen him looking at your arse as you went away.'

Was nothing private in this country? Donna came back and just laughed. 'Ignore her, Leif. That's an unusual name – where is that from?'

'Norwegian; my ancestors were from Scandinavia.'

I liked this girl – she was good looking, had a lovely arse and was interesting to talk to. Still, I was not going to be around long, I was off travelling soon, so I didn't want to get too involved. But I couldn't resist asking her, 'I'm here for a few more days; fancy a coffee sometime?'

'Coffee? No, thanks, mate, you're in Oz now. We drink beer here, mate, so if you're up for it I wouldn't say no to a schooner sometime.'

Schooner? What was she talking about, going on a ship sailing or something?

'Sorry, what is a schooner?'

'You are kidding me, right? You do not know what a schooner is? You know, middy, schooner, pint – they are glasses of beer; 7oz is a glass; 10oz is a middy, 15oz is a schooner and 20oz is a pint. But having said that, they are called different names in different states. Am I confusing you?'

'OK – let's meet for a schooner. What time are you free tonight?'

'Not tonight, hun – I will meet you around five-thirty this arvo, as pubs close at 10pm.'

'OK, where? It's three now; which pub do I meet you in?'

'Er, the Vic? It's not far from here; look, here's a map.' She pointed to the map on the reception desk. 'We are here: Evelyn Park Library; the pub is just there, see? Ya can't miss it. Listen, I've got to go, I'm busy – I've spent too much time yarning with you! Save it for later. Bye, hun.'

And then she was gone. Wow, you fool, I thought, you've done it again – arranging to meet a girl, and you've only been in Oz five minutes.

I went for a walk around the area as there wasn't enough time to go to the hotel and get back. I had picked up a brochure at the museum. I was in Subiaco and it was about two miles to the west of the centre of Perth. Its proper name was the City of Subiaco, and apparently it only became a city in 1952; it was first mentioned in the history annals in 1896, which is recent when you think we talk of UK history and go far back to events like 1066. I love history; it was one of my favourite subjects at school, where we were always told that we had no future without the past.

Anyway, I was there at the pub at five-thirty, and Donna was sitting outside in the sun with two beers on the table.

'Come on, Pom, you're late. Get that into yer,' she said, handing me the beer. Now, I have mentioned before I was not a beer man, but today I was maybe getting to change my mind. A nice cold glass of Swan Lager was indeed a great thirst-quencher, and to be bought one by a good-looking young woman was indeed an experience I had never encountered before.

We had a few more, and chatted away about this and that. Donna was very easy to talk to; she was one of those people you feel like you have known all your life after just a short while. I was getting a bit hungry and suggested we find somewhere to eat.

'OK, but we share the bill, right? Or forget it.'

We went to a little Italian place just around the corner; now, I hadn't ever eaten real Italian grub in Hull, so I did not know what to order. I was looking at the menu when the waiter came up and started talking in Italian. 'Buena sera; è pronto per ordinare?' – 'good evening; are you ready to order?'

'Potresti darci qualche minuto in più, per favore,' Donna answered, in fluent Italian. For you non-Italian speakers, that was, 'Could you give us a few more minutes, please?'

Now I was impressed. 'I did not know you could speak Italian!' I said, and then realised that was a bit of a stupid comment as I had only met her a few hours before.

'Oh, yes, my parents are New Australians – I was born in Italy twenty-one years ago but have been in Australia seventeen years; all my schooling has been here, but we still speak our native language at home. It was hard at first growing up as I could only speak Italian when we arrived, and I grew up learning two languages.'

I can speak two languages, I thought to myself – 'Hull' and 'English'.

We had a wonderful meal with some fantastic wine, an excellent pecorino white – and I was smitten.

'Are you ready to go, then? I will order a taxi.'

'No need, mate – I only live a five-minute walk away.'

We paid the bill and I set off to walk her home. There was a bit of chill in the air, and she was walking with her arms folded. I put my arm around her, and she did not attempt to pull away. She was right; it was not far to her house, which was an old colonial-style, single-storey building with a corrugated tin roof and a wide veranda going all the way around.

'Well, we are here.'

'Yes, I suppose we are,' was my response. It was that awkward moment when I did not know whether to hold my hand out to shake it, or grab her and stick the lips on her, or what. Donna made my mind up for me – she took my hands and kissed me on the lips, just touching them, and then moved her head back – not her body, just her head; her body was still close to me. I lowered my head, lifted her chin, and kissed her properly, and this time she did not move. It was an unreal moment in time.

'I am sorry; I must go in. Mum will be waiting up for me. Thank you, Leif, for a wonderful evening. I have enjoyed it.'

'Donna, can I see you again?' That's fucked it, son, you are hooked again, I thought.

'Naturalmente mi piacerebbe molto mi piaci molto, mi piacerebbe conoscere meglio.'

'What does that mean?'

She pulled a notepad out of her bag and quickly wrote it down. 'Look it up and find out; call me at the library any time. It's Donna Luciano – you did not know my surname.' She was right. I had not even asked her it.

I got back to the hotel. The guy on the reception looked a bit foreign; mind, thinking about it, most of the people I had met or seen looked foreign to me. I was clutching at straws here. I asked him if he spoke English, and he looked at me as if I was stupid.

'Yes, of course.'

'Do you speak Italian by any chance?'

'Si.' I knew that was yes.

'Would you do me a big favour and translate this for me, please?' I showed him the note.

He read it, looked at me and smiled. 'Of course – it says, "I would love to. I like you very much; would love to get to know you better."'

I must have blushed, and he added: 'Is she nice-looking Italian girl, sir?'

'Yes, she is.' Now I was in trouble.

I had a few things to do the next morning; I had to go and see the agents again, but perhaps I was not so keen on moving away from Perth as I had been the day before, though I needed a job to earn some money, I wasn't broke just yet; but not rich either.

I had narrowed the choice of agents down to three. One had nothing on his vacancies for anyone in Perth, another said he would enquire into it for me, and the last one, Drew McMahon, said that he had one vacancy just outside Perth; now, 'just outside' in Australian terms could have been 200 miles.

Now things were getting interesting. My forefathers had set off to travel to the 'Promised Land' from Norway to the USA but had got no further than Hull; could history be repeating itself? I had given them all my CV, and they were impressed. Now they had more details they would see what they could do. The third guy said: 'I have another one a bit nearer that could suit you down to the ground.'

'Oh right, where is that? What are they looking for?'

'It is in Fremantle, which is about fifteen miles away. It is the port city for Perth. The company is looking for a two-handed animal – a draughtsman used to industrial pipework, and who could also estimate the costs. Would you be interested?'

'Yes, sounds great – what else can you tell me about them?'

'The company's primary work comes from shipping and heavy industry, but they are looking at expanding to be a bit more diverse, spread their wings, so to speak. Would you like me to call them while you are here?'

'If you don't mind; I would love you to,' I said, and he pointed to a chair.

'Take a seat, Leif, let's see what we can do.'

He dialled the number and started talking to someone. As he did so he was nodding his head, and looking at me and smiling. He put his hand over the phone and said, 'They are very interested in you; are you willing to have a quick chat with them?'

'Yes – when do they want me to go for an interview?'

'Now – they would like a chat.'

Fuck me; I was not expecting that.

'OK, right – yes.'

He put his hand back over the phone and whispered, 'It's Doug Perry; he is the manager/owner of Perry Industrial.' Then he gave me the phone.

'Hello, Mr Perry, how are you?'

'G'day, mate – how're things? Welcome to Australia, mate – and it's Doug; forget all that "Mr" shit, OK?'

I was not used to all this friendly banter; I was used to stiff-upper-lip old English business rituals.

'Thank you, er, Doug – yes, I only arrived a few days ago. It's the first time I have been abroad, to be honest.'

'Bloody hell, mate – you could not have picked further to go on your first trip… 13,000 bleeding miles, good on yer! Anyway, cut the crap – Bluey tells me you are looking for a job, that right?'

'Yes,' I answered, somewhat nervously.

'OK, look, I was rapt with what he told me, you sound bloody good to me. I don't want to piss you about; let's meet up for a bloody interview. Can you get here today, this arvo? Where are you staying?'

I told him, and he said, 'Right, save you messing about – I will send our driver, Merv, out to collect you. No need to get fancy-dressed up; we are all bloody working men here – no shirts and bloody ties shit. Office attire is T-shirts and shorts office.'

He pronounced the word attire in a kind of British accent.

'Listen to me, taking the piss out of the Poms already. Will be at the hotel in an hour, say 1pm, OK?'

'Yes, that's fine. Thanks, Doug.'

'Wait till I give you the bloody job – depends on how bloody much you want before you thank me, mate,' he said, and then put the phone down.

Drew smiled and said, 'Well I think that went OK.'

We discussed what the agency wanted from me, which was nothing; they got a finder's fee from the client. We also talked about rates, as I hadn't a clue what to ask for; I had been on £2,500 a year, less stoppages, when I left home. Drew told me he thought the going rate for what they were looking could be as much as $8,000 a year, maybe more, which at the time was £4,000 plus benefits. I was stunned. He added, 'Perry are good payers, and excellent to work for. Not many leave once they are in. You might just have struck gold, Leif. I hope it goes OK; I believe it will. I know Doug well; he's a bit of a rough stone, likes a beer and is a real man's man, but I warn you, don't piss him about – he expects a good day's work for a bloody good day's pay. You will earn your money, but he will look after you if you look after him. Any questions?'

'Yes, I have one – what does "rapt" mean? I had no idea what he was talking about.'

'Very happy.'

'Oh, right, I see what you mean – as in rapture, or great joy. No one uses that term back home; well, not in my circle of friends.'

He wished me good luck, and shook my hand, as all Aussies do.

I rushed back to the hotel and was sitting in the reception at 1pm prompt when this guy, built like the proverbial brick, in a pair of shorts, singlet, working boots, baseball cap and sunglasses, walked in. I saw he was looking around when he spotted me near the cafe. He looked and smiled, and I walked over. 'Hello – are you Merv?'

'G'day, mate – yes, bloody Leif is it?'

'Yes'

'OK mate, pleased to meet you.'

He put out his hand; now, I thought my hands were big – his was like a leg of lamb with fingers. I thought he had broken my hand when he eventually let go.

'OK, blue – let's go.'

We arrived at the works in about thirty-five minutes, which I thought was pretty good. Doug came into the reception. 'G'day mate – thanks for coming.'

We sat chatting casually, after the formal stuff – that is, if you could call anything that Doug did traditional. Then he said, 'OK, blue – it is like this. I am not gonna give you a load of bullshit about this and bloody that – here is the offer, bloody take it or leave it, what is on the table today. If you don't like it after that – no dramas; you can always piss off, OK? Right, now, here it is: I will pay you 10,000 bucks a year, plus you will get a company Ute, a Holden, all fuel-free, even when travelling back and forth to work – none of your bloody Pommie shit, pure Aussie, mate; ten sickies.'

'What are sickies? I've never heard of them.'

'What're bloody sickies? You fair dinkum, mate? They are days when if you feel crook, you can ring up and let the company know you are ill, and you get paid for it. Fifteen days' annual leave plus the ten statutory holidays per year, working forty bloody hours week; if you work over your forty hours you will be paid cash in hand. How does that sound?'

'Er, well –'

'Fack me, Pom, that not enough? What more do you want, the bloody shirt off my back? OK, I will make it I will make it 11,000, final offer. Well, is it a deal or any more bloody questions?'

'Just one, Doug – why do us English keep being called Pommies? I have never heard the terminology used so much?'

'Bloody hell, mate... as far as I know, the word comes from the fact that many of Australia's first settlers were convicts, sentenced to transportation. The theory goes that upon arrival in the country they would be given a uniform with POHM emblazoned on the back, and that convicts with an extended stay on Australian soil would no longer have to wear the shirt and would often refer to newer entrants into the country as Poms. There is another one, mate – that it came from the Australian slang term for attacks on the English. The word 'pommie' derives from the pomegranate. The English were called limeys because they ate limes to ward off scurvy on the long sea voyages, but the pomegranate tag didn't originate that way. Pommie-grant is likely to have developed as a form of rhyming slang for immigrant. Take your pick, mate – now you have had your free bloody Aussie history lesson, do you want the bloody job or not?'

Before he could say any more, I said, 'Yes, it is a deal – when do I start?'

'Tomorrow, OK? Or do you need more time?'

'But it is Thursday tomorrow – can we make it Monday? Give me time to look for accommodation, as I am in a hotel, as you know.'

'Bloody good job I like you, Pom.'

It seemed that was now going to be my name – the Pom.

'OK, Monday it is. By the way, go and see Rosamond Real Estate – she is a bloody good mate of mine. I know they have some beaut rental units on Elizabeth Quay. I will ring her and tell her to look after you; see what she can do. I will tell her you will be going to see her tomorrow. OK, mate, now piss off – I have work to do. Can't be yapping to youse all bloody day. See ya Monday, Pom – 7am start. Don't be bloody late.'

I could not believe I was going to be paid £5,500 a year – that was £106 per week. I had never dreamt it could be that much. God, to think I had only been earning £1,500 a year back home; what had I been missing?

I went to see Rosamund, known as Ros, at the real estate agency the next morning. Doug had done the business; she took me to see a couple of units, as they called them – one was a three-bedroom place, which was far too big for me. We then looked at a smaller two-bed unit that was a bit more expensive, but nearer the town centre, and not too far from the beach and Langley Park, a little park right on the water-front. The rental was $300 a month, but it was fully furnished and ser-viced and included electricity and other costs. I had to put down three months' deposit, but Ros said Doug would take care of that; I would be paying him back out of my wages. Ros was an agent for Blue Cross Medical Insurance, so I also organised that through her. When I asked what the Blue Cross was for, it appeared it was just like our National Insurance back home, but this was private insurance to cover medical and other unexpected bills. The taxation side of things the company took care of so, bingo – I was now working, and well on the road to starting my new life in Australia.

I could not wait to see Donna to let her know what had happened and to thank her for her help. I tried ringing her at the library just after leaving Perry to tell her I had got a job and would be looking for a unit the next day, but she could not get time off to come with me, unfortunately. Now I had a place to live, I knew she would love it. I did ask myself why was I thinking about what she thought, and wondered if I was getting a bit too close. Still, I liked her.

I met Donna that night and we went for a celebration meal at another Italian restaurant, this time owned by her uncle Luigi. Once again she ordered in her native dialect; I must admit she sounded great. It just rolled off her tongue and seemed so sexy. We had another different wine that I had never heard of; I was getting to like this plonk.

After a beautiful night, we just walked home through the park, and sat on a bench under the stars. There was no one around but this incredible Italian beauty and me, holding hands. I was so happy in my new environment; things could not have been better.

Something had to spoil the party, though. It was then that Donna told me about her father. He was a bit of an Italian mobster with a tendency to show off. He was also determined that his only daughter would marry a 'good Italian boy', and if he knew she was seeing a half-breed Norwegian Pommie, he would go berserk.

Suddenly, I got this uneasy feeling around my groin, and it wasn't sexual arousal – it was the fear of losing my balls.

'Hey babe,' said Donna, 'don't look so serious. It's not like we are that close; we only just met. It's not like we were having sesso, is it?'

'Sesso? What's that? What are you talking about?'

'Sesso… you know – gli amanti: sex, lovers.'

'No, we aren't, yet,' I said; whoops… that was a slip of the tongue.

Her face changed very quickly, looking slightly annoyed.

'So, that is that your intention is it, Leif? To get me into bed? Is that all you want from me? Come on, be honest with me. I have never slept with anyone and have no intention to as I am saving myself for my husband to be, the man that I will devote the rest of my life to. Do you understand, Leif? Talk to me.'

Talk to me? I could not get a word in. I had never heard such a statement from any girl like that. I'd never listened to such words from anyone with such determination in their voice. I was impressed with her loyalty; it was like she was saying her vows in church.

CHAPTER 26

LARS
The Other One

21 years earlier – Altrincham, Cheshire, June 28, 1946

Jon was cradling his new son in his arms. He'd never thought the day would come when he would be able to hold a child of his own, but it had come at a price.

'Marjory, we do not realise how lucky we are to be blessed with such a gift. Well, not so much a gift, as we paid £500, but to be quite honest I would gladly have paid twice the amount had they asked for it. But when I happened to mention my brother was a detective, she kind of altered her stance, don't you think?'

Marjory told him to stop going on about the money, for if they could have had children, this would never have needed to happen. 'What shall we call him, Jon? Did you make your mind up?'

'I still like Sebastian; it has a ring to it – Sebastian Mellows.'

'But, Jon, I think that now we have heard that they were going to call him Lars… that sounds wonderful; it's different. Please, Jon. When I asked Freda where the name was from, she said something about Norway or Sweden, or somewhere in Scandinavia; it seems his ancestors were from there. That goes well too – Lars Mellows.'

'Marjory, we need to agree, and quickly; we must come up with a decision to get him registered before we send in the documents to Australia House in London.'

'Are you sure they will accept the papers we got from Freda?'

'Yes, no problem. She told me she had friends in the right places, and she has done this a few times. How do you think they bought that big house right on the front in Blackpool? That would not have been cheap. Stop worrying, dear; he is ours now, and no one can take him from us. Now just sit back and look forward to our new life down under. The immigration people told us we should be leaving hopefully within the next four months, as soon as we finalise the paperwork. We have sold our house, everything is organised, now stop worrying. You worry about not worrying! We're just waiting for the Johnsons to get their mortgage finalised. They thought it was all done and dusted, but someone in the chain had pulled out; it often happens. For goodness' sake, Marjory, please stop bloody worrying. Everything will be OK.'

Time and time again, she started to get on his nerves, forever going on about it; he wished they had never applied to emigrate.

'I told you, Marjory. It was because we needed another copy of his reference from the bank, along with Morrison's Mortgage, now that is all done and dusted. I reminded you that Australia House wanted to make sure we had no ties in the UK – that we were going there to make a new life.' He handed her the document. 'Just reread it; we are leaving on January 1, 1947; everything is packed, waiting to go. You're right about keeping his name; it gives that bit of history to the boy when he gets older. We will tell him about his past when it is time for him to know he was adopted. I just want to get to Australia; Lars will love it – new mum and dad, and new life. Fantastic.'

It was a crisp, bright morning, with the Harbour Bridge towering above them as the Marco Polo pulled into its berth alongside Circular Quay. The local ferries looked minute against the size of the liner as they pulled into their berths with their thousands of commuters, jostling to get off at the start of another day in the heart of Sydney.

Jon and Marjory could hear the hustle and bustle of people outside their cabin, excited about what was for most of them a new dawn. Jon asked Marjory if she had got everything, as it was time to disembark.

'We are here – our new home and our new beginning.' She smiled and hugged Jon. 'I have checked; there was nothing left in the cabin. Let's go.'

They picked up Lars and made their way to immigration and then through to customs. They had arranged to meet up with representatives from the Bank of New South Wales, with which Jon had secured employment when he applied to emigrate. As he was classed as a professional person, Jon's name had been forwarded by the Australian authorities to all the relevant financial institutions, and the bank contacted him with an offer. After quite a bit of negotiation and a couple of early morning telephone conversations, Jon chose to join the BNSW. They had arranged accommodation for an initial six months, close enough to travel to the bank's headquarters in the suburb of Glebe about two and a half miles from Circular Quay. He joined the bank as a manager and financial consultant, which was quite a senior position and well paid, far more than anything he had ever received back in the UK.

They were to be met by Christian Walters, senior personnel manager, and his assistant, Annette Whitlock; as they came through immigration, Jon spotted her standing with a card that read 'Mr & Mrs Mellows'. Jon waved at Annette and moved towards them, pleasantries were exchanged, and they moved out of the hustle of the crowd to one side towards the exit.

'You got your baggage with you, Jon?' asked Christian.

'It's over there; we collected it from the baggage claim and that porter has it,' said Jon, pointing towards a guy with a large barrow and four large cases.

'The other stuff is with the shipping company and will be delivered to the address we tell them, once we know where they are staying.'

'Right – G'day. I am Christian Walters.' He put out his hand. 'Call me Chris. And this is Annette Whitlock, my assistant – we are part of the personnel management team. Welcome to Australia and the BNSW – we use the four letters rather than saying the full version every time.'

CHAPTER 27

LEIF

Wish I Was Italian

Now, this was going to be a challenge; I wanted Donna far more than ever. 'I think you are worrying a bit early, for we have just met; we are friends – nothing more,' I told her. 'From what you have just told me the guy who wins your heart would be a fortunate man. I just wish I was Italian.' She then laughed and hit me on the arm. Jesus, she had a punch.

I walked her home, but did not stop too close to the house in case Pops spotted me. Six foot four, with blond hair – no way did I look Italian. She took my hand and looked up at me with those beautiful dark eyes, and then she went up on her toes and kissed me – our first real kiss, and it was good; oh yes, it was good.

'Mmmmm… Notte, mia cara,' she said. Here we go again, I thought; I need to get an Italian phrasebook. I bid her good night and watched her walk down the street towards her house.

The following morning my friendly translator was on reception, and I asked him what Donna had whispered as we parted last night. He smiled and said, 'Night, my darling.'

Wow… darling?

She wasn't working the following morning, so we arranged to meet at the central bus station to go out to see my new unit; Ros would meet us there with the keys and contract to sign, and then it was mine.

Twelve-thirty. I was standing outside the bus station, but still no Donna. I was getting a bit worried; had her dad found out about me?

Then this red Alfa Romeo pulled up. 'Leif! Leif!' I heard this voice calling. 'Come on, get in.'

'I didn't know you could drive, babe.'

'You never asked me. It's Dad's; he lets me borrow it now and again, and he has promised to buy me one later this year for my birthday. Nice, don't you think? I love it.'

I gave her directions, and we got out to Elizabeth Bay in no time. We pulled up outside the building.

'Hey, impressive. How did you find this place? It's a great spot.'

'I told you – Doug put me on to Ros, who is a mate of his. Come on, she will be waiting.'

We got the lift up to the second floor. 'Here we are – 205.' I rang the bell and Ros opened the door.

'G'day, Leif; welcome home.' I introduced her to Donna, and they both disappeared into the bedroom as I went out on to the balcony. I was just absorbing the view when Donna joined me. She put her arm around my waist and kissed me on the cheek.

'What a fantastic place, babe; I love it. When can I move in?'

I looked at her in amazement.

'Only joking, you galah – don't get worried.'

Some of the words these Australians used was bemusing; what the fuck was a galah when it was at home? I managed to ask Ros when Donna had gone to powder her nose. 'You never heard of a galah?' she said. 'It is an Australian cockatoo with a reputation for not being too bloody bright, mate – hence a galah is a stupid person.'

I had taken out a twelve-month lease with the option on my side to renew at the same rate; I signed all the relevant papers and Ros handed me the keys.

'There you go; I will get off. There is a bottle in the fridge to welcome you,' said Ros, and then she left, and we were alone.

Well, that's it, I thought; I've got to stay now, whether I want to or not. It suddenly hit me that I'd signed up to the unit for a year not knowing if I would like my new job or if they would like me. I told myself to get a grip and stop being so pessimistic.

The bottle turned out to be champagne, so I found some glasses, and sitting out on the balcony, everything seemed so perfect.

'Well, this is lovely, Donna. I never thought I would meet someone so quickly. I'd not been in the country five minutes and you come into my life.'

'Me neither; I wasn't looking. I had a lover a while back but it did not work out. Then, as you say, we meet.'

'Who was he? You want to talk about him?'

'No, I'd rather not; let's just call it a bad experience, shall we?'

With that she took my hand and started to kiss my fingers. Just watching her lips run up and down them, taking them into her mouth, and sucking them each one at a time – oh my god, it felt good. I wondered what else she could suck like that... No, Leif, not yet; it's too early, I told myself.

We stayed a couple of hours, before she dropped me off back at my hotel. It was only a fifteen-minute drive; brilliant, I thought – not far from Donna's place. She smiled and once again gave me a peck on the cheek, and before she drove off it was my turn to say, 'Notte, mia cara.'

On the Sunday I was up early, so I grabbed a cab and went to my unit to unpack. I went out for a walk to survey the area, looking for shops, bars, etc, and did a bit of shopping for basics. It seemed the right place to be. I found a burger bar so thought I would treat myself to a hefty half-pound special with fries, salad – the works. Then I headed back to the unit for an early night.

I woke up at 6am, had a bit of breakfast then went off to work. Doug had organised Merv to pick me up for my first day as I would be given my transport later. I didn't have a clue what a Ute was as I didn't know Aussie cars.

'G'day Pom! Get in, mate – gotta beat the traffic this time of a morning,' said Merv. Having said that, we were at the shop in two minutes.

Doug was talking to the foreman, going over some drawings. 'G'day, Pom. OK, mate, be with you in a sec. Grab a coffee – mine's two sugars.'

I went into a little room with a boiler, two fridges, a sink and store cupboard along with the usual kitchen utensils.

'Right – let's go into my office. I'll run through what I have in mind for you.' Doug grabbed my arm and led me in. As we had discussed at the initial interview, I was on a three-month trial, but he was confident that he had a 'gut feeling' about me.

We went through a few drawings and specifications of a job Doug had been pricing up; he showed me his calculations, scribbled on several sheets of paper, but I could not make head nor tail of them. After reading his numbers I asked him how he priced jobs up, and he said it was all in his head; he more or less guessed what it would cost, then doubled it. I could not believe it. I asked him to leave me to go through it my way for a couple of hours, and I would come back with my conclusions.

I had brought my book of norms for fabrication and installation of steelwork and pipework that I had created at my last job, as they were more or less in the same stream as him; I could not believe everything was in the estimator's head. First of all, I took a set of drawings for one structure he had already come up with a cost to include in the quotation. I put together a price to fabricate and install for material and labour only, not including overheads or management costs, or escalation and profit. I wanted to make sure I did not confuse Doug when I had to sit with him and explain how I came up with the working hours. It took me about half a day to write things down in a format I thought he would understand.

I was going through my figures when there was a knock on the door.

'Come in,' I said; it was Doug.

'G'day – how you doing?'

'OK. I have come up with a cost.'

We started to go through it step by step – how I had completed a material take-off per foot to give me total tonnage. I explained how I had broken it down into the light, medium and heavy sections – more working hours allowed for the fabrication of light steel per ton for the more substantial section, which is quite evident as heavy section weighs more per foot. He had already given me the cost of materials from his supplier.

He sat there, not saying a lot and just taking it all in; then he said, 'Have you compared it with my costs?'

Luckily, Doug had done one thing right – each of his drawings had a separate lump sum price written on the bottom. I asked him if his lump sum included overheads, plant, scaffold, management, supervision, consumables, craneage, painting or galvanising, or transport to site. He said no. I asked him how he added these items to the lump sum price; it was good that his lump sum terminology was for fabrication only. I was relieved when he said that.

'OK – where are your old contracts? Where is the one for this job? I need to see it so I can work out an all-inclusive cost, to see what you had put in for inclusions and exclusions.'

As I explained to him, his exclusions were more critical than his inclusions. He had to be more detailed in what he had quoted for, which would save arguments later on down the line. He went into another office and came back with a folder containing all the relevant documents.

Later that day he came back to see how I was getting on, and I told him it would be finished tomorrow afternoon. He just smiled and disappeared, still not commenting on what I had accomplished up to now.

The next afternoon I had finished my estimate after digging out the information from his documents and asking Angela, his secretary, for a little help on the cost of consumables, plant hire, and the rest. Now, she was more than just a secretary; she was his office manager and accountant, for she knew everything about the business that needed knowing.

Doug came in. 'Now then, young Pommie – how have you done, OK?'

'Well, according to my calculations, you were too expensive with your price for the job.'

'What? Are you bloody joking, mate? You're taking the piss. They said I was the cheapest. My mate who gave me the job told me all the other prices were a lot higher than mine; I was 20% lower.'

'Well, in that case, you don't need me; just keep doing it your way, or on the other hand if you want to do it my way, I was 10% higher than your price – but I had included the 10% profit.'

'OK, smart arse. Give it to me in a bloody language I can understand.'

'Well, if you take out the profit I had put in, you would have been 30% cheaper. Let us say their top quote was $25,000. Your price was $20,000. Well, my price including the 10% is $18,000; without the 10%, it's $16,000. The profit can always be added to the bid price dependent on how much work you have on at the time. Say all your overheads for the shop and management have been covered for the year – you do have a working year, don't you?' He nodded. 'Then your profit can always be reduced to ensure you get the job. On the other hand, say you don't want the job as you can't fit it in, but you don't want to be taken off the bid list by the relevant company, you add more profit to price yourself out; understand? What I am saying is you could be winning more work by reducing your cost. You may have done OK on this job, but on others you may well have been too expensive. Let me work a price out for a job you did not win. I'm not trying to beat any quote you put in; all I am doing is providing a quote or prices that are consistent and with a traceable breakdown. It's your choice.'

I took a quote for a project he did not win and came in under his original quote by $3,000.

Over the next few weeks, I had taken all of his actual costs and included them in a model to quote projects of any size for structural enquiries, along with a piping schedule.

Doug came into my office one day, and I asked him if he had any norms. 'Nah, mate – all in my head,' he said.

'Then I think we should get some time and motion study done to take a look at how long each of your workforce is taking to carry out the primary duties – such as cutting, welding assembly, etc., to ensure they are working productively. This will be even more important if you want to get into the pipework scenario.'

'Bloody hell, mate – I don't think they will like that. Might cause some strife. You are more or less saying they are a load of bludgers.'

'Bludgers? What are they?'

'Lazy bastards, mate. But they are a decent crew, mate; I don't want to go upsetting no one – they've been with me a long time. No, fack that;

we will leave it be, OK? Youse can still work to your norms that youse have brought with you; no problem with that. When we do get pipe jobs in, we can tell them we need them to do weld tests. I think we will need them to do pressure work anyway, won't we?'

'Yes, OK. We will go down that route; no worries.' No worries? I was picking up the lingo already.

I got home from work and found I had a cassette tape from Mum; we had started corresponding with tapes rather than sending letters. She told me she had been given the opportunity of getting a council house in Gipsyville; she and Billy had gone to look at it on Thursday. Although it needed some decorating done – an old lady had lived there and since passed away – it was in good nick. Mum went on and on about it – how beautiful the garden was, when a window box was the only garden she had at the two up, two down she was living in now. She said she had taken up the offer and would get the keys in three weeks. The only problem was the rent, for Mum had been paying ten shillings a week for years at Clarence Ave, and would go up to one pound and five shillings for the new place. Mum said Billy had agreed to give her more.

I had been telling her for years, that, although they were not married, she and Billy should be sharing all the costs, but she was too independent for her own good. It wasn't that Billy was greedy, far from it – but if he could get away with it, he would.

Funnily though, the big thing about the house for Mum was that it had a bathroom. She said she and Billy had just stood there staring at it, then both together said, 'Fucking hell, a bath!' Billy wanted to try it there and then – but there was no hot water, or they would have.

'Fancy having a bath every week instead of a strip wash in the kitchen sink,' Billy had said.

'Every day, you dirty bastard,' said Mum.

I laughed like fuck listening to them; they were still arguing but I loved them and missed them so much. I couldn't wait to get home and see them. Mum even said the new house had three bedrooms so I would have my own room and a place for an office if I needed it, and it also had a back boiler. But living in this heat, I was more into air conditioning nowadays.

CHAPTER 28

LARS
Settling in Sydney

C hris told Jon and Marjory about the arrangements that had made for them. 'You will be staying in a hotel close by, booked for one week, full board, all at the bank's expense, or until you find accommodation of your own. Seeing as Lars is only an infant, the hotel has provided a cot. They have only booked this for a week, which will give you time to look for a two-bedroom place, which the bank will pay for three months' rent on.'

Marjory looked at Jon; he raised his eyebrows, as if to say 'wow'. They followed Chris through to two waiting taxis – one for them, the other for their luggage. Nothing was spared; they were being treated like movie stars. They were walking to catch the cab, and Jon pulled Marjory's arm to slow her down, whispering, 'They never looked after us like this at the Royal Bank of Scotland during my ten years with them.'

The ride was not far as they soon pulled up outside the Langham hotel, one of Sydney's finest establishments. 'Here we are then – it's not the best in Sydney, but we always use this for our new employees. The place is kept clean and tidy, and the tucker is pretty good.'

'It looks fine, thank you, Chris – but what if we can't find a rental place within the week? What happens then?'

'Oh, don't worry – they won't throw you out on the street, but we have found that most people want to get settled and in their own place. Besides, there are quite a lot of places available; you won't find it hard, I'm sure. We have noticed that with some of the other Pommies working at the bank, they tended to stick together and all lived in the same area. They did not mingle with the other Australian families, which seems strange to me. Why travel halfway around the world to try and live the same as you did back home? Try to make friends, and get to know some of the locals – you will find most Australians and even New Australians are a friendly mob.'

It did not take Jon and Marjory long to settle in, and, after finding a beautiful two-bedroom apartment in Darling Harbour, they were soon living the Australian life.

Jon was doing well in his job; he seemed to be a bit of a snob and somewhat aloof when people first met him, but deep down, he was better for knowing. He heard a couple of the locals discussing him in the gents' toilets one day, while he was in a cubicle.

'What do you think of the new guy, Jon, mate?'

'He is OK, I suppose… typical bloody Pommie. A bit up himself – think they rule the bloody world.'

'They did, mate, but picked the worst bloody place to live in.' They both laughed at the joke and left.

I don't want to be thought of as arrogant or anything like that, Jon thought; I must try to be friendlier. Maybe even joining them for a beer on a Friday might be a good start.

Marjory had met a couple of ladies through Jon's work, and she had been invited round for afternoon tea on a few occasions, which was nice, but the Australian women seemed to drink more wine than tea, and she did not drink alcohol. When she had mentioned this to one of the girls, Abigail, she was told, 'We will soon bloody well alter you, my girl.'

Apart from that, everything was rosy. For a couple of years while Lars was growing up, Marjory was the stay-at-home wife. She had no need to work, and she couldn't even if she wanted to. Jon was right – she was not missing home at all. She had sent the odd letter back to her sister. Still, she was quite happy with her lot, and spent most of the time doing the tourist thing, taking baby Lars to see Sydney's sights; he especially loved Taronga Park Zoo as they had never been to a zoo, not even in London.

Lars was two when he first visited Taronga Park Zoo; the word Taronga is an aboriginal name for Beautiful View. They got the ferry from Circular Quay to Mosman on the harbour's north side; Lars loved the ferry ride. Marjory was reading the pamphlet about the history of Taronga. The first service to Taronga Zoo began on September 24, 1916, with a ferry taking the elephant Jessi across the harbour to her new home from the old zoo at Moore Park.

Marjory had settled down in Sydney and was enjoying her new life. There was lots of sunshine; it got a bit chilly during the winter months but nothing as severe as back in the UK. They had made the right decision to come all this way. They knew things were going to change, but it came a bit earlier than both of them thought it would.

Five years later

It was now 1952. One day, Jon arrived home from the bank. 'I have some news to tell you, dear. I have had a meeting with the personnel people, and they want me to take a position with a branch in Eden. It is our first move of many. We have been lucky; we have been in Sydney for five years, but the management thinks we are ready now. They told me that Eden was the gateway to the Sapphire Coast and the most southerly town on the New South Wales coast; it is supposed to be a lovely place, steeped in history. They told me the area housed one of the country's earliest whaling stations and is one of the state's busiest fishing ports. What do you think? I know it will be our first move, but we knew this was going to happen sooner or later, as I told you, and you must just get used to it.'

'I know, but I did not think it would be so quick – and why so far away, just when we are starting to make friends, dear?'

'It is better now than when Lars is in the middle of a school term. We are lucky he has not started school yet; it means it will be a fresh start for him in a new environment. It is supposed to be a great little town right on the coast not far from the Victorian border so it will be different for us all. It'll be good to get out of the big city and have some country air – the first time in our lives we have not been surrounded by concrete. As I said, Eden was an old whaling port, with a couple of local beaches; maybe we will all be able to learn to swim.'

Marjory accepted the move, as there was nothing she could do about it anyway.

They moved down to Eden, where the bank had its own house in the town not far from the beach. Mind, everything was not far from the beach; this was the focal point.

It was the first weekend they had gone down the beach area. 'Well, what do you think, Marjory? This is beautiful.'

'Jon, stop going on about the place. Yes, it is very friendly, and yes, I am accepting that we have had to move again, but let's just settle down, shall we? Stop mithering me'.

'My, you are becoming a typical Australian woman. That has not taken you long, being strong-willed and not taking any prisoners; you will be saying G'day next instead of hello.'

As time went by, Jon was proved right. All the family learnt to swim in the local rock pool at Thompson's Point, which they had read about recently in the local newspaper, the Eden Magnet. It was reported that Thompson's Point Baths had been built in 1905 and extended in about 1908. It was popular, and was reached by going down some wooden ramps from the cliff tops.

The town had a surf club that ran a Little Nippers Club, where children as young as five could learn to swim. They had found a ready-made social club based on the children; it was perfect. Marjory was accepted into the community. But after meeting some of the other English ladies, especially Gertrude, the wife of one of the members of a golf club they had visited in Sydney on a corporate day, she realised that it could be quite dull. She was always moaning about Australia and comparing it with England, saying things like, 'We did not do that back in England,' or 'We have much better ones than that back in England.'

CHAPTER 29

LARS
Eden and Beyond

This attitude used to get the locals' backs up. And rightly so. They were at a local football team's barbecue one weekend, and quite a few of the surf club members played for the club. One of the guys in the bank, Mitch, played for the team and had invited Jon and Marjory to join them.

'G'day, Marjory – how's youse today?' said Ronda, Mitch's wife. They were locals; it seemed that it was only managers who got moved about with the bank. Ronda was the women's secretary of the sub-junior football team and club social secretary. Anyone who wanted to know anything would see Ronda. 'Have you met all of the ladies? And I say that bloody loosely… come on; I will introduce you to a couple of them.'

They walked over to a group of women all sitting on the grass, dressed in shorts and bikini tops. They were a mixture of ages, from mid-forty to some over seventy, but all tanned and looking very healthy.

'Here you go, girls, this is Marjory; she's new in town. Her old fella is the new manager of the bank, so bloody look after her – we might need to borrow a few quid one day.'

'Hi, Marjory. Can we call you Marj? It sounds more informal. I am Lynn; that's Lorna over there.' Lorna waved and smiled. 'That's Leanne, and Robyn, the little one with the short hair, with her back to us.'

'Yes, Marj is fine. Are you all involved with the rugby team?'

'It's not rugby; that's what the wallabies play. It's footy, as in rugby league, and yes – we are all on the ladies' committee. Most of our fellas

237

have played, coached or been involved somehow since the club formed six years ago. Some coach a junior team; we have teams from under six to under-eighteen, and first grade, which is the men's league.'

'OK, I always thought rugby was rugby, but it doesn't matter. I will call it footy from now on, to save any confusion.'

'How old is your young fella? He is a big boy.'

'Oh, Lars – he is nearly six. Yes, he is big for his age. He has shot up ever since we arrived in Australia. Mind, he was only very young when we decided to come out here; only a few months old.' Marj did not want to get into too much conversation about having babies.

'Hey, Alan – another recruit for you. Lars here is nearly six; big bugger ain't he? You need another front-rower for your team, don't you? That's Alan, Robyn's hubby. He coaches the under six-team. You ought to get Lars playing the game, babe; he would love it.'

'I'm not sure, Lynn; he has never been involved in any sports. I think he is too young, to be honest.'

'They are never too young to start. Does he swim? There is a Little Nippers Club at the surf club; you ought to get him down there.

'It's not only him,' said Marjory. 'None of us knows how to swim. There's not a lot of call for it in Manchester, where we come from; it's a long way from the sea, and there's not much chance of drowning in the ship canal.'

'You all should get yourselves down there – we have lessons every Tuesday and Thursday evening. You need to be able to swim; it's second nature in Oz.'

'I will have a word with Jon; that's him over there with those other chaps.'

Of course, the men were all sitting around the keg drinking beer, and the women were seated away from the men; to Marjory this seemed to be an Aussie ritual.

She had read in the paper about the club and found that Eden was a rugby league town and that the Eden Tigers had played in competitive football for about six years. A lot of their ways were set in stone. When in Rome, do as the Romans do; makes life a hell of a lot easier, she thought.

Betty, who was rather large with blonde hair, was another one who was always going on and on, comparing Australia to England; why she ever emigrated God only knows, thought Marjory. She was getting on her nerves. The beer had been flowing, when one of the football players, Big Dick, shouted over, 'Hey, Betty – why don't you fack off back to England, you Pommie bitch; sick to death of hearing about facking Pommie land.' The atmosphere suddenly changed; then another voice said, 'Good on yer, Dick,' followed by murmured mutual agreement of 'Too bloody right.' With that Betty's husband, Bluey, came over and whispered something in her ear; she went bright red and got up and left, without saying goodbye.

Everyone thought 'Old Marj' was a 'decent Sheila', though. Hearing this pleased her no end, for she had always been quite meek, and never been an outgoing sort of person. She had always been a bit on the small side, being only five feet two inches, and slightly built; she had always been conscious of her skinny figure. She hated being seen in swimmers, as the Australians called a bathing costume. The thought of wearing a bikini terrified her. With Jon being over six feet tall, fifteen stone in weight, with a very straight, upright posture, he always reminded her of a guardsman – which is what really attracted her to him, but she still felt insignificant.

Nevertheless, they decided to try out for the swimming classes on the following Tuesday evening. They arrived early, and just hovered around the surf club entrance, looking for a face that they recognised. There was a group of guys all wearing funny hats, and then they spotted Wayne, the surf club coach. 'G'day, and welcome to the Eden Little Nippers Swimming Club. We call the adults little nippers too, as not to frighten the kids, who are also here to learn how to swim. We're all in the same boat, so to speak.'

There were the three of them and two other adults and five kids who never stopped jumping up and down and making a noise. Jon was not a 'kiddy' person but soon seemed to be joining in with whatever they were told to do and, after a few weeks, they were all swimming. They never went too far out and always had a float, but it was swimming, nevertheless. 'I would never have believed it, Marjory – you in a swimming costume, mixing with strangers, and swimming, actually swimming. I am so proud of you, dear.' Jon kissed her in public; that was another first.

Five years later – Tamworth, NSW

It was now 1957 and their second move had come about. Marjory looked out of the window overlooking the large front garden and thought, well, this is different. She wasn't sure if she would like it there as much as Eden, as she had never lived in a rural area before, and everything seemed to depend on the weather.

Jon was reading a pamphlet on Tamworth and its history. 'Marjory, do you know that the branch was one of the oldest branches of the Bank of New South Wales when it was opened in Tamworth on December 15, 1856? It was only the sixth branch, with Shepherd Smith as its manager. The first depositor was William McClelland, an innkeeper and gold buyer from the nearby town of Moonbi, who banked £182.' He read on. 'Just look at that – would you believe it was the first town in Australia to have electric street lights?'

They are certainly trying us out, Jon said to himself, but at least we are getting our five years out of a place, which is more than some others. For he had heard that one or two managers only lasted a couple of years before they were moved on. It was a good job we don't have to sell a house every time we move – that would be deadly, he thought.

He put the pamphlet down and walked over to Marjory, who was still daydreaming out of the window. 'Look on the positive side; think of all the money we are saving not having a mortgage round our necks – and we see Australia at their expense. Not many people can say that.'

Lars was lying on the sofa and could hear them talking; he thought it was all very exciting. The only problem was Lars could see there were no beaches; there was only the local river, the Peel river, named after some other Pommie bloke, Sir Robert Peel, the same guy who founded the police force in the UK.

The next day Marjory was sitting reading the documentation they had been given when they first arrived and what was expected of the senior management, moving from branch to branch. Marjory hated that word, 'expected'; she wished she had never said she would come to Australia. However, it was the best thing to do considering what they had done in buying Lars. She still felt guilty, knowing what that poor girl must have gone through in losing a child and being told it was still-born. They were never told anything about Lars's birth mother. They should never have found out that she had been told he was dead; that slipped out in conversation with that horrible woman Jon had done the deal with. How he ever found someone who could get them a baby, Marjory did not know, but he had, and she could not say no when Jon had suggested his plans.

Her mind wandered; she needed something to pass her time. She was bored, but dared not suggest getting a job. 'Bank managers' wives do not work,' Jon had always said when she mentioned getting employment.

Marjory's next thought was to wonder where Lars was. He was not yet home from school, and he was getting later and later every night. But with that, he walked in with a couple of his friends. 'Can the guys stay for a while, Mum?'

'Yes, dear, what time do they have to be home for tea?'

'Anytime – no worries. Cheers, Mum; we will be over at Scully Park, OK?'

'OK, off you go; don't be late for tea.'

The boys were off with a football in their hands. Lars loved his footy and was getting to be a decent player, which was to be expected as he was well over five feet tall and ten stone with an incredibly defined body for a boy his age.

It was five-thirty, and Jon came home. 'Hello, dear – had a good day?' he said, as he kissed Marjory on the cheek.

'Yes, same old, same old, Jon. What would you think if I got a part-time job?'

'Marjory, you know how I feel about you working in the community;

it is just not on. You will make friends, and then they will think that because you are their friend it gives them a right to preferential treatment from the bank because the manager is your husband. The answer is no; a definite no.'

'OK... I thought I would ask.'

Then Lars came back in. 'Tea ready, Mum? I am starving. Have I time for a shower before tea, or am I OK as I am?'

'No, go and have your shower. Dad's in the garden; he has nodded off, I think, so tea won't spoil. Go on, hurry up; throw me your footy gear, I will put it in the wash.'

'Here, I will strip off now.' With that, Lars dropped his shorts and pulled his shirt over his head. As he did so, Mrs Johnston from next door popped her head over the fence. 'My, what a beautiful specimen, Lars – you are a big boy for your age.' Then she burst out laughing.

Lars shot into the back hallway and to his room. 'Stop teasing him, Brenda,' said Marjory. 'He is very self-conscious about his body. With him being much bigger than all his mates, the poor boy feels that he is some kind of freak, I think. Anyway, what are you wanting?'

'We are having a barbie on Saturday – fancy coming round and joining us?'

'Yes, that will be nice. I will bring the coleslaw and wine – Jon only drinks wine. He's not got used to the Aussie beer even after all these years. Are you buying the meat? If so, we will pay our share for that.'

'No, don't worry; we have just got a yearling and filled the freezer, so more snags and cube roll than you can shake a stick at, no worries – see you Saturday, then, around four-ish, OK?'

'Right-o, Brenda – thanks again.'

They had just finished tea when Marjory informed Jon and Lars, 'We have been invited next door to a bit of a pool barbie thing on Saturday – you both OK with that?'

'Yes – that is very kind of them. What time?' said Jon.

'Oh, after four; the sun will have gone down a bit by then. All we have to take is our drinks and the coleslaw.'

'Mum, do I have to come? I would rather not, if that's OK?'

'Yes, Lars – you are going. Mike will be there – you get on with him, don't you? And I think Steph, Greta's daughter, will be there. You know her from school – she is your age, such a pretty girl; you get on well with her, don't you?'

Get on well? What a thing to say, Lars thought to himself. Mike is a dick; all he ever talks about is birds and wildlife and Steph, who is a bit older and going through puberty, is a nutcase. Mind, she's got massive tits, and she will be coming in her bikini, so it has some good points, he thought.

'OK, Mum, I'm in; I will go.'

Saturday came, and they were all next door. They had been there an hour or so when Greta and her husband Mel turned up, with Steph in tow.

'Sorry we are late, guys,' said Mel. 'Got a bloody puncture, had to change the wheel. Greta's car is rooted so we could not come in her wheels. I was covered in shit and grease so needed a shower.'

'That's OK, Mel – no drama. Grab a beer. What will you have, Greta? The usual – Pernod and lemon squash?'

'Yes, cheers, Brenda.'

Steph walked in, not saying a word.

'G'day Steph – how's you, OK?' said Brenda. 'You're quiet. What would you like to drink, coke?'

She nodded. She still hadn't said anything to anyone.

'I'm going for a swim – you coming too, Mike?' Lars said.

'Yes, OK – I will go and put my swimmers on.' He disappeared inside.

'Can I come too, Lars?' said Steph, as she took off her robe and bent over in front of Lars to take off her sandals.

'Yes, for sure, come on.'

Lars dived in the deep end of the pool and swam a length on his way back; he came up from under the water and, as he rose, he was fronted by the body of Steph. She looked into his eyes, knowing full well that she was affecting him. 'G'day Lars – like my new swimmers? I only got them yesterday. I only came because Mum told me youse would be here.' Her hand touched his thigh under the water.

He could not get out of the pool if he had wanted to; she was a big girl for fifteen.

The sun was going down, they had finished the barbecue and were sitting around drinking; the men were getting rowdier, the more beer they consumed.

'Isn't it funny, dear,' Jon said to Marjory, 'How quickly the sun goes down? It's like it switches off... not like back home when there is definite dusk. How unusual... it has always amazed me.' Lars looked at Jon; it was the first time he had seen him even drunk. He must have had a bit more red wine than usual.

Steph came and sat beside Lars on the grass; he was still in his swimmers. 'Lars, can I ask you something?' she whispered. 'One of the girls in my class has the hots for you. You know, Melanie, the one who is supposed to be a bit... well, you know.'

'What are you talking about, Steph? I am not interested in girls; well, not in the way you are talking. Melanie is a nice girl – why are you spreading rumours about her?'

CHAPTER 30

LEIF
Three Months Up

I t was soon October; three months had passed. I was thinking about what the outcome of my trial period was going to be when Doug called me into his office.

'Leif, come in, son – we need to have a chat regarding your initial three-month period.'

I was expecting some bad news, the way he had started the conversation.

'Don't look so worried. I am more than happy; not only have you brought some stability to my commercial department but your input to the drawing and design office has been outstanding. The work you put into the flood mitigation job for the new floodgates on the upper Swan River project, and its innovative design for the gates using railway lines and rubber seals, was unreal.'

I was amazed; I had not heard this side of Doug.

'I hope you have enjoyed your first three months and hope you will agree to extend your stay with Peters Industrial Engineering.' He put out his hand, and I shook it without hesitation. 'Bloody ripper, mate – thought some other bastards might have lured you away for more money.'

'No, I am pleased to be working for you, Doug. Thanks for taking me on full time.'

Later that week, I went in to pay my $300 rent money at Rosamond Real Estate when Ros came out of the back office.

'G'day, Leif, how are you? Got some good news – your rent has gone down, mate. It's now $150 a month, as your employer, Peters, directly subsidises the other half.'

'What are you talking about? I thought we had a sealed agreement. How does Doug know about the deal?'

'He owns the block, babe; he is the landlord, that's how. Just accept it.'

My luck could not have been any better – and my situation with Donna was on the up, too.

We had been out for a drive, and she had to call in to see her old man at his maintenance yard; he had a haulage company. I had not met him yet as it was still a secret relationship, me not being Italian the main contention.

We pulled up into the yard in her Fiat Tipo; she got out as her father appeared from under a ramp with a small truck on it. He was ranting about taking the engine and gearbox out due to some problem after a crash.

Donna introduced me to her father; we exchanged pleasantries.

'What's the problem, Mr Luciano? Can I help?'

He looked at me as if to say, 'What the fuck would you know?' Then he said, 'The truck was run off the road trying to avoid hitting a bloody big red out in the bush. The driver had to swerve to miss the kangaroo and hit a tree; the bodywork is rooted. The chassis is cracked and needs either a replacement or stiffener plates to strengthen the channel frame, but we can't get at the backside to fillet-weld up the plate. If we leave it, that will leave a stress point and eventually it will give and fail again. If the engine and gearbox need to come out, it'll be a bloody big job and will mean the truck being off the road longer, which means losing more bloody money.'

'Mind if I take a look, Mr Luciano? I think I might be able to help,' I said.

He looked at me kind of strangely.

'How do you mean?' he asked.

I looked under the ramps. 'OK, no problem – have you got an old wing mirror? Even just the glass would do; it'd make it a bit easier to place. Where is the welding equipment?' I took my jacket off and asked if he had any welder's leathers. I was given a jacket, which was bit tight, but it fitted. 'Leave me to it,' I said. 'Come back in an hour or two, and it should be fixed.'

I welded some rods together to make them twice as long as the twelve-inch regular size and bent them, so they were in kind of a loop, and I had the mirror strategically placed to enable me to see the area that needed welding. Luckily I could weld with both hands. I had learnt to do this when working on my apprenticeship a few years ago, but once you can weld, it is like riding a bike – you never forget.

When Donna came back, I was sitting having a beer with one of the mechanics and chatting about what I had just done.

'Some guy you got here, Donna – bloody magician; I've never seen anything like it. Takes a Pom to show us how to do something, that's for sure. Never seen a guy who was ambi... ambidect... oh, could use both his fucking hands.'

I got up and started to leave; it was embarrassing listening to his story. 'Come on, Donna, let's go before your old man comes in.'

With that, he came into the office. 'Hey, son – thank you so much! Great job. How the hell do you learn to do that? Never seen anything like it; my man reckons the welding was better than he could normally do. How much do I owe you?'

'Nothing; pleased I could help. Glad I was here before you had to take the engine out; I know what a problem that could have been.'

I was well in with him now; he came up and gave me a big hug, like only Italians can do. He gave Donna $30, telling her, 'Go buy the boy lunch!' Now you could have some lunch in those days for thirty bucks.

As we drove away, Donna said, 'I think he likes you; he's never done that before, and with you not being Italian... wow.'

I had been seeing Donna for a few months, and I felt we were getting closer. I had respected her decision about saving herself for the right man. Doing without was getting frustrating, I must admit, but I was happy, and so was she.

We had been out for a few beers; it was a hot steamy night, and we had gone back to my place. Donna had gone to the toilet, and I was standing on the balcony admiring the view over the river.

I had got changed into a pair of stubbie shorts and no shirt, enjoying the bit of a breeze blowing across from the south. I felt these arms around me and then bare breasts touching my back, along with moist lips in between my shoulder blades. Two hands went inside my shorts and pulled them down. I suddenly felt her bare thighs against the cheeks of my arse. Oh my god, Donna was naked; holding me close. I did not turn to face her; I was just enjoying the moment, the feel of her body, for I had not had the pleasure of seeing her naked, never mind touching her.

Eventually, I turned and looked. It was a far better sight than I could ever have imagined – long dark hair cascading down to her waist, perfect olive skin, breasts so firm. Her nipples, with dark areola – or headlamps, as some people say in Hull, were so sexy. A tuft of pubic hair been trimmed to perfection. I took her in my arms, and we kissed like never before.

I never even reached Featherstone that first time. We lay on my bed not talking, both thinking about the sacrifice Donna had made for me; her vow she had just broken, and how she would feel in the morning. She was lying across me, her head on my belly. I was looking at that perfectly formed arse and smooth back; I felt so good. We fell asleep that night, dreaming of what we had done. Well, I know I did.

On Sunday morning I awoke with the sun blazing through the blinds. Donna was lying next to me in the foetal position – body bent, her head bowed, and her legs drawn up to her chest almost in a ball; so peaceful, so beautiful. The dark hair on her body was ever so soft and just showing on her lovely skin; fuck, she was some beauty.

I got up; I was gagging for a drink, so I started to make some coffee when Donna walked in, still naked. 'Hi, babes, good morning.' She walked towards me, put her arms around my neck and kissed me. 'Grazie bambino, che il sesso era assolutamente fantastico. Meglio di quanto potessi mai immaginare.' I made a mental note to look that up in my new phrasebook. I supposed it meant something like 'thank you, baby, that sex was fantastic – better than I could ever imagine'. My thoughts exactly.

I was now worried what the local Cosa Nostra would do to me if it ever came out I had deflowered the daughter of one of leading Italian families in Perth. To make things worse, Donna now thought she had invented shagging; she could not get enough of it. Every time we were alone she wanted sex. Now, I was not one to knock a fuck back, for the one you missed, you could never get back, but enough was enough. I never in this world thought it would happen, but I was having to try to not see her so much during the week, only at weekends. What was I doing?

I was sitting around the canteen at work during lunch one day and heard two guys talking about footy, so I listened in. They mentioned Fremantle Roosters and South Perth Lions, so I butted in. 'Sorry, guys, don't want to interrupt, but do they play rugby league in Perth?'

'Yeah, of course they do – about eight clubs in the comp, mate. AFL is big round here, and rugby – but league, OK? Been going since the 1940s, the Roosters – they're one of the oldest clubs. Why? Fancy a game, mate? You ever played?'

'I have, yes; a few years ago now. Nearly turned pro when I was seventeen, but work came first.'

Wayne, one of the guys, overheard the conversation. It turned out he was on the Roosters committee. He chipped in, 'Get your ass down, mate – pre-season training starts this week. We'd love to see you there; looks like you need a bit of exercise, looking at yer.'

He was right; I had put a few pounds on. No exercise and all the Italian food I had been having; I needed to do something.

I happened to mention to Doug later on during the day about going down to the Roosters, and he was OK with it. Unlike the attitude I'd encountered back home, the Australians loved their sport and encouraged their employees in keeping fit.

'Go for it, mate – I sponsor the Roosters, used to play for them as front-rower a few years ago. They're a good set of guys – you will love it. By the way, you did not have that on your CV – you just said you liked sport.'

I told him about Paratec and not liking sportspeople, especially rugby players, working for them in case of injury.

'Bullshit,' was the comment.

I went down to training the following Monday. There was a decent turnout of players; all ages and level of fitness were on show, from youths to the middle-aged.

I was standing talking to Wayne when a guy with a whistle on a lanyard came over.

'G'day, mate – you must be Leif, the guy everyone has been talking about. I am Dennis Mountain, head coach. Welcome to the Roosters.' He put out his hand. I was taken back a bit by his comment.

'They tell me you played for that mob Hull KR over in Pommie land – that right?' I explained what had occurred when I was a mere youth, but he still seemed impressed. He asked me what position I preferred. I told him centre; he nodded and smiled.

'You look the part, son – let's see how you perform, OK?'

The training was hard – a lot harder than I'd imagined it would be, but it was enjoyable all the same. The guys made me welcome, and I felt at home with them – all except one guy who did not even speak, and when I asked who he was it appeared he was the star of the show, Terry O'Neil. It seems the Roosters had been his only club since he had arrived from NSW country team Kurri Kurri in Newcastle. He also played centre, so maybe he felt a bit threatened by the new kid on the block.

We trained for six weeks before we were split into two groups; there were only two teams plus an under-eighteens team. I was put with the reserve grade, which suited me as the new boy. Gus Scott was the coach. An ex-Roosters player, he had retired with injury but still turned out now and again when required at number six, or standoff.

We trained for another month before it was announced we would be playing a trial game. This would be among ourselves with a mixture of first-grade forwards and reserve-grade backs, versus reserve-grade forwards and first-grade backs. There were more than fifty players down so that meant competition would be fierce. We were told that, during the game – which was going to be played in four quarters of half an hour each – there would be a bit of mixing and matching, but not to worry about that as it would not define where we would be playing.

The club used selectors to pick the squads and the four coaches – head and assistant –for both teams. This was something I had never heard of back home; the directors decided the teams for Hull FC and Hull Kingston Rovers.

We played the game on the Sunday under lights at 8pm kick-off after the sun had gone down, finishing at 10pm. I'd never played that late in my life, so that was another new experience. I thought I did OK for my first game for a long time. I was a bit rusty but I scored two tries and put my winger in for a hat trick; everyone seemed pleased with my efforts, except you know who.

The only problem with me being involved with the Roosters was I had not seen Donna as much over the past few weeks. We had been training three nights a week, so the weekend was the only time we had met, apart from the odd Tuesday or Thursday night. I could tell she was not that happy about being a footy widow, but it was a good test of our relationship. She came round to my place one Thursday, and I cooked tea, we made love, in that order, and afterwards we lay on the bed making small talk.

'Leif, can I say something?'

'Sure, babe – what's up? Thought you had been a bit quiet.'

'Well, it's like this… I miss not seeing as much of you as I did before you started playing footy. Tell me if I am wrong, but do you prefer being with the guys more than with me? Do you still love me, or are you tired of me?'

'Donna, please – of course I love you. But it has been a long time since I have been involved in a rugby club or fact any club of any sort for years and, yes – I love it. The camaraderie and the craic of being among a bunch of guys was something I had missed, but did not know how much I had missed it, until now. To say I prefer being with the guys is daft; there is no comparison. Of course I'd rather be with you.'

She was pressuring me, no doubt about that, but I was a single guy with no real ties apart from a girlfriend whom I had known a few months, and the only girl I had met since coming to Australia. What was I going to do about it? I did not know.

'Look, you will see me every weekend. I hope you will be coming to the games with me and joining in the social life of the club; meeting new people, other girls – it will be great fun.'

I could see Donna had doubts, but she never actually said she was not interested.

I was busy at work. My first quote had gone in for an installation of four storage vessels, pumps and ancillary pipework, structural steelwork and walkways on a small chemical plant on the outskirts of Fremantle. It was not a big job, but still, it was big enough; we were doing it as a joint venture with an electrical contractor and a small piping company owned by an old guy that Doug knew quite well. Doug had told me he was hoping to buy the company as a going concern to add to Peters Industrial Engineering, as his friend wanted to retire. He was also contemplating buying an electrical/instrumentation contractor, an idea I told him to forget as my experience with E&I was that it was a speciality, and best left to the experts. OK, the piping or industrial pipework, had its expertise and often required a more technical specialist approach, but I could point him in the right direction there. I had sent out an enquiry to four piping contractors for the job and asked them to complete my bill as I had laid it out; it was different to the usual enquiry and I had to visit the four chosen ones whose names Doug had furnished me with. I had given them each the same enquiry documents, material lists, WB or work breakdown, etc; this was to ensure we were all singing from the same song sheet. One of them declined to bid, but the others came back with quotes and Doug's favourite for the job won it.

A week later, we got a letter of intent, telling us that we would be awarded the contract for the extension. One more week and we received the contract for the project, whose total all-inclusive value was

$145,000. We finished the job under budget in two weeks, which was less than the programme indicated. Doug was over the moon, and more enquiries started coming in. We were now on our way as a company offering more than just structural steel installation.

It was 1973, and I was reminded of home, and how much I was missing being on Hessle Road, when I got the news that the Hull trawler Ian Fleming had been lost on Christmas Day. She had been heading out to the treacherous White Sea off the Russian coast. The skipper decided to take the vessel through the Norwegian fjords to avoid the worst of the weather, but the trip was to end in tragedy as the Ian Fleming ran aground, hitting the Havosund Mountain. Two life rafts were launched after the grounding. Fifteen crewmen took one, and the skipper and five others took the other, but it had not inflated properly and capsized. Three men in this raft drowned – mate Terence Day, radio operator George Lee and engineer Dennis Colby. It was said at the time that they should have had a pilot to take the ship through the fjords, but it seems that one was not requested. When they ran aground, George Lee managed to make a mayday call for help, but no one knew where the ship was in the fjord. If it had not been for the radio operator's actions that dreadful night, all of the crew would have perished.

I had now been with Doug and Peters Industrial Engineering for three years; my salary had gone up to $15,000 year.

Then in early 1974 came another message from home – another trawler, the Gaul, had gone missing off the north coast of Norway on February 8. She had sailed from Hull on the morning of January 22. Mate George Petty became ill and was put ashore at Lødingen on the 26th. Maurice Spurgeon joined the crew on the 28th at Tromsø and arrived at the fishing grounds off the north coast of Norway the following day. On February 8, reports came in from other trawler skippers in the area saying it was very rough weather with heavy seas and gale-force winds. A message came back that the Gaul was 'laid and dodging' off the North Cape Bank, as was company policy. She reported to the Orsino on the 'Skipper's Freezer Schedule' – a summary of position, weather conditions, catch, and so on. A further report was due at 4.30pm but the Gaul alone, of the seventeen British United Trawlers ships in the area at the time, failed to report.

By the afternoon of February 10, British United Trawlers had alerted its insurance company, UK Trawlers Mutual, that the Gaul had been unable to communicate for two days. On the following morning, the insurance company sent out a message to all of its trawlers: 'To all vessels fishing North Bank, Norway – all vessels please report any contact with the Gaul last reported fishing North Bank. Nil reports not required.'

The aircraft carrier HMS Hermes was in the area and was ordered to begin searching. The search involved four other British ships, three Norwegian ships and nineteen trawlers, coordinated by the Hermes. No evidence of the missing Gaul was found, and the search was called off on the afternoon of February 15.

It always brought it home to me, as I had been brought up living with these tragedies, how much the men – who put their lives at risk to put fish on our tables – gave to us all.

I was still seeing Donna and was under pressure from her father to marry his daughter. He thought that our courtship had gone on long enough; he wanted grandchildren to add to his family tree, to keep the name Luciano going. There was just one problem – I was not ready. Yes, I was in love with her, but I was not ready to commit myself to be with the same woman for the rest of my life.

I received a letter from home on October 1 1974. This was unusual as we used to send tape recordings back and forth instead of writing a message. I would send one on the third Monday of every month and Mum would send one back on the first Monday. Hence, a letter meant either good or bad news.

It was terrible news. My grandfather Hans had passed away in his sleep aged seventy-nine, I could not believe I would be so upset after all that he had done to my mother, but I was devastated. Was it because I was a long way away from home, missing my family? I could not help myself – I just broke down in tears. I was inconsolable. I did not go to work; I never rang in, or anything. I just sat in my unit and didn't eat for three days.

Then there was a knock on the front door. I ignored it. They knocked again and again, but I still did not answer the door. I heard Doug's voice calling my name. 'Leif, I know you're there – open the bloody door!'

I was on the way to answer it when Doug shouted again, and then he pushed the door and barged in. 'What the fuck's going on, Leif? Jesus, mate – just look at the state of you. What's wrong? Why did you not ring in? What's happened?'

I broke down again, and dropped down on my haunches, sobbing. I told Doug about my grandfather. He picked me up and held me close, saying, 'So sorry, mate. Gee, you must have been close for it to affect you like this.'

But he was wrong; we weren't that close, and I could not tell him why I was so upset; why I did not know him that well, because of what had happened over the years. I should have been pleased he had gone, but at the end of the day I was his flesh and blood; he wasn't just my grand-father, he was my father. My true father had gone. Doug offered to pay for a flight home, but it was too late; he would have been buried by the time I got back, so I declined his offer.

I went back to work, and sort of got over the passing; yes, I was still having moments, but I was OK.

It was only three months after the news about my father that I had to deal with another personal tragedy.

Donna, my beautiful, beautiful Donna, was the victim of a head-on car crash, just outside Fremantle. She had been out visiting an old school friend when she came around a bend, and there was a semi-trail-er coming the other way. It seemed that her car had been on the wrong side of the road; she died instantly.

I found out as I was driving; I heard it on the car radio. It said a young woman driving a red Fiat had been fatally injured in a motor accident on the highway between the City of Swan and Perth. I just knew it was her. The place they mentioned was where her friend's family had prop-erty. I knew Donna had gone that day. My head was spinning; what could I do? How could I find out for sure? Should I ring the police, or ring her parents up? I had to go and see them, but what would I say? It was then I realised how alone I was. Yes, I had a circle of friends – the footy team, Doug, and the guys at work. But still, I had no one to hug me, cry with me; no brothers to call and tell them the tragic news that my baby, my best friend, had died and we hadn't had the chance to say goodbye. I didn't get to hold her close, or tell her how much I loved her. I broke down again.

Her parents did not have my telephone number as far as I knew; I had only met them about six times in the period I had known her. I was not even sure they approved of me not being an Italian Catholic boy, but now none of that mattered. I rang Doug; he was the nearest thing to a relative I had. He would know what to do.

'Hi, Doug, it's me, Leif.'

'Oh, hi, buddy.' He sounded different.

'Doug, I need some advice. It's about…'

Before I could finish he said, 'Donna – I know, mate. I am so sorry.'

How did he know? I had only just heard a news bulletin; how could he have found out?

'I am not even sure it is her; I only heard it on the radio, Doug. How come you know?' I was close to tears again, and starting to waffle.

'Stay there; are you at home?'

'Yes. Please – how do you know? How did you find out it was Donna?'

'I will be there in half an hour. Stay calm, mate; I will be there.'

He arrived and knocked on the door; it was open. I knew it was Donna by the look on his face. He grabbed me and pulled me close to him, then he burst out crying. That was all I needed. We both stood there crying, and I mean sobbing, for, I don't know, a good five minutes before Doug let go of me. 'Sit down, mate,' he said. 'I will tell you how I found out. I have a mate who is a policeman; he was first on the scene. He said he could not believe his eyes when he saw the wreck. She had had no chance – the car was embedded in the front of the Big Mack semi-trailer. She was on the wrong side of the road, just as you come over the brow of the hill. He would have been doing at least fifty miles per hour and her about the same.'

'But why, Doug? Why was she on the wrong side of the road? Did she lose control?'

'I don't know. The police could not understand why she was on the wrong side of the road; there were no other cars around. The truck driver was not hurt, just really shook up, but when interviewed stated she was there in front of him as he came over the hill. He said he didn't even get the chance to break until the last second, but it was way too late; he just pushed the car or what was left of it further back down the hill. What made it worse, with her father being in the transport game, he said he knew Donna and her car. My mate said he had been a cop for twenty years, but it was the first time he had ever been called to an RTA where he knew the person or persons involved; he was distraught by it. He knew Donna was in a relationship with you; that is why he rang me. He knew it was out of order and hoped it would not go any further, the fact that he contacted me before her parents were informed officially by the police department. I believe this has already been done, as it is a while since the accident had happened. I am so sorry, mate – so sorry. Why don't you come back to my place? It's better than being alone, mate. Come on – stay with us for a few days?'

We drove back to his house; I'd never been there before. As much as Doug was a bit of a lair, he was a private person when at home, and he had a heart as big as a lion. I was just numb; there was nothing either of us could say. I sat outside Doug's house on the veranda at the back, and he went inside and left me alone with my thoughts.

He came back with two beers. 'Here, mate – get this down you. I have called Peter, the policeman who was at the scene; he said he would call around here after he comes off shift to see you. Is that OK? Should be here in a couple of hours. Like I said, you could stay here the night, or longer if you don't want to be on your own, what with all your family being in Pommie land. Must be facking hard, mate. We have lots of room if you do not want to be alone; Maggs won't mind.'

Two hours later, Sgt Peter Nichols came round the back of the house near the pool and tennis courts. Doug introduced me.

'Thank you for coming to see me, Peter. Have you found out yet what happened?'

'Sorry for your loss, son, and no – we are none the wiser, mate. We just can't say at the moment. The car will be inspected, what's left of it, but you can imagine it is in a bit of a state.'

'What about Donna's mum and dad? Have they been told yet? Fuck, they will be in bits.'

'Yes, the officers who had gone to see Donna's parents got a radio call while they were there to tell them you had been informed, but they did not tell her parents that until after they had been told the bad news.'

There was not much more I could say or do, so we just sat there having a few more beers, and talking about Donna – what a fantastic beautiful person she was; why should it happen to her?

'There will be an inquest into the accident,' said Peter. 'It usually takes a couple of weeks before the findings are sent to the coroner. Up to now as far as I am concerned we believe it was an accident. I am so sorry, mate; you have my condolences. She was a beautiful young woman.'

I gave it a few days before I went to see Donna's parents. God, it was hard. They welcomed me into their home, Donna's home; they showed me her room. It was tough just being there. I could smell her perfume as soon as I walked in. I could feel her presence; there were photos of her all over the place. I was in pieces within minutes, and we just stood there hugging each other, crying uncontrollable tears.

I did not even have a decent photo of her. I was looking at one in a frame, and her mother said, 'You can take that if you want, Leif. Please, take it.' I hugged it to my chest and broke down again. The pain was unreal; there was a lump in my throat just above my breastbone. I had never known pain like it.

A few weeks passed, and there was an inquest. It was relatively quick, and the finding was accidental death.

Her funeral was the next thing; she was a practising Catholic and the service was arranged by her parents and their local priest. I needed to see Donna's parents again.

CHAPTER 31

LARS

Tweed Heads: Five Years Later – 1962

J on walked in to the kitchen. Marjory was at the sink washing some pots, daydreaming, and didn't hear him come in. Their third move was surely imminent; she hated thinking about it, but knew it would happen soon. He hugged her and kissed her on the back of her neck. 'I have some great news,' he whispered in her ear. 'Our time is up in Tamworth; we are being transferred again – this time up to the Queensland border to the Tweed Heads branch.'

Tweed Heads – where was that, she wondered. He could see that she was not too pleased, but all he could think of saying was, 'But it is twinned with Coolangatta, just across the border into Queensland.'

Marjory turned to Jon and told him it was OK to keep moving, but she felt sorry for Lars. 'He does not say much to us,' she said. She knew he was not happy with all this moving about from town to town. 'One of his friends' mothers, Mandy – Billy's mother – told me the other day Lars was telling Billy he was expecting to be leaving soon, as he has only got four to five years and he has to move again. Jon, we have loved it here; we have some lovely friends, and Lars will not be overjoyed to find out, for it will mean him finding another school and new footy team to join – do they play rugby up there?'

'Of course – they play rugby league up there, you mean you do not know?'

She reminded him that Lars's schooling should come first.

'Look – it does not matter; we are moving in four weeks and I am going up there on Monday to meet the staff and to look for a place to rent.'

'But, Jon, you are not listening to me – it is Lars I am worried about, we –'

'Marjory – how many times do I have to keep saying it is a good job? The bank is still paying for accommodation. Just think of what we are saving for when we do settle down in our own place – we mustn't grumble.'

Jon was starting to get a bit annoyed with Marjory. He had explained all this to her before they came to Australia. 'I will tell you again,' he said, 'it is the policy for branch managers to be moved around the state; they feel it keeps everyone on their toes and complacency doesn't creep in. Also, it does not give us managers much chance to be too well acquainted with the customers when negotiating mortgages, loans, etc.' He got up out of his chair to make his point. 'I do realise about his schooling. But they have always put him in the best schools available in the area and paid all the fees; you must not forget that. Not may boys would have had the same opportunities as Lars if their parents had to pay for their education. Lars certainly would not have had if we had to pay over the years. Just think about that, before you complain.'

'But, Jon, Lars told Billy he would be glad when the time came, and old enough to get away from us and do what he wants to do – "not the fucking bank". Those were his words, not mine. Don't forget, he is a star player in the under-fifteens team; they will miss him when he goes up north, that is for sure, and I know Lars will miss them. He's getting to that age now; I did hear he has a girlfriend called Gwen, and she is older than him, she is sixteen. He does not know we know, so don't you go saying anything, you understand? Jon, are you listening to what I am saying?'

'Marjory, of course; there was going to come the day when Lars started getting interested. All boys do it, even I did; I can remember my first.'

'Don't say another word; I don't want to hear about your sordid past, thank you very much.'

Lars walked in just as they finished speaking. Marjory asked him if he was ready for tea or whether he wanted to shower first.

'I will shower first, Mum, as I am all sweaty and I stink.'

'OK – but don't be long.'

Lars went to his bedroom at the back of the house and stripped. He stood in front of the mirror, looking at himself; he was not a narcissist but did realise he was a good-looking boy. He started touching himself, thinking about Gwen, his girlfriend, and how he was going to make love to her at her place for the first time tonight when her mum went out to work at the league's club. He thought he'd better get in a cold shower, before he had a happy ending.

Lars went back downstairs into the kitchen after his shower. 'That's better, Mum – what's for tea? I am starving.'

'You are always starving, son – it's schnitzel with fries and sweetcorn; your favourite.'

They had almost finished their evening meal. Jon put down his fork and folded his hands together. 'Right, now we are all together, we have something to tell you, Lars. I have to say I am sorry, but we are moving again. I know that is rather a blunt way of putting it, but that is the way it is. I am going up to Tweed Heads on Monday, and we are moving in four weeks. What do you think about that, Lars? It is near the beach and not far from Surfers Paradise.'

Lars sat there, not saying much; he was sick of it all. He'd had to put up with this all his life, keeping his mouth shut, just going along with the flow. Well, now was the time to say something. It would not make a bit of difference, but he had to say something. He knew he would still have to go, and leave his mates again, but this time it was a bit different. There was Gwen and all that went with her. He had found he liked being naked with her and the sex was incredible. These were things that did not matter before, but now girls were a big part of his life. In the past year things had changed – he had met Gwen. OK, she was no raving beauty, but to him, she was hot as hell. She was tall and gangly, more like a fashion model, and she had also introduced Lars to using his dick for more than just passing water through – and now they wanted to take him away. He sat there listening to them going on about the move and how great it would be, but that was it – he had heard enough. 'Mum, Dad, I have always gone along with whatever you have had to do. Well, now, this time I just want to say no. I am not going. Fuck it – why should I?'

There was utter silence. Jon and Marjory just looked at each other in disbelief. In fourteen years neither of them had ever sworn in front of the boy, and the first one to swear had been him. He had dared to declare what he thought in front of his parents.

Jon went red, stood up and was just going to blast Lars when Marjory butted in.

'Jon, please – not in front of the boy.'

'Not in front of the fucking boy? Didn't you hear what he just said? Are you deaf as well as fucking daft, woman? And you, fucking Lars – are you fucking mad as well?'

That did not go down too well, Lars thought. 'There is no reason to overreact, Dad. I was just passing an opinion – and the name's Lars, not fucking Lars.' He was on a roll now, so he gave them everything. 'I do not want to go. Tell the bank to fuck off. We are not leaving – have you no bollocks? You have been getting shit on ever since we came to this godforsaken fucking country. Why we ever left England I will never know, not that I knew much about it. You dragged me out here to a fucking land that is too hot, with spiders, snakes, fucking animals that want to kill you – even if you go swimming there are ten foot fucking fish that want to fucking eat you… and you say I am fucking mad!' Lars stood up to leave the table. 'Is that it, then? Is the family meeting over? Can I leave the table now, please?'

'No, you fucking can't leave the fucking table!' Marjory said. Both Lars and Jon turned to look at her, open-mouthed.

'I am not happy,' said Lars. 'This will be the last time I ever move. I will leave home first. You can take it from me, Dad, if you ever get another move, I am gone, understand?'

Marjory just smiled to calm him, as mothers do. She tried to explain to Lars that it was his father's job, but before she could say any more Lars butted in, 'I don't believe it – you haven't taken notice of one fucking word I have said, have you? I'm going to my room. I have heard enough.'

Three months later

'Here we are, dear,' said Jon. 'Now, isn't this nice. We have this lovely place for another five years, and they have promised no move for five years – isn't that nice of them, dear?'

I don't fucking believe it, Lars was thinking to himself. Will you please stop exaggerating the five years; I will be gone and fuck the pair of you. I will have left school, hopefully got into university or, even better, a job and my own place, and then I can please myself what I do and bollocks to you.

Lars was moved to yet another new school, this time Tweed River High School – the third and, as far as was concerned, last time that he would ever have to find new friends.

'G'day, how are you? I am Warren; looks like we are sitting together, mate.' He put out his hand to Lars.

'Hello – I am Lars Mellows. Yes, it is my first day. I've just moved to town. I was in Tamworth before this. The old man works in a bank and I've been moved more times than I care to remember, mate.'

'That must be great,' said Warren. 'Must be unreal getting to see different places instead of being stuck in same fucking town all your life. I can't wait to get away, me – eighteen, I will be gone, as soon as I leave school. I don't want to go to university – I'll just get a job, earn a few quid, and then go to Sydney. That's where I am heading – I want to get into a team in Sydney and be a semi-pro footy player. They will get me a job down there, and I will play for Australia one day, you'll see.'

Lars thought this kid was deluded – but fair play, he knew what he wanted to be. He thought about what he wanted to do when he left school. Deep down he did like travelling and meeting other people, so why not go and see the world, he thought; there must be more to see than Australia. Why not go back to England to see where he was born and find any relations? After all, he did not know his grandparents; they were never mentioned, so he decided to ask mum about them one day after getting home from school.

'Mum, can I ask you a question?'

She looked at him apprehensively. 'Yes, son?'

'Well, I have been wondering for quite a few years now – at school wherever we have been, all the kids often talk of their grandparents. You know, Nan and Pop, that sort of reference, and they often ask me how old mine are. I also say I haven't a clue as they are back in the "Old Dart", as you refer to England. Why do you not mention them? Are they dead?'

The colour drained from his mother's face. 'Er… well… it's a long story, dear. But I haven't got time to tell you now – lots to do, tea to prepare.'

Lars touched her on the arm; she tried to pull away. 'Why don't you or Dad ever tell me? It is 1962, and I do not think you have ever mentioned any of them – why? Mum, I don't think we have ever had a letter or a card all the time we have been here; well, at least the past five years, since I have taken notice. Are your mother and father still alive? What about Dad's? Or are you both orphans? It seems odd. Come on, now, Mum – what is the truth?'

'We will have a family meeting, dear. I will speak to your father about it when he gets home tonight from the bank, OK?'

'Mum, why do we have to have a meeting for everything? Just tell me – why all the secrets? Come on, Mum – every time I ask a question about England you both just close ranks; I am sick to death of it. Are you hiding something from me? What is going on?'

At around six o'clock, his father got home and called him into the kitchen.

'Now then – what's all this about you asking Mum about your grandparents? Why are you are interested in your family back home all of a sudden, son?'

'It's just at school I often get asked what it was like in England, and who my relations are – do we hear from them? Do they ever come to visit? Have I ever been back to the UK? That sort of thing – and I know nothing, Dad. It's embarrassing at times. Quite a few at school are Pommies as well; they all say they get presents from home when it is their birthdays, Christmas and the like, but we do not ever get letters or cards or anything. I just wondered why. I would love to know more about my past. Dad, you have a funny expression on your face same as Mum had when I asked her; is there some secret you need to tell me?'

'OK, after tea we will sit down and tell you everything, son. You are old enough to know now. It is time you found out the truth about your background, OK?'

'OK. I will be in my room – just give me a shout when tea is ready, please?'

Lars left them alone; he considered listening at the door to see what they had to say. There must be something they were keeping from him.

'Jon, what are we going to say? How much are you going to come out with? We can't tell him we bought him from his auntie, for God's sake. We can't say he has a twin brother somewhere. Oh, why did you have to say that we would go through it with him? Why?'

'Just leave it to me. I will do the talking. You just sit there and act dumb; you are pretty good at that. Just keep nodding and smiling, OK?'

After tea, they all sat around the table in the dining room. 'Right then, son,' said Jon, 'you want to know about your past – what do you want to know? Do you want to take notes while we talk? It may be an idea for future reference if you ever want to find your family tree. Genealogy is the correct name – or where your forefathers came from.'

'OK, good idea, Dad; I will be right back.' Lars shot off to his room to get a notepad and pencil. 'Right, OK – I am ready. Fire away, Dad. Start at the beginning. Why has this not been discussed before? I don't understand.'

CHAPTER 32

LARS
You Were Adopted

'Slow down, Lars; I will start from when you were born. The first thing you should know is you are adopted. Don't look so shocked – we had meant to tell you for years when the appropriate time came; when you started asking questions. Well, that time has come, son; you OK with that so far?'

'Wow, what can I say? I never knew... I had no idea.'

'We adopted you from an orphanage when you were a baby, only a few weeks old. We were told your mother died in childbirth, I am sorry to say, along with the other baby – you had a twin.'

Marjory could not believe what she was hearing, but kept her mouth shut.

'It was also a boy,' Jon went on. 'They were going to call him Leif; both names were taken from their Norwegian background. We were looking to adopt and were next on the list. We do not know anything about your natural parents; we think she was a single mum from Manchester but weren't told any more due to confidentiality rules or something. We were never told about either of the girl's parents, if indeed she had any, so that is why you never had grandparents, as ours passed away many years ago when we were both teenagers before me and your mother met.'

'Why did you not tell me before? Mum – you are not saying much. Why did you not say something before? How did they know it was going to be a boy? What if it had been a girl?'

'We don't know – we were never told. We only found out afterwards.

I suppose they must have had discussions with the poor young woman. It is so sad when something like this happens.'

Marjory looked at Jon, shaking her head.

'But we were so lucky to get you, son; we hope you can forgive us for not telling you sooner.'

'Is that it, then? No more secrets? It's OK, Dad. I understand why you have done it; it's a lot to take in, I suppose. Thank you for being so open and honest now. I love you both, and you know that I have always believed you are my parents – and you still are, for I have never had any other. Mind if I go to my room now, please?'

Lars sat on his bed; his head was spinning, trying to take in all that he had been told. Had his mum and dad's parents died when they were his age, or maybe a bit older? How did his dad have such an excellent education to become a bank manager? He wished he was in England; he could have done some enquiries, but it was a bit hard being 13,000 miles away. However, maybe one day he could go back and find his real grandparents if they were still alive. He needed to find out what orphanage he had been in when his mum and dad found him; there must be more to it than what they had told him. He thought about what Warren had said – that he was lucky to have seen many different places; he was now wondering what he could do.

Two years had flown by, and Lars had done well at school, picking up from where he'd left off in Tamworth. He was now playing under-seventeens for the Seagulls in group 18; he had also made the North Coast Representative team after starring in the Divisional games for the group. At six foot three and fourteen stone and with a quick turn of pace, he was the ideal build for a centre. He had been told that a couple of scouts from Sydney had been at the group games and also most of the Big League clubs were at the North Coast games against Newcastle and Queanbeyan, which is the ACT or Canberra to the outsider. Could he be good enough to get picked up by a Sydney team? It would be a dream come true. His coach, Mick Grogan, at the Seagulls told him once that he did not know how good he was. His actual words were

'Keep going the way you are, Lars, and you will make it pro, son – that's how good I think you are.'

The family was sitting having tea one evening, and Jon said, 'Have you any thoughts on what you intend doing when you leave college? Do you want to go to university?'

'Where did that come from, Dad? I don't even want to go to college; I want to leave as soon as I can, and get a job and earn some money.'

'There is more to life than money, son; you need a good education – you need to get a real job, in commerce or even banking.'

'What, like you? You mean being pushed about from pillar to post, at their beck and call? No, thank you. I have had enough of that life; I want to play footy or travel, maybe go back to the Old Dart and even find my ancestors.'

'No way is any son of mine going to leave school without a proper education, you hear me? You understand?'

'We will see, Dad,' said Lars.

He was now playing for both the under-seventeens teams and the odd game in the first team. The question about what he intended doing when he left school came up again, and this time it was Marjory's turn.

'Have you given any thought to what you are going to do next year when you are seventeen, dear?'

'Yes, Mum – I am leaving and going to look for a job. I fancy being a brickie; it's good money, and everyone is looking for them.'

'Your father won't like that, son; he will put his foot down. No way will he let you do a manual labour job – no way.'

'Mum, it is my life, and I will do as I want, not what he wants, so let's not have any more talks; I have made my mind up.'

'We will have a family meeting tonight when your father gets home. We will see what he has to say about this.'

'You know what happened at the last family meeting. I am a man now, Mum. I will do as I want. I'm sorry if that does not fit in with your plans for me to go to university and become a professional man. I feel the people who do the work on the tools in this country are far better thought of than the pen-pushers and guys who get dressed up in suits and ties. It is not for me, OK? Call a meeting, but don't expect me to be there.'

Later that evening after tea, Jon said, 'Can I have a word, son? I hear you have been talking to your mother about leaving school.'

'Yes, Dad – did Mum tell you what I said?'

'Yes, she did, and...'

'Then there's no need for a meeting. I have made my mind up; it's no good you trying to talk me out of it, no good you upsetting yourself, I am leaving school – end of story. Now can that be it? No more from you or Mum?'

'OK, but I am not happy.'

'Dad, I don't want to fall out with you or Mum over this, but it is what I want. Me – it's my life; just let me do it my way. If I fall flat on my face, then so be it. I promise you this, Dad, I will make you proud of me, believe me. Let me do it my way.'

With that, Lars hugged his father for perhaps the first time in his life. He stepped back, tears in his eyes. 'OK, my boy, I understand.'

Later that year, Lars left school. He had been offered an apprenticeship by one of the sponsors at the Seagulls, and jumped at the chance. He thought they would always want bricklayers and would be a reliable trade to be in; there would still be a demand for them years down the track.

Things were going well. Lars had been playing regular games in the reserve team and had been picked for the first team. He was standing with a group of guys watching the reserve grade before he went into the sheds to get stripped, when a man came over.

'G'day, mate – you Lars Mellows?'

'Yes, I am – why do you ask? Who are you?'

'The name's Jed Jackson – I am chief scout for the St George Dragons.' He put out his hand; Lars took it, and said, 'Hello.'

'We have been watching you for a while, son, and I won't beat about the bush – would you be interested in coming to Sydney and joining the Dragons? There is more to it than you just saying yes; we would have to speak to your parents, and also the Seagulls for you are their property and would require a transfer fee before you can join us.'

Lars thought about his job. 'I am an apprentice bricklayer,' he said. 'How will I go on getting a job there?'

Jed told him not to worry about minor details. 'All that would be sorted out; there are no full-time professional players. The fact is, guys with manual jobs tend to be the better players; they are naturally fit because of the work they do.'

'But I am not eighteen until June. I don't think I am ready for Sydney. Maybe in a year.'

'Lars – think about it, OK?'

CHAPTER 33

LEIF
The Funeral

I went round to see Donna's parents again, and was back in the family's living room. We were just numb. No one was saying anything. What could you say? I had never been in this situation before. Then her father said, 'Leif, you are not a Catholic boy, are you?'

'No, I am Church of England.' I'd nearly said atheist, but it wasn't the right time.

'That is OK; we knew already, although Donna did not tell us. We knew she was so in love with you; she never stopped talking about her new Pommie boyfriend. You do realise a Catholic funeral is a lot more complicated than a Church of England one, don't you? There are lots of things to take into consideration when organising one.'

He went over to a side cupboard and brought back a piece of paper that the priest had brought round. 'Here, take a look; we do not know where to begin. We will organise everything, but we would love you to have an input into it. Is that OK with you, son?'

I took the list from him; it was all foreign to me, which may sound a stupid statement, them being Italian, but I was so pleased that they wanted to include me as part of their family and to call me son. I was humbled when he said it.

'Please, Leif, take the list with you,' said Donna's mother. 'It will give you some idea. If you have any questions, just give us a call, or please come round anytime.'

Glancing at the list in front of me, it seemed quite daunting. It read:

1. The Last Rites
2. The Vigil
3. Catholic Funeral Mass (or Memorial Mass)
4. Dates Funeral Masses are Not Permitted
5. Organ Donation under Catholicism
6. Embalming
7. Catholic Views on Cremation
8. Rite of Committal
9. The Cost of a Catholic Funeral
10. Finding Catholic Funeral Directors

'Donna will not be cremated,' she added. 'Her body will be interred at our local church, the one she has attended since she was small.'

They held a vigil the evening before the funeral; close family, which included me, and friends gathered at their home to say prayers and remember Donna as she was.

The next day arrived, and it was as terrible as I thought it would be. I was invited to travel in the family cars following the hearse to the church; it was unbearable moving along slowly behind, when all I could see was the coffin, knowing that she was in there, knowing that I would never be able to feel her in my arms, smell her, touch her, listen to her go on and on about just about everything. It seemed that we would never get to the church. But when we did arrive, I wished I could go round again for I knew it was getting to that moment – the dreadful moment when I would see the body being lowered into the ground.

Oh, my god, how I loved that girl. Oh, how I wished we had been married. She would have been mine; she might never have gone to her mates – she might still be alive with me, her husband, the man who wanted to look after her for the rest of her life. Why did it happen?

I opened my eyes, and the car had stopped. There were hundreds of people there, people I had not seen, never mind met; all of them come to pay their respects to Donna.

The service seemed to last forever, and it was conducted in Italian, which was a family ritual. The book they gave us as we entered the church had her photograph on the front, the same one her mother had given me, and it also had the service laid out in both Italian and English so that everyone knew what was going on as they worked through it.

Her father said the eulogy and her brother Fabrizio, whom I did not even know existed, was there; he had flown in from the USA. By the look of him, he was older than Donna by quite a few years. He said a few words first in Italian then in English, which I thought was a nice gesture; he put it over well.

After the ceremony, the family, including me, was asked to remain in the church as we would go out after the mass and follow the cortège to the graveside for the actual burial.

That was the hardest thing I had ever done, as the priest said what he had to say, then we were then handed a box with soil in it and asked to throw some down on to the coffin along with the single roses we were all carrying. This was the end. I did not want to leave her; I felt like throwing myself on to the coffin. I know it was stupid, but I had this feeling she was calling me to join her. Fabrizio took my hand and said, 'Vieni, Leif, è finita – lei è a pace' – 'Come, Leif, it is over – she is at peace.' He hugged me and kissed me on both cheeks, and I answered him with 'Grazie, Fabrizio.' We walked out of the church; most of the guests had gone.

There was no going back to the local pub or club for a drink; everyone went home. We were taken back to their house where my Ute was. I was asked if I wanted to stay the night, but I declined the offer. They told me not to stop coming to see them, which I thought was a bit odd, as I had not seen a lot of them before, but I said I would, and I was made to promise such. Apparently, Leanne, Donna's friend, was the last person to see her alive before the accident, which in the cold light of day seemed odd. I needed to speak with Leanne to find out what happened that day, and if she knew anything that could piece together Donna's final hours alive. I did not even know her full name; only that they lived on a large farm outside Perth near the City of Swan, one of Perth's western suburbs.

I had lost a lot of time off work, but Doug had told me to take as much time as I needed. Whenever I had rung him to say I wasn't ready for work, 'No worries, mate' was his answer; he had been like a brother to me over this ordeal and I could not thank him enough.

Next day I went for a ride out to see if I could find Leanne, which would be like looking for a needle in a haystack as I had not contacted Donna's parents; they were in enough pain without me putting any more worry on them.

I called at the library on my way just to say hello and thank everyone one there for their support. I was talking to one of the girls, Tammy, and happened to mention Leanne. 'Oh, Leanne Thomas, you mean; I know her. I went to school with her and Donna.'

'Do you know her address, by any chance?'

'No, sorry, I don't, but if you call in at the Railway Hotel when you get there, just ask about the Thomas property; they will be sure to know. Everyone knows everyone in those small places.'

It took me about an hour to find the property, having been to the pub. People there knew the Thomases as the father Pete drank in there quite regularly. I pulled up outside the house, and as I got out of the Ute, a girl came out.

'Hello, Leif – sorry I missed you at the funeral. It was a great send-off for her, wasn't it?'

She did not seem that upset, which seemed odd; I thought that she and Donna had been closer than that.

'Can I talk to you, Leanne? I am trying to put together Donna's last day. I think you might be able to help me?'

'What you mean? What are you talking about? What do you think I should know?'

She seemed to be getting a bit worked up and not wanting to say much.

'OK, Leanne – I don't want to upset you.' I touched her arm, and she pulled away as if an electric shock had hit her.

'Hey, what's wrong?'

'Nothing – what could be wrong?'

Something did not fit. I was not sure what Leanne was not telling me, but I intended to find out.

I was there about half an hour trying to discover what was eating into Leanne, then suddenly she burst into tears. I put my arm around her shoulders, and she let me this time; she rested her head against my chest, and I just let her cry.

'I promised, Leif,' she said. 'I promised I would not tell anyone.'

'Tell them what?'

'I can't, Leif, please – don't ask me, please.' The tears started streaming; she was in a hell of a state. I waited once again for her to calm down.

'Is it something I should know? Does it concern me, Leanne? Is it about me?'

Or was there something about Donna she had not told me?

'Leanne, I need to know – please?'

'You mean you did not know about her?'

I was still holding her in my arms. 'Did I not know about what?'

'She was pregnant. She was having your baby, Leif. I was sworn to secrecy, but I assumed you already knew. She was so worried about how she was going to tell her parents and how they would react to the news.'

I let go of her. I could not believe what I was hearing. Why, oh why, didn't Donna tell me? Was she afraid of my reaction? All I could think of was my poor Donna keeping the secret to herself and the turmoil she would have been going through.

'Leanne, how was she when she left here on the day of the crash? Was she OK?'

'She was upset. She had broken down and cried a lot after she had told me the news, but seemed OK when we had talked about what she was going to tell her parents. Donna seemed settled, as if her mind was made up. That is what she said; she knew what she had to do. It was funny; she did something she did not usually do – she thanked me for listening to her and made me promise not to tell anyone, then she kissed me and said, "Goodbye, Leanne, I love you so much," then left.'

No one will ever know what happened after that. Had she been crying and could not see where she was going, or did she drive straight at the truck on the wrong side of the road? I kept it to myself and never did tell her parents; I asked Leanne to honour her final promise to Donna, and not tell anyone.

'The secret will go to my grave with me,' Leanne said as I got up to leave.

I moved out of my unit – it held too many memories – and stayed with Doug for another six months after Donna had died, but I was still not over her death. I was on the piss more, not eating, not looking after myself. My main worry was the fact that Leanne held the key to everything. If she were to tell the truth about Donna being pregnant I was a dead man. No way would the 'The Family' let me live, knowing that I had not only fucked their only daughter, but that I knew she was pregnant, and not told them.

I went in to see Doug one morning. I told him I had decided to get away from Perth, and away from Western Australia; it was too dangerous to stay. I made an excuse that there were too many memories there, and all that crap.

Doug understood. He was not happy, but thanked me for all I had done for him in the nearly four years with his company. He tried to talk me into staying, saying he was planning to make me a director with shares in the company; he even offered me more money, which was unreal considering I had had an annual increase of 10% plus the odd brown envelope when we had made a good profit on one or two of the projects we had undertaken. But I had decided there was more to life than money.

One of the main reasons for wanting to get away was Leanne – I did not trust her. I didn't think she had told me the whole truth about her relationship with Donna when they were at school.

I had been back to see Tammy at the library after meeting Leanne, and she asked how she was. I told her what I thought about her not being too cut up about Donna's death. Tammy looked surprised, and then said, 'She did not mention her and Donna being lovers, then?'

Now, talk about a shock. 'Fucking lovers… what you mean, like lesbian lovers?'

'Oh, yes, for about four years, I think. They started in their early teens and lasted quite a while, I believe. There were quite a few girls that way inclined, for it was a costly boarding school near Melbourne called Lady Madonna's All-Girls College.'

My mind went back to our club at Boulevard, but that was no comparison to this. I mean, we did it for fun; they did it because they were in love with each other.

'They were very, very close; it was a closed shop there in its little world. I believe that they slept together every night; well, I know they did. When the lights went out, you could hear girls scurrying from one bed to another; the noises through the night were unreal – giggling interrupted by the odd moan and odd, "Oh, yes". And before you ask – no, I was not into it. I tried it, yes, but I did not like it. I prefer men – always have done. To be fair I was a bit gutted when Donna got off with you, mate; thought I wouldn't mind going out with you myself, but now I am happily married, babe, so you are too late. Anyway, I felt that Donna and Leanne had grown out of it over the years, but there had been rumours that it was back on between them just before you hit the scene. It thought no more of it when she started seeing you regularly.'

I did not know what to say. Talk about not knowing the one you love; but once again, I learned another thing about life – bisexual women.

'So the story goes,' Tammy went on, 'when they left school and came back to Perth they still saw each other regularly; there was talk of them moving in together. One of my friends told me that Leanne talked about getting pregnant so that they could have a child to bring up as their own. Could you believe that, mate? I know she had a couple of boyfriends who were shagging her; one of them was my hubby before I met him. In those days, he was in a biker gang, and never took precautions. He said she was on the pill and was not that good a root, mind, so he reckons. She was about seventeen at the time, I think.'

She couldn't have done that, could she? I couldn't believe that she had lined me up to be a father of a child for her and Leanne and then ditch me. Why had it taken three years to get pregnant? Or had the light come on again with Leanne? Were they back together and was the stranger in town just the thing they were looking for? Leanne could not have kids, or so it seemed; not for want of trying, according to Tammy.

Or had Donna gone off women and fallen in love with me once she had discovered what sex with a man was like? But why go and see Leanne? Was it to tell her she was staying with me and their affair was over? I didn't know any of the answers; all I knew is I had to get away before the shit hit the fan.

I had saved up quite a few quid with being on a fair wage and my rent being low; it had been hard work, but still, I had loved every minute of it. I was leaving Perry Industrial Engineering in a better state than when I joined them. I had picked up my rugby career, finishing up top try scorer and captain of the Roosters.

I was looking for a new start and where better than Sydney NSW? But first, I needed a holiday. I would get the train across to Sydney via Adelaide; it would be a bit more expensive than flying, but I figured I may never do it again. I booked my tickets said my goodbyes to everyone in Fremantle.

Doug told me to come back if I changed my mind; there would always be a job for me. But no – I was off. I'd made my decision and was sticking to it this time.

I had a great time on the Indian Pacific; it took three days in all but was well worth the trip. I had booked a first-class sleeper with a cabin to myself. We left the East Perth Station heading for the Eastern Goldfields then to Kalgoorlie, before heading along the world's longest straight railway track – 297 miles across the Nullabor Plain to Port Augusta – and later on to Crystal Brook. People going to Adelaide had to change at Port Pirie, we then headed for Broken Hill and, finally, we landed in Sydney on Friday, June 27, 1975 – my birthday. I was now twenty-nine.

CHAPTER 34

LARS
St George

L ars was bubbling. Why St George? They were the biggest club in Sydney, for they had won every premiership to date since 1956, which was ten years without defeat, and they wanted him to join them. He could not believe it could be happening.

'Let's take it one step at a time, OK; we will look after everything,' said Jed. He asked Lars to ask his parents if he could come and have a word with them, as he was in the area for a couple of weeks, and he gave Lars his business card. Lars took it and looked at the St George emblem and the words, "Jed Jackson, Head of Recruitment" with a contact number. Jed had written his hotel number on the back to enable Lars to leave a message should he need to contact him. Lars could not wait to get home to tell his parents about St George.

After the game, Seagulls winning 36-2, Lars scoring a hat trick and being named man of the match, the coach walked over to him. 'Lars, can I have a word mate – in private, OK? I saw you talking to the St George guy before the game. Can I ask what he had to say? Did he approach you about going to Sydney, by any chance?' Lars did not reply. 'If he did, he was out of order; he should ask the club for permission to talk to you.'

Lars did not know what to say; should he tell the coach the truth and maybe blow his chance out of the water, or just bend the truth a little? He chose the latter option. 'Oh, him – he asked how I was and was I happy here playing for the Seagulls; he did congratulate me on the way

I was playing and said he had heard I was the star man down here, but never made any remarks about leaving. Why do you ask?'

'Look, Lars, this is serious stuff. If he did approach you in any way, he was out of order. He should have asked the club for permission to talk to with you; the club would take it very badly if another party had approached one of their players, as it is totally against the rules.'

'No, Mick, nothing like that happened; we just chatted, that's all.'

Lars did not know what to say, so he just lied.

When he got home, he went straight to his room; he lay on his bed looking at the card had had been given, dreaming of Kogarah Oval and being a Dragon. They were no doubt the best team in the competition and had been since 1954. They had never been beaten at Kogarah in twelve seasons, until 1965; they had only had five tries scored against them in eleven Grand Finals. He had to tell his mum and dad, but when? Now? Or leave it until it was definite? His head was in a spin. Why me, he kept asking himself. Others had done it. He was now worried about how to sort this mess out, as he had blatantly lied to Mick.

He decided to give Mr Jackson a call and tell him he was very interested in going south to Sydney. 'Hello, Mr Jackson, it's Lars – Lars Mellows from Tweed Heads; we spoke yesterday.'

'Oh, hi, son – what can I do for you? Have you been thinking about what I said yesterday? You interested in joining the Dragons?'

'I am not sure; my coach told me there could be trouble if they found out that you had approached me without talking to them first. I also told lies to cover for you if it fell through – what would happen to me?'

'So, you want to come? Have you told your parents yet, or your employers?'

'No, I haven't, as I'm not sure of what the procedure is from now on. I did not want to go telling them if there is no chance of it happening.'

'If you are sure, I can approach your club and ask them for permission to speak with you. I need to put my recommendations to the Dragons, for they need to sanction any details regarding organising employment as an apprentice bricklayer, as well as accommodation, and also how much they would be willing to pay as a transfer fee, as you are a Seagulls player. There should be no problem there; it happens all the time. They also need to contact your current employer to see if they will release you and, should things not work out, be willing to take you back on at a later date. We tend not to have any problems in the area of negotiations. It's good for public relations. There is a lot to do, but you must be 100% certain you want to make a move. First of all, tell your parents that you have decided you want to be a top-grade rugby league player, OK? Just leave it to me. I will ask you once again – are you positive about this decision to join the Dragons? Once the wheels are rolling, they don't want you changing your mind; are you OK with that?'

Lars thought for a minute and said, 'Yes, I am sure. How can I tell Mum and Dad if you haven't approached me yet?'

'OK, give me your phone number. I will ring the same time as I contact your club. When is the best time to catch them in?'

'It is best on an evening around 6pm any day; they don't do much. They are not into going into pubs or clubs; they mostly stay at home either reading or watching TV.'

'OK, no worries; I will ring them tomorrow night and will ring the chairman of Seagulls at the same time; I have his number.'

CHAPTER 35

LARS
A Dragon

J ed rang Lars's parents the following evening.

'Hello, Jon Mellows here – how can I help?'

'G'day, Jon – it's Jed Jackson. I am the head scout for the St George rugby league club in Sydney. I was hoping I could have a word with you; we have been watching your son for quite a few years now, going back to his junior years with West Tamworth, and we feel that we could help him in his development as a footy player.'

'Thank you for calling, Jed, and being so honest with us, but no – he won't be joining you. He has a good job here in Tweed Heads, and I would not let him give up his trade to go and be a footballer, as you Australians call them. Lars is too young to be leaving home; he is only eighteen; well, nearly nineteen. He only has two years to go, and he will be a tradesman. Sorry, but no, thank you.'

'Jon, may I call round and discuss what we can offer Lars? I hope you will meet me and let me explain the way we work.'

'Just a moment please; I will ask his mother; I won't keep you.'

There was a silence, but Jed could hear voices; one of them being Lars, and he was quite vocal. He heard something like, 'No chance! I am going whether you like it or not!' Then Jon came back.

'OK, Jed – Marjory has agreed to meet up; when would you like to come?'

'Tomorrow – is that any good? Around six; I am back in Sydney the following day so that would be great for me.'

'OK, tomorrow is good for us, Jed. I look forward to meeting you. Goodbye.'

The following night Jed was at Lars's home bang on six o'clock. He rang the doorbell, waited a few minutes, and Lars opened the door.

'G'day mate,' said Jed. 'Your mum and dad in? Any problems?' Then he whispered, 'Is everything OK?'

'Yes – they have a list of questions for you, but I will let them ask you; they might be warming to the idea, I hope?'

'You sure that's not just wishful thinking? Last night I heard you say something like, "no chance – I am going whether you like it or not".'

'Yes, I know, but I worked on them after Dad had spoken to you and I just need you to sell the Dragons to them. I'm still their baby and have never been away from them. I can understand how they are feeling, but it's not the end of the Earth, is it?'

We walked into the lounge room. Jon stood up to shake Jed's hand. 'Thank you for coming; this my wife, Marjory.'

'G'day, Marjory, pleased to meet you; thank you for inviting me to your home.'

'Right then, Jed,' said Jon, 'so you want to take our son away from us to play football in Sydney, do you?'

'Jon, we don't look at it in quite those terms. Yes, we want him to come live in Sydney, as St George is in the city. We play in the ARL competition, which is the highest, most competitive sport in the world and St George is – well, we feel it is – the best club in that competition. We attract the best players from around the world, and we pay them highly for their services.'

'Excellent – but Lars is only a boy. How do we know he will be well looked after? He has never lived on his own since he was born. Lars has never had to feed himself, buy his own clothes, nothing – he has relied on us, his parents, to look after him.'

'Jon, we bring to the club young boys from all over the country, mostly NSW and Queensland, but we do have one boy from Darwin in the Northern Territory. We have several families that take in our young men and sometimes older guys who have no ties; they move in rather than fend for themselves. The families we use are all long-term Dragons fans; some of them are retired people who have big homes with spare bedrooms and their children have flown the nest, giving them an income. We pay all costs and the boys are treated like sons – these families do all the washing, cooking – everything you would do for Lars, Marjory.'

She gave Lars a tender look, and smiled and nodded, smiling at Jed as well.

'I know that one of our families will have a vacancy at the end of this season. One of the boys living with them is getting married. He has already put a deposit on a house.'

'There are three guys already there and she has four spare rooms; the others are from Wauchope, which is in the mid-north coast – that's Karl Higgins, a front-rower; Grubby O'Neil, a winger from Ipswich in Queensland, and Ben Lismore from Taree – he is a hooker. So, you see they are from far and wide.'

'What about his job, Jed? He is into his apprenticeship as a bricklayer, as I told you. I don't want him throwing that away.'

'No problem there, Jon. I have spoken to our recruitment manager at Kogarah, and he said there would be no problem getting a company. I rang him first thing this morning, and he got back to me this arvo, telling me he had already got one of the club's main sponsors to offer Lars a job. Brickies are like the proverbial rocking horse shit – excuse the language, Marjory – no problems there.'

'Am I right in saying that you will have to pay a transfer fee to the Seagulls to sign Lars on because he plays for them?'

'Yes, you are right, but it is only a nominal sum, nothing to worry about. We also encourage the boys, should they not make the grade – and some don't for one reason or another – to return to their original club; the Seagulls in Lars's case.'

'What about insurance if he gets injured? How does he get paid if he is off work, or if he gets hurt and can't play again?'

'Jon, do you have to think like that? He won't get hurt, will you Lars,' chipped in Marjory.

'Of course, with a high-collision sport like rugby league, players do get injured. We have them insured and also pay any loss of income while they are off work, and I will point out that the company we have Lars lined up with is very good to its employees. They have to be to keep them; as I said earlier, bricklayers are in demand in Sydney. Also, he would not have a lot of travelling to do as most of their work is in the Kogarah and Sutherland shires area. I must point out we do not just take anyone; we sometimes ask players to come to the following pre-season and play a few trial games to prove themselves, but we also take pride in our recruitment systems, and as I said we have monitored Lars from afar. We have asked the right questions from his current coach and the scouts in this area, for we have scouts in every division in NSW and Queensland and there are twenty-eight of them; we search high and low to bring in the best of the best. I can promise you that no other club will look after Lars like the Dragons will. With regards to payments, I know you, as a bank manager, Jon; you will be thinking of the monitory side of things. He will be well looked after. I am not at liberty to discuss those things just yet but, believe me, we are one of the best clubs in Sydney; you don't win eleven premierships on the run by paying peanuts. Is there anything else you would like to know or questions I can answer? Marjory, have you anything you would like to know? Any worries you may have?'

'No, Jed, I think you have covered everything we had listed. It will be a sad day when Lars leaves us; we don't want him to leave home, but the youngsters must leave the nest one day, that is for sure. We just didn't think it would be so soon. Can you give us a while to discuss it, Jed, please?'

'Yes, no worries. You do not have to make a decision tonight, but we would like to know as soon as you can. We do have other targets on our list to add to our roster, but Lars is high on the list.'

'Yes, Jed – do you mind giving us say an hour to talk about it? Or what time are you leaving tomorrow to go back south?'

'I am leaving around seven-thirty; I have to stop at Coffs Harbour on the way down for an hour or so; we have a scout in the Mid North Coast I need to see.'

'An answer tonight would suit you better, then?'

'Yes, to be honest, it would. I will nip up the hotel for an hour and come back if that is OK?'

'Thank you, Jed, we appreciate that.'

Jed left the house, got in his car, and drove around the block and parked up.

'Well, Dad, what do you think? Can I go? I am going anyway, but would love it if you and Mum let me leave on good terms with your blessings, rather than any bad feeling between us. It is too good to knock back. Dad, Mum – talk to me.'

'Lars, will you give us a few minutes on our own, please? Just go up to your room for ten minutes?'

'OK, Mum.' Lars left them alone.

'Jon, I think he should go. As Lars says, the chance may never come again and if we said no, he would never forgive us. I do not know anything about football but the women at the bowling club say Lars is a great player; he is the team's star. Even in first grade, he is far above the rest of the players. We would be doing him an injustice if we try to get him to stay in Tweed Heads. He has followed us around ever since he was a boy moving from town to town; now it's our turn to repay that. I think we should give him our blessing.'

'Yes, you are right; I will call him. Lars, can you hear me? Can you come down, please?' Jon shouted.

Lars came into the lounge, not sure what the outcome would be.

Marjory stood up alongside Jon. 'Well, son, we have come to our decision, and you have our blessing, son. You go and fulfil your dreams. We want you to go to the Dragons. We love you so much, and you have done right by us over the years. I know there have been times when you did not want to leave, but we have dragged you away, all because of my job with the bank. Go, son, we will always love you – make us proud.'

'Thanks, Dad – oh fuck… thank you.'

'Mind your language, son; you aren't in Sydney yet.'

'Oh, sorry, Mum. Oh, thank you, thank you. I love you both so much – thank you.'

CHAPTER 36

LARS

Sydney at Last

Lars arrived in Sydney in January 1964. He was picked up at the station by Jed Jackson, the guy who had organised his signing from the Seagulls. It had all gone smoothly; the Dragons had paid a transfer fee that had never been publicly disclosed. Even Lars did not know what it was. He had asked Jed but he was told that it was not talked about; the club felt that if younger players were never told, there was never any extra pressure on them – everyone was equal.

Lars was taken round to Mr and Mrs Williamson's house, where he would be staying; it was in Kogarah, not far from the ground.

'Mrs Williamson, this is Lars, your new inmate. We hope you will look after him. You may need to get some more tucker in, by the size of him; he's a bit smaller than Freddie, who has just left you, eh?'

'Too right, Jed – he is a bloody giant. G'day, Lars, and welcome to your new home, mate. My name's Becky and the old fella is Marty; he is out just at the moment, but he won't be long. Come on in, let's get you settled.'

'Thank you, Mrs Williamson.'

'Becky – we don't have that shit here, son, it's Becky. Come on – want a drink or something to eat? Dinner is not until six-thirty, when the rest of the boys get in from work. Did Jed explain the training times to you? They are training three nights a week at present and Saturday mornings, but I suppose one of the coaches will be down to see you sometime today. Now, this is your room; we don't have guys sharing here, we have enough room to give you all one each. The bathroom is across there on the landing – here you are; it faces the front of the house. The road may be a bit noisy but you will get used to that. When do you start work? Have they got you fixed up with a job yet? They usually do; bloody smart people down there, mate. You have chosen the right club, that's for sure. Mind, we might be a bit biased; we've been Dragons supporters for, bloody hell, must be fifty years or more. I'm going on; tell me to stop yapping, Lars, they all do.'

'That's OK, Becky, I don't mind. I am going to see two companies tomorrow about a job. One is Home Bricks Builders and the other is Stockwell's Builders – they are both willing to take me on as an apprentice to finish my time.'

'What do you do for a quid, Lars?'

'I am a brickie in my third year.'

'Dardy – good trade to have; scarce as hen's teeth, mate. That's a bloody job for life. Right, I will leave you in peace. Come down when you are ready, and I will put the jug on. I have some cakes in the oven – be nice with a sanger. Got some corned beef if you fancy one?'

'No thanks, Becky, not right now; might have a bit of a snooze, if that's OK?'

'No worries, darl, you must be buggered after travelling all that way. You get your head down. I'll give you a call when dinner is on.'

Lars nodded off, until he was woken by footsteps outside the room, and two guys talking and laughing. He had a quick shower and went downstairs. The house was an old brick-built two-storey colonial-style place with a veranda all the way around, as well as a massive garden and a pool. There was no air-conditioning but big fans in every room.

Marty was home now, and he was sitting in a rocking chair on the veranda with a stubby in his hand. G'day mate – you must be the new guy. Lars, isn't it?'

'Yes – I guess you must be Marty. Pleased to meet you; thank you for letting me stay with you.'

'No worries, mate. Becky told you the house rules, I assume?'

'No, she never mentioned anything.'

'Not bloody surprised – there are none. Just behave; no bother or you're out on your ear OK?' He then started laughing. 'No worries, mate – only taking the piss; you will get used to me.'

With that the other two guys he had heard earlier – who turned out to be Ben Lismore and Grubby O'Neil – came down along with Karl, who was a typical front-rower, built like the proverbial brick dunny. Now, Lars was big, but this guy was massive.

'G'day, guys – come and meet your new Dragon. This is Lars; he plays centre. Bloody big enough to join you in the pack, Karl.'

We all introduced ourselves, and grabbed a drink and went out and sat around a table in the back garden near the pool.

'Welcome to the Dragon's den, Lars – you have joined the slave trade, mate, until they want to be shut of you. Still, you could have picked a worse outfit. I have been here three seasons now, just got into first grade and I love it. The game is the easy part of the week; training is bloody hard, but after a while, you get used to it. I've never been so fit in my life.'

'Is it that bad, Karl? The training, I mean.'

'My facking oath, mate, but I believe it is like that at every club in Sydney and the pre-season sorts out the bludgers from the genuine guys. I for one love it; I must be a bit of a masochist – I just love the pain,' he laughed.

'I bloody hate it,' said Grubby. 'Mind, I have never been a lover of training even at my old club up in Ipswich; that was hard enough. But when I got here, jeez, it just about rooted me. Now that bastard over there –' he pointed at Ben. 'He thrives on it. Mind, all bloody rakes are wrong in the facking head, or they would never put their heads in a scrum.'

'Me, wrong in the facking head?' said Ben. 'We all are for putting ourselves through it, but you just have to if you wanna be a star and get big money. There is one thing for sure with this outfit; you do the right thing by them, they will do it for you. Look at Raper and Changa, and the Magic Dragon Gasnier, they must be on megabucks – we must try and get to their standards. Anyways, what do you do for a quid, Lars?'

'I am a brickie – still an apprentice; got two interviews tomorrow.'

'Oh right, who with? I am working for Home Bricks Builders, not a bad outfit.'

'That is one of them; the other is Stockwell's Builders.'

'Go with them, mate – Stockwell's were chock-a-block when I came down, so I got settled in with HBB and just never bothered to move, but they reckon that other mob are one of the best in Sydney.'

'So you would pick them?'

'My bloody oath I would; fair dinkum, they are the best. But if you do join them, you earn your money. The guys are flat out like a lizard drinking, all bloody day, in all weathers.'

'Be no good for me,' said Karl. 'Out in that bloody sun all day – fack that for a game; prefer indoors in the shop.'

'What do you do, Karl?'

'Boilermaker mate, general hand; I work for a steel fabricator over in Matraville. Been there three years. It does for me, sat on my ass, with my head in a bucket; no pressure, spot on.'

'Before you ask mate, I am a plumber,' said Grubby. 'Work for a local guy, love it –wouldn't swap it for the world. No heavy lifting, nothing too bloody strenuous; an easy life, that's all I want. All the exercise I need is at training and playing footy, and the odd Sheila under me,' he said, winking and touching his nose.

'You will find out tomorrow night how bloody hard it is,' said Ben, 'but don't let us put you off, Lars. You will love it once you get into it. You will hate the coach and the trainers with a vengeance, but it's all for your own good because if you don't do it, you will be on the next train back to Tweed Heads, mate, that is for sure.'

The next morning Lars was up for breakfast around seven; the guys had already gone off to work. One of the Dragons' personnel people, Mike, was picking him up at eight to take him for the interviews; they were due at Home Bricks Builders first, then Stockwell's at eleven. Mike arrived on time and they set off for HBB's offices just outside Kogarah. Lars had a good chat with the company's owner, Peter Williams. He gave Lars the impression he was doing him a favour by employing him just because he was playing for the Dragons.

They arrived early at Stockwell's office, where they were offered a drink in the office cafeteria; it was a nice gesture, which impressed Lars. Bang on eleven, the boss arrived, 'G'day, you must be Lars. Pleased to meet you, son – welcome to Dragons country.' It was a completely different approach from the other guy at HBB. 'I am Ron Stockwell,' he said, and put out his hand. 'I am the owner of the company; come on into my office – we need to chat. You need any more drinks or anything? No? OK, come on then.'

On entering his office, it was clear to Lars that Ron was a Dragons fan; there were photographs all over the walls going back years. Lars stopped to look at them in amazement. 'I take it you follow the Dragons, then, Ron?'

'My bloody oath, mate – have been going since I was a kid. My old man followed them and, going back to my grandfather, he barracked for the Red V. Anyway, let's talk about you; why did you join the club?' He was far more interested in how Lars started playing back in Eden, and his life in Tamworth – anything but work.

'Well, son, suppose we better talk about your position here. We are quite willing to take you on as an apprentice to finish your time with us and then hopefully keep you on for as long as you want to stay. Now I know that may sound a bit blasé, but we look after our men – for if they are a load of bludgers, I don't make money. Then I am not a happy man. I am not a slave driver; I do not ask my men to do anything I would not do. We offer a fair day's pay for a fair day's work. Don't take the piss out of Ron and I won't take the piss out of you; that understood?'

Lars nodded. 'Yes, Ron,' was all he could manage to say.

'Good, good – as long as we understand each other. Then, in that case, I would like to ask you if you would join my merry band.' Ron put out his hand again. 'Welcome to Stockwell's. Now here's the bit I don't like having to tell you – how much I am going to pay you, so I get my accounts person to come in and go through the figures.' He picked up the phone. 'Oh, hi, Jean, can you come in and bring Lars Mellows' file with you, please? Yes – that is the one, the apprentice we are taking on. Yes, OK, right away. Jean will go through it all with you. It's all beyond me. So that's that done – I have to go out now. Jean will fill you in on where you will be working, and all that dreary stuff. Catch you later, son.'

Lars was gobsmacked; Ron he was a whirlwind – footy and Drag-ons-mad. What a great guy, he thought; how lucky he was to get a job with him.

A few minutes later a lady came in the room, with sleek, short blonde hair. 'G'day, Lars. I am Jean Atkins, the accounts person for the company. I deal with wages, etc. If you want to know anything, just see me, OK?'

They went through the payment terms; Lars would be on more than he was getting in Tweed Heads, plus they paid a company bonus on profits made every Christmas, so he had just started at the right time. Jean said it had averaged a month's salary or four weeks' average of a tradesman's wage. Lars would be working in gangs of brickies, and once up to speed, he would be on the same bonus payment as them. He had already been doing that in his last job, but after what Ben had told him he was a bit worried about whether he would be quick enough, but only time would tell. He was due to start work the following Monday on a new subdivision outside of Kogarah, and would be picked up at the top of his street by one of the other guys on site who lived close – Mario, a New Australian guy.

CHAPTER 37

LEIF
Another State

It was July 1975 and winter in NSW – bloody cold and lots of rain about, not the best for holidays, and once again I was starting a new chapter in my life. I was out of work but had a few quid in my pocket, so I was not that bothered about what I did or where I did it. I intended to see some of the city before I looked for work anyway.

I did all the tourist things for a couple of weeks. I had booked a seedy little hotel in the Kings Cross area of the city, Sydney's answer to London's Soho, with lots of bars, clubs, pubs and ladies of the night – which suited me. I was not looking for a long-term relationship; just a one-night stand would do nicely, thank you. Quite a few parties were going on in the pubs around the area, with hen parties and lots of girls just out for a good time.

Chinatown was also an excellent place to pick up girls on an evening, and at the time Sydney was awash with Asian girls – Thai, Chinese, Korean, Japanese, Philippine, Singaporean – you name them, they were there for the taking. I had been in Sydney a few weeks and had tried most of what there was to offer. I found that the Thais were the best in bed, and the Chinese a bit too regimental – but the Singapore girls were the best-looking of the lot.

One of them was stunning; her father was British and mother from Singapore. She was at university in Sydney training to be a doctor. Leia Tan was her name, and we met in a bar in the Rocks area of the city.

I met her in the Fortune of War, one of the oldest pubs in the town, and she was on a girls-only night. There was six of them, all from Singapore, and they were sitting at a table near me. As I was alone, they asked if they could take the two chairs near me to go around their table; it was a chance to start chatting to the one sitting nearest me, who was Leia, although I did not know her name at the time. Anyway, we talked, and she turned her chair to join my table, which I did not object to one little bit.

She was beautiful – really gorgeous. It was her eyes that did it for me: they were almost jet-black. They were mesmerising me. What was also a hell of a turn-on was her long black hair almost down to her waist, against her pale skin. We chatted for ages and I was gutted when the other girls said they were going to another bar before heading to a party, as one of them was going back to Singapore for she had finished her studies in Australia.

Leia wrote something on the back of a beer mat and gave it to me, saying, 'This is where the party is at; please come – be there around eleven, OK?'

I read the note; it was not far from the hotel I had moved to, which was more of an apartment hotel; not five-star but a bit better than the first one.

I had nothing to lose. I had a few more beers in the Fortune then headed back towards the Cross, about half an hour's walk. It was not a bad night and I could stop off en route at a few bars on the way, for the party was at some accommodation near St Vincent's Hospital.

Leia was at the Garvan Institute of Medical Science studying to be a researcher; she must have had a hell of a brain to get into that place as it was a small research department of the hospital.

After a while looking for the house, I turned the corner, and there it was; I knew that must be the party, as it was bouncing. I had picked up a bottle of Bundaberg Rum from a pub along the way as I did not want to turn up empty-handed. I had grown to like this stuff; it was not quite the single malt but a lot cheaper and had the same effect.

No one questioned another stranger joining in the party fun, especially if he was fully loaded. I spotted Leia over in the corner with a couple of guys; she looked as if she had had a few too many. I worked my way over to her, and she spotted me. 'Hiya, Leify baby, you found us then?'

'Yes, sorry I am late, babe. Hi, guys – see you already met my girl-friend, Leia?' They took one look at me – six-four, fifteen stone – and decided they had gone off her all of a sudden.

'Oh, I did not realise I was your girlfriend – when did that happen?'

'First time I saw you, Leia, that's when.'

I found out that the Aussie birds never really got what we Brits call 'chatted up'; a bit of flattery got you everywhere.

'Sounds good to me,' she said as she staggered into my arms. She had had enough drink, so I walked and carried her all at the same time out of the house and stood her against the wall outside. It was not far to my hotel but too far to walk with her, so I hailed a passing cab. We got back to my place. There was no night porter, as we had an outside door key to let ourselves in. I brought her to the lift, and she was still half awake, so I managed to get her into the flat, and sat her on the sofa. I went to make some coffee, and when I came back she was fast asleep, so I picked her up and carried her to bed. I undressed her, but left her bra and panties on. I could not help but just look at her body lying on my bed, half naked – it was a sight to behold; she was even better than I had hoped. My god, she was awesome. I put the covers over her and went to sleep on the sofa, which was a bit short for me but I managed to get a decent night's sleep.

I woke up as the sun was shining through the blinds, and my eyes would not focus, but my nose was working OK; the first thing I smelt was coffee brewing. I got up, and did the usual things a guy does when he first wakes up – scratches his balls and takes a leak. Then I saw her sitting in the window – that classic look, wearing one of my shirts. She had watched too many old movies; all she needed was a lit cigarette.

'Hi,' she said.

'Morning – how are you this beautiful day?'

.She just giggled as girls do, and said, 'Thank you, Leif. You could have done anything to me last night, and I would not have known.'

'If you weren't awake to enjoy me, why bother?'

She blushed; and looked to the floor; then she bit her bottom lip. She was so sexy.

I went over to the stove. 'Coffee ready – want some?'

She nodded, and swung those long legs off the window ledge and stood up. Wow – she was still at least five-eight in bare feet, and what bare feet. My shirt was only fastened with a couple of buttons and was ten sizes too big for her, but she still looked good.

She was sitting on the sofa when I came back with the coffee. I poured out the drinks. 'Milk, sugar?'

'Please,' she said.

I sat down beside her; all I had on was footy shorts and a vest.

'Leif, can I ask you a question? Why did you not try and have sex with me last night? Most men would have taken advantage of me.'

'Why did you come back to my place? Or didn't you know you were coming back here – were you that drunk?'

'I did not realise until this morning where I was or who I was with. I had got up in the night and seen you asleep on the sofa and went back to bed.'

'So you weren't worried I would try it on while you were asleep or try to wake you up?'

'No, I trusted you. I think you would have tried when you undressed me – it was you who undressed me, wasn't it?'

'Yes, I had that pleasure; it was me and enjoyed every minute of it.' I laughed, and she bit her bottom lip again, which was such a turn-on.

'I love it when you say things like that. I have never had a boy say stuff like that; it's sexy and so lovely to hear.'

'That's OK, I mean it, babe. You are beautiful. I am glad you spent the night with me; we must do it again sometime. Why not tonight? What are you doing today, or even this week?'

That shook her. Go in for the kill, son, I thought; see what she says – dumb boys don't get anything.

'I have nothing planned this week. I don't go back until next Monday the seventh; why do you ask?'

'OK, great – why not hang out with me here for a week or so? We can take it slowly, just as you want it– no pressure. But if you want fun, just say so; you know what I mean.'

'Can I go to my place to get some more clothes? It is not far. This sounds like fun to me; I've never done this before, just gone off with a stranger – it's exciting.'

'I tell you what – I will hire a car and we can go out to the beaches away up the coast a bit. Maybe hire a van on the beach, and bring swimmers with you, OK?'

'Let's have some breakfast first. I am hungry – what have you got, anything?' she asked.

I went to the deli on the corner and got some food – ham, eggs and a French stick – and dashed back, then we ate the lot.

'Right – I'm nipping in the shower,' I said.

'Mmmm… why waste the water? I will join you.'

Now that was out of this world, I can tell you. We did not have sex – just showered together, washing each other's backs and nether regions with lots of shower gel. It was really erotic, very sensual, and the nearest thing to sex as the water ran down our bodies.

We went out for the day. We grabbed a cab and went to her place first to collect some gear. It was a beautiful afternoon, and we took the ferry out to Watsons Bay for fish and chips at Doyle's, and then back to Circular Quay. We were in bed early that night and got up first thing as we had decided to leave the following day.

We dressed and went to collect a hire car. I picked a Holden Torana, a two-door which was a bit sporty but big enough for the two of us, and set off up the coast. We drove for a couple of hours past Gosford and further north. I'd not been up this way yet, and the roads were not the best. It was supposed to be the Pacific Highway, but not many bits were dual carriageway. We saw a sign for the Hunter Valley, and I asked if she had ever been up here; she said no, but was happy to go anywhere. We turned off the highway heading for Cessnock, and lo and behold, there was a sign for Kurri Kurri, where my best mate at the Roosters was from; we had to see what the place was like.

We pulled up outside the Chelmsford Hotel, which looked OK, but there was another one called the Kurri Kurri Hotel not far away; this one seemed a bit better, with more people around, and that was always a good sign, plus on the walls there were a few photos of the local footy team. I asked if they had a room for the night, and the guy looked at Leia and smiled. 'You want a double, mate? I can let you have the bridal suite for couple of extra bucks, mate.' I nodded. 'No worries, blue – it's all yours; number thirteen, unlucky for some.' He had a sense of humour this bastard, I liked him; he handed me the key. 'Twenty-five bucks, mate, including brekkie in the morning if you're up; it finishes at three-thirty in the arvo. Your room is at the back of the pub away from the noise, to make sure no one can hear you.'

One or two guys sitting at the bar were having a good laugh, and one said, 'Ignore the bastard, he is always the bloody same. No wonder no one stays here; haven't had visitors here since Clancy's offsider died.'

I hadn't a clue what he was talking about; must be bush talk, I thought. I was sure I'd heard someone say that once before and still didn't know what it meant.

We went up to the room; it was quite spacious with a four-poster bed, shower and toilet in the room. The bath was actually in the room itself – a big double cast-iron freestanding tub that was near the window, which opened up on to fields.

'I'm hungry, are you?' I said. 'Come on, let's go and have a bar meal. I am starving.'

The food was spot on. I had a T-bone steak and Leia had the gammon, which was like a dinner plate; in fact, it did not fit on the plate along with the fries and salad. I was chatting to the barman, Cec, and asked him if he knew of a Terry O'Neil from around these parts.

'I don't remember the name,' he said, 'but I have only been here ten years. Maybe some of the other guys might know him – most of them come in for the six o'clock rush after work; you should ask again later.'

We had decided to go for a drive around the area up to Cessnock and the vineyards, where we did a bit of wine tasting, but not too much as I was driving. I could not be too careful now the breathalyser had just come out.

We got back to the hotel at about six-thirty, and went up for a shower before tea.

As we entered the room, we both read each other's minds; I started to run the bath as Leia got undressed. Wow, she sure was stunning; the more I saw of her, the more I liked her. I held her hand as she got into the bathtub and lowered her body under the bubbles. I quickly stripped and joined her. I lay at the end without the taps, and she got between my legs, lying back against my chest. Her soft skin felt incredible against my body, with the hot water encapsulating us both; it had to happen.

We made love in the bathtub; it was difficult, as there was not enough room, but hey – we managed it, and I didn't get past Halifax, to be honest. I wanted her so much. 'Oh, why did you do that, Leif? I am on the pill, it's OK – you could have gone all the way. Next time, OK?' she said with a smile and rolling those beautiful black eyes. 'You promise?'

I nodded, like a good boy.

We went down for a meal about eight-thirty, and there were quite a few guys in the bar but no one in the lounge, so we went in there as it was not as loud. We had just sat down and a guy I had not seen before came over. 'G'day, mate – are you the guy asking about Terry O'Neil? He was an old mate of mine; we played together down here, hmm, a few years back now. How do you know him? Haven't seen or heard of him for many a long year.'

'He is in Perth – been there a few years now. He was playing for the Roosters in the local comp there.'

'Gee – he will be getting on a bit now, I suppose; must be in his early forties, I reckon. I am thirty-nine, and he was older than me. I got on OK with the guy, but he could be a queer bugger. One day he talked, next time you saw him he looked right through you, but he'd do you no harm all the same, fella. I have a team photo with him on it – I will bring it tomorrow night if you are still here, OK?'

I thanked him, and only afterwards realised I hadn't asked his name.

We had another day exploring the area; we passed through a place called Maitland, which had a rugby team called the Pumpkin Pickers; what a strange name! The football season had just finished, and I had not seen a game even in my few weeks in Sydney; I had not bothered. We were looking for a bar meal and were advised to try the leagues club; we found it and went in. We had to sign in as guests, just in case you dropped the jackpot on the pokies, whatever that was. All of this was new to me. I looked at the photographs of all the past teams, and one of the barmen came over.

'Some right sides up there, mate; won some premierships, that lot. See that one there? They won the comp last season – beat Lakes in the Grand Final.'

'Very impressive. Anyway, we are off – just thought we would call in for a feed as we were passing.'

'OK – where you heading? Some nice spots around the area; Nelson's Bay is a beautiful place. Or you heading up to Coffs Harbour, or Byron Bay? Mind, that's a fair drive.'

We said we did not know if we were going that far north, to be honest, but would see how we go. We had lunch and then headed off over to the Newcastle beach areas for a look.

We returned to Kurri around six-thirty. Leia was starting to run the bath again and then she stripped off. Just watching her walking around the room was unreal; she was so light on her feet, like she had a spring in each foot. She was standing in front of the big mirror on the wall; at the right angle I could see front and back at the same time. She saw me watching her.

'What's wrong, babe? Do you like watching me being naked?'

I nodded. She turned her head and looked at me; I was lying on my bed with 'him' in my hand.

'Oh yes, I see you do, by the look of him,' she said, pointing at my groin. She walked over to the bed and sat next to me, running her hand up my inner thigh. We never did get to use the bath. I got as far as Warrington, but did not get off; I went right through until it stopped at the station.

I was thinking it was turning out to be a perfect trip; I didn't want it to end, but knew it would so I told myself enjoy it while we could. We still had six days to fill before we had to be back in Sydney.

The next day around one o'clock, the guy asking about Terry O'Neil walked into the pub. He told us his name was Max MacDonald.

'G'day – glad I found you here. Here's that team photo I was on about last night.' He took it out of an envelope. Oh no, not family photos, I thought; we wanted to get away. We had decided to go up to Northavon, just north of Newcastle, on the recommendation of one of the other guys in the pub; he had told us it was a great spot, with great beaches. It was about a three-hour drive, so we wanted to be away early. I told Max he had been lucky to catch us as we were just about to leave,

'OK, no worries – I was just hoping you might have seen this woman with Terry; it's my wife – she fucked off with him, leaving me with two kids, mate. Never heard from her since, the bastard.'

I didn't know what to say. I looked at the photos; he had half a dozen family-type pictures at the beach, in the yard, at the house – the usual happy family groups, but I had not seen her and could quite honestly tell Max the same. He had such a sad expression.

'The kids are grown up now; it was about ten years since she shot through,' he said, shaking his head. 'OK, thanks for your time anyway.'

We shook hands and off he went. We finished breakfast and paid the bill, having said goodbye to our hosts, and left the Hunter Valley with some fond memories. It turned out to be a beautiful morning when we headed for the Pacific Highway and the Hexham Bridge. Now this area was known for the biggest mosquito in Australia, the Hexham Grey. The saying went that if you were unlucky to be bitten by one, you would scratch for two weeks. Luckily we never encountered any and made sure the car windows were up as we passed through.

I was gagging for a drink, so we pulled up at Bulahdelah for a while just to stretch our legs. Leia was dressed just in a pair of short shorts and a vest along with thongs. We walked into a pub, and every guy's head turned to watch her as she walked past. I felt so chuffed that she was with me and that everyone hated me, thinking, look at that lucky bastard, wish I was halfway with him.

'G'day, mate – what are you having?' said the barman, not even looking at me as he spoke.

'Schooner of black and a dry white wine please.' We got our drinks and went out into the beer garden; there was a nice gentle breeze, which just tempered the hot sun. Leia sat on a lounge chair stretching her long legs out. God, she looked beautiful, with her pale skin, her almond eyes, and long black hair; she had taken her grip out and let it fall its full length nearly down to her arse. That perfect bubble arse; I was just sitting perving on her, thinking they were right – I was one lucky bastard. How was I going to let her go after this week was over? Or would she stay with me? Why was I even thinking this? I did not know what I was going to do, so why should she?

We finished our drinks and set off again. It was not a long way to the Haven, and we arrived within an hour and a half or so.

CHAPTER 38

LARS

Pig Chasing: A Year Later

It was the end of the season summer coming on, and Lars was spending as much time as he could down the beach. His Mum and Dad had begging him to come back to Tweed Heads. He arrived home late after a long drive.

'Oh, Lars, oh baby – it's so good to see you; oh, come here, let me kiss you.'

'Give over, Mum; I'm not a kid any more.'

Marjory was hanging on to him, hugging him and kissing his face. 'Hello, Dad,' Lars said, looking over her head.

'Hi, son – good to see you home. Marjory, get off the boy; let him go, for God's sake.'

They talked about this and that; Lars had rung home a few times, so there was not that much to say, really. 'Oh, by the way, he said, 'I am not here for the two full weeks of my annual leave; I am going to a wedding to a friend of mine from the Dragons. His brother is getting married so I will be leaving next Tuesday. Thought I would let you know now, OK?'

'Oh, Lars – do you have to, dear? It's been so long. Do you have to go to this wedding?'

'Yes, Mum. I have promised; I can't let Karl down now, can I? We have become quite close friends. He is a bit of a loner, and I see more of him than any of the other guys in the team. We hang around a lot together, more like brothers than just mates. I have agreed to go for the weekend; it is the second one of my two at home, so I can call on the way back down south.'

'How come you only got two weeks off? You told me you had more leave due.'

'Yes, I have – I have worked a few public holidays, and I have not had a sickie all year. I can take them in bulk but what with training and working I don't get that much chance.'

Lars spent the rest of the week meeting a few old mates, but a lot of them had either moved away to Brisbane or Sydney. A couple had gone over to Perth and Western Australia. Jed had gone overseas. They were all a little bit older than Lars, only a year or so, but at that age it made a lot of difference. He went down the beach to a surf for a couple of days.

Then Tuesday came, and it was time to say goodbye once again. Marjory was in tears; Jon, as usual, did not say a lot; he had not said that much the whole of the time Lars was there, but that was nothing new.

Lars arrived at Karl's place mid-afternoon after about four hours driving. There'd been a crash on the Pacific Highway, causing traffic mayhem.

'G'day, mate – thanks for coming. Wanna beer? You look fucked, mate – long drive?'

'Yeah, I fucking hate driving. I'll have a Tooheys if you got one; been drinking that XXXX, which gives me a bad head.'

'There ya go, mate, get that inta ya – cheers,' They clicked stubbies. 'Tonight we are having a barbie with Mum, Dad and my sister; keep your hands off her, she is only seventeen. But you will love her, mate. On Wednesday, we are going pig chasing up on a mate of mine's old fella's property up the mountain. Should be a beaut day – he has got three crazy fucking dogs, mate; facking wild they are, youse'll love it. Friday it's Mick's buck show; we were going to have it tomorrow but there's been a change of plan.'

Karl's mum, Mary, came in. 'G'day – youse must be the Lars I have heard about; pleased to meet you, son.' She walked over and hugged Lars; he felt like he'd been wrapped in the arms of a bear. He could see where Karl got his build from; she was solid.

'G'day, Mrs Higgins – pleased to meet you.'

'Nah, none of that Mrs malarkey, it's Mary and Fred the buff head over there.' She pointed at another giant walking through the back gate.

'Is Fred Karl's father? Well, I think he is?' said Lars, laughing.

Fred called over. 'Welcome to our home, son; any friend of our boy's is a friend of ours.'

'OK,' said Mary, 'I suppose you will want a shower. Come on, I'll show you your room.'

'Thanks, Mary, I will just get my bag out of the van.'

'Fred, go and get Lars's port from his van and bring it up to the room, OK?'

'Is it open, Lars?'

Lars threw Fred the keys and off he went, Mary taking him by the hand like a school kid.

'Here you go.' Mary opened the door. The room was huge with a big double bed with a solid frame made out of a tree, like a snooker table with a mattress on top.

'Jeez, Mary – I've never seen a bed as big as that. You need a ladder to get into it!'

'Yes – Fred made them all. We have one in every room. Why have single beds, bloody nuisance having different sizes of Manchester. Have them all the same size, then you can swap and change them as you like. Dinner is at 6pm prompt – if you wanna have a nap, no worries, just get your head down. I will get Karl to give you a shout if you don't come down before.'

Mary disappeared and left Lars on the bed; it was so comfy, with big fluffy pillows, that it didn't take him long to nod off. When he awoke, he could hear the sound of a girl singing; she had a great voice. He got off the bed and looked out the window; there she was, sitting on a swing chair playing the guitar and singing the Seekers song A World of our Own. She sounded just like Judith Durham. It could have been a record. Not only did she have a great voice but the package it came in was equally as good. She was beautiful – who was this girl? Could it be Karl's sister? She looked nothing like the rest of the family. Lars just had to meet her. He had a shower and changed into a pair of old footy shorts and singlet and headed out into the back yard; she was still playing the guitar. She heard him walking across the gravel path.

'G'day, you must be Lars. Mum said you had arrived. I'm Beth, Karl's sister.' She got off the swing, put her guitar down, and came over and hugged Lars, kissing him on the cheek.

'Wow – now that is some greeting. Very pleased to meet you, Beth; you have a wonderful voice, and your playing was unreal – how long you been playing?'

She blushed, dipped her head and looked away. 'Er, about eight years, I suppose. I started when I was around nine. Dad plays a twelve-string banjo in a bit of a band, mostly country stuff, you know, Slim Dusty, Hank Williams, that sort of stuff. He loves Earl Scruggs and he does a great *Ballad of Jed Clampett* – you know the tune?'

'Yes, I do. I love that Seekers song you were singing. They are a great band. Will you play it again for me, please?'

'Ooh, OK then, you sure you want me to sing it again?' she frowned, as if she doubted that she was any good.

'Yes, I love it, and the way you sing.'

Just then, Karl came out. 'You pestering my baby sister there, Lars? I warned you.' Then bellowed out a laugh.

'No, Beth is going to sing for me again. She is great – you never told me that.'

'Yep, you are right about that – she will be a country star one day, won't you, babe?' said Karl, putting his arm around her and kissing her forehead. 'Come on, let's hear you again.'

Beth sang the song. What a singer, Lars thought – Karl could be right.

They had dinner, and then went back outside for coffee. It was a beautiful summer night, with just a nice breeze, and they all sat around talking as the sun went down.

'Well, I am ready for bed,' said Mary. 'I don't know about you young ones, but I have a big day tomorrow; lots to do for the wedding. I will say goodnight. You coming too, Fred, or you having a drop of Bundy before you come up? Make it one if you are – don't want you snoring all night.'

'Maybe just the one, Mary,' said Fred, winking across at us. 'Just the one. What about you boys? You want some of the liquid gold?'

'No, thanks – not for me,' Lars and Karl said in unison.

'I am off to bed,' said Karl. 'Don't forget, Lars, we have to be up at four – got to be up at Benny's for six if we are going to get out before it gets too hot.'

'Yes, OK, Karl, I will be up soon. I'll finish this beer. See you in the morning.'

Fred had his one Bundy; then off he went, leaving Lars with Beth. He was about to head up to bed when Beth said, 'You leaving me on my own, Lars? I'm not tired. Stay up a bit longer, keep me company. I don't get chance to speak with any new guys around here. Tell me about city life and how is my Karl doing? He never tells me anything. I miss him so much. Come over here and sit on the sofa with me, please.'

Lars walked over and sat next to her; she shuffled up to him. It was getting a bit chilly now the sun had gone in, with the sound of the crickets and the odd call from a bullfrog coming from the bush. He hadn't realised how much he had missed country towns so much since Tamworth; the still of the night, the smell of eucalyptus… it felt so good.

She lay her head on his shoulder and looked up at him. He knew what she wanted, but not tonight. Lars looked at his watch. 'Sorry, Beth – I must go. Got to be up early in the morning.' He gave her a hug and a peck on the cheek. 'Come on – bed. Let's go.'

'You mean you want me to come to bed with you?'

'No, I don't. Your room, young lady – now come on, or are you staying there all night?'

Beth got up and took his hand walking up the stairs; she was in the next room. 'Goodnight, Beth, see you tomorrow,' said Lars, making sure it was loud enough for everyone to hear.

The following morning he was up at four, and he went down to the kitchen. Mary was at the stove, cooking breakfast. 'What you having, Lars? Karl's having his favourite –beans on toast with fried eggs on top; you want the same?'

'Yes, that will be great, Mary, thank you.'

'Coffee or tea? There is juice in the fridge if you prefer a cold drink?'

'Coffee, thanks, Mary. It's OK, I'll make it.'

'Like hell you will – you're a guest. It is my kitchen; now, sit down there.' She pointed at the chair next to Karl. 'Won't be long – how many eggs? Three enough or do you want four, like piggy there?'

'Three will be fine, thank you.'

They had breakfast and set off to the property owned by the father of Wayne, one of Karl's mates. It was a dirt road leading up into the hills above Wauchope and the Broken Bago State Forest. They pulled into the yard, and the sound of dogs barking filled the air.

'Listen to those bastards getting excited, mate – they know what's going on; they are ready for the hunt.'

'What we doing, Karl? You say pig chasing… what sort of pigs?'

'Wild boar, mate, it's great fun; have you never done it?'

'Never heard of it, never mind done it – what happens? Isn't it dangerous? They are wild animals – surely it has got to be dangerous?'

'Can be, mate, but do as you are told and stay in the truck, and you should be OK. Leave it to Wayne and me.'

'G'day Karl,' said Wayne, walking over to them. 'How the fack are ya, mate? Long time no see! Was choked when I got your call about setting up a pig run. Haven't done it for a while, but looking forward to it; a bloody good day for it n'all.'

They hugged, slapping each other on the back like two grizzly bears fighting. Wayne was in his early twenties and the same size and build as Karl; he might have been carrying a few more pounds but still looked fit.

'This is my mate from the Dragons – Lars Mellows. Wayne Merest, meet Lars.'

They shook hands; it was another vice-like grip, leaving Lars's hand numb.

'Right then, let's get the truck loaded with the gear and dogs. Need to put their protective collars on first. Don't want to try and put them on when they get a sniff of the pigs, as they will take your bloody fingers off. Right, Lars, you handled guns before, I take it?'

He shook his head. 'No, I haven't – what sort of guns?'

'We have two, both Winchesters, model 94 30-30 automatic, and the model 70 30-06; the 30-30 is lever-action, the other a bolt action. You mean you never been shooting?'

'No, Wayne, I haven't, but I'm a quick learner.'

Wayne shot a quizzical look at Karl. 'OK, I will show you how to load them, but you better not try using one – you're liable to kill some poor bastard.'

Lars had his lessons in loading and found it easy; Wayne watched him load another couple. 'OK, mate, you got the job. I'll get the dogs. Come on, we better get going.'

They went round to the kennel, where there were three dogs, which looked like American bulldogs to Lars.

'Wayne, what kind of dogs do you use in hunting pigs? Are they specially trained?'

'Yes, mate – they must be able to work as a team. They have to find the pig, flush it out from the thick bush, grab it by the ear to slow it, and then hold it down so we can kill it.'

'What happens if the dog bites the pig instead of grabbing its ear?'

'If it attacks and bites the pig during the hunt, it is no good to us as it is not fair on the pig; it is a bigger risk of injury to us, the pig and the other dogs. Our three work well as a team; we have had them since they were pups. They are part of our family just as any other pet dog. The easiest way of hunting feral pigs with dogs is when the dog flushes out the pig and chases it until it is facked or cornered. When the pig has been "bailed up" – which means the pig has stopped and is facing the dogs – we then move in to shoot the pig at close range. But that is not always the case in the open ground where we have to chase the pigs.'

'Why the big collar? What's that for?'

'Two reasons – one, it protects the dog from the tusks of the pig; some of these wild boar have long tusks that they attack with, mainly aiming for the neck of the dog. Secondly, if the pig takes off running we chase it with the truck, and when we get alongside we throw the dog off to grab the pig; you will see when we get going.'

'You throw the dog off a moving truck?'

Wayne looked puzzled. 'Yes, why not? We don't go that fast – only the same speed as the pig. And hopefully by that time they are facked.'

The dogs were fussing around, being quite friendly. Lars was amazed that these hunters were not yapping and barking, but that was to change.

'Wayne, do you always kill the pigs?'

'No – sometimes if we get a younger male – not a piglet, just a bit older – we can sell them to pork breeders. They make the breed a bit more healthy and hardier when the piglets are born. Pigs are very much like humans; they tend to pick up illnesses quite easily; a bit of wild boar blood in their systems hardens them up, and often the meat tastes even better.'

They got into the dense bushland and let one of the dogs go. It was not long before they heard a rumbling and a boar shot out in front of them, with the dog on the chase. Lars was holding on for grim death as they sped along the dirt track. As they got close, Wayne lowered one of the other dogs down, and within seconds it had grabbed the boar's ear, slowing it down until it was pinned to the floor. Wayne got off the truck with a gun, and, bang, it was dead. He had to pull Charlie off the pig; it was not a happy dog.

Wayne threw the carcass on the back of the truck and off they went again. This time, the three dogs got on the back of the truck with Charlie and Bluey out looking for prey. They were riding along nice and slow, and suddenly another boar shot out. Off went the three dogs, like parachute jumpers without the chutes. They chased it a while until the pig ran back into the thicker brush, and they stopped the truck and followed the squealing Patch. He had grabbed the pig's ear, and all three dogs were trying to attach themselves to the ears. The pig was putting up a hell of a fight. Its tusks were huge, and it was throwing its head around trying to slash the dogs. But it was getting tired, and one bullet in the head dropped him like a stone.

They drove around for a few more hours getting two more pigs; Bluey would not let go of the last one's ear, so Wayne had to cut it off. Bluey jumped off the truck when they got back, proudly showing off his prize for the day.

Wayne's mother Anne came out. 'G'day, boys – you enjoy your day? Look like youse did OK by the look of things – that will feed the dogs for a few weeks, that's for sure.'

'You mean humans don't eat the meat?' said Lars.

'No – the boars are only any good for ding sausages, as they are quite rank,' said Wayne. The sows and younger ones can be brought back alive and put into pens. We feed them grain to get the gamy taste out of their flesh, then eat them as normal pork, or as I said earlier, use them for breeding.'

While Karl and Wayne butchered the meat and Anne put it all in the deep freeze, Lars sat back just taking in the setting sun; he had certainly enjoyed his day's hunting. 'Thanks, Wayne, for a beaut day,' said Lars. 'See you later, Anne – see you at the wedding, no doubt; see you tomorrow arvo, Wayne.'

When Lars got back he went straight to his room, had a shower and crashed out on the bed. He managed to get down for dinner – no roast pork, but another barbecue. A great T-bone steak washed down with a cold beer finished off a perfect day.

The next night was the buck show – all the boys met up in the Hastings Hotel, which stood on the corner of two of the main roads through the town. It was the usual routine – drink as much as you can, as quickly as you can, and go home legless. They managed this quite quickly, and the last thing Lars remembered was being carried by Karl and Wayne along the main street, being followed by a police car.

He woke up at six-thirty the next morning, head pounding, swearing never to drink again; the only difference was, he was in the barn, with two cows for company – and naked. Lars thought it was the groom who was supposed to finish up in this state, not him.

'G'day, mate – you OK? You look a bit rough around the edges, son.'

It was Fred. Lars looked at him, squinting as the sun was in his eyes.

'What happened? Why am I here like this?'

'The boys thought that, being a city slicker, you would bear the brunt of the joke for the night, and apart from that you had a few technicolour yawns when you got back. They thought it safer if you slept out here. Here, put your strides on, son – go and have a shower. Breakfast is on the go; big day today. Mick is shitting himself, poor bugger, nervous as hell, but once he gets it over with he will be right. You haven't met his lady have you? Cheryl, beautiful girl from a good family as well. He is one lucky guy; they make a great couple.'

They got to the church; Lars had gone in his van, as the rest of the family had gone in their car and there was no room for him. As he entered, he was shown to his seat by one of the ushers, of which there were eight – all Cheryl's brothers. They looked like the Ned Kelly gang in their maroon suits, and half of them had long hair and bushy beards. When they were all seated, the music started. Karl and Mick were standing at the front; Mick was another giant – were they all built like this up here? Must have been the mountain air, Lars thought.

Lars was sitting on the end of a row, and as Cheryl and her father passed him, he could see what Fred meant; she was stunning. What a beauty; Mick was one lucky man.

During the ceremony, one of the ushers, the middle brother, Glen, caught Lars's eye. He had been told he was a mad gambler who would bet on anything. As the wedding was on a Saturday afternoon, he was missing out on his horse racing. Lars noticed he had an earpiece in, listening to the racing on his radio, and hidden in his hymnbook was the day's TAB tickets folded up small; Glen had made sure he would not miss any of his runners. Then came the part where the vows were exchanged; everyone listened to the bride and groom, going through their rehearsed speeches – everyone bar Glen, that is. Just as the vicar said, 'I now pronounce you man and wife,' a voice shouted out, 'You fucking beauty! Yesssssss! Get in there! There was no doubt Glen's horse had won.

The wedding went well and they all finished up at the reception in the Hastings Hotel. Beth came over. 'Hi, Lars, you enjoyed your day? You were a bit pissed last night; you looked well away when I saw you in the barn.'

'You saw me in the barn? What time was that?'

'Oh, I don't know – I heard the boys coming in and making a noise, and Karl saying, "Fuck him – put him in the barn, don't want him chundering in his bed – Mum would kill us," or words similar. I won't tell Mum what I saw, but it was very nice by the way; just wish it was mine.' She started to walk away, smiling as she turned to look back at Lars. 'Oh, by the way, my bedroom door does not have a lock on it.'

She is sixteen, Lars – don't be even tempted, he told himself. He had a good night's sleep – the best he had had for three days – as he needed to be up early for the long drive back to Sydney. He packed his bag and headed to go downstairs, and as he closed his bedroom door, Beth's opened. She was standing there in her bra and knickers. 'You never came in, Lars – why?'

'Beth, go in and get dressed – someone might come up and see you. Just get dressed. I told you last night you are too young for me, much too young – now go.'

He left her sulking as he went down. The rest of the family were sitting having breakfast – once again, the full monty. 'Morning all – everyone OK? I must thank you for inviting me for the weekend. It's been wonderful – the wedding, the day's hunting – bloody awesome, thanks again.'

'No worries, mate – it's been a pleasure to meet you. Any time you want to visit, just give us a call; you're more than welcome. What do you want for brekkie, mate?'

'Oh, just a coffee and some toast, thanks. I have eaten far too much over the past few days. I would not eat that much in a week at home.'

He finished his breakfast as Beth came down barefoot and wearing a cut top, showing her midriff and shorts; she was no doubt beautiful.

'OK, I must be off,' said Lars. They said their farewells and he had just got to his van and opened the back door to throw his bags in when Beth appeared. She put her arms around his neck and kissed him. 'Hope you come again, Lars Mellows – make it in, say, two years – will I be old enough then? I think I will be, don't you?' She turned and left.

CHAPTER 39

LEIF

The Man from Snowy River

We had a drive around searching for some accommodation, when we saw a sign for 'Beach Cabins', turned off the road and followed the track about a mile or so.

It was starting to get dark, and there was a storm brewing; you could smell the rain in the air. We had to stop as a koala with its joey on her back crossed the road; it moved slowly as if every step was going to be its last. She turned halfway across and looked at us, more or less saying thank you.

A bit further along the rain started to tumble down, for when it rained it rained, then as suddenly as it started, it stopped. We continued through the bush and came out on a secluded bay; there was no sign of civilisation – no telegraph poles, just the sound of running water over rocks and the call of a kookaburra, sounding like fiendish laughter, somewhere in the gum trees.

The sign was right – the 'Beach Cabins' were right on the beach. We parked the car at the office and went for a look at the units, which could not have been any closer to the sea. You stepped out of your front door on to the sand, and the view was unreal. We entered the ramshackle lean-to hut; it had no windows – open-plan, you would call it nowadays – and it had an office-bar/cafe, and the kitchen was in the back. We could sense the distinctive smell of freshly baked bread, which reminded me that we had not eaten yet. There were numerous posters on the wall advertising the north coast area, the usual advertisements for Tooheys and Resch's beers, and yet no one around but the sound of Slim Dusty coming from a cassette player on the shelf.

'And Clancy of the Overflow came down to lend a hand,
No better horseman ever held the reins.
For never horse could throw him while saddle-girths would stand,
He learnt to ride while droving on the plains.'

Being a Dusty fan I recognised the lyrics that he had set to music; they were from a poem *The Man from Snowy River*, by Banjo Paterson, a well-known old Australian bush poet.

I heard a voice coming from a back room; a man was talking to someone about a Veterans' reunion on Anzac Day, and I heard the 'Nam' mentioned. I could tell by his drawl that he was from far North Queensland, maybe as far up as Cape Tribulation, around 1,200 miles north of Brisbane. The further north you travelled, the slower they talked.

The man entered the outer office area; he stood at least six feet two, broad at the shoulder, and his nose leaned over, almost resting on his right cheekbone. That must have taken a mean right hook, I thought. His weather-beaten face had more wrinkles than a sharpie dog, complete with an earring. He was wearing a vest, and his once muscled arms now showed the skin hanging like chicken wings; his pecs, once firm, now resembled a pair of saddlebags resting on his chest. His skin was like leather due to too much sun. He must once have been a cane cutter and keen surfer in his younger days, as his hair was bleached and straggly, and this along with a full beard gave him the look of a pirate. He had big, rough hands, and bent fingers showing signs of arthritis. I noticed the tops of his ears had been removed; he must have been diagnosed with melanoma at some time, a common sight in Australia. Another thing that struck me was his feet looked more like hooves; he couldn't have worn shoes for years. The soles of his feet must have been half an inch thick and spread out like a flat tyre, and his toes were more like a hand, straight as a die. As we left the office, I noticed that on his shoulder was a long scar from the top to just below his armpit, and as he turned, you could see a bullet hole. I assumed he had received it when serving in Vietnam around 1964 after being called up for compulsory national service, an era that was a really hard time for the 20-year-old men of Australia. They were conscripted using a sortition or lottery based on their date of birth. They were obligated to give two years' continuous full-time service followed by a further three years on the active reserve list.

G'day, how can I help?'

'Hi – have you any vacancies? We are looking for somewhere to stay for a couple of nights.'

He just nodded, his steely blue eyes almost cutting through me.

'Sure, no worries – you want basic or deluxe?'

'What's the difference?'

'Ten bucks a night for deluxe – with that, you get running water, a dunny, a shower and electric all included. The other is a box with a door in it.' He laughed, looked at Leia and said, 'Suppose it's deluxe.'

He stood up, smiled, and picked up some keys off the rack. He headed for the door, gesturing for us to follow him, and put on an old Akubra Cattleman pelt hat, years of sweat and grease showing through. As we left the office we had to walk on a gravel/stone chip path, which was bad enough with flip-flops on, but he never missed a step.

'Bar opens at 4pm until you can't drink any more,' he went on. 'Pub grub, meals – the usual tucker – burgers, fish and chips, schnitzel, chicken, freshly made pizzas, and we make our own bread. If it's not on the menu you can't have it. There you go, mate – wanna spot or not?'

'You make it sound a very attractive proposition; how much for two nights?'

'Twenty-five bucks a night or if you book three nights minimum I will do it for sixty. The longer you stay, the cheaper it is, so four nights is seventy-five and so on; stay as long as you like. I am sure your pretty little lady here will be only too happy to stay.'

I was thinking, bloody hell – if you stayed a month, they would end up paying you.

We booked for three nights with the proviso that if we decided to stay longer we would get the appropriate discount. 'Wino' took us to our cabin, and as we walked along the beach he said, 'You got a choice –

this one here or the one right at yon end.' This one was kind of set back and surrounded by trees, with the stream alongside it, running down to the sea. 'That is usually five bucks a night more because you got a bit more privacy; it's even got a thunder-box and shower inside, and blinds on the windows.' He winked at me. 'But if you stay four nights I won't charge you, OK?'

'If we book five, what's the bonus?' I said.

'Tell you what I will do, son – a full week, or seven nights, is a maximum of 120 bucks; that's less than eighteen a night. The longer youse stay, the cheaper it gets. What yer reckon, folks? Fancy a few days in Paradise Found and first beer's on me for the two of ya, OK?'

It finished up as five nights – and what a five nights. It was fantastic, that's all I can say; we lived in swimmers for much of the full five days. The next day eight of the other cabins were all taken by a group of couples from Wollongong. They all made us welcome, and we joined in with their barbecues. They had brought their meat from home with them, as two of them worked at an abattoir. I'd never eaten so much cubed roll steak in my life – that's fillet, to us Poms that's fillet. We chipped in for the beers, which we bought from the bar. The more we drank, the cheaper it was; all we did was eat, drink, dance and sleep for five days solid. I was well and truly rooted after it.

The little stream next to our cabin became our bath. As it was freshwater the soap would create a lather and it was better than using the showers in the cabins; that's if you had one. The pressure wasn't that good anyway, so we all finished up in the stream. It was bloody cold but freshened you up first thing in a morning. It was no good if you were shy – it was all off and in, and that went for everyone; there were some beautiful views, I can tell you.

After our five beautiful days, we set off to go back to Sydney. Leia was very quiet on our journey; most of the time she had been singing along with the music on the radio, her feet up on the dashboard showing her beautiful long legs. Fuck, they turned me on, but not now; she was very subdued.

'What's wrong, babe? You are quiet; something bothering you?'

She just shook her head, said, 'Nah, I'm OK,' and then nothing.

We had travelled without a break as we approached the harbour bridge. I asked her if she wanted dropping at hers or mine, and she said 'Mine' without even thinking about it.

Had I done something wrong? What was eating her? She had not acted this way all the time we were away. I needed an answer. As we got to her apartment block I pulled in to the car park; she was sitting still with her belt on, looking away from me, I touched her arm, and she pulled away. 'Hey, baby – come on, what's wrong?' She turned towards me with tears in her eyes, and then hugged me.

'I don't want it to end, Leif. I didn't intend for it to be like this. I only came away for fun; I thought it might be exciting going away with a stranger. I have always been impulsive, but it was not supposed to finish with me falling for you. All I wanted it to be was a free week away. I knew you would want sex, but so did I – I love it, can't get enough – and you are not only a good-looking guy, you sure can root, so that was a bonus. I have rooted worse-looking guys than you, believe me.'

I took that as a compliment, but I also did not want to get into a relationship. I had gone away with the same idea as her, that it would just a bit of fun. I had only asked the initial question about seeing each other for a week as a joke, but she had jumped at the chance. I really thought my luck had changed.

It seems that I now had a problem – how to get rid of her, for she was a career girl with a very unusual profession; not one you could jump in to anywhere, so she would be tied to living in Sydney. I did not want to be in the area; I wanted to do what I had intended to do before I met Donna – to travel around Australia – and look how that turned out. I wasn't getting any younger; I was thirty next birthday. What was I to do?

I dropped Leia at her place, and told her I would ring her in a couple of days when I had sorted a couple of job interviews out, which was a lie. I thought that in a few days she might have cooled down, not missed me and realised it was OK. She was some girl. Having said that, I was not in love with her; it had to end. I did not do a lot on Monday as I was still getting over the last week's partying. I needed to get my head right and find a job; I could not keep this pace up. I still was worried about ending it with Leia, but I did not want to get involved. Half of me did; well, the bottom half. Yet, in my head, I did not want a relationship.

I rang Doug back in Perth the next day to see how things were.

'G'day, mate – how are ya? Pleased you have rung. I won't beat about the bush, mate – there is a bit of a problem, blue.'

'Why, what's wrong? What's happened.'

'You are in strife, mate. Donna's old man has been told that she was having your child, that she was pregnant – not that it makes that much difference now she is dead – but the fact is he thinks you knew and you drove her to commit suicide, and then shot through after the accident. It seems that her mate Leanne has spilt the beans to some girl pissed in a bar; the girl just happened to be a cousin of Donna's and went straight to her uncle and told him. What makes things worse, they were sorting out Donna's room and personal effects and found her diary. She'd written that she did not want the child, but knew you did not want to marry her, and there were also intimate details of her relationship with her lover. It proved that she had got herself pregnant to be with her girlfriend, as they had promised each other, but she had fallen in love with you. Still, she also wanted Leanne, something her parents didn't know about, and the final words of her diary, the day before the accident, read, "I know what to do to end it."'

'That does not mean she committed suicide,' I said. 'There is no proof there it was an accident. I don't believe Donna drove straight at the truck with the intentions of killing herself and the baby.'

There was a silence, and then Doug said, 'They rang me asking if you had been in touch, and I told them that I knew you had gone on the train to either Adelaide or Sydney, I wasn't sure which, but I told them that before they came out with the news about Donna. My advice, mate, is get out of the way – do not stop in Sydney for the Italians are everywhere. They have "family" in every state. Move on, mate, and don't look back.'

That was it – I had to get away. I packed my bags went to the local travel agency and booked a one-way flight to Brisbane. I would ring Leia when I got up there, giving her even more time to forget me.

The flight left Sydney at six-thirty the next morning. I left the keys to the apartment in the mailbox with a letter telling them I had had to go back to the UK urgently as my grandmother had died, hoping that if the Italians had got a sniff of me, this would put them off the trail. To say I was crapping myself was an understatement, if you have never had a death sentence placed on you, I would not advise it for it is not a nice feeling, believe me.

CHAPTER 40

LARS

Surprise Guest – Two Years Later

J on and Marjory had moved again since Lars had gone to Sydney. They had been transferred to Maitland, near Newcastle; Jon was hoping this might be his last move as he was fifty-nine, and Marjory forty-seven. Lars kept in touch, but was quite happy to be on his own. Being an only child helped to make spending time alone relatively straightforward; in fact, he preferred it.

Time had flown, and he had now completed his apprenticeship and was now a fully time-served bricklayer, He was also a member of the St George first-grade squad, playing in the ARL. He wasn't what you'd call a superstar player, as he played more reserve grade than first, but he was still in the first-team squad. The Seagulls had reluctantly released him from his contract, and he was now living his dream of playing alongside legends of the game such as Graham Langland, Johnny Raper and Billy Smith. He had also managed to rent his own place, so he was not tied to his parents' situation, where they moved about every five years or so. He had a regular girlfriend, Carol Masters, whom he'd met through footy; she worked at the Taj Mahal or St George Leagues Club in Kogarah (it was called the Taj Mahal because of the extensive use of white marble in the building).

Lars would hit the beach at weekends and sleep in the back of the van with Carol; he had kitted it out with the latest cassette/radio and cupboards, making it quite a home from home. Even if the bed was small in width, it was big enough for both of them. It was a living he'd become used to – burgers, fries, coke, sex, along with weed, which was freely available to most surfers if you knew the right people.

Carol was a beautiful, blonde typical Australian girl; tall, brown all over, and lived in a bikini during the summer months. She had the sexiest voice, which had a kind of husky hoarseness to it. Most nights were spent down the beach drinking wine and smoking grass.

When Lars used to see her during the week on reception at the leagues club, people would not think butter would melt in her mouth, but they couldn't have been more wrong. Things were good between them; Lars had been seeing Carol for the past year. Carol was talking about getting married, but Lars was quite happy just being close friends. He thought the world of her and the sex was great; what was the need to get married?

One night he was at her place, watching TV. She called over to him from the kitchen. 'Lars, are we going down the beach tonight, as usual? It's Friday, and I have a new bikini I want to wear; got it yesterday.'

'OK, let's see it – go put it on.'

'No, Mum will be home soon; we can't do anything, and I know that's what you have in mind – you want to root, you are always horny. You would fuck for Australia if it was an Olympic sport.'

'No, babe – England, and thanks for the compliment. By the way, you're not so bad yourself. You even said it's the most fun you can have without laughing. Go put it on – go on, let's see it.'

She disappeared into her bedroom, and came out five minutes later wearing the bikini. It was just big enough to call it a bikini – the bra was two three-inch squares attached by straps just enough to cover her nipples, and the bottom wasn't much bigger. Black in colour, it went well against her golden tan. 'Fuck me, babe, you look awesome. Where the fuck did you get that from?'

'In town – the new sports store in the Victoria building on George Street. You like it? I think it's great; only thing is you can't swim in it, it's just for posing in.'

Lars was adjusting his shorts as he was getting quite excited about watching her. She saw him getting hard and said, 'I told you no, you are not getting it, we haven't time – mind, the way you shoot your load we might have.' She laughed, as she was always mocking him, for he did suffer a bit from PES, or premature ejaculation syndrome. She kept asking him to see someone about it, but he would not admit that he had a problem.

What he would admit to, what turned him on the most, was women's feet. Now, Carol had the most beautiful feet he had ever seen – and he had seen a few, for it was the first thing I looked at in a girl. He didn't know why; he always had done. He'd started noticing them when he was in his teens. As he got older, he just loved a girl to make him climax using her feet. He had read about foot fetishes a porn magazine.

It had taken some convincing to get Carol into it, but now she loved it as well. She was five feet eleven and took a size eight shoe. She had long, slim feet with straight toes and painted nails, and Lars loved nothing more than just lying back and watching her feet, rubbing up and down his shaft, her toes gripping it like fingers. If only he could last that bit longer.

'Come on, Carol just a quick one,' he said, as he slipped his shorts down. She walked over to him, already barefoot, standing there in her new bikini. Even she felt sexy, and she started to act like a stripper dancing in front of him. She slipped her top off, which didn't need much effort. She was dancing in the skimpy bottoms, her long legs apart, rubbing her groin. She lifted her foot on to Lars, touching his thigh, and then moved over to his scrotum with the top of her foot. His penis jerked; it was glistening already. She was thinking that she needn't worry about Mum coming home and catching them; this wouldn't take that long. Why couldn't he last that bit longer? It was a good job Robby, the captain of the third grade, was better, or she would have to look elsewhere for satisfaction. She touched the head of his penis, and that was it. Lars just laid back, eyes closed, with that smile men give when they have ejaculated.

'OK, babe, go get cleaned up – I'm taking a shower,' said Carol, as she dropped the bottom of her bikini, stroking herself.

Lars opened his eyes. 'You love that, don't you? It wouldn't surprise me if you were a lezzo!'

That might be fun; that's the one thing I haven't tried, Carol thought.

*

Lars had gone up the north coast again to another wedding – this time in Taree. One of Karl's mates was getting married, and they went up for his buck show. They had booked into a motel for the night in the centre of town. They were meeting in the Manning River Hotel, having checked into the motel just after lunch, and went for a walk for a few cold ones; Lars did not want too many as he was expecting a big night.

They went back to the motel, and as usual, after a few beers, Lars crashed out. He was woken up by Karl banging on the door. 'Lars, wake up you bludger – get your facking ass up. We are ready to go.'

Lars opened the door, still bleary-eyed, then realised he was naked; it was lucky there was no one around.

'Get dressed, come on – we are ready to hit the town.'

'Who is we? There is only you and me here?'

'OK, smartarse – we are meeting the rest of the guys, don't you re-member? Down at the Manning. Come on, how long are you gonna be?'

'Look – you go. I will come after I have got my head together. I need a shower. You go, and I will find you. It's not a big place for fuck's sake; you go.'

'OK, don't be too long and don't lie back on the bed; you will only fall asleep again. I know you, reckon you would sleep for Aussie.'

Lars had his shower, put on clean briefs, a fresh pair of shorts and a T-shirt, and set off out of the door. He was just turning the key when a door opened a few rooms up. A gorgeous woman came out and turned to walk towards him. He thought he knew her face.

'G'day, Lars – how the fack are ya, mate. You don't recognise me, do you?'

'No, I am sorry, but wish I did. Do we know each other?' The voice seemed familiar but he was not sure of the face, and the body he did not know, for sure.

'It's Beth, Karl's sister. Don't tell me you have forgotten me already. It has only been two years – you must remember me?'

How she had changed, Lars thought – she was hot when she was six-

330

teen, but now, what a gorgeous young woman she was.

'Beth! I did not know you! What a transformation. How are you? Come here – kiss me.

'Oh, you want to kiss me now, do you? That has changed a bit since the last time we met.'

'You were only a child then, Beth; now it's a different scenario, for sure.'

'I said one day I would be old enough. Am I old enough now? Karl told me you were coming up for the wedding. He does not know I have come; he does not know I went to school with Melanie, the bride, and that I had an invite.'

'Who are you with? You alone or with a boyfriend?'

'No, I am alone. I only came for one reason, Lars, and you can guess what that is?'

'Me? Is that what you are saying, Beth? Well, I am truly honoured. We must do something about it. Where are the girls meeting? Not the Manning, I suppose – the guys are in there; well, starting in there.'

'No, we are starting in the Exchange, then going on a bit of a crawl round. We'll be in the Manning later – I know a couple of the girls are meeting their guys in there.'

'You want to meet me there or come back here?'

She looked away from Lars as if to see if anyone was listening. But there was no one else around.

'What time?'

'Pubs close at ten, but I suppose the guys will be going down the river with a couple of flagons.'

She walked past Lars and said, with a smile, 'OK, ten, don't drink too much. Looking forward to getting to know you better this time, Lars; two years is a long wait.'

He went to meet the guys at the Manning, but made out he had a funny tummy which was why he had been a bit late getting there. He had a few beers but kept missing a round, despite the old unwritten Aussie law, 'slob rule' – that you don't miss a shout until everyone has finished.

It was about nine-thirty, maybe a bit later, and the girls came into the room at the back of the pub; the men were in the saloon bar. Lars spotted Beth. He could see her looking through the door between the two bars; she had made sure she was standing where he could see her.

He went to the toilet, and as he went out of the bar into the passageway, she came out of the room. There was no one else there, which was quite unusual seeing as it was going on closing time. 'Hi – fancy seeing you here!'

'Yes, are you ready for off?'

'OK, I'm going myself, catch you later,' Lars said, just in case someone did suddenly appear and hear the conversation.

'OK, Lars – bye… nice seeing you again,' said Beth, and she went into the ladies.

Lars headed back to the motel. He had been in his room around a quarter of an hour when there was a knock on the door. It was Karl. 'Come on, mate – we are going down the river. What's fucking wrong with you, miserable bastard. It's a fucking buck show! Come on, get your arse down there. There are another three guys in the taxi.'

'No, mate, I've got the runs. My sorry arse is like a fucking Japanese flag. No way – I'm off to bed. Go on, enjoy yourselves. I have had enough; I'll see you in the morning.'

'Ah, fack you then, your facking loss! See ya in the morning, mate.' Then he was gone. Lars looked out of the window and watched the car drive away.

Another knock. It was Beth.

They did not even speak; they attacked each other, undressing as they did so, not that Lars had much to take off. They were naked, and for both, it had been worth the wait. Beth was even more beautiful than Lars had remembered. Her figure now was like that of a curvy model. She was perfect.

'You like what you see, Lars?'

'Too fucking right I do – come here.'

They kissed and moved to the bed. What a lover she was – for Lars, she was the best yet. He'd never been drained by a girl like she did. He lost count of how many times they did it, but he was well and truly rooted. He fell asleep, and she left and went back to her room.

The next morning, at breakfast, she was sitting with Karl, who looked as rough as a bear's behind.

'Hi, Lars. I didn't see you last night; where were you?' she said.

'Oh, hi Beth – I didn't know you were here! Were you in the pub last night, in the back room? I saw a few girls in there; never saw you, mind. You have changed a bit – all grown up now.'

'Keep your hands off my sister, Lars,' said Karl. 'She is not for the likes of you, mate; she is too bloody good for you.'

'Thanks for those kind words, mate. With friends like you, I don't need fucking enemies.'

'Only joking, mate – pity you two don't get together. You might even get your chance if Beth wins a place at uni in Sydney, eh, Beth?'

'You never know, maybe another couple of years,' said Lars, 'but it's a long time between drinks, mate.'

He just smiled, for they both knew a lot more than Karl did.

CHAPTER 41

LEIF
Queensland – New Beginning

S hortly before eight o'clock on an overcast Wednesday morning, the TAA airliner departed Kingsford Smith airport, scheduled to arrive in Brisbane later that morning.

We arrived on time, and I had to pay excess baggage to take all my stuff with me; I didn't want to leave any evidence.

Here I was, late September, and yet again making a new start in a new state – the Sunshine State. I took the bus into the city and booked into a hotel for the night; I scoured the telephone directory of Brisbane looking for employment agencies, as I needed to get a job.

I had made a list of six that I thought may help me get a start in Queensland. The next morning I rang all of them, and they all told me to get my CV to them. Here we go again, I thought. It was lucky I still had some copies left from when I made my CV out for Peters Engineering. I wondered whether to put them on it, and supposed I better had or they'd ask me where had I been for nearly four years. I needed a reference anyway. Or did I? I was confused; this was a new experience.

Three of the agencies were within a square mile of the central business district, so I decided to make a personal visit to see how I would get on.

The first one was a bit unhelpful. The manager wasn't in, and all I got from the young girl at reception was, 'Leave your CV with us; if it's OK, we will get in touch.'

The second one was a bit better. I managed to speak with the manager, and he said there would be no problem if I wrote out who I had been working for recently, as they would add that to my CV and transfer the information on to their model, and that is what would be sent out to their clients. Because of my experience in quite a few disciplines, he thought I could well fit the bill for four companies that he knew were looking for staff. I was getting discouraged, mainly because I had a lot on my mind and had never had to look for work in my life. I did not know that you could get knocked back. How could anyone dare to think I was not good enough to be taken on? I knew that was stupid, of course.

The third one was not much better; they took my details and said they would contact me if anything came up, and the fourth one was a total waste of time. I was pissed off now. I knew there were many employment agencies in Brisbane, and if I had to go round them all it would take me months.

The fifth one was more helpful. Techmaster were the most friendly and offered to rewrite my CV for me there and then, asking one of their typists to sit with me and let me dictate the amendment to my CV. She would copy the remaining information with a couple of alterations, for a more up to date version. Michael Evans, the guy I was meeting, went through the options he had on the books at the time. One was on the outskirts of Brisbane; one was in Gladstone, 300 miles away, and another was in Mount Isa nearly 1,200 miles away. These sounded good to me, with Mount Isa looking the favourite. Michael explained the three positions and what the companies were looking for; to me, the money was not the main thing – it was getting out of the way for a few months.

I discounted the Brisbane position for obvious reasons. He told me it would take a few days for him to get an answer back from both the remaining companies; I left him my hotel number and just had to wait. He did say, about the Mount Isa position, that it could be a while, maybe a month, before they wanted anyone on site, but they were good payers and they might have something to offer in between in one of their other offices.

I heard nothing for three days and was starting to look for another option if there was one. Working my way around the central business district looking for other employment opportunities, I had been thinking about Leia and wondering how she was. It seemed I was getting soft, but we had had a great time; I needed to get a message to her.

Then I had an idea. I wrote a letter home to Mum. In the letter I put another note, for Leia, to be posted back to her from the UK. If she thought I had gone home, giving the same excuse as I had given my hotel – that my Grandma had passed away – if anyone did trace me back to her, it would show I had returned home. It was a cunning plan...

It had been a while since I had written home, and the tapes had stopped a bit back. I couldn't remember when I had last contacted Mum; it must have been well over a year. I explained to her what had gone on, but I never mentioned the Italians were looking for me; I only told her about the accident, and that I had moved away as I had too many memories in Perth, met a girl on the rebound in Sydney, but had been offered a job back home, hoping she would forget me. I told Mum I would be in touch once I got sorted out.

When I got back to the hotel, there was a message at reception from Michael at Techmaster. He would like to speak to me, as he had received some interest from a couple of companies. I rang him and said I would be there that day.

'G'day mate – thanks for coming in. I have some good news for you. Well, I think it is good; you may not.'

I listened to what he had to say; the two jobs were different. Still, both interested me, and one was back on the drawing board as a design draughtsman for a wide-ranging engineering company in Gladstone. They were a bit like Peters Engineering, wanting to move away from their public image.

The second position was for a project manager installing a new process plant in Mount Isa; they were looking for someone who could cover the whole installation using local contractors and labour, both mechanical and E&I. They were very interested in me, having read my CV and references; they had offices in Melbourne, Brisbane and another in Sydney. The Melbourne office had contacted Doug Peters, and he had sent a reference for me, for which I needed to thank him the next time I spoke to him.

The package they offered was excellent – more or less the same money I had been on, but with the bonus of free accommodation, a fully furnished three-bedroom house, and a car.

They wanted to do a telephone interview before flying me up to Mount Isa in their private plane, which sounded good. There was only one downside – they did not want me on-site until August, but they wanted an informal chat just to throw a few things at me. Would I be willing? Well after the Doug Perry scenario, why not, I thought.

Michael had contacted the Melbourne office and was told the guy in Mount Isa was away on another project and would not be back in that office until the following Monday. I could not do much about that as it was out of my hands, so I agreed to wait; I had nothing to lose as there was not much else coming to grab my attention. I told Michael I would still be looking elsewhere for an opening and if one came up, they might miss out. He said there was always the Gladstone position, and they were very keen on talking to me, but I was trying to hedge my bets. If I was honest with myself, I did not want to be back on the boards, and the other job sounded very interesting, as long as the money was OK.

I was in my room at the hotel, waiting for the call from the company. The phone rang bang on 10am.

'Hi, Leif, is it?'

I thought that seemed a stupid question, as he had rung me.

'My name is Rick Thomas, HR manager.'

'Yes, good morning, Rick. How are you?'

'Fine, fine – first of all, thank you for agreeing to this call. Just an informal chat to tick a few boxes. Company policy, no need to worry.'

Just a chat, my arse, I thought; I bet he had my CV in front of him. I could tell he was asking me questions relating to what was shown on it, trying to catch me out and making sure there were no lies or fantasies on there. Luckily for me I had only had the two jobs, so I didn't have a lot to hide. It took about half an hour to complete the phone session.

'Well, that just about sums it up, Leif. We will be in touch through

Techmaster after I have talked to the guys on site. Will you be available, all things being equal, for a full interview, all expenses paid – including a sum to cover for the day or days in Mount Isa – at a time to be confirmed?'

'Yes, certainly.'

'Great, great – then I will let you go. Thanks for your time; we will be in touch.'

Michael at Techmaster rang me the following Thursday, saying they wanted me to go up to Mount Isa for a final interview, and the next date that they could fit in was August 15. I said I would have to think about it, as this was over a month since I had first had a conversation with Techmaster about work, and my funds were running down a bit. He said he would have a word but could not promise anything.

Two days later, when he rang me back, he said they had pulled a few strings, and had rescheduled the interview to enable me to fly up there sooner. They had arranged for their plane to be in Brisbane on Wednesday, August 6.

CHAPTER 42

LARS

All Change – A Year Later

Lars was now twenty-two, and he had split from Carol, who had gone to Melbourne. She had met a woman in the fashion industry who needed a PA, which meant moving away as most of the industry was in Victoria. Carol used to do swimsuit modelling and was at a job in the city when this woman had seen her and had talked. Carol had always wanted to travel; the opportunity was too good to turn down.

Carol had met the woman, Abigail Donaldson, at a couple of functions; she was originally from Sydney and followed the Dragons as a girl. She used to come to games when she was in Sydney. She was a good-looking woman in her early forties, but one thing Lars had noticed was that she was never with a guy whenever she came to the club, which seemed odd for a woman like her – loaded, own business, but no guy. Still, when you are in that position of power, you can pick and choose, he thought. He did wonder if Carol was now batting for the other side.

As a Dragons player there was no lack of a bit on the side for Lars, either. There were always young girls at the footy hanging about after the game, and even at training they used to turn up, for 'lifts home'. He had his own set of wheels – a Holden panel van that he used at weekends, especially during the summer when he spent most of his free time at the beach. He loved surfing, even though he had to travel about ten miles to Cronulla for some decent waves.

Lars had a new girl, Maya, who was seven years older than him. She was just his type – tall and slim, with dark hair, almost black. She also had her own business, a fleet of concrete trucks she ran with her father. He was is getting on a bit, as he had had Maya later in life, and his wife had sadly died of cancer. Maya was an only child, and more like a man than a woman – she loved a beer and hanging out with the guys, and was a real tomboy but older with it. Lars met her one day when she visited a site he was working on in the city. He had been made a leading hand brickie, and had just walked into the site office as she was coming out. It was a scorching day; he was only wearing a pair of stubby shorts and his safety boots and helmet. They bumped into each other as Lars opened the door to the cabin. Maya had held her hands up, and then put them on his chest. What with footy training and his job, he had kept himself in great physical shape; Maya must have thought he was a fine specimen of a man. He had put his hands around her waist; their first embrace, so to speak.

'Well, hello, and who are you, young man?'

'Whoops, I am sorry,' said Lars, as their bodies touched.

'No need to be sorry; I'm certainly not.'

'G'day – I'm Lars Mellows.'

'Oh, you play footy don't you, at Kogarah? I have seen your name some-where. Dad follows the Dragons; I think he has mentioned you as well.'

He was impressed that she had heard of him. 'Yes, I do. Don't you like footy at all? You should come down to a game, it's great – you will love it.'

'Well, are you asking me out? We have just met, and you are hitting on me. I like your style, son, and you don't even know my name. I'm Maya Brooksbank; very pleased to meet you, Lars.' She held out her hand, and Lars responded by taking it in both hands. 'Well, I accept your invitation. Never knock back a beer, I always say; you may never get it another time. When you at Kogarah again?'

Lars was a bit taken aback; he had never been out with an older wom-an, but she was certainly fit for her age.

'Oh, this week we have the Eels at home. I'm in reserve grade. I could meet you after my game, if I'm not a reserve for the firsts, that is. In any case, we can have a few beers, maybe a meal after the game at the Taj, OK?'

It felt so natural for Lars, talking to her like that.

CHAPTER 43

LEIF
Mount Isa

It was a hot and humid day, and the temperature was heading for the high twenties. As I arrived at the airport, a private one just outside of Brisbane, only one plane was on the tarmac being made ready; it was a Piper PA-30 Twin Comanche six-passenger aircraft.

I had never been on a small plane before and was a bit apprehensive, but much to my delight everything went really smoothly. I helped myself to coffee and biscuits, as there was no hostess on board, but it all seemed very well organised. There was just the pilot – a guy named Liam – and me. Liam just happened to be another Pom – they got everywhere – he was ex-RAF and had been in Australia five years, four of them working for Mount Engineering. His job was to fly all the high-ranking staff about from project to project, mainly on the east coast; we landed in Mount Isa at 10am.

Tony Rogers of Mount Engineering met me. He was general manager of the North Queensland office and wanted to chat with me away from the office environment. The reason was, he was a Pom too. From the Leeds area originally, he had been in Australia for fifteen years; his background was in the mining industry, working his way from the tools as a mechanical fitter. Most of his working life had been in the West Riding collieries – typical mining stock, ex-amateur rugby player, had trials with 'Fev', that is Featherstone Rovers to you and me, but he liked his ale too much. He was another foreign language speaker, same as old Dot from Withernsea – all thee and thou and t'owld cock, if you know what I mean. He had read my CV and, being a Pom, he had chosen me from a few other candidates put forward. He was honest about it, saying us Poms had to look each other, as he put it.

He told me that after my phone interview, Rick Thomas had been very impressed with my performance. Tony wanted to have a word with me to tell me more or less what I needed to say at the interview, which would be in front of three other people the following morning; they had booked me a room at the Holiday Inn and I needed to be at the offices for eight o'clock.

Once again, the agency only got a finder's fee. It was down to me to negotiate my salary; Tony told me that they would pay over the odds to get the right guy. He told me exactly what to ask for, and to lay on the fact that I had served an apprenticeship and been on the tools, as well as having worked on on-site installations both as a tradesman and management. They were looking for someone with a multi-disciplinary background and who had QS experience. I ticked all of these boxes, but they just needed to hear it.

The interview lasted about two hours; they asked me if I had any questions, to which I had said, no, not at this moment in time. We discussed terms and conditions, and I was asked if I would leave the room and return after lunch at one o'clock.

I was in the town side of the city as the area was split in two. The town side and the mine side, as they were known, were divided by the Leichhardt river. The offices were in the central business district. I had a walk round, went for a coffee and chatted to a few people. It seemed like there was a big Irish contingent; there was even an Irish club. I liked it; it seemed like an excellent place to get lost for a few months.

I arrived back at the offices in good time for the resitting of the interview team. I went in, and the chairman, who happened to be Tony, asked me to take a seat. 'Thank you for your patience,' he said. 'We have reached a decision, and we would like to make you an offer. We do feel that the salary you have asked for was a little high, and that our offer is fair.' Tony had told me to ask for more so they could offer less, but it was still more than the salary I had been told by the agent, and more than what I had been on with Peter's Engineering.

'We realise that you may well be disappointed that we have not come to the party with the basic salary. We feel that we can offer a completion bonus of 30% of the top line, which compensates the basic, if you see out the contract duration of twelve months. Along with the other benefits, we feel it is a great package.'

'I would like to thank you,' I said, 'Can I sleep on it? I have another offer on the table and would like to compare the two side by side, back at my hotel.'

Tony then looked at each of the panel, and he then asked that they give me time to take the offer away and go over it and return with my decision the next day. He said this was something he would do if the panel were keen on getting me after the interview; he also said he would try to get me a bit more money before we met the next day.

They agreed and were asked to be back at the office at nine the next morning. I would usually have bitten their hands off, but was being led by Tony, and could not thank him enough for what he had done for me. As he had said, 'Us Pommies need to stick together.'

There was still a bit of a Pommie-hating thing in Australia, even though it went back to the First Fleet and the way the government treated the indigenous and early immigrants; it seemed stupid, but it was still there.

I had a great meal that night and a few beers to celebrate my new job – the one I would accept the next morning. I arrived at the office first thing and was sitting in reception when the rest of the panel arrived, each saying the usual 'G'day' as they came in and shaking my hand in a friendly manner. The phone rang and the receptionist, a girl called Scarlet, answered it, and she asked me to go in. At precisely 9am the panel offered me a seat and Tony asked me for my decision.

'I have compared the two offers,' I said, 'and my only reservation was that the other offer was more than what yours was; would you consider increasing the amount being offered?'

Tony looked across the panel. 'The offer they had on the table was what they thought was a generous one,' he said.

This had surprised me, for he did not say that before. Had I put too much trust in him?

'Could you give us a minute, please, Leif?' Tony added.

I left the room and about ten minutes after, I was asked back in.

'Well Leif,' said Tony, 'we have discussed your request and come up with this increased offer. We will give you 15% more now, but reduce the bonus down to 25% – how does that sound?'

I smiled. Yes, he could be trusted – that was the 10% they had knocked off my request, for which Tony had told me to ask.

'In that case,' I said, 'how can I refuse? I would love to accept your offer and look forward very much to working with Mount Engineering.'

They all stood up at once and came round to my side of the desk to shake hands on the deal; then Tony told me he would take me to see the house that I would be allocated to me after meeting the personnel team to go through the contract and sign up.

The house was in a great area; it was a fully furnished three-bed bungalow with air-conditioning, a swimming pool and even a barbecue in a covered area in the yard. It was on the town side of the modern growing city. One thing I had noticed was that there seemed to be more men than women. I asked Tony if what I had perceived was right, and he said it was and had been for a while, due to the influx of labour that had come to the area and not left. 'But us Poms know how to chat up a bird,' he laughed. 'Not like the Aussie guys; their chat-up lines are, "G'day, babe – fancy a root?"'

'Yes, I have noticed that,' I smiled.

'Don't worry, mate – if you know where to go it's easy to get your leg over. I've never missed out. I'll take you where it's laid on like a fucking smorgasbord.'

It's funny, that was never mentioned in the interview or the information pack that HR had handed me; if it had been, I might have settled for less money.

It was agreed that I would start a week on Monday and I would be flown up again on the company plane on the Friday before, August 15, to give me time to settle in.

I was taken straight to my new home, and the company car had been delivered – a very nice Holden Premier saloon V6, white, as usual; I needed it in that weather. The fridge was full of food, including a few beers, and the freezer was full of meat. Had they forgotten anything? I didn't think so; they seemed to look after their staff, this mob.

I unpacked my gear, not that I had many clothes. It's funny how my fashion tastes had changed since I had come to Australia; I used to wear trousers and shirts, even a suit, when I went out on the pull or was just relaxing. Now it was a pair of shorts, flip-flops and T-shirt or even vest, depending on where I was going. At work I also wore shorts and long socks and a shirt with an open-neck collar and no tie; I loved this country.

I was restless, so I decided I would go for a drive in my new motor and pick up some more beers from the bottle shop when I found one. I passed one pub, but then came upon the Boyd Hotel, so thought I would pull up and take a look. It was more like a Wild West pub; the beer was OK, so I had a couple and got into a conversation with the barmaid. She was in her mid-forties, I reckoned, and she told me there were three pubs of note in Mount Isa – the 'top pub' (Mount Isa Hotel), the 'bottom pub' (Argent Hotel), and in between on the corners of West and Marian streets stood the iconic Hotel Boyd – 'Boydies' – the one I was in. I thought I would save the other two until I did a bit more research of the guys at work.

When I got back home – it sounded odd calling it home, but it was the first time I had my own house, and a decent one, with a swimming pool – I couldn't wait to write to Mum and tell her all about it. I had one or two reservations, to be honest, but maybe at the back of my mind was the Italian thing and the way I had just dropped Leia. Maybe one day we could meet again once the dust had settled.

Sunday was another hot day; I did nothing but lie about the house with the air-con fully on, and go for a swim in my pool. This was the life, I thought to myself; I wondered what the poor people were doing.

But it was soon back to reality, and back to work. I got there early and had to wait to get in as the offices were closed. I was sitting outside in the car, with the engine running and the air-con on, when I saw the receptionist Scarlet go in using her pass; I hadn't noticed the pass reader on the wall.

'Hi, Leif, how are you' she said. 'Did you have a good weekend? Welcome to Mount Isa.'

She was a good-looking girl – tall, dark, perhaps a bit Italian? Whoops, stay away, mate, I thought. 'Hi, Scarlet, how are you – OK? You're looking nice; it is a pleasure to come to work.' You smooth bastard, I said to myself. Some things never change – remember Tony's words: Aussie guys don't know how to chat up women.

She smiled, blushed and looked down, so she lost eye contact, which was, I thought, a good sign that she liked someone flirting with her.

Tony was the next person in, then most of the staff arrived well before the seven-thirty starting time. I was shown to my office – not just a desk, which was a pleasant surprise – and I went through the induction, had a photo taken for my pass, and I was done.

Tony rang me on the internal phone and summoned me to his office.

'Nah then, Leif – everything fine? I saw they delivered the car no problem, House OK? Did they fill fridge up? Everything hunky-dory?'

'Great, thanks, Tony – that was a surprise, much appreciated.'

'No worries, t'owld cock, that is standard procedure for any new starts coming up to the area.'

We got down to the job at hand; they gave me all the contract details and copies of everything and told me to go back to the office and peruse the information, and we would meet up in a couple of days to discuss the project. Back in my office, I was sitting reading the documentation when the phone rang; it was Scarlet.

'Hi, Leif – fancy a coffee? I've just put the jug on.'

'Yes, please – white, one sugar.'

'OK, no drama – be right there.'

Now, that sounded nice; was that par for the course, her offering to bring me a coffee? Don't knock it, son, was my thought.

She knocked at the door and came in. 'There you are – coffee, one sugar, as requested; enjoy.'

I watched her arse as she turned to leave; mmm, she was hot. Get on with the job, Leif, I told myself; no more Italians.

I looked at the contract: it gave a complete breakdown with $123,000 for shop fabrication; we were supplying all materials as a free issue. The remaining cost covered all other items including craneage and scaffolding, with an estimated total cost of just over $5 million including $493,000 contingency and $460,000 profit.

Having read all that, my arse suddenly got tight. I hadn't realised this was such a big project. My salary wasn't included, as head office staff came out of a separate pot altogether. I had worked out a schedule showing the breakdown of costs for the site for every month and the QA manager came to see me the following day to discuss my thoughts as there was a pre-construction site meeting due to be held the next Friday morning.

The next day I met the site manager, site QS, general foreman, and senior site supervisor. I was informed that all the installation was to be carried out by local contractors chosen from a list of companies that had done work for them previously, on fixed price quotations.

As with most projects, it was down to me to ensure that any extra work was kept to a minimum. Any claims would be taken care of there and then as none would be left in abeyance; this had been laid out in the ITT documentation sent out for bids. I was given the proposals they had already received back from the contractors, which was usual in the contracting industry. The middle one had been chosen of the three received for the separate disciplines, mechanical, E&I and civil, which was the minimal as the site was a building already in place.

The client's main civil contract had been built and handed over to us a couple of months previously with all interface points already in place, including the electrical substation. That was a relief, for tying into the existing plant would be a hell of a lot easier.

It was usual the practice, kind of an unwritten law, to choose the middle quote; you never took the top price as nine out of ten companies didn't want the job and had put in a high bid to keep the client happy and give them a chance of being considered for future enquires. You never took the bottom quote as most likely the company had either missed something or, even worse, once they had got the job they would try to hit you with extras from day one. It was a common practice with UK contractors; I know, I have done it.

Things were going great on the job; it was only about half an hour's drive out of town to the site. The plant was to be a forerunner for what they hoped would be a new type of copper refining subsidiary developing the Isa Process copper refining technology, which was to be known as The Mountchild process. It was hopefully going to be the preferred copper refining process technology. It was brought about by replacing copper cathode-starter-sheets with stainless sheets, and allowing a very labour-intensive process to be mechanised. I won't go into any more detail, as I will bore you to death.

A few months had passed. I had really enjoyed my stay up to now; the only thing lacking was women. I had lived like a monk, and my right hand was my best friend so far. There was not even a bordello to visit, although having said that I did not have the time; I had been working seven days a week for the past two months at least.

I reminded Tony one night at the pub after work of his comment about him taking me where it was 'laid on like a fucking smorgasbord'.

'But you –' he cut me off.

'OK, I know what I said. You mean you have not had a fuck since you been here? I don't believe it; you not tapped up Scarlet yet? Fuck me, mate, she adores you.'

This was music to my ears. 'I thought she was engaged to a guy who works for us?'

'She was, but they broke up just after you started; did you not notice her fingers were clear now? Get in there, son; she is fucking fit. But if you fancy a bit of rough, go out to the local dance on Friday – it's the last Friday of every month. In fact,' he said, looking at his watch, 'it is tonight – fancy going?'

We arrived at the hall about nine-thirty after having a few beers and Bundies, and, sure enough, Tony was right – quite there was quite an array of talent to be seen. There was one good-looking girl, but the guys sniffing round here were like bees round a honey pot. I was told many years ago to go for the ones with buck-teeth and glasses, as no other fucker wants them, and they are usually grateful when you tap them up. Tony and I decided to split up to survey the talent pool rather than trying to find two at the same time. I was wandering around eyeing up the talent, so to speak, and bingo – sitting on her own was 'Miss Buck Teeth and Glasses, 1978'. Honestly, she was that buck-toothed that she could have eaten an apple through a tennis racket. She had a beautiful body, though, and great legs as far as I could see, as they were kind of tucked under her chair.

I noticed no one was dancing – or, what I knew of as dancing; it was more old-time waltzing or foxtrot, which put me off a bit as I was no Lionel Blair or Fred Astaire. I walked over to her table and asked in my best English, 'Hello – is it OK if I join you? Seats are a bit hard to come by.' She looked up at me with her vivid green eyes; I had never seen anything so beautiful. I had read a poem once somewhere; I don't know where, but it came to my lips. 'Your eyes are like an ever-flowing stream, and I want to float in them forever.'

'You pissed, mate?' she answered. 'Another sweet-talking Pom – yes, sit your ass down, mate. Not seen you here before – you new in town? Where are you working. I am Glynis – Glynis O'Rourke… and you are?'

'Er, Leif – Leif Askenes-Daniels. I'm working at the mine; been here three months. So pleased to meet you, Glynis – can I buy you a drink?' I had noticed her glass was nearly empty.

'OK, mate, I'll have another Bundaberg and coke, thanks – not too much coke and only two ice cubes.'

I went to the bar and bumped into Tony on the way back. 'Oh, I see you met Glynis – then you will be OK tonight, mate. She is a widow; her old man got killed in an accident a year or so ago, and she got a lump sum of compo that set her up for life. She has a truck she leases out and lives not far from you. Great shag, but don't go down on her; she will break your neck if she climaxes with you in there. Great legs – she does a lot of running.'

I got back to the table. 'Here we are then – Bundy and coke; not much ice, as requested.'

'So, you single, then, Leif? That's an odd name; where is that from?'

I told her the story I'd told a thousand times before. We chatted for about an hour then she said, 'Right – I am off; wanna come back to my place for a nightcap and a root? Let's not beat about the bush, mate – I need some dick. Not had a root for a couple of weeks now, and you seem like a decent guy. I've not fucked a Pommie, and I love big, tall men.'

I just sat there and could not say a word for a moment; I was just about to take a sip on my drink but downed the lot in one swig. 'Why not, Glynis? I have not had such a good offer for quite a while.'

We went outside. I had not seen her standing up; she must have been at least five foot eleven, maybe bigger, and she had a solid body. She grabbed me, which was like being tackled in a rugby match, and stuck the lips on me. I was a bit wary; I thought my lips might come away with a few lacerations, and it felt like I was being kissed by a vacuum cleaner, but fuck, it was beautiful.

'Great kisser, mate,' she said. 'We will get on; get in my truck – let's go.'

We arrived at her place. Tony was right – it was not far away from my house; only a fifteen-minute, as I found out the following morning. Tony was also right in saying she was a great shag. In fact, I would say even better than great – she was awesome. I only reached Hull FC the first time; mind, I hadn't had sex for three months or so, but the second and third times I got to Wigan and even Workington. What a woman; I'd never had sex like it. She got up, early leaving me in bed, and came back with coffee. What a sight, standing there by the side of the bed stark-naked; I will say again – what a fantastic body. She was not muscular like a bodybuilder but solid, with no spare flesh and a belly that was flat as a pancake. She was more athletic, I would say, like a swimmer, with streamlined, trimmed pubes that were pure blonde, with just a wisp of hair on her body arms and legs. What set it all off was those nipples, which must have been half an inch think and long, surrounded by large, dark brown rings, all perfectly proportioned.

I had a shower and then went into the kitchen. Glynis was sitting on the deck, sunbathing, still naked. Her garden was beautiful, with a manicured lawn, flower beds all neat and tidy, and the fence was about eight feet high with no one overlooking the yard.

'Hi, babe – come on, grab a chair; you sunbathe much?'

'I do,' I said.

'I love it too, but I must use plenty of creams. Here – while you're up, put some on my back, please.'

She let the back down on the bed and rolled over; I started to put cream on her back. Nothing moved as I rubbed it on; it was like massaging a tree trunk. 'Don't be shy – put some on my arse, will you? Don't want a red butt, do I? And don't be slipping any fingers in when you're down there either,' she giggled. 'Are you going to strip off with me, Leif? Never know where it might lead to.'

I stripped off, and it was clear that I was already getting to enjoy it. She stroked me as I bent over to move the sunbed. 'Wanna give the ferret another run, Leif?' she said.

I did not get back to my place until late that afternoon, and to say I was well and truly fucked would be an understatement. I was still in bed on the Sunday morning wondering what I was going to do with myself when there was a knock on the door. It was Glynis, running on the spot.

'G'day, Leif – just thought I would say hello. I'm on my way back home; what are you doing this arvo? You busy? Fancy coming round for a beer around dinner time?' – that's tea time if you're from Hull. 'I will light the barbie, OK.'

I thought for a minute; that was long enough.

'Yes, OK, I will be there. What time? Five, no worries?'

'Yes, great. See ya then – byeee!' She ran off down the street.

What was I letting myself in to? I went, and sure enough there was beer, food and sex in abundance; it was another great evening. I made my excuses about having to be up early the next morning as I had to be at work before six, which stopped me staying all night again. I could not have stood another night of depravity; my balls ached, and my dick was so sore from Glynis's muscles gripping me. I'd had sex with some of the horniest women I've ever known, including those who did it for a living, but this woman was something else.

CHAPTER 44

LEIF

Problems in More Ways Than One

I had to go to the office for the monthly report meeting before going on-site. I was standing chatting to Scarlet when Tony walked in.

'Morning all, had a good weekend then, everyone?'

We both said 'not too bad', but I sounded a bit more happy than Scarlet.'

'How was Glynis, Pom, OK?'

Scarlet looked daggers at me as I had just told her I was getting lonely being on my own. I was doing the groundwork for my next adventure.

'Yes, she was OK. I left just after I saw you at the bar; her boyfriend turned up. Seemed like a nice girl, but not my type.' Scarlet smiled. Wow – got out of that one.

'You ready then? The rest are in the conference room. Scarlet, leave the man alone – and you, Leif, why not ask the girl out? You know you fancy the lass.' I looked at her, and she had the biggest smile you could wish to see.

'I will see you later, Scarlet, OK?'

As I got up, I said to Tony before we went into the room, 'You bas-tard – what did you say that for? You embarrassed the girl – she is only a kid.'

'She is older than you imagine; she's twenty-four or five, I think, and she has the hots for you.'

We had the meeting, and everyone was happy with my report along with all the other project managers present, so things were OK.

Christmas holidays did not slow the project down; we only had one week off from Christmas Eve to January 2, then it was back into it. By this time I had given up on Glynis; if I'd stayed seeing her she would have killed me. There had already been another three guys who were servicing her needs. She was unreal and no doubt she would have found another four if we were all to have disappeared.

I had been seeing Scarlet for about five weeks, and everything was going fine. They say you should not have office romances, as it's not ethical, but I only saw her a couple of times a week at work, so it's not as if we worked together; that was my excuse, anyway.

Scarlet was a wonderful girl. She was not Italian, which was a bonus – she was from Australian stock, with a bit of indigenous blood in her, but she was the youngest of six children; the only girl from way back. Her five brothers were all mineworkers – either maintenance or local contract workers, as were most of the people in Mount Isa. The remaining population were mostly contractors who came and went as required, to top up the locals.

We had made love quite a few times but we didn't go over the top and not until we had been out a few times; I left it to Scarlet to decide when she wanted to go to bed with me. She was not a virgin; she had been with her previous boyfriend quite a few years, but things were rocky with them just before I appeared on the scene. He had told her he did not want to see her any more the weekend I rolled into town.

Maybe she fancied me as a bit of a rebound scenario; that I do not know, but she was a good-looking girl. There must have been quite a few local boys who would have fitted the bill. It just happened to be a sweet-talking Pom who arrived on his white stallion – well, white Holden Premier V6.

The job had been going great; we were hitting our targets on the installation of the plant, until one day the general foreman Kenny Morgan came into the office telling me he was having problems with the labour of the structural company. He told me their supervisor, Vince Flanagan, had threatened him.

'What did you say to him?'

'I told him I wanted him off the site.'

I told Kenny I would handle this, and I would see their manager and have the man removed. I went to the company's site office; the manager knew nothing of the confrontation until I told him. He called the supervisor in question on his radio and asked him to come to the offices. A few minutes later, this guy came in. I cordially introduced myself – no swearing, not being smart. I asked him his side of the story, and he started slowly, and precisely, relating the same story as Kenny had told me – apart from the bit about telling Kenny that if he did not fuck off and let him do it his way, he would break his legs, or a lump of steel might accidentally fall off a scaffold. He did not mention that he had been cutting corners on safety by removing some scaffolding that should have been done by the scaffolding company, as written in safety procedures.

Having listened to him, I asked him about the scaffold; he denied having done it.

'OK, Vince, you are saying my general foreman is not telling the truth? Well, I don't believe you either and want you off the job immediately.'

He looked at his manager, who shrugged his shoulders, and with that he took a swing at me and caught me on the jaw. I shook my head and said, 'Nice one, Vince – if that's the best you can do, you're in for the biggest hiding of your life.' He went the colour of bad shit. I turned to his manager and said, 'You saw what happened – he struck me; that is immediate dismissal on any job in the world. Now you get rid of him, or you and your company are off the job; I will cancel the contract and see you and him in court.'

Stan, the manager, apologised. I could see he was worried. He told Vince to get his gear and leave the site, and he asked for his site pass and his company van keys. He then called security and had him removed.

Within hours it was all around the site – don't mess with the Pommie boss; big Vince cracked him and never dropped him. We had no more trouble from anyone else; not that we had before. Later that day I got a phone call from Tony asking me what had gone on. I told him and asked him how he had found out about it. He said the MD of the relevant company had contacted him, thanking us for getting rid of 'Big Vince' – they had been trying to sack him for a few years, but no one had the bottle; he was a known thug. 'Watch yourself when out in the town, he might come looking for you,' Tony warned me.

'Don't worry, mate, I can take care of myself; you had to be able to where I was brought up.'

I was in the pub at the weekend having a few schooners and, lo and behold, who should walk in with one of his mates from the site, but Big Vince. He had had a few beers and was full of himself, mouthing it off to anyone who wanted to listen. I was facing the bar sitting on a stool, when I heard him say, 'Hey, Pommie bastard! I want you now – outside.'

I turned; he had a bottle in his hand, and he was not holding it like he was drinking it. I just smiled and in one movement grabbed the lapels on his jacket and gave him the good old Liverpool kiss – or head-butted him, for those that are not aware of the Aussie terminology. His nose disappeared, and blood went everywhere. His mate who was standing on his right-hand side made a quick move but was in perfect range for my right hook, which dropped him like a stone. They did not come back for more. One of the guys in the pub said, 'Fack me, mate – you know how to use yourself! Never seen a sweeter headbutt in my life, and the right hook was spot on, blue. Well done! Never did like that bludger, Vince, 'bout time someone levelled him. Can I buy you a beer, mate?'

Within five minutes two policemen came in, and the two bodies were still lying in front of the bar; both now conscious, but only just. The landlord, Alan, told police they were fighting with each other, a statement I don't think they believed, but they had also had bother with them previously and were happy to take them and lock them up. They pushed them into the back of a police van, and I carried on with my beer; I never bought another one all night.

I got a phone call on the job the following Monday from one of the local rugby league teams in the town asking me if I fancied a football game; they had heard I used to play a bit and I could handle myself, but I declined the offer. I was loving my time in Mount Isa. I had been here for three months; the job was a piece of piss. I had altered one or two of the procedures – I had more of the larger diameter pipework fabricated in the shop rather than on site, along with the ducting manufactured in larger spools with supports and flange units already welded on instead of welded on site. This reduced a lot of the site installation hours and gave me a few brownie points.

My love life was spot on, but not with Scarlet – she had gone back with her boyfriend and was getting married in a few weeks, and she was pregnant; not mine, by the way – she had been getting the best of both worlds as we were both giving her one.

I had met another girl who had come to town, Melanie Randerson, or Mel, for short. She also was a contractor – a process engineer from Byron Bay in NSW, which I was told was supposed to be a great place to live. She had come on a short four-month contract to set up the plant we were installing; she had gotten her degree at Brisbane University and had travelled quite a bit to a few different countries, including the UK. She'd worked at Saltend, near Hull, believe it or not, and knew loads of places I used to frequent.

We got talking at work one day, then had a few dates – a few beers, then meals, and it had to happen – she moved in with me. It saved her a few quid on travelling to work – well, that was my excuse. Mel was just what I needed in my life; she was twenty-nine, the same age as me, a travelling contractor, and she could cook, which was not something I had really mastered. I was OK with basic Hessle Road food, but she could cook anything. Along with that, she was a great lover; she actually taught me things I did not know.

I rang Doug in Perth to see what had gone on over the past six months or so. He told me it had gone quiet; Donna's family had heard I had gone back to the UK, but how they knew that I didn't know. It bothered me how had they found out; only my hotel and Leia had been told. Had they found Leia? Had they done anything to hurt her to force her to tell them where I was? Maybe they had seen her, and she had the letter I had got Mum to send. I never asked Mum; she was due a message, but it would just have to wait. I thought about trying to phone home but there was the time difference and the chance of catching Mum in was minimal. Then I had the idea of giving Leia a call; I could make out I was calling from the UK, and she would never know. I could get her at work at the hospital.

The next day I got the number in Sydney. I got through, and the operator asked me for the extension. I had no idea; I just asked for Leia Tan and told her what she did and what department she was in. I asked her to hurry as I was calling from the UK.

She came back to me. 'Sorry, Leia no longer works here.'

'What – when did she leave? Any follow-on address? Any idea where she has gone?'

'You can try hospital administration, but I must warn you they usually don't give out personal information,' was all she could add.

I was gutted. How could I find out where Leia had gone? Was she OK? Had she got my letter? I was worried, and blaming myself for just leaving her like that.

About two weeks later, a letter arrived from Mum, saying all the usual stuff about how the weather was back home and how Billy was still a dozy bastard, but she loved him. Then she said she had sent my letter to Leia and was annoyed at me for asking her to do it; Mum thought she was lying for me, as she put it. Then she said that Leia had not replied to her. What did she mean? Why should she? What had she done? I only asked her to post a fucking letter, not become pen-pals with Leia. Then I read that she had put her address on the back of the envelope, with a note saying 'if not delivered, please return to…' Holy fuck, that was all I needed. Mother, what have you done? I thought. I had supposedly left Australia to get away from people, and she was sending them an address to find me. Perhaps I was just being a bit paranoid, but deep down I was worried.

It was three months later, mid-July, and the job was coming to an end in front of schedule and well within the price, which made me the blue-eyed boy. All of the construction was completed, and we were down to minor contract changes, so earning even more for the company.

Mel was still living with me; we were making quite a 'nice couple', as we were often told. I was enjoying a type of married life without the ties; it was nice cuddling up every night and waking up with a belly full of bum – and a nice bum, I must add. Life was good for old Leif Askenes-Daniels. It was also coming to the end of Mel's contract and she had been looking for another opportunity but was not having much success. One night we were sitting watching TV, and she said, 'I think our time together may be coming to an end, babe. I will be sorry to leave here; I have loved this job for more reasons than just the work, but the main reason is you – I never thought I would ever fall in love again,'

I asked her what she meant by 'again'; it was an odd statement, for although we had lived together now for quite a few weeks, I did not know her, not deep down. She told me she had had a regular boyfriend, a teenage sweetheart, to be exact, back in Byron Bay, and they had been together from being fourteen up to them being twenty. They were madly in love, he was a local football star who played representative football for the North Coast and was tipped to go to Sydney, but he got a bad injury that finished his career. He became a pisshead and went off the rails, and they broke up.

'I got a degree in engineering and went travelling the world, and I have never had a serious relationship since,' said Mel. 'I did not want to be hurt again, so it was just casual sex. I go back to Byron Bay in between jobs and stay with my parents, until the next project comes up. Unfortunately living with you for the past months I have got the same view as you; it is great waking up to the same person every day. We have got on well; too well, it seems, for we both now feelings for each other, I did not want it to happen, but it has.'

I put my arm around her and kissed her forehead; she started to cry.

It was now August, and Mel had finished the job and had gone back home to NSW. I had promised to see her when it was possible, as I did not know what was happening to me at the end of the job, and whether Mount had anything for me. No one had said anything; they had kept the cards close to their chest. All the paperwork for the job had been completed and the plant was working at the levels required to hand over to the client, so we had a party to celebrate. 'Well mate,' I said to Tony, 'what's happening next? You haven't said much lately – what's going on?'

'I have not said anything because we have been waiting for a couple of jobs to come through, so I have not had much to tell you, mate. I did not want to bullshit you as we are friends; well, I like to think we are, and so far nothing has borne fruit, not here anyway. The company has a job coming off in New Zealand and has asked me if I am interested in going over there, but I am not sure yet; even I may be moving on.'

'So things are not looking good for me, then?'

'To be honest, Leif, the answer is no. I may also tell you now; you will be getting paid off in two weeks, you know what the contracting game is like – one door shuts, the other smacks you in the fucking mouth. You will be getting the completion bonus you were promised plus a month in hand and six weeks' holiday pay.'

I tried working it out in my head. I had started on $16,000 a year, so 30% of that was nearly $6,000, then ten weeks' holiday pay and a week in place of notice was nearly $4,000 so it was almost a $10,000 payoff. They paid the tax on it, that was the deal. I had saved $6,000 during my four years with Doug in Perth, and I'd saved $8,000 on this job. There was also the money I had earned from my brief football career in Perth when I was paid in cash, which was $2,000 that I had kept in an old wallet. This gave me about $26,350 in the bank, give or take a few quid.

What should I do? Look for more work over here or was it time to go back home to the UK? I more money in the bank than I had ever had, or dreamed, of having – £14,000 would be worth a fortune back home. I decided to spend some holiday time in Australia before I made up my mind. I said my goodbyes to everyone in Mount Isa and headed back to Brisbane, and booked into a decent hotel for a week.

I rang Mel's number in Ballina, but there was no answer, so I had a good look around the city and looked up Michael at Techmaster; I rang him to tell him I was finished at Mount, and we met for a few beers one afternoon. He already knew, as it was common practice for employers to let the agency that had found them know that they were releasing them, which was a nice touch, I thought. Michael told me he had nothing now as things were a bit quiet, but would be contacting all their offices to see if any suitable positions were available, within Oceania and beyond.

I thought I would hire a car and drive down the coast via Surfers Paradise; it was only a couple of hours. I decided to stay there a week and then head on to Byron Bay and hopefully catch up with Mel.

CHAPTER 45

LARS
Mayabrook

Nearly a year had passed. Lars had been seeing Maya regularly; you could say they were an item. As he had his own place, she would stay over a couple of nights during the week when she could and most weekends. Lars had decided that he was in love with her; he had never felt this way with any of the younger girls he had been in relationships with, but Maya was different. Maybe it was because she was older and much more experienced in more ways than one. She knew what she wanted out of life and, by hell, made sure she got it.

Lars was now a foreman brickie and had met quite a few of her drivers, who all reckoned she was a hard taskmaster at work, and he could believe that, for she paid well but expected 150% for the dollar; she was firm but fair. Her father had been ill and therefore was not doing a lot of work himself; she ran the business full time.

As he was not getting as much game time now, Lars was thinking of moving on, but it just depended on the Dennis Tutty court case result, which was due the coming summer. Tutty had taken his current club, Balmain, to court because they would not put him on the transfer list, hoping that another club would buy him to play for them. Lars thought he would hang out with the Dragons until that was sorted, plus he had a good job – the construction industry was booming, and bricklayers were as in short supply, about the same as rocking horse shit. He was earning good money now and what with his footy earnings he had just moved into a bigger unit and things were looking good.

Maya was teaching him more about life than he thought he would ever know; she had suggested he start his own building business, and she would fund the enterprise, though she would be a partner; she was not doing it for nothing. She was good to him – but not that good. Another thing she was excellent at was making love – he had never been to such places as she had taken him when he first met her; she had seduced him – the older woman and the boy syndrome – and had him naked on his knees. Maya had also been naked apart from her panties, and she'd slowly slipped them off. Lars could not believe his eyes – she was trimmed; he had never seen pubic hair cut and above the mound was a tattoo with 'Welcome to Paradise' just above the hairline. She had taken his head in her hands and pushed him down on her, saying, 'Oh yes… mmm…' and would not let him up; he was nearly suffocated. She then took him; he had nothing to do, as she did all the work. He just lay there, hoping he could last out. But Maya was talented; she knew when he was close, and when he did let go, it was like a thousand sparrows flying out of his dick.

The news came out about the Dennis Tutty legal action, which had begun in May 1969. He had fought for more than two years for the right for players to transfer to another club. The New South Wales Equity Court granted Tutty's application to have the league's transfer system declared invalid, deeming it an 'unreasonable restraint of trade'. The league had appealed to the High Court of Australia, but on December 13, 1971, the High Court's judgment upheld the Equity Court's decision.

After two years of sitting out of the game and waiting for a legal conclusion, Tutty returned to play for Balmain during 1971. He played seventeen games but did not receive any remuneration from the club. Tutty was free to play for the Penrith Panthers.

A couple of agents approached Lars. He had now realised that there could be big money to be earned from these new rulings. Before this, there wasn't such a thing as an agent; players had done their own negotiations, if there were any to do, for transfer fees were the norm. Clubs bought and sold players similar to the slave trade; a player was theirs until they decided to sell them or give them a free transfer, which did not happen very often.

Lars was not sure what to do. He was in the throes of starting his own construction company with Maya. He had contacted a couple of developers who would start work on a couple of new sub-divisions out in Sydney's western suburbs. They had promised that they would get the job, dependent on cost and a percentage of the profits for them. It was agreed that their cut would be built into the quotation. It was a no-brainer; everyone was a winner, and it was just how they could hide the numbers from the taxman.

It seemed like Lars's football career was over. He had done OK; he'd never been a superstar but had made a name for himself. He had played eighty first-grade games in the seven years with the Dragons, and never been injured, so in total he had played more than a hundred games for the club and had never played in the third grade; he'd always been in the first-team squad, and considering some of the stars he had played alongside that was some achievement. But things had changed, and he had gone down the pecking order; he was now looking to his future after football, and Maya was offering that opportunity.

Lars and Maya took the plunge and started up Mayabrook Construction, unsure if they were doing the right thing; there were many competitors in Sydney's construction game. It was a dog-eat-dog situation trying to win work off established companies that were well in with most of their customers.

A Year Later

Things began to look up after around twelve months of trading; they had not undercut most of the competitors, as the award rates were set in stone. The labour costs were more or less the same for every company it was the overheads and profit that they trimmed; they went on the principle that, the more work they got, the more they made. They weren't creaming a big profit off every project, and the clients loved it. They had also spread their wings and opened an office in Wollongong about an hour's drive from Sydney; the city had a booming population, mostly Italian immigrants looking for work and homes to live in. Mayabrook was lucky enough to pick up some blocks of land by pulling in a few favours that Maya's father had done over the years. But the gamble had paid off, and things were booming.

It was a Friday afternoon, and Lars was in his local, yarning with a few of the guys from one of their sites. He missed the banter, or the craic, as it was so often called, so he used to try to get to each of the sites at least once a month, to shout the guys a few beers. This particular afternoon he had gone to the bar and a guy he did not know came over to him. 'G'day, mate – you Lars Mellows?'

'Yes, I am – who is asking? How can I help?'

'I thought it was you when you walked into the pub; seen you play a few times for the Dragons, mate. Good player, enjoyed watching you; I felt for you as I think you should have got more first-team games. Oh, I'm Freddie Norman – pleased to meet you; I live not far away.'

'Well, thank you – I appreciate your thoughts, mate, but that's footy. That is what you get when you are the top club and can draw the best players; they can't all get in the first grade. I enjoyed my time, and got out while I could still walk.'

'You done all right, anyway, by's the look of things. I was talking to a few of your guys the other Friday arvo; they reckon you are a good guy to work for. That's some shout, mate – good on yer.'

'Well, thank you. What you after, a job? What are you – a chippy or brickie?'

'Nah, mate, nothing like that; I thought we might be able to help each other, that's all. I often get the chance of some cheap meat.' He looked around to make sure no one was listening. 'I work for a freezer company delivering pre-packed meat and veggies to people who hire the deep freezers off them. You know the script – they hire the unit and order meat and stuff as and when they need it.'

'Oh, right, yes – I have heard of the system. Never got into it myself but I do know it's a good idea – but why are you asking me?'

'Just thought you might be interested in a bit of cheap meat, if you know what I mean? I can get you brand-new American-style deep freezes if you haven't got one; I know a guy who deals in them, if you're interested, that is?'

Now, Lars was always interested in a deal, and this sounded OK, but could he trust Freddie? He needed to ask around the guys from the site.

'When do you need to know? I need to ask the boss if she fancies one. No good me ordering a freezer if we have nowhere to put the bloody thing.'

'OK, no worries, mate; just ring me on that number.' He handed a slip of paper over. 'Just ask for Freddie.'

'When would the best time to deliver it if I do want one?'

'Of an evening mate – you got a big garage at your place?'

'Yes, as a matter of fact we do – holds two cars and a bit to spare.'

'Perfect – you could put one of the bigger units in there. Good deal, mate. One thing – you need to have the freezer running for at least twenty-four hours before you can fill it. Anyway, I got to shoot through, just give us a shout mate. Nice talking to ya.'

Billy, our site foreman, came over, 'See Freddie has been into you about a freezer by any chance?'

'Yes, he has – how did you guess?'

'I got one off him a few months back – it was a good deal and first-class tucker, mate; he even gives you the company order form to top up the bloody thing – he must be earning a bloody fortune.'

'So he is kosher then? It's OK?'

'My bloody oath it is. He's a bit of a larrikin but he is fair dinkum. Get into him, mate. I got a super freezer for 150 bucks, and the meat and stuff was another fifty.'

'How much meat was there? Is it good stuff, good quality?'

'I reckon – there was a full yearling and a heap of snags, bloody beautiful. The cheaper cuts are supplied as mince and burgers. Half a lamb, some chump chops, they were beautiful cooked slow. It's all good gear, mate, you won't be disappointed; cost me a hundred just for a yearling last time I got one, never mind the bloody freezer.'

'I will have to give him a call; he gave me his number.'

'You won't need to – he will be back. He has gone down the road to the other pub. That guy is not as stupid as he looks, mate; he knew you would ask some of us guys about him, see if anyone would give him a reference. He will be back; in fact, he has just pulled up outside – look.'

I looked out of the pub window and, sure enough, Freddie was getting out of a panel van.

'So you are back – that did not take long?'

'I got a Sheila I see on a Friday arvo, but her hubby was home. His car was on the drive – bastard; needed a root as well. Any thoughts on my offer, mate? You won't get it better anywhere else.'

'OK – count me in. When can you deliver the freezer? Can you tie in with the guy who supplies the unit?'

'Yes, it's cash on delivery, that all right? He will deliver it Sunday night, OK? What's your address? Like I said, you need to have it on for twenty-four hours before putting anything in it. I will deliver the meat on Monday night – will be late, OK, around ten.'

'Why so late?'

'Don't ask – it is the way it is.'

'Do I get a chance of ordering what we want?'

'Not the first lot, but I know it will be a mixture – beef, lamb, hogget, chooks; we prefer to do it like that so gives you an idea of what the quality is. It makes it better for both of us when you reorder.'

'What about veggie? What do you supply in that line?'

'To be fair dinkum it's a waste of money. You're better filling it with meat. At these prices you can afford to pay top dollar for the other stuff, but if you want it's up to you.'

'OK, Freddie; how will I know when your man is coming with the freezer?'

'He will ring you an hour before delivery; you won't meet him. Leave the garage door open when he rings you, put the money on the top of the driver's side wheel of your car – is that your Ute out there?'

'Yes, it is.'

'Great – just leave the money in an envelope; 150 bucks. Don't worry, we are honest; well, a bit honest. We won't rob you, mate; we don't want to get a bad name. I will deliver the meat on Monday night around the same time, maybe a bit later, but I will ring you. I will need you to help me unload the van; when I get there don't want to hang about – nosy neighbours and all that.'

'That sounds good to me.' Lars put out his hand, and they shook on the deal.

'OK, blue – I got to shoot through; see you on Monday.'

Lars got home after the pub and Maya was waiting for him, with dinner ready. 'Where the hell have you been? The chook's just about burnt to a crisp. Thought I would do a roast for a change.'

'Sorry, babe, got caught up yarning, you know how it is; I could eat a bloody horse, babe.'

He told Maya about the freezer and the deal he had struck.

'Unreal,' she said. 'I was only thinking about getting a new freezer; that small chest one we have is not big enough. It is fine for the two of us, but you can't get the deals on bulk buying.'

'Well, you will now.'

It was Sunday night and they had just gone to bed; it was gone eleven when the phone rang.

'Hello, can I help you?'

'G'day – freezer man here, mate. Sorry, we will be thirty minutes late, OK?'

The phone went dead, and half an hour later they heard the sound of a van or truck. Then it stopped, and they could only hear the sound of footsteps; no voices. They listened to the garage door closing. The engine started up again, and they were gone. Lars and Maya got up and went down to see what they had got.

'Bloody hell, Lars, that's worth a fortune – they are over 500 bucks. How much did you pay for it?'

'150 – looks OK to me.'

'My bloody oath it does! So when are we getting the meat and stuff? Tomorrow, you said?'

'Yes, Freddie is bringing it himself around the same time. I think he works the night shift at the warehouse or cold store loading vans ready for the following morning for the regular drivers to take out. We will see when he turns up.'

Once again it was late, but still no Freddie. 'He can't be coming now; it's gone midnight,' said Maya. 'Did he say he would ring you?'

'Yes, he said he would give us half an hour or so's notice. I can't understand it; he must have got waylaid.'

They went back to bed, and Lars was woken by the doorbell ringing. He looked at his watch; it was three-thirty. What was going on? He went to the door and there stood Freddie. 'Come on, mate, I'm sorry I am late – got tied up at work. Bloody shift manager came back and I almost shit myself, but he was pissed; he kept me talking for a bloody hour and I couldn't get rid of the bastard. He facks off home or to some Sheila he has on the side, and we don't see him all bloody night; anyway, I am here – come on, let's get this lot unloaded.'

Lars could not believe the amount of meat Freddie had brought; they could not get it all in the freezer, so they left out a load of snags and small T-bone steaks.

CHAPTER 46

LEIF
Surfers Paradise

The surfers were unreal; it was coming on spring, and a bit off-season, but there were still lots of bikinis about – what a place. I'd not had a bit of fresh for a few weeks now and was feeling a bit edgy around the groin area. It was ten o'clock on a Monday morning, the sun was coming out and people were starting to go on the beach. There were women out for the day with their children – best kindergarten in the world. Some older people were walking along the esplanade doing their exercise routines; it was a perfect day. I was sitting on the beach near Eileen Peters Park on the esplanade, enjoying the views, when this volleyball smacked me behind the head, knocking off my sunglasses.

'Sorry, mate – jeez, you OK?' a voice said. I looked up, and wow – this girl was standing there in a yellow bikini, showing off the most beautiful golden tan on a fantastic frame. She was gorgeous.

'That's OK, I'm fine,' I said, as I handed her the ball, touching her fingers that little bit longer than required, which was always a good way of telling whether a girl was interested. Had I a chance? She was only late teens, early twenties at a guess, and I was twenty-nine, but once again dumb boys didn't get nowt as they used to say at home, and the Pommie charm started to flow.

'Oh, you a Pom, then? Where are you from? My parents are from Leeds, but I was born here.'

'I'm from Hull originally – been out here five years, so we are both Yorkies in a way.'

She threw the ball to her mates and sat in front of me; I could see what she had for breakfast as she sat down.

'I love listening to your accent; my name is Steph, short for Stephanie, but I hate that. Steph Longbottom, don't laugh – I hate my surname, but I am stuck with it suppose.'

Quick as a flash, I replied, 'I think you have a lovely bottom, Steph – it goes along with the rest of you,'

She gave that look that all women give when they love being flattered. 'Thank you.' Before she could say anything else, I said, 'Leif is the name – Leif Askenes-Daniels.'

'Wow, that's some mouthful,' she said.

I had to bite my lip before answering. But once again I had to describe where the name came from, my heritage and all that. It was getting quite warm. 'Well, I fancy a swim to cool down a bit, you coming?' I said.

She got up in front of me, and as she rose to her feet, her legs spread. Her bikini bottom stretched the material against her, showing what is sometimes described as her camel-toe. She ran off towards the water's edge, encouraging me to join her; she was straight in diving under the surf as the waves broke on the beach – a real Aussie girl. They love the water, and don't worry about getting their hair wet with saltwater. I followed her in, and as I came up from under a wave she was standing right in front of me. I was rubbing the seawater out of my eyes as our faces met, close enough to kiss, but I did not attempt to. I could smell the sweetness of her breath. She jumped up and wrapped her arms and legs around me like a baby chimp would, and was trying to pull me under the next wave. I could feel the heat of her against my hip as she pulled me over; my, it felt so good. We messed around in the surf like two kids, play-fighting and wrestling; people watching probably thought we were uncle and niece as I must have been ten years older than her, but I didn't care.

We got back to where I had been sitting; she ran to where her friends had been, but they had gone. She gathered up her bag and towel and went off for a shower; no one worried about leaving stuff around on the beach as no one would pinch it. She came back, still drying herself; the little droplets of water still on her brown skin looked so sexy.

'My friends have gone; they must have got fed up with waiting for me. Still, I loved it in the surf. Too bad; I will catch up with them later.'

'Do you live local, are you from Surfers?'

'Yes, not far – Mermaid Waters, just along the beach, about half an hour on the bus.'

'I can drop you off if you like, it's no bother,' I said, but she declined my offer, saying she wasn't ready to go home yet and would be getting a burger or something as she was out for the day. It didn't matter what time she got back. Was this a hint, or something? Should I go in for the kill or not? We had only just met; mind, I did fancy her, she was a good-looking girl.

'Where are you staying, Leif? Is it close?'

'Yes, just across the road – a small motel. Well, it's more of a poolside apartment; they have a restaurant/cafe that does great burgers – fancy joining me for a feed?'

'Yes, thank you – I'd love to,' said Steph, without hesitation. 'Can I use your shower to get this sand off me, please?'

Now, this was getting too good.

'Yes, of course you can. I could do to freshen up myself.'

We left the beach and walked a couple of hundred yards to my hotel, around the side to the pool and into my apartment; luckily there was no one around to see me taking this gorgeous young girl into my room.

'You want to go first or shall I go in the shower?' I asked her as I threw my bag on the floor and kicked off my thongs.

'You go first if you like; I'll follow you.'

Was that a promise? Or just what it meant – that she would come in after I have finished? I went into the bathroom and did not lock the door; I left it a little bit open, just in case, or was I pushing my luck? I was under the shower lathering myself with gel, but there was no movement, and I did not hear anything. I washed the soap out of my eyes and rinsed off. OK, she had not taken the hint; I had got it all wrong. I dried myself off and came out of the bathroom.

Steph was sitting on the bed with a towel wrapped around round her. Her bikini was in the sink; she had washed it out along with my swimmers. 'OK you finished in there?' she smiled.

'Yep, all yours – if you want your back washing, give me a shout,' I said jokingly.

'Mmm… sounds good, but I think I will give it a miss today, thank you, Leif.' She touched me on the shoulder as she walked past; it was more of a stroke than just touching. I did not push my luck; she was a nice girl, and I told myself to just enjoy her company – there was more to life than just sex.

She came out of the shower, all dried and with her hair wrapped in a towel. There was a bedroom in the apartment, and she had put her clothes in there already. I had seen them when I had gone to get dressed – no bra, skimpy panties and shorts with a sleeveless top, along with her makeup bag. She was out for the day, as she had said.

I was sitting on the balcony, a glass of wine in my hand, a bottle in a bucket of ice, when she reappeared. 'Fancy a drink before we eat, Steph?'

'Oh, yes, please – not a big one, though; I get rat-arsed easy, mate.'

She sat, still wrapped in a towel, sipping her wine, then said, 'I better get into some clothes before I get a chill; the sun is going down. You know what it is like out here – you don't get dusk as you do in the northern hemisphere; one minute it is light, then bang – it's dark.'

Steph disappeared into the bedroom; within minutes, she was back dressed. She looked and smelt wonderful.

'Wow, you scrub up well, lass.'

She laughed. 'That's one of my dad's favourite sayings, Leif; long time since I heard that.'

'Why a long time?'

That was when she told me he had passed away two years before with cancer. You know those moments when you are not sure what to say – you can't say 'sorry for your loss', as it was a while ago, but you need to say something. I was just about to speak when she said, 'It's OK, you don't have to say anything. I'm getting used to it now; I still miss him so much, but that's life. As he used to say, 'Shit happens.'

She had tears in her eyes. I grabbed her and hugged her, and she put her arms around me and lay her head on my chest; it felt so good holding her. I kissed the top of her forehead.

She pulled away and looked up at me. 'Thanks Leif,' she said, and smiled a beautiful smile. I was so tempted to kiss her; believe me, I was tempted, but I thought better of it once again.

'Come on, I am starving; could eat a bloody horse,' I said as I grabbed her hand to go out of the sliding door, but she let go of it as she walked out. I locked it, and as I caught up with her, she grabbed my hand back; that was the nearest I got to any signal from Steph.

'Fancy anything more than a burger? My treat. I have enjoyed your company today, babe.'

'Oh, well – if you are shouting it's up to you, Leif; I won't say no.'

I did not know the area at all, so I asked her if she knew of any restaurant or bar that did good food.

'I love Italian,' she said. Wow – Italian… I'd not eaten Italian since Donna, and I did not know if I could face it, but it was over a year ago; I had to move on.

'OK – Italian's fine for me,' I said.

'Right then, there is a great little one just down here,' said Steph, as we turned off the esplanade into a side street.

As we approached it, I could see 'Luigi's' in neon lights in the window – now there was a coincidence. It had the usual red, white and green decor with Dean Martin in the background singing 'That's Amore'; some things never changed. We had an aperitif before the starter, and then I had calamari, while Steph had garlic mushrooms; now, there was a passion killer. Both of us had pasta as main meals – and very nice too, washed down with a bottle of asti spumante.

Afterwards we walked along the esplanade towards my hotel; Steph hadn't mentioned going home. We stopped across the street from my hotel. Not a word was spoken, and she was still holding my hand when I said, 'I will drop you off if you want me to, or get you a cab?' Steph just squeezed my hand and turned to cross the street towards the hotel, and we strolled around the side of reception to the pool area, which was floodlit in dim light. I opened the door, and we stepped inside.

She put her bag on the chair and turned to me. 'Leif, thank you for a wonderful day – let's finish it properly.' With that she undid her shorts and let them drop to the floor, and put her arms around my neck. I softly kissed her; this was our first sexual kiss, and, oh my, it was good. My hands stroked her beautiful arse and I lifted her top over her head. Her breasts were white compared with her tanned body, along with a white arse and shaved mound. God, she was beautiful. We went to sit on the sofa in the living area; the moment was close when suddenly she got up and stood in front of me.

'Leif, sorry – I need to ring Mum to tell her I won't be home. She will worry if I leave it too late. She went over and picked up the phone beside the sink. 'Hi, Mum, listen – I won't be home tonight. I am stay-ing at one of the girls' houses; we are having a few drinks as Melanie is going away. You know Mel, the one who works at Woolworths? You know… yes, that's her – didn't you know? Oh, thought you did… yes – I will give her your love. Don't worry, I will be OK… Yes, Mum, I love you too… bye, Mum – love you to the moon and back… bye – bye… love you.'

I was still dressed, but that did not last long. We went into the bed-room and lay together, touching, exploring, kissing, licking every part of each other's bodies. I went all the way to Wigan and never left the train; my god, she was good.

I woke up during the night and watched her sleeping; she looked so sweet and innocent just lying there. I could not believe what a beau-tiful, skilful lover she was. I slept like a baby and never heard another thing – and when I woke up it was daylight and she had gone. I had not heard her leave. I was gutted. I needed to see her again, but she had just disappeared.

She had left a note on the side of the desk, which read, 'Thank you, Leif – sorry I had to leave, but I am at work on an early shift today. Will be in touch, love Steph XXX.'

I drove up and down the esplanade to Mermaid Waters, and I looked in the phone book for the name Longbottom, but there was none to be found. Was it her real name? Was I just a one-night stand? I don't know, but I never saw her again. She was a girl I will never forget.

I checked out of my hotel around eleven o'clock. It was a gorgeous spring day as I set off for Byron Bay, and it was another two to three hours' drive down the coast over the border at Coolangatta through Brunswick Heads where I stopped for breakfast, following the Pacific Highway as far as Ewingdales Road. I turned off heading towards the bay.

I found a motel right on the beach on Bay Street and booked in for three nights initially as I didn't know how long I would stay; it was a great spot on the fantastic beach right opposite the surf club. I unpacked my gear and thought I would go for a walk to stretch my legs after the drive. I wandered around along the beachfront, and it was around two when I started to feel a bit hungry, so I called in the Great Northern on Johnson Street for a bar meal; there were not a lot in but the grand old pub must have been there years. I was sitting on a barstool minding my own business when a guy walked up for a beer.

'G'day, mate, how's you, OK?'

'Fine, thanks,' I said, and he remarked about me being a long way from home considering I was a Pommie.

'Where you from, mate? I know's youse a Pom, but were in the Old Dart you from?'

'A place called Hull originally; that's in the north of England, East Yorkshire.'

'Yes, heard of it, mate – good footy team ain't there? In fact, isn't that the only place with two footy teams in the same town, am I right?' He rubbed his chin while thinking.

'Yes, but Leeds has Leeds, Hunslet and Bramley. Also, Manchester has Swinton and Salford.'

I started to get a yarn on with this guy; he seemed very knowledge-able about rugby league and England. We must have sat for a couple of hours discussing the game; he had heard of Johnny Whiteley, Hull FC and Rovers, and what a great team the Poms were – he loved the way they played. Billy Boston was his all-time favourite player, how the game had changed, and he thought Roger Millward was the best half-back he had ever seen, compared with Tommy Raudonikis. He even said he was better than Billy Smith, the magnificent St George half-back. He also hated Alex Murphy, but did acknowledge that he wasn't a bad player. We moved out into the beer garden and had a few schooners as the afternoon wore on, and we shook hands a few times as strangers do when getting close to the wind. 'Everyone knows me as Skippy, mate – been here all my bloody life mate. Must go or will be strife when I gets home, bloody women.'

He was gone as quickly as he'd appeared. The barmaid came up to clear the glasses. 'Take no notice of old Skip, mate – he is a bloody nuisance at times but means no harm. Can't get rid of the bastard once he starts. You just visiting, then? On hols, are you?' All the usual questions a Pom got when visiting in Australia.

I told her I was looking for an old workmate whom I knew lived in Byron Bay but hadn't got her address, and was just hoping I could look her up while I was in the area.

'What's her name, mate? Might know her – it's not that big a place, Byron.' I told her Melanie Randerson, that she was about twenty-eight, and started to describe her.

'Oh yes, Mel – I know her. She lives with her gran now up Cowper Street, near the sports field; she is a lovely girl, known her most of her life. Was a pity about her husband dying like that, and so sad what with her mother passing away suddenly. You knew about her hubby, didn't you?'

I told her that Mel had told me all about it, but I didn't know about her mother.

'It was only a couple of weeks ago; she had a massive heart attack and dropped dead in the garden. No warning, just bang – gone. Terrible it was, so sad.'

She smiled that smile when someone has been discussing the passing of another and doesn't know what else to say, and went back into the pub with the empty glasses. 'Hope you go and see Mel,' she said. 'She would love to see you; I know she would.'

Maybe she did not want visitors, but I thought I should go and see her. She hadn't said anything about her being married, only about a boyfriend and how he became a pisshead; was this the guy she married? Mel had also told me she was staying with her parents, not just her mother. You would not say 'parent' if there were only one of them, would you? You would say father or mother, I thought.

With that, Stella, the barmaid came back out. 'You still here, babe? Want another beer? It's not waitress service, but if you want one I will bring it out. Tooheys New, wasn't it?'

'OK, yes, please – I will have another.' I needed to get to know more about the mysterious Mel; were any more things she had not wanted me to know?

Stella returned with my beer. 'There you go, babe. I have put it on your tab; just settle up when you're ready.'

I stopped her just before she walked away. 'Stella, can I ask you a few questions about Mel? I don't want to go barging in on her after such a tragic time. I did not know her that well.' I was lying, of course; I knew every inch of her – how could I forget? 'Why does she live with her gran? What about her father, where is he? Her husband – I forgot what she said about him. I know he was a good football player but had a serious injury, I know that, but she did not elaborate on it.'

'I am no gossip spreader, babe, but her father left her mother when she was only young, about twenty years ago I reckon. Right bastard if you ask me – fancy leaving a woman pregnant an' all. No wonder she lost the baby, but no one would have thought he would have done that.'

I was intrigued. 'Done what? What did he do?'

'Bloody went and hung himself down at the football oval in the boiler room. He used to go down there, instead of going home, and when he was pissed, he'd sleep it off in there, especially on winter nights when it was a bit cold as it was always warm in there. The boiler was forever fired up; an old, wood-fired one, it was. He was a kind of unpaid caretaker used to keep dressing sheds clean, and stoked the old boiler up; they found him hanging from the rafters. Old Skippy you were yarning to, he found him – ask him next time you see him, if you're here that is; he will tell you all about that night.'

I did not know what to say. Stella must have thought I was a right idiot not remembering all that; I'd just told her I knew Mel's father had died but not in such a tragic way.

I decided I must see her; it would be wrong not to. I asked Stella if she knew Mel's gran's telephone number, but she didn't.

'I'll tell you what, mate – she doesn't live far from me. I can call in and see her if you want? She doesn't get about much now. I will ask her for her number and tell her I can call her now and again for a yarn, make some excuse up.'

I thanked her for her help, but wondered whether Mel was still there, or had she moved on again? Stella answered that question when she told me, 'Call in here tomorrow I start at twelve. If Mel's home, do you want me to tell her you are here or save it as a surprise for her?'

'Save it, be nice – but see if you can find out when is the best time to catch her in if possible, please.'

I wanted to see her face as she opened the door. I had no intentions of ringing her.

The next day I was in the Northern, just after twelve, and Stella was behind the bar. Skippy was holding court with some more tourists; he waved as I walked in, and I acknowledged him but kept walking.

CHAPTER 47

LARS

Hi-Fi – Three Years Later

T hings had gone a lot better than either of them would have imagined. It was 1974, and Mayabrook Construction had been active for nearly three years now and was doing very well. It had gone from nothing to employing more than 100 men on several sites around Sydney and the south coast of NSW; thanks to Maya's contacts and Lars's hard work they had broken into the competitive construction market with a vengeance.

Lars and Maya were now living together in a brand-new house on Sydney's North Shore; it had cost more than $100,000 when the average house price was $34,000. Both were driving imported BMW saloon cars and drank more wine than beer now but, deep down, they never forgot who they were.

One day they were in a store in Sydney looking at some new furniture. Lars was in the hi-fi department looking at a new system with quadraphonic sound, when he heard someone say, 'You can't afford that bastard, mate.' He looked around. It was Freddie, the meat man; he had still been supplying them meat, along with anything else they needed that had fallen off the back of a truck.

'G'day, Freddie – how's you mate? What are you doing in here? Bit a bit out of your league,' said Lars.

'You never know, Lars – I am spreading my wings, a bit going upmarket, mate. Never say never! You fancy one of those systems, do you? I might just know where I can get my hands on one if you are interested?'

'We are looking at furniture for a den we have in our new place; we have put it up at the bottom of the garden. Oh, sorry – you have never seen our new house in daylight, have you? I am after a pool table as well if you know anyone that supplies them?'

'Just might. I know a few guys in the pub trade that are in that game. Just leave it with me. I don't do furniture, mate, sorry – too bulky, needs too many hands for delivery and all that. Can you leave it a few weeks? How soon do you want it?'

'Well, this hi-fi I'm looking at is on a month's delivery,' said Lars, pointing to a unit in the corner. 'They are just out and hard to get hold of. The sales guy has quoted four weeks, maybe longer. They sold the last one only yesterday, and have none in stock, only the display unit. He was showing me who had purchased it in his sales book, trying to prove he was not making up the story. But he didn't not show their name; he covered that up.'

'OK, leave it with me. I will go and have a look at it and get some information off him to make sure I have the right model and everything – don't want to get the wrong system for you, do I?'

'OK, Freddie – give us a ring; we are on the same number. Oh, you know that, don't you?'

A couple of weeks went by; Lars and Maya were sitting having a beer when the phone rang.

'G'day, Lars Mellows – can I help you? Oh, hi, Freddie. Yes – couple of weeks? Great– how much is it going to cost me? How much! You got to be taking the piss – no way. Are you sure? Fair dinkum, yes, of course, I will have it. No, it's not too expensive; you sure? OK, I will have it… no, I won't tell anyone where I got it from. I understand, mate… you know any business we do is always kept – yes, that's right our – secret. Good on yer, Freddie. OK – ring me when you are bringing it, and I know it will be at night, no problem.'

'I take it that was Freddie,' said Maya. 'What you up to now? It won't be legal if he has anything to do with it, that is for sure.'

'Remember when we in town looking at furniture and I was looking at that expensive hi-fi system that you said we could not afford? Well,

384

Freddie can get us one. Of course, it's not legal, but at 200 bucks it's legal.'

'How much – 200? It was nearly 800 dollars; how can he get that one at that price?'

'Don't ask. He has noses in every trough. It'll be knocked off from some warehouse or supplier.'

The following week, three in the morning as usual, they got a phone call. 'Freddie, how you doing? OK, great – yes, what? OK, half an hour. No, I won't put the outside lights on, no worries.'

When it arrived, they carried it in the house. It was the same system as Lars had looked at, more like a piece of furniture than a music system, enclosed in a teak cabinet, with two speakers to match. He paid Freddie his ill-gotten gains; he was only in the house a matter of minutes, and off he went.

They put the lights out and went back to bed. They never bothered examining the system, assuming it was all OK as there were no marks or damage; they could not have sent it back anyway. The next morning, Lars got up and went out to pick up the paper from the front garden. He was reading the back page when Maya shouted from inside the house, 'Lars – come in here, quick! Just look at this – you will never believe it!'

'Why? What's up? What the hell is wrong... you OK?'

She had turned the news on, and the broadcaster was talking about a burglary that had happened sometime the night before in the affluent area of Potts Point. The place had been just about emptied. The owners had been away on holiday and it was the gardener who had found the damaged back door where the burglars had got in; it seems the alarm system had been turned off but they could not understand how. Lars and Maya looked at the new hi-fi and opened the cabinet doors; it was full of LPs and in the drawers were cassettes that had been recorded, along with original bought ones.

'The little bastard – Freddie has sold us stolen goods, Lars. Can you believe it? How the hell does he think we will accept that?'

'We have to now. No way will he take it back. He can't take it back to the owners and the police will be looking at all known fences. We will just have to keep it; it may not be from there anyway.'

'Lars, look here.' She handed him some paperwork for the system, including the warranty and purchase invoice; it had a Potts Point address on it. 'Just look at the name. I can't believe we have some stolen goods belonging to him, can you?'

'No, but we won't be advertising the fact either; they would lock us up and throw the bloody key away.'

He set up the system in the den; it had an unbelievable sound. He put on one of their 'new' LPs, which was something he would never have bought – *Train Sounds from Around the World*. He sat in his recliner and pressed the remote to play. He heard the system start to work and then came the sound – it was some Pommie bloke describing what he was about to hear. 'The Flying Scotsman, travelling from London to Edinburgh, went 392 miles in less than seven hours.' And then Lars heard it; it was like the train was travelling around the den as the sound came out of the different speakers. It was the best 200 bucks he had ever spent.

CHAPTER 48

LEIF

Finding Mel

'**G**'day, Stella – any news for me? Find anything out?'

She ignored my question. 'Tooheys again, mate?'

'Yes, please – schooner.'

She pulled the beer and handed it over. 'You going out in the beer garden?' She winked, and I took the hint.

'Yes, I think so. It's a nice day, might as well.'

I went outside, and there was no one around. I picked a table with an umbrella for a bit of shade; it was also in a corner away from the main route through.

Five or ten minutes later, Stella came out. 'Thought it better if I gave you the news on your own. Loose lips sink ships, all that shite – you know what I mean?'

I wondered why all the secrecy, but I didn't know Stella; she might have been a bit of a drama queen.

'Well,' she said, 'here is the number – she lives at 29 Cowper Street; mind, I told you that yesterday.' She handed me a piece of paper with a number written on it, but no name. 'Now, Mel seems to spend most of her time out of the house; it seems she is working at the surf club as a lifeguard co-ordinator or something like that, I'm not really sure, but is always home by six-thirty to give her gran her tea – hope that helps?'

I thanked Stella and kissed her on the cheek,

'Get out of here, you sweet-talking Pommie bastard!' she said, and went away laughing. With that, Skippy had spotted me on his way to the toilets. 'G'day, Leif – you OK, blue? Be with you in a mo, mate – just having a yarn with some Ham Shanks, bloody nuisance; want to know the far end of a fart.'

I supposed I had better have a word, and maybe find out about the hanging story Stella had mentioned.

A few minutes later Skippy came out, clutching a half-empty glass. I knew what was coming next. 'G'day – shout you a beer, mate, while I am up?' he said.

'No, here, I will get them – was just about to get another.' I started to get up, and Stella came out. 'Do us a favour, Stella – can you get us a couple of beers please? Put them on my tab, OK?'

She nodded and looked at Skippy with disdain. 'OK – same again, Skip?'

'Yes, thanks – good on yer, Leif.' He joined me at the table.

'Glad you're here, Skippy. Stella was telling me you know a bit about Mel Randerson's father's accident, that right?'

'No bloody accident, mate – he topped his bloody self. I found the poor bugger, you know; fair shook me up an' all.' The beers arrived. 'Just telling Leif here about Mel's father down at the footy ground,' Skippy said to Stella. 'Fair dinkum, it was terrible – never forget the look on his face, all blue and tongue hanging out.'

'All right Skippy, I don't want to hear the bloody gory details, thank you,' said Stella as she turned to walk away, shaking her head.

'Right – where was I? Yes, that's right – I used to be the strapper for the football team a few years back. I had gone down to the ground to drop some gear off on my way to work. Cheers mate,' he said, taking a mouth full of beer. 'I was in the dressing sheds sorting some stuff out when I heard this banging coming from the boiler house round the back; you know the footy ground, don't you? Oh no, of course not, stupid bugger, how the hell would you know? Anyway I went round the back and the door was not open; it was locked from the inside. Now, that was unusual – no one ever locked the bloody thing. I told the club about it on many occasion, but no one took any bloody notice.'

'OK, never mind the bloody lock – what happened?'

'Oh, yes, right – anyway I tried to open the door, no bloody chance, and I could smell piss. Yes, definitely piss – seemed odd to me. I was worried as I knew Mary's hubby was dossing down in there now and again when he was pissed and frightened to go home to her. I managed to get the door open, didn't take much; it was a bloody old wooden door, it must be fifty bloody years old, I reckon.'

'For fuck's sake, Skippy – get on with the story will you? What happened?'

'OK, OK, let me tell you.' He took a gulp of his beer. 'I managed to get the door open and went round the back of the boiler. As I said, I had noticed was the stench of urine. I thought to myself, bloody hell, he was supposed to keep this clean, and he must have been using some bucket or something as a urinal. I went round the back of the boiler; it was a real home from home – he had done it out like a little flat, with a camp bed and small paraffin stove. I hadn't realised he was spending so much time there; things must have been real crook at home with Mary; there was even a bloody frying pan hung on the wall. Still, fair dinkum, mate – this was not the only thing hanging. For on the other side of the boiler, I found him swinging from the rafters like a lantern on a square-rigger. He had hanged himself, and he had left a farewell message: "Tell Mary I am sorry, I love her so much – she doesn't deserve me." Fack me, mate, it shook me up, I can tell you; I will never forget the look on his face.'

'Yes, you already said. Jesus, mate – that must have been fucking awful for you?'

'Bloody oath, mate, but what can you do, blue? Shit happens. He must have been in some state in his head.'

'Well, thank you for sharing that with me, Skippy. Sorry to bring back so many bad memories; it must give you fucking nightmares thinking about it?'

'No dramas, mate; I am glad to be able to talk about it, to be honest.' He downed his beer. 'Fancy another cold one before I go? My shout this time, OK? Don't want the reputation of being a bloody bludger, you know.'

I had another schooner and then made my way back to the hotel, I walked past the surf club on my way to see if I could spot Mel, but nothing. I had to wait until the evening, and patience was something I was not issued with; I lay around the hotel pool, had a swim, then lay around some more; the bloody time just didn't seem to pass quickly enough. I got a local map from the hotel reception; Cowper Street was not far away – I could walk it. It was about fifteen minutes on the far side of the sports ground. I set off at six-thirty, which would ensure she was home when I got there and would not pass me if she was in the car, or bump into me walking.

I was right – it took me exactly sixteen minutes to get to the house; there was a car in the drive – a Torana LC two-door, bright yellow; wouldn't miss that. I was nervous; why, I wasn't sure. I'd never felt like this before. I walked up to the front door; it was a wooden-clad building, as most of the houses down the street were the same design. I knocked. Both the door and the fly screen were closed. No answer. I waited a few minutes, which seemed like an hour, then knocked again. I heard a voice. It was Mel. My heart missed a beat; she was home. 'Won't be a second, hang on – I will be there.' I stood at the side of the door to make sure she came out to see who it was. I heard the lock turn, the squeak of the door as it opened, and then the wobble of the fly screen.

She stepped out; it was her, as beautiful as I remembered. She had lost weight, and looked fit; her hair was bit longer but it suited her. It had only been four months or so but seemed like a lifetime. Mel's expression when she saw me was priceless – she just grabbed me and hugged me. 'Oh, baby! What are you doing here? When did you arrive?'

She let go of me and kissed me. Oh, how I remembered that kiss. I hadn't spoken a word yet; she just kept standing back looking at me, then hugging me again. I guessed she was pleased to see me after all. 'How did you find me? Why didn't you ring? You had my number. I gave you it, didn't I? Yes, I know I gave it to you – did you lose it?'

I told her to calm down and let me get a word in.

Eventually, she said, 'Oh, sorry – come in; mind the house, it's a mess.

I wish you had rung me. Nan! Guess who is here? It's Leif – I told you about him, from Mount Isa, you remember?'

An elderly-sounding voice came back. 'Who is it, dear? Mount Isa? Who, dear?'

We were out on the back porch by now; Nan was sitting at the table eating her evening meal. 'Hello, Nan – pleased to meet you,' I said, and bent over and gave her a peck on the cheek. She gave a chuckle and a smile; she must have been in her early seventies, I supposed.

'G'day, young man – it's a long time since a handsome young Pommie gave me a kiss; what's your name?'

Here we go again, I thought. 'Leif – Leif Askenes-Daniels and, yes, I am a Pommie, but have a lot of Norwegian blood in me,' I said, before she asked.

Same reply as always. 'Hell of a mouthful that name, young man.'

Mel asked me if I wanted something to drink or eat. I said, 'A beer would be good if you have one, please?'

'No worries – be right back.'

Mel returned with my beer and one for herself; her nan decided she had eaten enough and wanted to go inside, mumbling something about being a gooseberry as she went in. We were sitting on a sofa on the back porch and Mel held my hand, saying how good it was to see me, how much she had missed me, and she'd wondered if we would ever meet again – all the things two friends, not lovers, would say to each other after a few months apart. We talked and talked most of the evening about the good times at Mount, and then I had to ask her, 'Why didn't you tell me you had been married, Mel?'

She went quiet and let go of my hand, which was the first time she had not held it since I arrived.

'How did you find out about that? Who told you? No one knew up in Mount Isa. How did you find out?' She sounded angry.

I told her about meeting Stella in the Northern and how we had got talking. I said I'd only told Stella we had been workmates, nothing else. I did not mention her father or knowing about her mother passing away not long ago; I was going to let her tell me that. She seemed satisfied; her attitude changed back to the Mel I'd known a few months ago. She told me the full story, and about her mother – and then the tears arrived. I took her in my arms and held her as she sobbed. The thought of her mother was still painful, as so it should be; you only get one mother and when they go, part of you goes with them.

'What was it she died of, Mel?'

'A broken heart. I suppose they told you about my father leaving Mum and then committing suicide down at the football stadium?'

'Yes, they did. I am so sorry. Why didn't you tell me that as well? Another secret.'

'I did not think I needed to; it was all in the past. What did they tell you about him, my father, that is?'

'They told me what happened, and that he was a pisshead. I won't go on; I do not need you to go through it all again. But your husband – that was a shock to me more than your father; you told me about the relationship, but you never mentioned marriage. I don't think you even mentioned his name.'

'He was called Warren; his mates called him Rabbits.'

'Rabbits, how come?'

'You know, Rabbit – warren… where they live.'

'Oh, right – typical Australian.'

'It only lasted a year; we were married young. He had been a bit of a larrikin, always joking, life of the party – that sort of guy. He died on a motorbike. He went around a bend too fast and hit a tree, killed outright. I got over it by blocking it out of my mind. I am sorry I did not tell you, believe me, I am – but life was so good up the Mount I did not want to spoil it. Will you forgive me, please, Leif?'

Her nan was her mother's mother; she was seventy-six, and did not look it, to be fair, but she also had a bad heart. It had been in failure for years and she was always tired; everything was an effort, which was why she didn't get out much. Mel said she had no one but her, which was why she was still here in Byron Bay. If she left she did not know what would happen to her. It had been OK when her mum was alive – Mel was always there; she only lived round the corner in Kingsley Street, and was still living there on and off, but now she spent most of the time here at her nan's house.

'Come on, we will go for a walk,' said Mel. 'I will show you where I was born.' She looked in on Nan, who was asleep in front of the TV. 'She will be fine; she stays like that until midnight, then goes to bed saying she's tired.'

We walked around the corner to Mel's house, which was a brick building like thousands of similarly built structures thrown up around Australia in the 1950s. We went inside; it the first time we had been alone together. She had held my hand all the way while we were walking and now we were alone she retook my hand, and kissed my fingers. A tingle went through me; it felt so good to be with Mel again. I didn't know how I was going to repeat my goodbye. I thought it was a mistake to have tried to find her, but there was something there between us – something more substantial than just being lovers. What the fuck was I going to do?

We sat on the sofa like two young kids, holding hands and looking into each other's eyes – no sexual contact, no ripping each other's clothes off, just two people who were deeply in love; it was the first time I had admitted to myself that I was in fact in love with this girl.

I stayed in Byron Bay for another month, eventually moving into Mel's house after a week in the hotel. I did not want to leave but, deep down, I knew I would have to. I had taken the hire car back to Avis; they had a depot there. It cost me a one-way rental fee, but that was OK – it was cheaper than hiring it for a month. I told the agency guy that I would be hiring another car shortly.

I was in contact with Michael at Techmaster and a few other agencies, but I was not trying too hard. It was not costing me much to live at Mel's; therefore, money was not flowing out of the bank. I had been in the Bay longer than I expected to be and Christmas was getting close. I knew I must start looking for a job in the new year or make the ultimate decision to stay or go home to the UK.

I rang Doug up in Perth to see how things were in his part of the world; he told me he had not heard anything for quite a while. He told me one bit of good news, or sad news, depending on how you looked at it – Donna's father had passed away, some said of a broken heart after losing his only daughter in such tragic circumstances. I had to admit I was relieved; it meant the pressure was surely off from the Italians. Could I rest easy now the head of the Luciano family had gone? I didn't know, but at least he would not be chasing me, I figured.

Doug seemed to think the same as me. He even asked me if I would return to Perth and join him again. I was tempted, but said I would think about it. He asked me if I would give him an answer as quickly as I could, as he had many inquiries due to come in; he said it was booming on the west coast.

I had a phone call from an agency in Sydney – one I had contacted that dealt in Asia, Malaysia, Thailand and Singapore, where it seemed that work was kicking off; they were looking for experienced personnel and asked if I was interested in a position in Malaysia as a piping engineer/designer for Shell BV, a subsidiary of the Royal Dutch/Shell consortium working for Petronas, the Malaysian state-owned oil company in Sarawak.

Ken, the agent, told me the work was on a new plant built in the area. It was for a full design and build project from FEED (front-end engineering design) through to construction; they were manning up with all engineering disciplines. The subsidiary, Asean Bintulu Fertilizer (ABF), was based in Sarawak and it intended to be the largest exporter of ammonia and urea all over the world.

When Mel found out about my offer she was both pleased for me, but sad at the same time as she knew I would be saying goodbye once again.

I had waited until we were back at her place after leaving Nan at home before I had told her the news. She said she was happy as Larry, but I could see in her eyes that she was lying. She went into the kitchen, saying, 'I will put the billy on and make a coffee.' When she came back with the drinks I could see she had been crying. I took the cups from her and held her hands, and she just crumbled into my arms,

'Leif, I don't want you to go, babe – I love you so much.' That was the first time she had ever said it. 'I love you – please don't go. Stay with me – you can get work here; we can manage on both our wages coming in.' She knew she was on a losing wicket but was giving it a fair go.

'Mel, how can I get a job here? There is nothing for me here.' Those were the wrong words. The look she gave me was enough to wish me dead.

'What do mean, nothing for you here? What about me? Why are you here, you bastard? Get out, go on – fuck off! Get out of my house.'

How could I talk my way out of this one? Come on, think about it, you stupid idiot, I was saying to myself. Mel had gone to the bedroom and slammed the door, nearly taking it off its hinges. I followed her, but she had locked it.

'Mel, open the door, please, Mel – I am sorry. They were not the right words; it's not what I meant. I meant no work for me, not you, baby – please, open the door. Let me in, please, Mel.'

I could hear her sobbing in the room – deep sobs, like when a baby cries. She sounded so sad. I felt terrible; I was nearly in tears myself. 'Please, baby, let me in – we need to talk; we can't end it like this. I love you, baby, please.'

There was no response, so I went and lay on the sofa. I must have nodded off for something woke me. She was moving – I heard the bedroom lock turn, and I got up. I went to her room, and she had gone back to the bed and was lying in the foetal position, still sobbing. She looked so fragile, as if I had smashed her with my hands. I went over to her. I put my hand on her shoulder, and she shrugged away. She did not want me, but why was the door unlocked? I touched her again, this time more gently. 'Baby, please,' She turned and looked at me; her eyes were red, full of tears, and streaks down her face. Her nose was running, and her face was wet all over; she looked so sad. I went to hug her; she did not resist, and lay her head on my chest.

'I'm sorry, baby – you know I did not mean you when I said there was nothing here for me, I meant work – you know I did, don't you? How could you believe I meant you?'

Mel had not spoken; it was like she wanted to talk, but nothing was coming out; as if she was frightened to speak in case she broke down again. Finally, she said, 'It's not just you, Leif, it's me. I want to go with you. I want to get back in to doing what I love, my work – but I can't because of Nan. I can't leave her. What would she do? She has no one but me. When you said there was nothing here for you, it just brought it home to me. I have been thinking like that ever since Mum died and I had to take over caring for Nan. I love her to bits, but I am not cut out to be a nursemaid. I feel like I am imprisoned; if it weren't for the job I would have gone crazy.'

I was thinking of what to say. I hadn't realised how she was feeling, there'd been no hints from Mel. Now I was feeling bad. 'Let's go for a beer, Mel – clear our heads and get out of here for a while; maybe it will help.' She surprised me by agreeing to go out, and we both had separate showers. Mel put on a bit of makeup, which was something she did not often do, and we took her car and went to the Northern, which had become my favourite watering hole.

'Well, look who's here! G'day, you two – been a while since I have seen you, Mel,' said Stella as we walked into the lounge. 'What will it be, two schooners of the usual, Leif?'

'No, just one and a large chardonnay please,' said Mel.

'Go over to a booth, you two – I will bring them over.'

We went and sat down. Stella came over with her drink as well. 'I shouted these; a bit of a celebration. Mind if I join you?'

There was no doubt Stella had lightened up the mood. 'What you so bubbly about, Stella? Won the bloody lottery, have you?' I said.

'My bloody oath – might as well have. I just managed to get Mum in a home. Been thinking about it for years. I am not getting any younger and starting to feel the pressure. Mum needs twenty-four-hour care, not that she is crook or on her last legs as she sleeps most of the day, but I need a break from it; I'm beginning to feel like I am a prisoner in my own home.'

Now, where had I heard that lately?

CHAPTER 49

LARS

Keeping in Touch

Lars used to regularly keep in touch with his mother and father, but, like most kids who had flown the nest, it was not enough. He had been up to Maitland at least every two months and gone out to the vineyards for lunch, taken them shopping into Newcastle, trying to do the right thing and give them a bit back for what they had done for him over the years.

However, the fact they had lied to him still hurt him, as did moving every four to five years. OK, he often thought he was a bit selfish in his belief, but that is what you get when you are brought up as an only child. Lars knew other kids who were only ones, and they had had a similar upbringing – they had been spoilt rotten, as a way of making up for the fact they had been moved around a lot and had to keep making new friends. His father was a disciplinarian, or he'd tried to be; his mother was soft and had always given in to him, but he had tried to do the right thing, for, after all, it was his father's job that made them move.

Things had changed, and Lars had not been in touch as much as he had been. Once or twice his mother had contacted him and given him a rollicking for not ringing, but work was taking up most of his time. He kept saying to himself he must get back up there.

Maya came into the kitchen; Lars was at the table looking at some enquiry papers for a new contract they were going to quote.

'Hi, babe, had a good day?' she said, as she kissed him on the cheek.'

She opened the fridge. 'Wanna beer?'

'Yes, please; I'll have a Crown Lager, thanks.'

'You look pensive; what's up, mate?' said Maya, sitting down next to him.

'I am a bit. I am worried about Mum and Dad; they have not been in touch. They must be sulking; the old fella is probably still brooding about me not taking the same route as him into the banking sector and being an ordinary bricklayer, then to top it all I come to Sydney and leave them at the age of eighteen – it still gets to him.'

'You must get to see them, babe. Do the right thing; take some time off and get up there.'

Lars phoned his parents up the following day thinking that everything was OK, apart from the fact he had not been in touch for a while. He told Maya that he had phoned his mum and left a message, again and again, the following couple of days.

'That was the fourth time this week,' he said. He couldn't understand why they were ignoring him. 'I can't remember this ever happening before. You are right. I have to go up to Maitland to find out what's going on.'

Jon was in his mid-sixties now and Marjory was ten years younger, yet sadly did not look it; they had lived on the Hunter for a good few years, which was the longest they had been anywhere. Jon had been asked to move on to other bank branches, but he was not a healthy man. He had had a few heart warnings lately. On numerous occasions, his doctor had told him to try to slow down take it easy, even think about early retirement. He would get a decent pension from the bank, especially if he had to retire through ill health; they would not be short of money, or 'skint', as the Pommies used to describe being broke.

Lars knew he had not kept in touch as much as he should have, but something always cropped up; what with business and footy, he just never seemed to have the time. He decided he had to go and see them.

Lars arrived in Maitland around three-thirty and pulled in to the drive on Brook Street, Telarah. No one seemed to be around; he was getting worried now – what had happened? Had someone been taken ill, or died, even? Something must be deeply wrong.

He tried knocking at the next-door neighbours, the Watsons, but there was no one there either. He sat around for an hour or so until it was gone six, thinking his father should be home from the bank by now – or did they stay open late some days? He hadn't a clue.

Then they both turned up in the same car. His mum got out first as Lars got out of his car, but there were no smiles or greetings, just 'Hello, how long have you been waiting?' – as if Lars were a tradesman they had booked and they had not been there to meet him.

'Is that all I get, Mum? What the fuck's going on?'

'Come in, then,' Marjory said, and Lars heard a voice behind him.

'Don't swear in front of your mother. I won't have it, you hear.'

'I'm sorry,' said Lars, 'but I was worried about you. Why have you not returned my calls or even written? I have not heard anything from you for months now.'

Marjory was still quiet. Jon was scowling and mumbling to himself. Then Marjory said, 'Why did you not call in to see us when you were up here? When you were in Kurri, staying at the Chelmsford Hotel. You were there for a week with some woman, managed to go to the vineyards and even came into Maitland, but never let us know you were coming or stopped by to say hello. Why, Lars? How could you not visit your parents? What have we done wrong to deserve such treatment?'

'I haven't a clue what you are talking about! I was not in Kurri. I have never been to Kurri in my life. Where did you get that idea from, for heaven's sake?'

'A guy came into the bank about some business and had said he had seen you,' said Jon. 'He noticed the photograph in my office of you in your Dragons gear. He said that he had seen you in the pub in Kurri; he'd never actually spoken to you or the girl you were with, but had seen you a few times in the bar during your stay there.'

'He must have been mistaken,' said Lars. 'I swear on the Bible that we've never been up to Kurri. Must be someone who looks a bit like me. I mean, it's not hard – blond, tall surfer build – must be hundreds of guys who fit that description in NSW, never mind Australia.'

'Don't think we are stupid; we believe that you not only came up to Maitland, you then went up to the bay and stayed there for a few days. We know all about it; there's no reason to lie. What secrets you are keeping from us? We don't deserve to be treated like this.'

Lars just could not understand what was going on; his mind was in a whirl. He had not been up to the Hunter, and had only ever driven past on the highway years ago. He had never been out of Sydney for years. He decided to go out to Kurri Kurri and make some enquiries. He told his mum and dad he would not be staying with them – not with the atmosphere the way it was. Marjory started crying. 'You think I am a liar and I am not,' said Lars. 'I am telling the truth, but you won't have it'

He left without saying another word. He decided to book into a local motel for the night and travel out to Kurri the following day. He had a walk around Maitland, and went for a beer in the Belmore Hotel, where he found the leagues club and signed in. At the bar were lots of photographs of former players; he spotted one of Robert Finch, who was in his third year with the Dragons. He had joined them after the 1973 Newcastle Grand Final, and promised to be a great centre and club man. Lars knew him quite well; he was a great guy both on and off the field.

He sat at the bar and got talking with a couple of guys. One said, 'I think we have met before, mate – you from around these parts?'

Lars told him he was from Sydney, but originally a Pom, and that he'd come out to Australia when he was only ten months old but had been around NSW a bit as his father worked for a bank.

The man was sure he had met Lars somewhere before he but did not press the subject. Lars was starting to become quite concerned about this case of mistaken identity. It was happening too often; people would stare at him, then cock their head to the side, like a dog does when it's listening to a sound it is not sure of, purse their lips and shake their head. Then they'd walk away, often looking back.

Lars had few beers with these two guys and spent quite a pleasant evening, but he was getting quite weary, what with the travel and the hassle he had had with his parents, so he went back to his motel for the night. After a fitful sleep, the next morning he had a shower, packed his things and went out to the car.

He drove into town and found a cafe for breakfast, and as he was walking back to the car park, he passed a guy in the street, who nodded and said, 'G'day.' Lars thought he'd said 'Leif', too, and turned around, but the man had got into the passenger side of a car and was gone.

CHAPTER 50

LARS

Kurri Kurri

Leif – that was what they were going to call my twin brother, the one who had died at birth, thought Lars. He felt a cold chill go up his spine. He recalled his mother telling him the story about what happened all those years ago in Manchester back in the Old Dart, as some called it. Or perhaps he'd been mistaken; he must have misheard.

Lars headed to Kurri, a typical small country mining town, and had a drive around. He found the footy ground, which was small, and very enclosed – a bit like the old photographs he'd seen of Pommie grounds, where the crowd was close to the pitch. He thought it would have been intimidating for opposing teams when they played there.

There was a man cutting the grass. Lars sat on a bench and watched him for a while as he pushed the mower up and down the pitch on the other side, working his way towards him.

'G'day, how're things, mate, OK? Mind if I ask why you are sitting in the ground when no one from the club is about?'

'G'day – no reason; as it was a beautiful morning I was just killing time. I love watching other people work, and there's nothing better than the smell of cut grass to relax you, that's all, mate.'

He laughed. 'Mind if I ask where you're from? You look familiar. I seem to know your face from somewhere?'

'I used to play footy down in Sydney for a while, St George, lower grades mostly. I did play a bit of first grade, but there are a lot of good players there, mate – you needed to be on your game 100%. My father is a bank manager in Maitland; he has a photo of me in his office – you might have seen that?'

'Nope – seen you before some bloody where. Never mind, it will come to me. Any way, must get on; nice talking to you, young fella. You take care now, and if you fancy a game with Kurri, come down, son – good enough for the Dragons, good enough for us.'

'Oh, OK – you can't chat awhile then? I'd like to know a bit more about the area.'

'OK, mate, I can spare you a few more minutes. The Kurri team are nicknamed the Bulldogs. We once had the great Johnny Raper coach us; we were one of his clubs he had after he finished playing with St George. He also played for West Newcastle, then coached them before moving on to coach Cronulla and finally Newtown Jets, where it all began in 1957. A guy once told me why the great Dragons team were that good; he said the majority of them thought winning a game of footy was better than sex. For if you lose a game, it's gone and can never be got back. But miss a root, it doesn't matter – youse can get a root anytime. Now that's some statement, mate.'

'Yes, I suppose that is one way of looking at it. I know John well, but I did not know that much about him. I love footy, especially rugby league; it is my Pommie blood in me that makes me love it so much. My birth mother came from Hull, although my adopted parents were from Manchester. I enjoyed watching some of the old GB touring teams come out to visit Australia and New Zealand. There have been a few Poms play in the Newcastle competition – Nat Silcock, the former St Helens and Wigan prop, coached South Newcastle in the 1961-62 seasons, I seem to remember. Then a guy, I believe he was from Hull, called Keith Pollard, played for Maitland a few seasons. He was here from 1971 to last season, a decent front-rower, helped win them two grand finals. Another couple of Poms played for Waratah around the same time. I seem to recall their names... hang on... er, yes, Alwyn Walters and Tony Finch, that's them. I have heard that another Pom is taking over at South Newcastle next year... oh fack, what's his name, er... Terry Clawson, another ex-GB International – must be getting on now though?'

Lars told the man, who'd said his name was Buddy, that he had heard of Malcolm Reilly, Phil Lowe, Roger Millward, Alan Burwell, and Paul Rose all playing in Sydney – the last three were from Hull; that's why he knew their names. They sat for ages just talking about footy; Lars had forgotten what he was doing in town.

He left old Buddy to finish off his grass cutting, apologising for holding him up too long, but he said, 'I don't mind – I can talk about the old days forever.' They said their goodbyes and Lars set off to find the Chelmsford Hotel.

He got booked in for a night and went and had some lunch. He noticed the landlord looking at him strangely, as if he wanted to say something, or was Lars just getting paranoid? He went into the bar – the schnitzel looked good, and he could see one or two people eating it, so he ordered the same with salad and fries. He took his beer and sat at a table looking out over the main road. When he'd finished eating, the landlord came into the bar; he still had that same look in his eyes.

'Enjoy your meal? Was everything OK? Could I have a word, please – could you give me a minute?'

'Yes, it was very nice, thank you. How can I help? Something wrong?'

'Have you ever been here before, or I do I know you?' said the landlord. 'I thought I knew your face. Didn't you stay here with a young lady a while back? I never forget a face or a pretty young Sheila – she was a stunner. Er… Leia, they called her.'

'No, I haven't. You have me mistaken for someone else. I have never been in the Hunter region in my life.'

'Come to think of it, I'm not too sure, but I think the other guy had a Pommie accent; he looked very much like you.'

'It was not me – as I say, I've never been up this way.'

'He could have been your twin, mate.'

This was too much of a coincidence; Lars had to go back and see his parents and get this sorted out. He spent another night in the pub, and the landlord introduced him to another guy who had met Leif. That name was beginning to eat into Lars; how could it be that a guy who looked like him and seemed to be a Pommie was called that name?

He had a terrible night's sleep again, and decided he had to get back to his parents and talk about what he had found out. But he had arranged to meet this other guy the next day. He rang his parents before he went back to see if the tension had petered out. Marjory answered the phone, and there was still a tense edge to her voice.

'Hi, Mum, just thought I would give you a call see if things had settled down a bit. I think I need to come back and talk about the situation. I have some more information to prove I had never been up to Maitland and this area, is that OK?'

She asked him to hang on a second while she spoke to Jon. Lars heard the phone go down, voices in another room mumbling, then he heard footsteps coming back; this time it was Jon.

'Hello, Lars, your mother just told me you wanted to come back. It's OK to come as long as you control your language in front of Mum and do not upset her in any way.'

'OK, I agree, but I don't know if my news will upset you both – that will depend on you. I will be there after lunch towards mid-afternoon as I have someone to see this morning. OK?'

He drove out to a house on the road to Cessnock at Chinaman Hollow, and met up with Max MacDonald, the guy who had spoken with this so-called Leif for quite a while when he had visited Kurri. They had a good chat and Max told Lars lots about Leif, and how had played footy out in Perth, the full story. Had Lars found his long-lost brother? The one who had supposedly died at childbirth? He was beginning to wonder. Lars could not wait to get to see his parents and sort this out once and for all.

It was about three-thirty when Lars arrived; Jon and Marjory were sitting in the garden having afternoon tea, which was an English ritual they'd brought out to Australia with them and loved it – three-tier cake stand, sandwiches – no crusts – on the bottom plate, pork pies and quiche on the middle and cakes on the top, washed down with Earl Grey tea. It always made Marjory think of home, which Lars found a bit hard to understand.

Lars said hello and kissed her on the cheek, then sat down at the table.

Marjory offered him tea in a china cup, another item that was about as well-travelled as he was – she had brought out with her a full bone-china dinner set; it had travelled 13,000 miles and gone on numerous moves from town to town, without any breakage or even a chip.

'Mum, Dad, I have something to ask, and I want the truth this time,' said Lars, putting the emphasis on 'this time'. 'I have been talking to someone who lives out near Kurri, someone who I believe has spoken to Leif, my brother – not only spoken to but had a long conversation with, and who seems to know a lot more than me about my past.'

Marjory went white, and Jon went bright red.

'Look, Dad – don't lie to me again. Just come out with it – or shall I tell you my version? Or should I say the version from Max, the guy from Kurri, and you can tell me if he is lying or not.'

Lars told them what Max said about Leif's mother, who was from Hull in East Yorkshire, how she had run away from home to Blackpool in Lancashire, had twins, and was told that one had died – but he had actually been sold to some people from Manchester, and that was all he knew. Marjory and Jon were deathly quiet.

'You do not have to say any more. I know this is the truth. Why the fuck have you lied to me all these years? And don't you dare say, "don't swear in front of Mum" – I will say what the fuck I like. You two don't deserve any respect, the way you have cheated me from knowing my heritage, telling me lies all these years. Why? Are you ashamed of what you did, buying a baby because you could not produce one yourselves? I hate you. I hope I never see you two again – fuck you.'

Lars walked out; he could hear Marjory shouting for him to go back, but he had meant what he said; he never wanted to see them again.

How could he find any more information on his brother? He hadn't a clue how to start. He thought about going to Perth. He sat in his hotel thinking about what he had said to his parents, thinking he had been a bit harsh with them – but he was heartbroken about the lies they had told him all those years. He had gone through life having to try to explain why he did not have grandparents, brothers or cousins. He'd never had the joy of grandparents spoiling him, or any brothers or sisters to share fun times. He felt like he was a slave – some piece of meat they had bought to use as they liked, just to satisfy the fact that they could not produce a child of their own. It made him hate them more and more.

The only person he hated more was the person who had stolen him from his mother and sold him – the person who had so cruelly told his mother he was dead. Lars couldn't stop thinking about the heartbreak she must have gone through at the time, and the pain they must have caused her – making her think she was not able to bear two healthy boys, and that one had been so disfigured they could not even show her the body. Lars hoped that whoever had sold him was dead and had gone to hell, but if they were still alive, he vowed to find them and make them pay, one way or the other.

He made up his mind to go to Perth to see what he could find out; surely someone would help. He had one or two leads that he could follow up, which Max had given him – the local team he played for, and the guy who gave him a job with his company in Fremantle. Hopefully they were still in existence. Lars rang Maya back in Sydney. She said she was missing him, but agreed that he should stay; she could do without him for a few more days. 'Whatever it takes,' she said, 'to either find your long-lost brother or at least get closure.'

CHAPTER 51

LEIF
Malaysia

We chatted for a while, but I could tell that both Mel and I were thinking the same thing – could this be an opening for us both? Stella had told us all about the care home she had got for her mum; the costs, how she went about selling it to her mum, everything that we needed to know.

'Better get back to yacka,' Stella said, 'or they will think I'm bludging on 'em. Nice chatting to youse two.'

I spoke first as she left us to ourselves.

'You thinking same as me, babe? Would you consider moving your nan into care? You could sell her house to cover the costs, or rent it out – bet you could get a good price, especially during the holiday season. It's not far from beaches, yet secluded enough.'

'Bloody hell, Leif, you don't mess about. Let's get some details first; I would have to ask Nan if she fancies it. We will have to break it slowly on her.'

I liked the way she said we, not me; it meant we were back on, and there was a hope we could be back together and working together.

Mel rang in and booked a day off as she was owed a few due to the extra hours she had put in previously. We went to visit the same home that Stella's mum was going in, for a couple of reasons; one, if Stella thought it was OK, it must be all right, and secondly, Nan was an old friend of Stella's mum, so at least she would know one person in there.

We went to the home; it was very friendly and looked clean and smelt

OK, not like some care homes. Not that I had been in many, but Mel had, and she said it was OK. We got all the details, looked at various options, and came away very happy.

The main thing was that Nan's house would have to be sold to pay for the costs. Mel needed to get a real estate agent to look at the house, or maybe even both of their homes, for Mel had decided that if both places had to go then so be it, for she had no intentions of staying around Byron Bay if she had a chance to go travelling again. She went to see Stella at her home just on the off chance that she would be in with her mum, just for a chat and to see how her mother was taking the news that she was going in a home.

She said she was looking forward to it. 'Lots of my friends I haven't seen for years are in there,' she added. 'It will be great to be with them all again.'

We explained the situation with Mel's mum, and Stella's mum suggested she come to visit for a yarn. Things were moving fast, maybe too fast, but the old saying, 'strike while the iron is hot' came to mind.

Mel contacted 'The Real Estate Man' – I kid you not, that was his name – and arranged a visit.

'G'day – I am Steve Luckwell from TREM; thanks for your call.' We explained the situation, and after a few questions, he said, 'I see, so you are thinking of putting your nan's house on the market? Have you any idea what you might be asking for it?'

'Not a clue,' said Mel. 'That is why we contacted you; we have had some good recommendations from guys down the surf club. We are in your hands – what do you think?'

'I need to see the place first, obviously. I can come in the morning – well, any time, but the morning suits me, OK?'

After making a tour of the property, Steve called round the next day; we made our excuses to Nan and went to Mel's house.

'Well, first impressions,' said Steve, 'it needs a bit of sprucing up and a coat of paint. You need that whichever way you go, sales or rental. Why are you getting rid of it, without sounding blunt?'

'My nan is living with me and looks like she will be going into a care home, and we are thinking of looking at doing something with both our properties, as I look like going overseas with work.'

'OK, well, my first thoughts are that we run a management company that looks after lots of holiday homes in the area; I would suggest that you rent the two places out. The joint income from both houses will more than cover the costs of the care home, plus you will still keep the equity in the houses. We can manage the rental for you, for a fee, of course, but at least that will cut out any hassle. The second option I can offer would be to sell just one of the houses and rent the other out; I would suggest selling your house as it is newer than your mum's and would sell easier, as not much work is needed. Then Nan's home just needs a coat of paint and some modern furniture putting in.'

'I could do that before we go overseas – it should not take long,' I chipped in.

'That is that sorted, then; doing that would attract the younger family set, seeing as it is only ten minutes from the beach. Put in an outside shower, split the larger bedrooms into separate twins to give more occupancy – gives you lots to look at?'

Steve agreed to come back and look at the two options; we could just tell Nan we were redecorating the other house to go on the rental market, and she would not be any wiser.

Mel took her nan round to see Stella's mum, Mary; they hadn't seen each other for years, but it was just as if they had met yesterday. They got straight into talking about old friends, their departed husbands, everyone from the past. It was Mary who brought up the subject of her going into a home; she called it her 'friends club', which even to me sounded better than a care home. She told Nan how much better it would be than living more or less alone; there would always be someone at her 'beck and call' with cups of tea when she wanted it.

Nan came away talking about it and even said to Mel, 'Would you mind if I did the same as Mary and joined her friends club?'

Mel said she would think about it and look into it for her.

It was not long after – weeks rather than months – and Nan had joined Mary in the 'friends club', and Mel's house was under offer. I had redecorated 'Nan's Cottage', as advertised as in the holiday accommodation vacancies, complete with new outside shower. It now slept six people with an en-suite to two of the bedrooms and sink in the other, all with hot running water.

Steve had handled all the paperwork and done a great job. OK, they were taking a decent lump for the service, but it had put no strain whatsoever on Mel and her mum.

I had contacted all the employment agencies again, but this time I was sending two CVs to them. At Techire, the company dealing with the Petronas in Malaysia project, Ken was still looking for staff, including process engineers, which seemed to be in short supply. After a few weeks of negotiation, we were asked if we could go up to their office in Brisbane for a formal interview as they liked the look of both of our CVs. We drove up the following week and as far as we were concerned both had positive vibes after coming out of their office. We drove back to the Bay, full of confidence that we had done OK.

This proved correct, for two days later we received a phone call from Peter Mathews, the manager of Techire in Brisbane, saying that there would be an offer of employment package in the post today if we were willing to join them. I accepted the offer on behalf of both of us, as Mel was still working at the surf club.

I kept quiet about the phone call until after tea; we were sitting on the veranda of Nan's cottage, having a relaxing glass of wine, talking about what type of day we had. I was still finishing off bits and pieces around the place, mainly in the garden.

We were putting in a swimming pool, not in the ground, but one that would have a deck around it about four feet high that you could access off the veranda; it was just about finished, with only the handrail to install. Mel was telling me about her day when I interrupted her. 'Er, oh… by the way, that job in Malaysia – we both got accepted. I told them on the phone that we would be willing to travel out to Sarawak after our injections and visa had come through – OK?'

'You are joking, aren't you? Both of us together? You mean we are going on the same project together?'

'Looks that way, babe – happy?'

'Too fucking right I am! Oh, baby!'

She jumped on me, sat across my legs, and kissed me; it was the most sensual kiss that she had given me for weeks. I could feel the heat of her on my groin, and I started to enjoy it. She could tell I was by the way I had grown in the last few minutes. She started grinding into me, and I closed my eyes. She threw her head back, her hair falling back.

'Leif, oh, baby – mmm, that feels so good. I want you to make love to me right now, here in the open air.'

She got off me, dropped her panties while I slipped off my shorts and briefs, and then she came back, lowering herself on to me and guiding me in. She was already wet; it went in easily. I felt myself get hotter as it slid in; I felt her muscles gripping me... oh fuck – Castleford... mmm... Wheldon Road... slowly I went from ground to ground past Keighley Lawkholme Lane... Rochdale on to Swinton Station Road... oh fuck, she was getting up speed now. She climaxed again, and I felt her body tremble as we went through the station. My legs were aching, and my toes were curled. Oh no... I wasn't going to reach Wigan, that was for sure. Our mouths were welded together as Mel did it again; she screamed out, 'Oh, fuck, yes!' We were at Warrington Wilderspool. The train came to a slow halt.

We just sat there, me still in the station. I was well and truly delighted; the journey had been well worth it. I could feel her heartbeat through my penis; it was so sexy, just staying coupled like Siamese twins joined by the sexual organs. I could feel myself going limp inside her; it tickled Mel, who was working her arse muscles, squeezing every drop out of me and smiling at me, gently kissing me all over my face, lips, nose, brows and cheeks, smoothly moving from spot to spot.

I heard a great sigh of satisfaction. 'Mmm, Mel... I need a shower, babe. Get off me, please' She shook her head, not speaking; just that smile. She started biting her bottom lip and grinding again. I was getting horny too, but it was tickling like hell. I think that was nature's way of telling a man, no more; you can't do it straight away, have a spell, mate – but this temptress had other ideas. We were both, for want of a better word, moist from the previous journey. Then I heard the front doorbell ring. Mel never moved; she just gripped me again and shook her head.

'Hello? Anyone home?' It was Stella. Luckily the back gate was locked and could not be opened from the outside. 'Hello! Anyone home?' she said again. She was at the back gate this time; she must have tried the front door and found it locked because usually she just shouted once, and then come in. We heard her say to herself, 'Oh, fuck it; I'll have to come back.' Mel was giggling, her body was shaking; I had my hand over her mouth to keep her silent, but the movement of her body with laughing was unreal. I told myself I must get her to giggle more often when we were making love – it was awesome. We heard Stella walk away, muttering to herself, as we both came together – oh god, I never even made Barrow in Furness, Craven Park.

As we were lying naked together and outside, we headed straight into my new shower. I thought we must do this more often – and that it was a good job the fence around the garden was seven feet tall with no houses overlooking it. It would have been a good thing to put in the advertisement – 'secluded garden with pool, good for shagging', which reminded me to get that handrail finished.

We filled in all the relevant forms for the visas and sent them back; we would be allocated a bungalow in Bintulu, the biggest port and in-dustrial area that had been chosen for more investment. It was a twelve-month contract. We were paid in US dollars, tax-free, into any bank of our choice. We would be earning nearly $40,000 tax-free between us plus a per diem living allowance of $25 paid in ringgits – that was $250 per week plus housing and all utilities free. Plus, there was a big incentive of a 25% tax-free bonus when we completed our initial con-tract, with a clause saying that if we were offered an extension, we had to take it, but the bonus increased to 40%; we could only be asked once and the length of time would be cast in stone. Shared transport was available for private use, but travel to and from the site offices where we would be based was by company shuttle bus.

We landed in Kuching International Airport at eight in the morning,

Malaysian time; we would change planes and fly on to Bintulu, where we would be met by a company representative to drive us to the complex. We boarded the Fokker 27 aircraft to fly the 330 miles to Bintulu, which would take about one to two hours give or take, dependent on winds.

When we arrived, we boarded a company minibus. The weather was humid, like entering a sauna. It was a good job the bus had air-conditioning, or we would have been soaked by the time we had driven the twelve miles to the complex and been shown our new home for the next twelve months or possibly longer,

It was the weekend and, as Malaysia was mainly a Christian country, we had the Saturday and Sunday to settle in; the fridge and freezer had been filled with what they imagined we would need for the first week or so. We both felt a bit apprehensive, wondering what the hell we had done, as we sat on the sofa in what I can only say was a very sparsely furnished house. We had no personal touches, no photos – only one of Mel, her mum and nan. I had none at all; mind, the ones I used to have were years out of date. I must remember to ask Mum to send me the latest one of them all, I thought, but then she might have got upset as I think she was hoping I would be returning home sooner than later. Initially, it was only two years I was coming for. It was over four now, and looking like being five at least; it was best to forget the photos.

'It's OK – what do you think, Mel?' I could tell that she disagreed. She did not reply, so that was the answer.

Monday came, and we got the bus at the designated stop only 100 yards from the house. It took fifteen minutes to get to the site offices, where we met the rest of the team at the Monday morning meeting.

Our new boss was called Gerry Howston; he was an American from Dallas, Texas, and seemed to be OK, not full of bullshit as I had imagined all Yanks to be. We had to introduce ourselves as he went around the table, each one in turn saying who they were and what discipline they were. Peter McNally, head design engineer, was to be my gaffer, the one I would answer to. Gail Frankish, head process engineer, would be Mel's boss. Gail batted for the other side; she had short hair, cut nearly as short as Yul Brynner. Well, maybe I'm exaggerating a bit, but she was definitely lesbian material.

There were fifteen of us sitting around the table, each giving a brief run-down of their past experiences. Most of the crew had been on site a while; only me and Mel were the greenhorns, as Gerry had so kindly pointed out.

I was taken away to the design/drawing office, and Mel disappeared with 'Yul', as I had nicknamed her, to the process office in another block.

Peter seemed OK; he was a Kiwi from Christchurch. We got on quite well. I have this thing about me, right or wrong, that I can take an instant dislike to someone, and nine out ten times I am right; this time I liked the guy. He explained that all the design from process to installation was done on-site, unlike many projects. They had their on-site fabrication facility and installation teams for every discipline. It sounded great, and I was looking forward to getting stuck in; Peter was putting me in charge of piping design, which included working with structural/support design, piping fabrication and installation. They had already done a FEED estimate and came up with the +/- 50% costing. The more detailed scope for the job was now needed, starting with the process department coming up with the answers. Mel had taken the place of one guy who had left; it seemed he did not get on with Gail.

It was now November; we had been in Malaysia six months. The time had flown by, and we were both enjoying our lives in Sarawak. Everything was going as well as we had hoped it would, and 200% better than when we had first arrived back in May. We had an excellent social life, which we had not thought was possible, but had made some new friends – mostly single people, but one or two relationships had developed on the project, being a mixed Christian group of people who had gotten together. No disrespect to other religions, I must add.

We had both joined the gym and where as fit as we had ever been, even having a personal trainer who was a great help; we worked out two to three times a week. There was an indoor fifty-yard pool, sauna, the works – had nothing been spared on the project? There was also a shopping mall, even a burger bar on the campus. The local pub was OK, I suppose; I couldn't ask for the Rovers Return, but it was fine; often one of the more talented guys off the job would give a live performance and a sing-song.

I was still getting tapes from home. Mel had been talking to Mum, if you can imagine talking to someone who is not there and can't answer back, and will not hear what you are saying for possibly a month – but still, we were conversing over the miles. It was even better when we listened to Mum and Billy. Whoever had come on the mic, Mel kept having to rewind it to listen again. She could not understand the Hessle Road accent. What's 'bairns'? What is, 'It's silin' down... and I gorrit fer nowt'? When Mum asked Mel, 'Ayer gorra bruvva?' it was hilarious, but Mel was learning – she even used to try to mimic Mum; in particular, if I complained about something, she would say 'Yer forever mernin' in a cross Hull/Aussie accent.

After a year, the job was well on. It looked like Mel might not be getting an offer of an extension to her contract, but I had already been approached, which had led to a bit of an unsettling atmosphere in the house. There were married couples on the job where the wives did not work, but you had to be married, not just living together; it was a strange rule, but that was how it was. We had discussed marriage at length on a few occasions, and decided to see the head man and ask if there could be a change to the rule if we were engaged to be married. Would that suffice? We wanted to see the project out as it was looking that Mel would be paid off before me. I looked like getting a maximum of six more months out of the job, which meant the big finishing bonus of 40%.

A couple of days passed, and Gerry Howston asked to see us about our request. 'Listen guys, it's like this,' he said. 'I understand your predicament, and I am sympathetic, but unfortunately, the company rules do not permit unmarried couples living together in one house – is not acceptable.'

'But we have lived together under one roof already.'

'No, you don't understand – you were sharing a house,' said Gerry.

'Not living together. We had known but turned a blind eye to as you both came on the job together, not at separate times, and it was easy just to put two people in one house at the same time. The company head office didn't know we had done that, so what they didn't know didn't hurt them, but if Mel got finished, she would get her bonus of 25% paid up in full. But if you left, you would not get any as they need you to complete the project, which means a six-month extension – but no more than six months maximum; understand now?'

I did understand; but they had me by the balls here.

'I do have one other thing up my sleeve. Mel – would you be willing to stay on as a technical clerk and help with producing the completion packs and works manuals for a few months longer? At a reduced rate of 10% of your starting salary. If you do this, you will get 40% of your original salary guaranteed.'

It was a no-brainer. Gerry guaranteed that once the six months were up or earlier, he would ensure each of us would be paid up with all relevant bonus payments owed, with flights to any destination in the world.

He was true to his word – the job went great, we completed the hand-over in four months. It was a good job Mel had stayed; there were one or two hiccups with the process side not getting the right results, which was beyond me. I never knew how and why it worked.

CHAPTER 52

LARS
Perth

It was a beautiful sunny day as Lars arrived at Perth Airport early on a Monday morning. He went to the Avis desk, hired a car, and then set off to find a Fremantle hotel. He had decided to make this his base, for if he needed to go into Perth, it was not a long way to travel.

The Fremantle Roosters were still playing, and Lars found a telephone number to contact the club. The man he spoke to did not recall anyone called Leif playing for the club. He said had not been on the committee or followed the club that long, but Dennis Mountain was still the coach and knew that he had been there for quite a few years and could help him. He gave Lars Dennis's number, and he arranged a meeting with him for the following Wednesday evening.

When they met up, Dennis he could not get over the likeness. 'Bloody hell, mate – it would be hard to tell you apart.'

Lars knew then that his brother was still alive; everything his parents had told him had been a lie. He wanted to meet his flesh and blood. He was almost in tears as Dennis told him all about Leif; they talked for at least two hours.

'He was an outstanding footballer, the same build as you. I can't believe the likeness. Are you the same style as him, mate? What a womaniser he was; he loved the Sheilas!'

Well, we've got one thing in common, thought Lars.

'Would you like to go down tomorrow night and meet some of the guys who played with Leif when he was here?'

'Oh, great – yes, please. I would love to; the more I can find out, the better.'

Lars drove around hoping to find where Leif used to work, to see if he could find the guy who had given him his first break in Australia. He was hoping he might be able to point him in the direction of some of Leif's friends, or even girlfriends, for he'd been told that Leif spread himself about a bit; they also said one of his girlfriends had died tragically in a car crash and that not long after, Leif had left Perth and disappeared. No one knew where and why; it appeared to be a dead-end there with the footy guys. Leif had undoubtedly made an impression on the club. Lars could not believe he played centre, the same as him; it was surreal. The more he thought about him, the more determined he was to find him.

He found the company Perry Industrial, and from the outside, it looked a prosperous outfit, with a smart office block and what looked like a fabrication shop and storage yard to the side. Lars went into the reception, and a girl behind the desk was typing. She looked up and asked if she could help.

Then she gave a kind of scream and ran around the desk, grabbing Lars and giving him a great hug and kiss, full on the lips. 'Oh, what a wonderful surprise! Why didn't you ring us and tell us you were in town? Oh, Doug will be over the moon when he sees you!'

Then she stood back and suddenly acted as if he was a stranger. 'There is something different,' she said. 'You have changed, Leif.'

Had this woman been one of the girls Leif had spread his seeds with? Why did she notice a difference? Lars thought he should drop his pants and see if there was any difference there, but then thought better of it.

'Wait a minute,' the receptionist said, 'you have got a hell of an Aussie accent now – how come? You have not been out here that long.'

'I am sorry, but I am not Leif,' Lars told her, adding that he believed he was his brother – but she did not have a clue what he was talking about. Doug was not in but was expected back any time; he had gone to look at a job in Perth. The receptionist, Angela, seemed to Lars to have been very friendly with Leif, to say the least. They talked about the days when Leif joined the company and what a great guy he was, fantastic at his job, that sort of thing. She also told him about Donna Luciano, the girl who had died in the accident; how Leif was besotted with her and how he had taken it badly when she was killed. Then Doug walked through the door.

'Well, I'll be fucked! You bastard – why didn't you ring to tell us you were in Perth?' He gave Lars a massive hug.

Angela could not hold it in any longer. 'Doug – it's not Leif, it's Lars, his brother.' Doug let go of Lars as if he was a red-hot lump of coal.

'What are you talking about? I know Leif Askenes when I see him. Are you mad, girl?' Doug was smiling, but it was not a genuine smile. Lars got the feeling Doug knew the story but did not want to believe it, or maybe he did not know; he was not sure.

He invited Lars into his office and closed the door; he wanted to know what Angela was talking about, so Lars went through it all again. Doug did not let on that he knew the story, but when Lars had finished, he got up and hugged him again, this time a bit longer. Lars could feel the love he had for Leif coming through to him.

Doug told Lars lots more than he could ever imagine – why Leif had left Perth so quickly after the car crash, about the Italian Mafia, how Leif had gone to Sydney and then up to Mount Isa. He more or less told him Leif's life story from leaving Hull to going to Queensland; after that he had lost touch with him. As far as he knew, Leif had disappeared after Mount Isa.

'One more thing,' said Doug. 'Get out of Perth as soon as you can, for if the Luciano family hear you are in the area, they may well come gunning for you – with an emphasis on the gunning! If anyone didn't know you were his brother, they would swear blind you were Leif, and ask no questions.'

Lars needed to know more. He wanted to visit Donna's family but wasn't sure whether that would be a good move. He slept on it, and then decided to leave Perth. He had enough information to keep him going. Doug had given him details of the company Leif worked for in Mount Isa, so he would contact them to see if they could enlighten him on where Leif went to after he left there.

CHAPTER 53

LARS

Possibly the Hunter Valley

Lars flew back to Sydney and did nothing about his quest for a few months as business was booming, so he had to put Leif on hold for a while.

Things had gone quiet, although they were still busy enough to take on more staff, both trades and supervision. The management had also increased; they now had dedicated project managers who did most of the work Lars used to do. He and Maya were now looking at other businesses to break into; they did not want to put all their eggs in one basket. They thought about opening a Brisbane company – or possibly in the Hunter Valley area, for Maitland had impressed him. It was a country town, but not far from the industrial city of Newcastle.

One thing that was eating at Lars was the number of high-rise buildings that were going up all over the place. He wanted to get into this type of construction, and one thing he'd spotted was that they all needed tower cranes. While Lars was in Maitland, he went for a beer, and got talking with a guy called Billy.

'How long you lived in Maitland, mate?' said Lars.

'All my bloody life – never been farther than Newcastle.'

'Bloody hell – what do you do for a quid, then?'

'I work for a company who manufacture tower and overhead cranes, including the sections for tower-type.'

'Any good? They busy? Plenty of work on, then?'

'My bloody oath, mate – we can't turn out enough of them. We are sending four of the sections every night five nights a week, fifty-two weeks of the year apart from Christmas.'

Now, this sounded good to Lars.

'Why you so bloody interested in cranes, mate? What do you do?'

'Well, I own a construction company in Sydney and I'm looking at moving into something else, and you have given me an idea, mate.'

'I don't know if you are interested,' said Billy, 'and I may be talking out of school, mate, but I've heard a whisper that the boss, who is getting on a bit, is looking to retire. It's only a whisper. But where there is smoke, often there is fire.'

'How long has he worked for them?'

'Five years, mate, along with most of the workforce; even longer for one or two of the guys.'

That was always a good sign of the type of guy who runs a company, Lars thought.

He went back to Maitland another day and went to see the company that built the cranes; it was easy to find them. He looked up engineering companies in the phone book and then, with a list in hand, had a ride around the town's industrial area looking at each company until he found the right one. It was on a corner block, which made it easy to survey. Lars drove around, took his camera out and took a few snaps for future reference. He thought it was very well designed; if he copied it as near as possible, it would save a lot of work later. The place looked impressive – the huge fabrication shop must have been half a football field long by a hundred feet wide, all open to the sides to let the air in, and there were two overhead cranes. One went over the materials stockyard to enable the beams and such to be brought in the shop without any real handling problems. They also had a small Iron Fairy mobile crane, along with a side-loading forklift; no expense had been spared when setting up the works, that was for sure. It looked like they were swamped with work; quite a number of guys were working inside the fabrication shop. On the other side, there was what looked like a machine shop with lathes and drilling machinery. From what Lars could see, they also manufactured overhead crane crabs and hoists, from small ones to those a driver could sit in and overlook the workforce below.

Lars was hugely impressed. He wanted to find out whether the boss did want to offload, and if so, he would buy this company if it was possible. If not, he'd start his own in competition with them. He went into the car park, where some striking vehicles were parked, including a big BMW 7 series. Lars had not seen many of these in Sydney, never mind the bush.

He introduced himself to the girl in reception, asking if he could see someone relating to purchasing; he was asked to take a seat, and someone would be out to see him. Five minutes passed and a man came out – Mr Lawrence, the manager of the company. 'Sorry I took some time,' he said, 'I have my big boss up from Sydney and was a little tied up – but how can I help?'

Lars explained who he was and what he was looking for in the construction industry, explaining that they were looking to branch out into civil engineering on high rises after being quite successful in housebuilding.

Mr Lawrence suggested Lars speak with his boss, Bruce Burke; he thought he might like to sit in on the discussion. He disappeared and a few minutes later came back and asked Lars to go through to the boardroom, where Mr Burke was waiting. He was a very well dressed elderly gentleman with silver hair and well-groomed in a costly looking suit that looked cashmere to Lars. He stood and offered his hand. 'Hello, Mr Mellows is it? Very pleased to meet you.'

In a well-spoken, almost English, accent, Mr Burke told Lars he had been brought up in Melbourne and moved to NSW in 1955; he had become fed up with the big city life and picked Maitland to start his engineering business. He got straight to the point and asked Lars what he was looking for; he seemed to Lars to be a really genuine sort of guy. Mr Burke explained how he got into manufacturing cranes and all the other gear, including mining, conveyors and mechanical handling equipment. 'I think you are here on more of a scouting mission than anything else by the questions you have asked,' he said. 'This could be your lucky day, son.'

He told Lars that he had seen him driving around the site and taking photographs.

Lars realised that was why Mr Burke had asked him in. He wanted to know why he was spying on his operation. Lars told him about his company and that he was looking at expanding his business interests by getting into the engineering industry, and possibly the crane hire business. Lars told Mr Burke what his thoughts were on building his own fleet of tower cranes rather than hiring them in. He found him so easy to talk to, as if they had known each other for years.

'Have you any literature on this company of yours that I could have a look at, please?' said Mr Burke.

'Yes, I always carry my company brochure with me in the car. Just excuse me; I will go and get you a copy.'

Lars went out and returned with a couple of brochures. Mr Burke looked through them, reading silently, nodding as he worked through them. He put them down on the desk and sat back; he was an intense guy, this Bruce Burke, thought Lars.

'OK, tell me why you want to buy my company – for, listening to you, that is obvious. No way have you come in here wanting to purchase a tower crane. You could have done that just by asking for a copy of my brochure, or even just a telephone call.'

He listened as Lars laid out his plans.

'I like you, son. I appreciate your honesty – it takes audacity to come in here and tell me all your plans, even after I told you I had seen you were taking photographs of my set-up here in Maitland. I have another similar business in Queensland – Ipswich, to be precise – more into mining equipment, large conveyor plant, that sort of thing. I also have had an ongoing contract to supply the jack-up sections and in-ground anchor beams for Laufkran, a prominent German tower crane manufacturer that imports the main lifting housing and jibs into Australia, which in itself is a good earner for us, without the overhead equipment we manufacture.'

He stopped for a while, looking out of the window. After a few moments, he said: 'OK, Lars, I am not getting any younger, and I have no children, for I was adopted – I've no family to leave all this to when I die; only my wife, who is not too good health-wise herself. I have long been thinking of retiring to spend more time with her in her last few years, for I believe she is terminally ill. I think she is keeping it to herself.'

Lars was engrossed in his story.

'But I don't want to sell my companies; I still want to be involved. I want you to think about joining me in this company as a shareholder or partner – what do you think? I know it may seem a bit bold, the fact that we have only just met, but I have all my life used my instinct to help me through, and I believe that we could work together.'

Lars was speechless for a moment; this had not even been in his head, and he was already a partner in a company with Maya. Then he spoke. 'Mr Burke, I am already a shareholder with my partner in our construction company in Sydney. I would have to discuss it with her before making any decisions, for she is an equal partner and whatever we need to put in your company will be part of her money. Can we meet again in, say, two weeks?'

'Lars, it is you who interests me; it is you who I want in this company. No disrespect to your partner. And as far as putting money in, that is not a big problem, but I would need 100% of your time for at least six months. For I would want you to take over the company and its running, I would take a backward step, still overseeing, but not giving all my time as I have been doing running between sites – that would be your job. We have a great staff working for us, first-class managers looking after the plants; I want you to oversee it all.'

Bruce agreed to a meeting in two weeks, and told Lars to bring Maya with him. He would lay out his plans, and get on to his solicitor to draw up a draft document for them to go through. Lars left the building still a bit shell-shocked; he needed to get back to Maya as soon as possible.

CHAPTER 54

LARS

LBM Engineering – A Year Later

'Well, what do you think, Maya? I believe we have made the right decision; Bruce has been unreal in letting us join his company – we are now partners in LBM Engineering. All we have to do now is attend the final meeting to sign the contracts. It has taken us twelve months, a little longer than we'd thought, but it has gone OK. Bruce owns 49% of the company, and we own 51% – I never thought he would give us the majority, but he has every confidence in us. He even though went through our history, unbeknown to us, before he agreed. Let's be honest, our other business has come on leaps and bounds just through his input and knowledge – he did not have to help us, as he has no involvement, and we did not pay a cent for his consultancy. I thought he might have wanted to take Mayabrook Construction under the LBM banner, but he didn't. Come on – we have the final meeting today downtown to sign everything.'

They walked into the offices of Clarkson and Clarkson Solicitors at eleven in the morning on October 26, 1978, to complete the contracts. All the hard work and travel Lars had put in over the past twelve months – flying up to Queensland and back to Sydney, up to Maitland and back to Sydney, hours in planes and behind the wheel of his car – today would make it all worth it.

'Good morning Lars, Maya,' Bruce said as they walked through the doors. He kissed Maya on the cheek as he always did, shaking hands with Lars.

'Hi, Bruce, good to see you again. Everything sorted, I hope? Let us get it done, shall we?'

They took their places in the boardroom of these old-world offices, with their teak-panelled walls. Lars thought they must have been the same since the building was first built back in the nineteenth century, for the offices were down in the Rocks area of the city. Clarkson was an old established solicitor going back nearly as early as the building they were in. The company was started in 1900 after brothers Percival and Robert Clarkson had emigrated to Australia in 1899. Bruce had given Lars a brochure on the company; it had been in the Clarkson family name ever since, as sons and daughters joined them, most of them having been back to England to university, either Oxford or the London Metropolitan, to study and gain degrees.

Everything went to plan; they were only in the offices less than an hour; all the contracts signed, sealed and completed, they were now officially partners in LBM. Part of the LBM company was a crane hire company, LBM Lifting Services. They had built five New Tower cranes and had them on hire in Sydney, complete with drivers on a day's work payback. This was proving to be a very lucrative business; they did have to pay out the cost of manufacture, but that was nothing compared with the return they were receiving. They had another five on the drawing board and ten other overhead cranes for new-build factories in NSW and Queensland; their Ipswich plant was booming, with orders for mining equipment as there was a boom going on up in North Queensland. They were negotiating the takeover of a Newcastle company specialising in mining and bulk handling equipment. Things were moving fast, and now with Bruce on board using his contacts, the future looked bright.

Quite a few companies were breaking into the crane hire field in Sydney and NSW in general, but luckily for them, they were the only ones building their Tower Cranes, and it was paying dividends; they could not produce enough. One of the big Swiss companies was getting a foothold, but it had to import its units from Europe, and what with transport cost and import duty LBM was on a par with them as they manufactured everything in house, which enabled them to keep the costs down. They also had a bit of an advantage on labour costs as the government did not let crane drivers/operators in as immigrants, so the local labour would instead work for them than foreign-owned companies.

Things were OK with Maya and Lars, but with him being away most of the previous year, he had strayed on occasion. He had felt guilty, and could not get away from them fast enough, yet he always seemed to want more. Sometimes he had stayed away for up to three weeks up in Queensland, and most of the time he scored. He met these other women at social functions or beers out with the guys after work, as they often finished at clubs.

One girl he got a bit too close to was a girl in Brisbane called Leanne Thompson. She worked for a small company that Bruce dealt with; a supplier of steel and fastenings. They met at a pub after work. She was a bit of a tomboy who always wore working clothes; Lars never saw her in a dress or skirt at work – she always wore jeans and a polo shirt, and he never took much notice of her. That was until this one afternoon in the pub. She had been to a funeral and had come back to the pub for the wake; this time she was wearing feminine clothes that showed off her body; Lars thought she looked stunning. He was standing at the bar, and she came over. 'G'day, mate, how are you, OK? Not seen you in the office this last couple of weeks – you ignoring me?'

'No, I did not need to visit, but if I'd realised you looked like that I would be in there every day. You look beautiful, Leanne – you should wear clothes like that all the time.'

'Well, thank you, kind sir. I don't get many compliments at work and don't see many guys. I don't know why – I'm not that ugly, am I?'

'Don't be so stupid. I wish you were my girl, that's for sure. Pity I am married; I would be round like a flash, you believe me.'

'Don't let being married stop you. I am not the jealous type. Just ask, Lars – all you have to do is ask. I have fancied you since the first time you came into the office; I am game if you are, mate – just say when and where.'

Lars did – and it went on for quite a few weeks. He got the feeling she was hearing wedding bells at times, and he knew that he had to get away. No-strings fun was all it was supposed to be about; they had agreed on that before they started seeing each other. Lars was getting too involved; he I had to let her down easily. The last thing he needed was her contacting Maya through work. After about three months of regular meets, Lars told Leanne he would not be returning so regularly as his time was coming to an end with Burksteel; she accepted it and said she was sorry he was going, but she had enjoyed his company – especially between the sheets.

CHAPTER 55

LEIF

Back to Australia – 1978

We got our notice and left on September 25, 1978 and flew to Singapore for a holiday first. We had booked at the Mandarin Orchard Hotel on Orchard Road. This was when it was the in-place to be seen – it was either here or Raffles. But this was one of the newest; it had only opened in 1972, and was the tallest building at the time. Construction of the second tower had been completed in 1973.

We had a wonderfully relaxing time. To be fair, there was not a lot to do in Singapore, but still, it was nice to be pampered for a week before we went back to Oz. One thing I must say is it was spotless; the whole country was clean as a whistle.

I was standing at the hotel pool bar one day. Mel had been late up and said she would come down after her shower. I overheard a conversation between two guys sat near me just as Mel walked through the doors to the pool area.

'Don't look now, mate,' said one of the guys, 'but just look at this thing walking up now. She is fucking stunning.'

'Where?' said the other guy.

'Behind you. Don't turn. Fuck, she is coming to the bar. God, I would love to get into her knickers – she is gorgeous. Some lucky bastard is hanging out of her.'

With that she walked up to me, passing these two guys, and kissed me on the cheek. They were spot on; she looked fucking awesome. I looked over at the two guys, who winked and mouthed, 'Lucky bastard.' They smiled as we walked past them to go to some beds by the pool, and I touched one on the shoulder as we walked. Mel was in front of me. He looked up, and I just said, 'You were right, mate.'

'Who are those two guys? You know them?' Mel asked me.

'Oh, them – I had just been chatting about something while you came down and he was right, what he had said. That's all; nowt to talk about.'

We had lunch that day by the pool; it was a great afternoon. Later we went back and made love. It was terrific just being with Mel, and that guy was right – I was a lucky bastard. I didn't need him to tell me, but it was nice to hear.

We left Singapore for Australia on October 4, arriving at ten-thirty at night. We stayed overnight in Brisbane before driving down to Byron Bay and home the next day. Mel had asked the agents not to let 'Nan's Cottage' after the end of September as we intended to live there for a few months until we got sorted.

We got home at midday on the Wednesday, unpacked, and went straight round to the home to see Nan. Mel had been getting the odd letter from her; it was hard for her to write at her age. But Mel had sent a message at least once a month anyway. When we arrived at the home, we went into the office to talk with the manager, Emily. Nan had written to Mel on three separate occasions. Still, we had never received her letters; Emily had even tried telephoning the work number we gave them but could not get through. There had been a gradual decline in Nan's health after about three months, which was when the letters had stopped coming. Emily said Nan had dementia, and that it had come on quicker than she had ever seen in a person. Nan was not ill with it, but was Emily was positive she suffered from the disease. She warned us that she might not know us when we went in to meet her.

'She is in the main lounge right now, so please take it slow with her,' she added.

We were both shaken; Mel was close to tears as we left the office. Nan was sitting on her own, not talking to anyone, and I let Mel go up to her first.

'Hi, Nan,' she said, but there was no response. She tried again. 'Hi, Nan, it's me, Mel – hello.' Nan just looked at her blankly.

Then Nan said, 'Hello – who are you, dear? Is tea ready? I am hungry. I never had any breakfast, you know; I was in bed.'

I was standing just behind Nan; I hadn't said anything yet as I didn't want to confuse her.

'How are you today?' Mel said, without using the word Nan. Then she told her a few more things about the day in general – the weather, how had she been, had she seen Mary, that sort of thing. Nan was OK with that, but she hadn't a clue who was talking to her. It was so sad to see the look on Mel's face. I then came around her side and said hello, and she just looked at me, not a clue. Nan asked me if I was here to see someone; she'd never seen me before – was I new here? It seemed she was OK in herself, but she just did not know either of us, which was just awful.

It made me think of home and how my mother was; she had no one now but Billy, as both my grandparents had already passed away. We did not push Nan, but Mel was upset about it. She was saying she should never have left her, that she'd gone away only thinking of herself and never considered Nan when she decided to go back to working overseas. I was just going to say something, then decided I'd better keep my mouth shut. I thought it was not the right time to butt in; Mel was hurting. I would not be able to comfort her, for it was my fault she had come with me to Malaysia, my idea to sell her family home and put Nan away like some dog into kennels.

We went round to Stella's to see if she was home, and on the way we called to see her mother in the home. She was sitting with some other old dears playing cards, but did not see us so we did not annoy her. When we got to Stella's a guy answered the door.

'G'day, mate – can I help you?'

'Yes – is Stella in, please? We are old friends of hers.'

'Just gone to the shops to get some bits and bobs; shouldn't be too long.'

'OK, we will call back later – just tell her Leif and Mel have called.

She will know who we are, OK?'

We both had no idea who the new guy in Stella's life was; when we'd left, Stella was not into men after her husband had left her years before. It had been a very rocky marriage, according to Nan. We went back later, and Stella introduced us to the new man – his name was Craig, and he was from Melbourne; he had come up for a holiday and stayed for a few days and been there ever since. Stella met him in the Northern when he came in for a drink, got chatting and next thing you know he had moved in; this was just after her mother, Mary, had gone in the home.

Stella told Mel they had just hit it off; she'd not had a man in her life for so long, not even casual affairs, but she was in love again. She also explained what had happened to Nan. She had gone down pretty quickly after Mel and I had gone to Malaysia; everyone in the home thought Nan would pull out of it, but her depression had just become gradually worse. Stella said the home had done everything it could to contact Mel but just never got a reply; it was as if we had just disappeared off the face of the earth. Mel was distraught and just broke down. It was terrible to see, and I again realised we had done this to Nan by putting her into the home and changing her life entirely so that Mel could come with me.

We went back to the home the next day to talk with the staff about the situation. We were told that one of the worst things to happen to anyone with Alzheimer's or dementia was to move them from their environment to a new place, as it kind of escalated the disease. How true this was I did not know. But within sixteen months Nan had gone downhill fast, for one reason or another. When we got back to the house, it blew up.

'That's it – I am bringing Nan home. I will never leave her again, and if it means us splitting up, so be it. I am sorry, but Nan comes first, no matter what.'

'Mel, let's just calm down. Let's not make any rash decisions. I know how you must be feeling, but don't blame yourself – it could have happened at any time.'

'I am sorry, Leif, I have made up my mind. I am sorry, but I wish we had never gone.'

I had never split up with a woman like this and was at a loss as to what to do, but I decided that it was best we split up. I saw no future for us under those terms. How could the past sixteen months be just wiped off? The great time we had in Sarawak – just gone and forgotten, just like that?

Within two weeks Nan was back home, and I was gone. Mel had tried to come round a bit, but it was no good – Nan was now back, and no way would she change her mind. I had packed my things and decided to go down to Sydney. We said our goodbyes on the veranda, and as we kissed for the last time my heart was aching. She turned away and went inside without looking back, and I was gone.

I hung around Sydney for a week or so before deciding to go back to the UK; I was cash-rich – I had more money than I had ever had. I booked a flight to Manchester via Bangkok and on Saturday, October 28, 1978, I left Australia.

CHAPTER 56

LEIF
Bangkok

October 1978 – *Silver Lady* by David Soul was in the top five of the UK's hit parade. I was thirty-two, still unmarried and free as a bird. I had rung Mum up from Sydney, told her I was coming home and would see her in a couple of weeks once I had booked a flight. I explained what had gone on, not in great detail, but still let her know the script.

I arrived in Bangkok late on a Friday night; getting off the plane was like walking into an oven. The humidity must have been 100%. I got a taxi into the city centre – well, not so much the centre but the tourist area of Sukhumvit, where the soldiers from the Vietnam war used to frequent as Bangkok was the place to go for R&R. I needed some of this in bucketloads.

I had an open ticket; all I needed to do was give the airline a ring a few days before I wanted to leave and they could find me a seat, as being a single traveller was easier for them to accommodate than couples or families.

I booked in at the Chavalit Hotel right on Sukhumvit Road; it was an old hotel the US servicemen used to use. If it was good enough for them, it was good enough for me; it was cheap, anyway. I booked in for a week to try it out, I thought I could always move on if need be.

I went down the Soi Cowboy. I had read a lot about Bangkok, and according to the information, there were three red-light districts, and this was supposed to be the best; it wasn't rumoured to be as seedy as others. I didn't know about that, but it looked OK to me. There were plenty of bars with fanny on tap as well as beer. I had a wander around and I was surprised as it wasn't a big street, only about 150 yards long. I walked into a bar and met this guy, as you do, and we were sitting enjoying the scenery, so to speak; it was just getting dark and the lights were coming on. He nodded, as guys do in faraway places when you are alone, and said, 'Where you from, bud? I recognise that accent.'

'Same as you – Hull,' was my reply.

'Fucking hell – you sound like an Aussie, pal. How long have you been out here?'

'Phew… since '71. I've picked up a bit of the twang, I know, but I never mixed with many Poms. I've no family out here, so I've mainly been with Aussies. What about you, are you on holiday or working?'

'I am in between jobs, mate. I work on drilling rigs; I am a tool pusher. Thought I would come here for some R&R. I've been here before; this is my fifth time. I work mainly in the USA, a month on and a month off.'

'Don't you ever go back home to Hull? I mean, where is home?'

'Nah, not very often, fuck all there. I am due to go back but not sure when. What is there in Hull? Bloody cold weather, freezing your bollocks off. Prefer coming here. Can't beat it, mate; the girls are fucking awesome and know what they have to do – no pissing about like the tarts at home. It's a fucking mortgage just to take them out nowadays, and you still might not get your leg over at the end of the night. Fuck that for a game of soldiers.'

'I am on my way home – we should get together for a few beers. Where do you drink when you are home?'

'Oh, mostly in town. I go in King Edward a lot, or Spencers; White Horse, not a bad boozer. Good idea, yeah, be nice.'

I wrote my name and Mum's phone number on a piece of paper and handed it to him with her address. He put it in his wallet; at least he didn't just put it in his pocket.

'OK, mate, I will get in touch. Might be a few months but let's call it a date,' he laughed.

One thing that stood out when talking to him, a typical Hull guy, was every other word was 'fucking'. He just couldn't help it.

'When did you get here, then?' I asked him.

'Yesterday, late on; this is my first night out, just looking for some fucking meat. I usually pick one and keep her for as long as I am here. I had one six weeks last time; she was spot on – had her own scooter, saved on taxis. She moved into the hotel with me. She only had a fucking hovel on the other side of town, so I got her for next to fuck all, fed her and fucked her. She drove me around on the back of her scooter, went to places other tourists would never find, ate well where the locals eat, was a good deal – would have cost me more in car hire costs.'

Typical Hully gully watching the pennies, I thought, but he was right. He was a heavy-set guy, five-eleven, I suppose, broken nose; been around the block by his look, but seemed a decent enough guy.

'Do you always do that? Hire one for a week or whatever?'

'Of course I fucking do. I know a guy now who finds them for me; fancy one? He is coming here in an hour or so, see if he can find you what you are looking for – big, little, slim, fat – he can get one to suit whatever you want, boy or girl or fucking mixture.'

'Sounds good to me – how long he will be before he gets here? I could do with my leg over.'

'Don't rush it, mate – you have plenty of time. As I said, about an hour, no fixed time. He knows I am here to meet him; he will turn up when he can, never lets me down, and they are always good, clean girls or boys. You ever fancied ladyboy? Katoey, that is what the local name for them is; you can't tell them from girls, to be honest. I have been with a few – they are unreal, but everyone to their personal taste.'

He carried on to tell me that ladyboys were usually taller than the natural Thai girls, so their feet were generally in proportion. They were also more effeminate than girls, always flicking their hair back and smiling all the time; they often had a high-pitched voice. I was getting the idea he preferred a katoey to a regular girl, but I was not bothered – a dick is a dick, and I am not that way inclined. We had few more beers, and lo and behold the man arrived. He introduced me to him, and then said, 'Oh, I don't even know your name, bud – I'm Freddie Walters, and you are?'

'Leif... don't ask – Norwegian. Leif Daniels.' I left out the middle bit.

'OK, Leif, this is Pino – he is the guy I was talking about. Don't be shy, just tell him what you are looking for and for how long – he will match your needs.' He laughed again.

We discussed our needs; Freddie wasn't that bothered – any girl would do as long as she was clean and decent with a scooter. I was a bit more detailed in what I thought I would like but emphasised I didn't want a katoey. I told him tall, slim, and pretty, with long hair, not over twenty-five and with her own transport – a car, preferably, or scooter would do. He said girls with vehicles were costly as they did not earn a lot of money, but could provide one if I was willing to pay the extra. I asked him what was he talking about as an extra; he said it was about $50.

'A day or a week?'

'A day,' was his reply.

As I was going to be there for at least ten days, possibly longer dependent on how it went, $500 seemed a lot to pay for car hire. Thinking about what Freddy had said about girls with scooters, I thought that might be more fun, so I opted for the scooter mob. We agreed on a $20 a day to be paid to him, which was $200 up front. He wanted it in US dollars, which I had to go and get from the exchange booth. He said he would be back in two hours with the girls as ordered; all we had to do was have the money, and if it went over the first ten days he would lower the rate. Pino headed off, and I said to Freddie I was going for a walk and would meet him back there in two hours as I needed to get some US dollars.

I had a wander around and got back in good time. Pino had not got back yet, and Freddie had not moved from the same stool. A few minutes later, two scooters turned up with two adorable Thai girls driving them, with Pino on the back of one, who happened to be mine. He introduced me to the girls who both gave the usual greeting of putting both hands together and bowing. Freddie did the same, so I followed suit. Areva and Intera were the girls' names. It seemed that Intera was to be my companion for the next ten days. She was just what I had asked for – even more. Slim, beautiful face, not a blemish on her skin, almond eyes, and her hair was tied up; I could not wait to see it fall upon her shoulders. She had a body any model would be proud of. The perfume she was wearing I did not recognise but it just got to me; it was kind of musky with a hint of mandarin. I once heard someone comparing perfume to the sensation of rubbing raw silk against the cheek; well, Intera's did that to me. She had a rucksack on her back with what I assumed was her clothes and necessities for ten days.

We sat chatting, getting to know each other. It quite unreal thinking about it, like buying a puppy – but one who answered you back. She was a brainy girl; she was saving up to go abroad to university when she could and doing what she did was one way of saving the pennies. She did not feel she was doing wrong; it was one way of learning English. It was a way of making a living, plus she loved sex, which made it easier, I suppose. She did not feel she was a prostitute, she was just a girl having fun and meeting men other than Thai men, who said she had no interest in. We decided to go and have a meal then head back to my hotel, which was 'girl-friendly' so no one would ask questions when we walked in together.

What a civilised country this Thailand is, I thought; more places should be the same, unlike Hull where prostitution was a seedy back alley kind of thing. There was only one street where working girls touted for punters, which was Waterhouse Lane in the city centre. Before 1960 it was legal. But all I was sure about was I did not want a ladyboy; that was not for me – I didn't fancy fucking a bloke. I was not gay, and did not want to try it in case I liked it.

The girls Pino had found where both of the feminine kind, no doubt about that. We had got back to my hotel no problem and just walked in, hand in hand, like any average couple. We entered the lift; we were alone for the first time, no one watching us. Intera looked up at me and smiled. I bent down and kissed her gently on the lips, and she never pulled away. She just kissed – and what a kiss. It was so soft. Her tongue tip came between her lips and mine corresponded, just touching. I pulled away and squeezed her hand, as the lift stopped on our floor.

As we walked, out an elderly couple were waiting to enter. The man, who appeared to be European, smiled at me, with a look that said, 'I know what you are doing, you lucky bastard.' His companion, who I assumed to be his wife, just looked away in disgust. I smiled at her on purpose, just to wind her up, knowing that as soon as she got in the lift, she would have a go at her old man.

We entered my room, and Intera said she needed to powder her nose; how sweet – that is what she said. I asked her if she wanted a beer, wine or coffee.

'Coffee, please,' was her reply; her wish was my command.

She came back out of the bathroom, and I could not believe my eyes – what a stunning sight. She had changed into what used to be called baby doll pyjamas, but these were see-through, in black silk. She still had her heels on, and she smiled and did a little pose and twirl has she walked towards me. Wigan looked a long way away, and I very much doubted that I would get anywhere near.

One thing that had been discussed earlier was that any form of intercourse had to be using a condom; now, I was not used to such things. I had used them, but didn't particularly like them. Still, we used one; she put it on for me, gently stroking me to make me ready, then sliding it on. Then she climbed aboard. Oh, god, she was good. She made love to me – her movements were so smooth, like a ballet dancer, slow and intense. I was going to enjoy these next few days of her, that was for sure.

The next day we got up around ten. I woke up first, and she was lying next to me naked, asleep, on her belly. Her gorgeous bubble arse and slim waist – it was beautiful just watching her breathing; her body rising and falling, just that little bit. I leant over and kissed her back, stroking her spine, running my finger down to the crack of her arse and running my hand over the rump. It was solid, yet soft to touch; I wondered whether she must work out or was she just naturally fit?

We went for breakfast, and it was great watching the faces of the people in the café, mostly the men perving on her as she glided through; she seemed to float as she walked. We then went outside, and her scooter was still there. She unlocked the chain, which was about an inch thick with a solid-looking padlock, and off we went through the traffic. We didn't wear helmets and there didn't seem to be any rules of the road; you just pointed at where you wanted to go and hoped to get there. The three-wheeler tuk-tuks were the main problem – they were everywhere.

I was glad she was driving, not me, but we got to our destination safely.

Intera had decided we should visit all the tourist attractions such as the Grand Palace, which was a must-see, and Chinatown – we had a fantastic night out there. We also visited Wat Pho Temple of the Reclining Buddha, the Muay Thai boxing gymnasium, and the Dusit Palace, the home of Thai Royal Family. We had a great day down at Bang Lamphu, which is home to Khao San Road, the backpackers' paradise, with great bars and nightlife. I had a fantastic week with my new friend and I would miss her, but life went on, and I was going home after six years of being away. I had booked my return flight for Wednesday, November 8, to arrive back in London the same day; I never could get my head around these travel times.

Our last night together I will never forget; we went to our favourite Thai restaurant. Having tried a few different dishes in the past few days, I had my favourite again. Phat kaphrao is one of the staples of street food, combining meat flash-fried with holy basil (the eponymous kaphrao) and a generous helping of fresh chilli and garlic. It must always be eaten with rice and crowned with a fried egg; to me, it will always be a reminder of a Thai one-dish meal. Intera had sam tam. She told me its origins lay in Thailand's rural north-east, and this dish had strips of crunchy unripe papaya bruised in a mortar and pestle with tomato, long beans, chilli, lime and fish sauce. It is one of Thailand's favourite dishes and just has to be eaten with a basket of sticky rice; I tried it once before, and it would always have been my second choice.

On our last night of passion, we were getting undressed as we got through the door to our room, and then we lay on the bed just caressing each other. She suggested we shower together first. We were still wrapped in each other's arms as we got under the water, and it felt so good soaping each other down and the hot water cascading down our bodies. I just ran my hands all over her wet body, pulling her close to me; oh god, I was at Doncaster already.

We dried each other off, then got into our robes, opened a bottle of wine, and sat on the balcony; we did not want to rush it.

We had just about finished the bottle, and Intera said, 'Leif, I want you now. Please, Leif – make love to me, baby, now.' How could anyone refuse such a plea? I went to the bedside drawer to take out a condom; she said, 'No, not now – let's not. I want to feel him inside me.' Wigan nearly arrived there and then.

We made love like never before. It was no doubt the best sex I had ever had, and when we got to Central Park, I was well and truly fucked.

The next morning, I did not want her to leave me, but she said she had to go; it was just a business transaction, but she had loved every second of it, that I would always be in her memory and would I keep in touch with her. I promised I would. She gave me her parents' address, saying they would always be there even if she was not at home for a few days. That was the end of our holiday together – for 'holidays' was how she classed her business transactions. We kissed goodbye, and she left.

I hung about Bangkok for a few more days. I saw Freddie again in the same bar, and asked him if he had seen Intera, or indeed Pino, but he hadn't. I gave him my mother's phone number to contact us the next time he was in Hull or found any news on Intera, but I was unsure if I ever he would.

One thing I did know was that I had fallen in love with my Intera, for she had got into my heart without a doubt. I had to see her again, just to hold her once again in my arms. I needed her, but I could not find Pino, I asked around, but no one had seen him for days. I just had to find her again, but how?

THE END

THE ASKENES TRILOGY: BOOK TWO
THE MOST BEAUTIFUL GIRL IN THE WORLD

CHAPTER 1

LEIF
Back Home Again

I t was November 6, the day after Bonfire Night, and the plane landed at ten-thirty in the morning. I lifted the window blind, and it was pissing down. I had come from a humid 32C to a damp, cold November day that felt like a winter's day. What had I done?

I got through passport control, customs and was out of the arrivals hall in about three-quarters of an hour. I had decided to hire a car and drive up to Hull the next day, having booked a hotel near the airport rather than do it all in one go. I was shattered. I'd been cramped up in baggage class with my six-foot four frame stretched to the limit; it was a good job I'd had a seat with plenty of legroom. I had struck lucky there; I think when I checked in early the girl on the desk took pity on me and allocated me that seat.

I took the shuttle bus to my hotel, went for a meal and a few beers, hit the sack and woke up eight hours later. I hadn't even rung home yet to tell them I was back safely; they did not realise I was coming home that particular day; all they knew was I was coming back sometime that month. I rang Mum, and luckily she was in.

'Hi, Mum, it's me, Leif.' It was a bit stupid saying who I was, as the

word 'Mum' would have given her a clue. After all, I was her only son...
but, there again, I wasn't.

'Oh, Leif! It's great to hear your voice. Where are you? It's a clear line.'

'Mum, it should be – I'm in London. I will be home this afternoon.'

She asked me all the usual questions, and I told her I would tell her
everything when I saw her later. Just as I was about to say goodbye, she
said she had had a phone call from a bloke; his name was Freddie something and he was calling from Bangkok, but he said he would call back.

To be continued...

Lightning Source UK Ltd.
Milton Keynes UK
UKHW010107070521
383232UK00002B/14

9 781649 697703